SINGING WATERS

Singing Waters

A NOVEL BY

Ann Bridge

NEW YORK   THE MACMILLAN COMPANY   1946

For

RACHEL

With Love

SINGING WATERS

1

AS the train, leaving Domodossola, corkscrewed its way through the gorges and began to emerge into more open country, Nils Larsen put down his book and turned to look out of the window of his sleeper. The countryside was still on a tilt, and harsh with cliff and rock; but there were steep small fields, and scattered sparsely among them, in groups, there were also houses. These Nils considered with the surprise which never failed to overtake him at the beauty of Italian rural architecture. Nothing could be simpler than the houses themselves, solid, with flattish roofs of brown pantiles; but their severe shape, and the way they were grouped—above a bridge, round a church, high on a bluff— gave them a quality that was profoundly satisfying. "Extraordinary!" Nils muttered to himself—"They can't put a foot wrong in architecture! And yet in politics—my God!" He began to recall the small houses of the people in other countries which were politically less tiresome than Italy; the brick villas of Southern England, the untidy shacks of the Eastern States, the prim squalor of French villages, even the rather tedious brown reiteration of Swiss chalets. Oh well, there was nothing wrong with chalets, aesthetically, he thought, for Nils had a quite passionate admiration for the political genius of the Swiss, and wished to defend them even from his own thoughts—but they had not got what these houses had got, insanitary as they certainly were, the firm authoritative stamp of actual beauty. Why was it? How come? These houses—there, look at that lot, standing together above that great sweep of retaining wall —hadn't been designed by architects or arty people; peasants

3

had built them for peasants' use, with no thought but to get a good strong house perched where there was space for it, near other houses for company if possible; and the result was this succession of perfect groups, satisfying the eye and the soul. One saw such beauty in Spain, one saw it in Mexico, and occasionally in French Catalonia; was it then a Latin gift?

A handbell resounded outside in the corridor. Nils, hungry, took up his book and his pouch of papers, and began to make his way along the train towards the restaurant car. In the next coach he overtook a woman, also in search of breakfast, evidently; he could only see her back, but the cut of her black dress, the set of her hat, her gossamer stockings and high-heeled shoes, to say nothing of the enormous size of the patent-leather handbag tucked under her arm, proclaimed the extreme of fashion; the fragrance of an expensive scent filled the corridor behind her as she passed. Nils sniffed it a little derisively as he followed—he had not much use for fashionable expensively-scented women. This one had a good figure, though, supple and elastic; and as they passed through coach after coach he was struck by the way she walked. The train, curving through still hilly country, swayed a good deal—it was hard to keep one's balance. But this fashionable woman, perched up as she was on those idiotic heels, kept hers amazingly; her supple body gave to each lurch of the train, paused, and recovered itself with what Nils recognised as great muscular strength, and a trained power of balance as well. So mountaineers and ski-runners walk—funny that she should walk like a mountaineer, in those clothes. In spite of himself Nils became interested in the woman, and began to look forward to seeing her face. She must be English or American—no other race had those slender thighs, and the long smooth sweep from shoulder to waist—except a few Hungarians, of course. Nils had a theory about these three nations—that their characteristic figures were due to the fact

4

that for generations, for centuries, the women had joined the men in their field sports, riding and walking for pleasure unencumbered by heavy loads; a particular social system had produced a particular physical type. But this woman was tall for a Hungarian, he thought. Would she be beautiful?

As he asked the question, he got a sort of answer to it. They were at the end of one coach when a man came round the corner from the next, walking fast; he checked on seeing the woman and politely flattened himself against the panelled wall to let her pass; drawing herself up to her narrowest, she slid past him with averted head, that yet sketched the faintest gesture of acknowledgement of his civility—the man for his part both bowed and frankly gaped after her. Nils grinned to himself. The other man thought her beautiful, anyhow—and that faint movement of her head was the typical gesture of the beautiful woman, mechanically acknowledging the accustomed tribute of bows and stares. "If she turns out to be really beautiful, she will be an Englishwoman; if she is only tolerably good-looking, she will be an American" Nils said to himself, still grinning; he was familiar with that skilful trick of well-bred, well-dressed American girls of acting the part of reigning beauties so well that they were accorded the treatment due to beauty itself.

They reached the restaurant car at last. It was fairly full, and the head steward, seeing them enter together, ushered them to the only vacant table for two. The woman sat down, propping her huge bag against the window, and without so much as a glance at Nils began to study the menu—Nils, putting his pouch on the floor, at last was able to take a look at her face.

What he saw, when he did so, for the moment drove all thoughts of whether she was beautiful or not out of his head. He was appalled by a sense of latent misery in it. This was such a shock that he examined her more carefully, wondering just what had given him that impression. Her actual expression was not one of misery; it was rather of a slightly

5

vacant discontent, such as he had often seen on the faces of very fashionable women in restaurants in many capitals—women whose way of living had given them habitually the cream of material life, the best food, wine, clothes, and jewels, leaving them, it seemed, at last with nothing but a slightly supercilious distaste for these things. He had often wondered, since they continued to wear the clothes, decorate themselves with the jewels, and consume the food and wine, whether this distaste was genuine or merely assumed in order the better to impose themselves on those who ministered to them—waiters, *vendeuses,* and the men who paid for it all; a grin usually came over Nils' rather severe wide legal mouth when he saw one of these women, recalling Margery Sharp's immortal vignette of The Disgusted Lady in *The Nutmeg Tree.* It was perhaps part of the protective mechanism of those who live always in the public eye—not in the sense that statesmen and royalties do, whose actions are of some public importance, but in the curious modern fashion by which the politically obscure rich live mainly in public, being forever seen, forever described and photographed—the vulgar competitive publicity of "Society" where the capital S denotes its complete divorcement from human society at large.

But in the case of the woman now sitting opposite to him, he felt that it was more than that; his first swift impression was not mistaken, he was sure, though he could not justify it by anything definite. As she ordered coffee, orange juice and toast in a bored weary tone from a grovelling subservient waiter, he now turned his attention to her actual features. No—not really beautiful. Or was she, actually? It was a curious face, short and very square, with a wide white forehead, rather prominent cheekbones, and a neat short nose that was just not ignobly too small—the slightly flaring nostrils gave it sensitiveness and some distinction. Her hair was of so beautiful and strange a colour that it was certainly natural—a very dark gold, stuck smooth and close to her

6

small head, with green shadows between the faint perfect waves; her eyes were dark gold too, like deep topazes, with the same illusion of green in them. The mouth, distorted as it was by the supercilious expression, was nevertheless fairly good; at least it was of a respectable size. Nils always looked for size in features, disliking and despising the petite and the miniature as unworthy and unwholesome. Well, yes— for all its oddness, the face was sufficiently near to beauty for her to be an Englishwoman, yet it was more a Central European type; but the cosmopolitan perfection of her dressing, lying all over her thick as lacquer, gave nothing away as to her nationality; she had spoken to the waiter in very good Italian. She belonged obviously to a good, as well as to the merely expensive class; her pearls were real, so were the diamonds on her breast and her left wrist. Nils was too widely experienced to fall ever into the common error of supposing that no Englishwomen dress really well; on the contrary, he knew that when, admittedly unusually, they turned their attention seriously to clothes, they dressed superlatively. But, as he ate his breakfast, he was forced to admit that he had no idea from what country this ultimate product of material civilisation sprang. They became completely international, these women, dressing in Paris, London, and New York; having their hair and faces arranged in Paris, London, and New York; living in huge hotels and eating in the most expensive restaurants in Paris, London, New York, Nice, Vienna, and Budapest; and in all these places dancing, attracting stares and men, playing bridge and being discontented. In spite of his original impression of her misery, he looked at last with undisguised hostility at the woman across the table, as she sat staring vacantly out of the window, dangling a piece of toast in her long scarlet-tipped fingers. At that moment she happened to turn her head and glance at him. His feeling must, unpardonably, have been visible on his face, for he saw a startled look of astonishment appear in her eyes before, with

7

a brusque movement, she turned to look out of the window again, while a slow blush, visible behind the faint careful make-up, crept over her cheeks, her temples, and even the white forehead.

Nils was very much ashamed. It was permissible to despise spoilt discontented ladies, but not to be rude to them. He wondered what he could do to make some amends—while he was still pondering various gambits, she reached for that enormous bag and took out a malachite cigarette case and a long malachite cigarette-holder, bordered round the top with rose diamonds; both the bag and cigarette-case, he noticed, bore the initials G. T., the one in gold, the other also in diamonds. However here was his chance; he whipped out his lighter, and as she fitted a cigarette into the holder he leant forward assiduously, saying "Permit me."

With a cold glance at him she said "Thank you," lit her cigarette, and looked out of the window again.

Nils however was not going to leave it at that—that was insufficient. He recognised that he would probably, deservedly, be snubbed, but he was going to say something else; his willingness to risk the snub would in itself constitute an apology. Following her glance out of the window to where Lago Maggiore lay spread shining in the morning sun he said—"The Borromean Islands are very picturesque, aren't they? I wonder who Saint Charles Borromeo was? One sees the islands so often, but one never hears anything about him. Do you know?"

She half-glanced at him, faintly surprised again, and then turned back to the window. For a moment he thought she was going to do the thing thoroughly, and not answer at all, but after a perceptible pause—"He was a Cardinal," she said vaguely, without turning her head. "He was made one when he was twenty-three and became Archbishop of Milan forty days later. And when there was plague in Milan he gave all his bedding to the sick and slept on the floor."

8

"But you know a lot about him," he said, surprised; "usually it is so hard to find out about saints."

"It isn't really," she said in her flat, bored voice—"there's that book, you know—a sort of Almanach de Gotha of Saints."

Nils didn't know, and didn't really want to. He was thinking about her voice. She had no definite accent of any kind, but the intonation was not quite English—it very faintly resembled the American tone, as distinct from the accent.

"I should like to get onto the islands," he said, wishing to make her speak again, "instead of always rushing past."

"They're not worth it," she said, still looking out of the window—"They're frightfully dull."

"Oh, have you been on them? That is very interesting—I have never met anyone before who had been on the Borromean Islands."

She looked at him again, coldly, for a moment, and then picked up her bag.

"We used to go there for picnics when I was a child," she said, rising. "It was very boring." And again sketching the faintest gesture of a bow, she walked out of the restaurant car.

When his bill was brought Nils asked the steward, whom he knew well, as he did all the attendants on the Orient Express, if he knew who the lady was?

"She is not with you, then, Signor Larsen? I thought you were together."

"Now, Francesco, when did you ever know me to travel with a lady?"

The man laughed. "Quite true, Signor, but one must make a beginning! No, I do not know this lady—I have not seen her before."

"She said she had lived here as a child. Find out her name, will you?"

"Certainly, Signor Larsen. And does Signor Larsen desire to sit somewhere else at lunch?"

9

"No, no—put us together again," Nils said, putting a tip into the man's hand.

During the morning the steward came along to Nils' sleeper to say that the sleeping-car attendant reported the lady's name to be Mrs. Thurston, that she was travelling on a British passport, had "a mountain" of luggage, and a maid in the second class; they were going to Istanbul. Not diplomatic—the labels were ordinary labels. She was going to lunch at the last service. Nils for his part had got out his papers, and read some reports on the labour situation in Sofia, which he was going to investigate for the International Labour Office at Geneva. When he had finished with these and made some notes, he lowered the window and sat in the full draught; it was the beginning of May, and the air was warm and sweet, with a rich Southern sweetness. Would that poor discontented creature enjoy a thing like that, he wondered? Probably not—it would disarrange her hair.

At Milan he got out and bought a couple of papers. From 1935 onwards the Italian press had been vitriolic against the English, the French, and the League of Nations in general— now, a year later, it was still the same. Addis Ababa had fallen, the Emperor Haile Selassie had just fled to England; sanctions were still in force, but half-heartedly; ham-strung by the proposals of the Hoare-Laval Treaty, in spite of the vigour with which the British public had repudiated these, and the Foreign Secretary's consequent resignation, sanctions no longer "had what it takes". Meanwhile the Italian press was trumpeting about its new Empire, breathing out defiance against all other nations, and boasting of what its "eight million bayonets" would do when the time came; there were threatening or tendentious articles about Yugo-Slavia, Albania, and the Adriatic Littoral generally. The papers were disagreeable and dismaying reading for anyone of peaceful and sensible views on international relations; on any man of taste the vulgar bragging and boasting could only produce a quite emetic effect. Nils grunted as he read,

10

and finally threw the cheap ill-smelling sheets down dis-
gustedly, and leaned out of the window again—the poison
of greed, ambition, and vulgarity had not tainted the Italian
air, and the houses and small towns of the Lombard plain
were as delightful as those he had seen up on the mountains
that morning. No vulgarity here—and none among those
peasants working in the fields. How had it come in to the
mental life of the nation to this odious extent? It was a quite
un-Italian characteristic. He thought of Italy's past, and the
flowering of art and literature and the graces of actual living
in her small Republics and tiny city-states, like Florence and
Pisa and Siena. No vulgarity there either, though there
had been vice, crime, and small wars a-plenty; it had only
come in, seemingly, since Italy became one nation, and went
on to aim at being a great power. It wasn't only Mussolini
who had introduced it; it had begun with d'Annunzio's lec-
ture campaign, from 1915 onwards. Tremendous, those
speeches of his—made, like those of Demosthenes or Pericles,
in the open air, to crowds of students and citizens; terrific
power, shattering invective. Nils remembered the Master
referring to Nitti as "Questo leccosudice Bolognese." But
it was about then that wealthy Italians started having "Per
la Piu Grande Italia" stamped on their notepaper, which
was a perfect example of the crudest vulgarity.

A Greater Italy—was there some connection, then, he wondered, between *size* and vulgarity? The sharp contrast between the elegance of the little city-states and the blatancy
of a United Italy looked as if there were. His mind ran
rapidly over Europe, surveying the various nations. Plenty
of blatancy and boasting in Germany certainly—while the
little countries, Belgium, Holland, Denmark, Norway, his
own Sweden, Finland, were all quiet, modest, efficiently
democratic, civil-spoken; and, except Finland, all monarchies. Even Britain, great power as she was, showed no vulgarity in public life—was that because, for all her Empire,
she was geographically a little country too?

11

He wasn't sure about all this. What was vulgarity, anyway? Any form of ostentation, of course; not wealth itself—he remembered the modesty and simplicity of many great American millionaires, like J. P. Morgan, Junior, carrying his cigarettes round in a paper packet—but the display of it, a sort of indecent exposure of wealth. Any form of pretence: the poor or poorer aping the rich, the ill-born giving themselves the airs of the great, typists trying to dress like film stars—oh those cheap high-heeled shoes, the sham jewellery, the greasy hair dressed à la Dietrich!—and, also, weak and not very heroic nations, like Italy, pretending to be great powers and prating of their future feats of arms. Yes, the essence of vulgarity seemed to lie in the pretence at being, or the attempt to be, something that one really was not, with the resulting lack of ease and dignity and taste. Peasants were never vulgar—on the contrary, they had ease and dignity to a high degree. And ease and dignity, though no one praised them in the modern world, were real values, conferring incalculable benefits on their possessors; because they were the outward and visible signs of an inward and spiritual balance, a poise, a being adjusted to and at home in one's universe, and satisfied with it. Why were people always trying now to improve the material condition of peasants, without giving a thought to what they might be taking away by so doing? Because, he supposed, the modern world, even the humanitarian and philanthropic side of it, thought wholly in material terms.

Why, he asked himself again, remembering Milan through which he had just passed, and its factories and slums—why had the artisans in large towns so much less ease and dignity than peasants? Size again, he supposed; a village was of manageable proportions, like small states; small enough for human intelligence and goodwill to exercise some measure of control and direction, small enough for all the parts to be visible at once and so for all the individuals and classes in it to be fully and humanly aware of one another. Small

12

industries tended to afford a better life to the individuals working in them than huge concerns. This was positive fact, not speculation; Nils had been inspecting mills and factories the world over for years, and here he was sure of his ground. He thought of the rural or semi-rural industries of Hungary and Yugo-Slavia, the single factory in the village, and the good life led by the workers in it. There might be no vita-glass in the windows, and the workers did not come to it in cars or on bicycles—they came on their feet, along the muddy or dusty village street, with geese on the grass by the roadside, and the village pigs going out in a great drove to pasture, and neighbours greeting them from the door-steps. This was better than going in a tram through leagues of hideous brick, as in Bolton or Wigan or Turin; it was better even than bowling to work in mass-produced cars, like their compatriots in Pittsburg or Detroit. Better because these peasant artisans were all the time intimately conscious of their true relationship to the two ultimate bases of human life—the earth, our Mother, on and by whom we live, and our fellow-men. Equably poised in their relationship to them, too; poised in their universe, as the artisans in great cities somehow and deplorably were not. And no amount of model dwellings or electric washers or cheap delicious food out of tins could replace to the town worker that loss of poise and awareness.

He had left the door of his compartment open to enjoy the rush of air; a gust of fragrance and a passing step warned him that Mrs. Thurston had just gone by. He rose and went after her. As he gathered up his pouch the thought struck him—"Is *she* vulgar?" Not sure, he thought; she is accustomed to a world where diamond initials are the normal thing—it may not be ostentation. Out in the corridor, there was her graceful athletic figure before him, moving with its beautiful strength, walking like a mountaineer—no, she is not; not fundamentally, he thought. She may live with vulgarity, and it may even have tainted her mind; but her body knows better, still has its share of the old wisdom. I wonder if she has borne children, or if her false modern values have prevented her. And again he wondered what her nationality was.

She looked up with an expression of surprise when the steward showed him into the chair opposite hers.

"It is a lovely day," said Nils, firmly assuming acquaintance and the right to conversation.

"It's very hot in here," she said, in rather drawling tones of protest. "I can't think why they don't have air-conditioning in these cars."

"For the reason, it is not necessary," said Nils; "in Europe there is neither great heat nor great cold." He beckoned the steward and asked him to open the top of the window. "Do you like air-conditioning?" he asked her then.

She raised her eyes from the menu.

"Of course. Doesn't everyone?"

"Not I!" he said, firmly. "With air-conditioning one is too cold or too hot, always; I prefer to control the temperature in my compartment myself. And I like to be able to open the window if I want to. Did you open your window this morning? The air was sweet."

"The smuts come in," she said, discontentedly. "They don't in air-conditioned cars." And she turned to the waiter to order her lunch. Now she will ask for something they haven't got, Nils thought, and his grin appeared again—but recalling his misdemeanour at breakfast he suppressed it, and listened with a blank face while she expressed a wish for tunny-fish, which was not on the menu, as a hors-d'œuvre. There was none. She pouted; the waiter was visibly desolated. That sort of lady should have whatever she desired, by rights.

"Drink some wine with me, Madame—it is quite good!" Nils said. "Do you like red or white?"

"Wine makes one so hot," she drawled again, in exhausted protest.

14

"Nonsense—pardon, Madame," said Nils. He turned to the waiter and ordered his own lunch, and a flask of Chianti. "Since people in semi-hot countries, like Italy and France, habitually drink wine, it must be the right thing to drink in these climates," he went on. "Have you not found in travelling that one keeps in health by eating what the inhabitants of any country regularly eat? In China, at least once a day rice; in Hungary, plenty of paprika; in Scotland, whisky. Do you not find this?"

Now how will she answer that? he thought. She lives in international hotels and eats their international food, I will bet, and knows nothing of local diet.

"I never thought about it," she said, without interest. Then to his surprise she added—"When we were children we used to eat polenta in the peasants' houses, but it was nasty as it was; it was only nice if you let it get cold, and then toasted it—then it was rather like corn bread, only soggier."

"How came you to be brought up in Italy? You are not Italian?"

"No—my mother's second husband was an Italian, so we lived quite a lot in Italy, till she divorced him," she said. "He had a villa by Maggiore."

"That is how you came to picnic on the Iles Borromées," he said with a smile; he said it really to gain time to make up his mind whether he could ask another question. He decided to risk it, and when she had given an uninterested "Yes," he asked:

"Was your mother American?"

Hitherto she had opposed a sort of dreary blankness, like that of the worst type of English debutante, to all his gambits; at the pertinacity of this question he could almost see the feminine in her rouse itself to a skirmish, even with such an unworthy opponent as himself, a big sub-blond man in the early forties, not dashing in either face or dress— but a man, and displaying a certain persistence of interest in her.

15

"Yes," she said, with a gleam of amusement in those green-shot topaz eyes. "I suppose the divorces gave you that idea?"

"No—your voice," he said.

She looked annoyed.

"You are not going to suggest that I have an American accent?" she said, pronouncing the word like an English-woman.

He smiled.

"No—it was the intonation; what the French call 'accent tonique'. I noticed it this morning. But since we are discussing your ancestry, may I also ask if your father was not English?"

That pleased her, as he had guessed it would. There is a curious element of glamour which in America and on the Continent of Europe still hangs about an Englishman, unglamorous as they may seem to their countrymen and to themselves. The gleam of amusement appeared in her eyes again.

"Yes. But what made you think that?"

Can I possibly tell her? he thought. Yes, why not? It is not rude, if it is a little enterprising—and he told her how he had followed her along the corridor to breakfast, unable to see her face, and of the meeting with the man, and how he had decided that if she was beautiful she would be English, and if she was not, American.

"So, when I sat down and saw you, I decided that there was an English strain," he added.

She laughed, with a slight blush.

"Very neatly turned, if it is only half a one," she said.

"Have a glass of wine," said Nils, taking up the Chianti flask—he couldn't stay the course long on those lines, and wanted to make it clear that he didn't intend to try.

"Thank you."

"But you have lived in England too?"

"After I married, for a while—oh, I've lived more or less

16

all over the place; America, Italy, England," she said vaguely.

"Which did you like best?"

"They're all much the same, I think," she said. "I mean, some things are better in America—the trains, and train food, and the baths; you get better meat in England, of course, and better wine in France. And for scent and clothes Paris is really ahead of anywhere else."

He looked at her thoughtfully. She was really very pretty while she talked; she moved her lips beautifully with each syllable, though the sounds were so undistinguished, and her toneless voice if anything rather ugly—speech took away that distorting line of discontent from her mouth. But her lack of interest was fantastic.

"Those are all material things," he said—"baths and trains and food. But what about the people?—the inhabitants of the countries? Which of those do you like best?"

"I don't think there's a lot of difference in people, actually," she said, still with that vacant look. "They all do much the same things. Italians talk more than Americans, and Americans more than Englishmen. English people play the best bridge, I find."

He looked at her with severity. "You astound me," he said shortly.

"Why on earth?" she said, startled.

"Either you are lying, or there is something strangely wrong with you," Nils said. "In each country there are other variations than baths and food, and how much men talk! There are differences in the social structure, the intellectual outlook, the emotional tone; and they are interesting and very important. Anyone who knows three countries well must be aware of these things unless he is congenitally cretinous—even poor peasant emigrants from Central Europe are aware of another mental atmosphere in America. You are not a cretin—so I do not understand how anyone can speak as you do unless they are mentally diseased."

17

She had a great capacity for lack of expression—deliberate, he had begun to think—but at this attack she looked at him with genuine astonishment. Then—

"Perhaps I am mentally diseased," she said, with a cold little laugh. "Are you a doctor?"

"No. It would distress me to think that," he said, eyeing her.

"I just don't happen to be much interested in people, that's all," she said. "I suppose people have a right not to be interested, if they don't want to."

"In the sense that they have a right to commit suicide, yes," said Nils. "But all the churches, and the laws of most nations, hold suicide to be a crime."

For the first time, she spoke with energy. "I've always thought that a perfectly damnable law," she said. "What business is it of the Church *or* the State, if someone is through with life and wants to pass out?"

So I was right at breakfast! was Nils' first thought. Aloud he said, rather slowly—"I imagine the legal position based itself formerly on the State's need of man-power and woman-power, so that to deprive one's country of a healthy person was a crime against the State. That is perhaps a little out of date, since so many countries now suffer from overcrowding and unemployment. But the Churches were and are thinking of the soul. Self-annihilation must always seem an unworthy thing—selfish, cowardly; a denial of one's duties and responsibilities to others, a denial of that glorious thing, courage, for one's self."

She played with her rings, in silence; Nils watched her dropped eyelids. He noticed that her eyelashes were very thick and dark; artificially curled, but not blackened. Her eyebrows were not darkened either, though they were plucked. At length she looked up at him, with a small smile.

"So you think I'm committing mental suicide by being bored most of the time?" she said.

18

"If you are speaking the truth about the extent of your boredom, I mean exactly that."

"Why shouldn't I be speaking the truth?"

"No, the question is rather—Why should you speak it, to me? There are plenty of reasons why you should not; reticence, a wish to conceal, or affectation."

"And which do you think is my reason?"

"Affectation," said Nils promptly,—"if you are lying, that is. But I think you are in part speaking what you have come to believe is the truth. I mean, your mind has lied to *you*, first."

When he brought out the word "affectation," so pat and brisk, she laughed out loud, a real genuine laugh.

"You are a most extraordinary person," she said then, her face still gay from her laughter. "Do you always talk like this to people in trains?"

"No—I very seldom talk to women in trains at all. If I get into conversation with a man, we talk politics. I have never talked so to anyone in a train before—but then I have never before met a mental suicide in a train," said Nils, also smiling.

Her face darkened at the word—really it was getting quite expressive, he thought.

"Suicide isn't a joke," she said, coldly.

"My dear lady, to whom do you say it? If I didn't think mental suicide, even, a crime, a tragedy, why do you suppose I have, so unwarrantably, been lecturing a total stranger about it?"

"I can't *think* why you have, anyway," she said, more naturally than she had yet spoken.

"I think it must be because interference is my profession," he said, with a smile.

"What *is* your profession? They don't have professors of interference yet! Are you"—suddenly she looked suspicious —"some sort of Gallup Poll person?"

He laughed. "No, no—I can reassure you. I am on the

19

staff of the I.L.O. So I go about interfering with factories and working conditions all the time."

"What does I.L.O. stand for?" she asked, getting out a cigarette.

Oh God, oh God, Nils thought—there you are! She knows three countries and two continents, and she has never heard of the I.L.O.

"International Labour Office, at Geneva," he said.

"Oh—a League of Nations thing," she said, looking vacant again.

"Where do you get your money from?" Nils asked her sharply.

"Land!" she said triumphantly—"land in England!"

"There isn't much money in land in England today," Nils said thoughtfully. "Are you sure there isn't any coal on it?"

She laughed. "You're too sharp! Yes, there is coal on it, as a matter of fact."

"And how much do you know about your miners' lives and conditions of work? Have you ever been down a mine?"

"No—but all that is controlled—there are inspectors and things," she said. "Their houses are all right, too; the two villages are models, as a matter of fact; people come from all over the place to see them. There aren't only the best pit-head baths in England, but each cottage has its own bath-room, and a stove that heats the water. And the coal is free, of course."

The funny energetic pride with which she said all this was in extraordinary contrast with the lackadaisicalness of most of her speech. She loves, or did love, her husband, Nils thought—and the mines are his.

"English labour conditions are ahead of any others in the world, of course," he said.

She raised the fine eyebrows.

"Ahead of American ones? When most of them live in those poky little houses, with brick floors that have to be scrubbed, and no washing machines, and walking to work?"

He smiled.

"You are thinking in terms of material things as apparently you always do," he said. "I was really thinking of the others—wage rates and the way they are regulated, the machinery for settling industrial disputes, and above all the power of English Trade Unions and their sense of political responsibility. It all goes so smoothly, with so much good will and mutual self-respect. There is nothing like it in the world—certainly there is nothing like it in America as yet. Though we in Scandinavia are not so bad," he added with a touch of complacency.

"I don't see what good power and political responsibility do, if people still have to live under horrid conditions and scrub dirty floors," she objected.

He looked at her thoughtfully. "How curious that is," he said—"You live in Italy, you have lived in England, and yet you do not understand Europe at all. In Europe we don't think labour a hardship in itself; only excessive labour. In fact we are more positive; we know, and have retained our knowledge, that working with the hands is a good thing for anyone—it confers virtue and power."

"You do say extraordinary things! How can it confer *virtue*?" she asked, with slightly mocking incredulity.

"Manual labour is a two-way thing," he answered. "Have you any real lace?—perhaps your wedding veil? I know that young women no longer wear lace."

"I have some very lovely lace, as a matter of fact," she said.

"Machine-made?"

"Of course not—Duchesse and Point d'Alençon."

"Real Point d'Alençon?"

"Naturally," she said scornfully. And then began to laugh. "I see where you are taking me! But that's rather different. Lace-making is an art."

"Excuse me, no," said Nils. "In Nottingham or Lille they could copy your Duchesse lace, in exactly the same pattern, in the same fine linen thread, on a machine. The Point d'Alençon, no—that must have the needle-point on it. But the machine-made would not have either the beauty or the money value of the other. You and I both know exactly what we mean by 'real lace'—we mean hand-made lace. And those absurd shoes of yours are made by hand, and so, I would wager, are your underclothes. I fancy your stockings, your suspender-belt and the seams of your dress are the only things on you sewn by machine."

She laughed, a little reluctantly.

"You know too much!" she said. "Of course hand-made things are better and more expensive, but I don't see what that has to do with scrubbing floors."

"Much," said Nils. "I tell you the work of the hands is a two-way. You can't define the merit of real lace, but you can recognise it, and that it comes from the work of the human hand. It has a virtue and a value that the machine cannot give. And in the reverse direction, working with the hands gives to the worker some virtue and power that cannot be had any other way."

For once she seemed interested. "And you mean that people work, over here, to get this virtue, as you call it?"

"Not consciously—no. Europeans work because they always have; but instinctively and fundamentally they like work, and take a pride in a floor or table well scrubbed, and in bread kneaded or linen washed with their own hands. What is wholly absent from their consciousness is any sense that manual labour is beneath their dignity, or a hardship; and there is very present too a distrust of machine-made things, and a contempt for those who cannot use their hands with competence and skill."

"That seems a frightfully uncivilised attitude, to me," she said. "Why use your hands to wash things if a machine will do it as well? Surely the whole point of civilisation is that machinery will do most of the work for us?"

"Good God!" Nils said. "What a conception of civilisation!"

"It's a very ordinary one," she said defensively.

"It is a false one," he said severely, "based on a very common modern confusion of thought between civilisation and mechanisation. Has it not occurred to you that there can be such a thing as a highly mechanised barbarism?"

Evidently it had not, for she fairly gaped at him when he said that.

"Mechanised *bar*barism!" she said. "You have the strangest ideas."

"Civilisation is an affair of the mind and the soul, and of human and social relationships. Machinery is incidental to it," he said. "By itself, it gives nothing and takes away nothing—it entirely depends on whether society controls it or is controlled by it. But do not go on imagining that ice-boxes and electric washers and a jade-green telephone by your bed are the marks of civilisation, or have anything to do with it at all."

She considered this, frowning a little. Evidently what Arnold Bennett called "the intolerable effort of conscious thought" was an unwonted exertion to her. At last—

"Then you think there should be no machinery?" she said, a little contemptuously, as one who throws out a *reductio ad absurdum* to crush an opponent.

"I have not said so, but upon my soul, I sometimes wonder if we should not be better without it. No—as things are, it is only that we should be careful not to let machinery swamp life. That we should be sure, when we are confronted with a fresh mechanical contrivance, that we are not losing more than we gain by adopting it."

"What could we lose? What sort of thing?"

How curious it is, he thought, how she swings to and fro between genuine interest in a new idea, and lazy contempt for it.

"The printing press," he said, "has conferred untold benefits on mankind by spreading great literature and noble ideas; but universal literacy in Britain, for example, has

23

robbed a nation of its power of memory, or almost; and the daily press in America, with its flood of columnists and commentators, has utterly debauched the power of independent thought in a people naturally shrewd. That is an example of both the gains and the losses, and that is why I said that it is a question of control. So too many electric washers and sweepers mean that women lose the use of their hands, as too many cars mean that people lose the use of their legs. Women's hands should not be empty; there should be vessels in them, or brushes, or needles! There is something sterile about empty hands, or hands which only hold cards!" he said with sudden contempt—"as there is about empty wombs. In both cases women are in the wrong relation to life—and so they are nervous, restless, miserable. They take up culture, they take up Causes, but Life passes them by. They gain the whole world—on the radio—and lose their souls. And what shall a man—or a woman—give in exchange for his soul?"

He spoke at last with real passion, and this time it was she who looked at him, in speculation. It was all quite new to her, this, he could see that; and while half the time she resisted these strange ideas, his conviction—probably in conjunction with his evident interest in her, that expressed itself so unusually, without gallantry—drew her back, each time, to question a little further, to consider the novel view of life that he put before her. She sat looking at him, turning her huge rings on her white fingers—then, with a sudden movement, she dropped her hands into her lap. Nils was touched by the childish abruptness of the gesture, and a little flattered that his words about empty hands should so have gone home; it was almost a gesture of surrender to his argument. But he said nothing; he waited to see how she would tackle the thing in words, which for all her apparent sophistication she used so incompetently.

"It seems to me that you're trying to put the clock back," she said at last. "I—ordinary people—feel that cars and ice-boxes and less drudgery for women are a good thing. Leisure is a practical thing, anyhow—not like this virtue of yours."

"What do you—and the other ordinary people—use your extra leisure for?" he asked.

"Oh, I don't know—well, for amusing oneself, or reading. Women in America today have all sorts of interests, clubs and lectures and so on, that they couldn't have if they were drudging around all day."

"And what about their flavour, their tang, their individuality? Do they create their own beauty, in dress or in the home, or in music? Or do they get it mass-produced, by mail order, from Sears Roebuck, and over the radio?"

She laughed a little.

"They do dress a bit alike," she admitted. "Oh, I don't know—I don't really understand what you mean by this virtue of yours."

"Why don't you take a look at European civilisation? It's obvious you never have," he said.

"On the contrary, I know most of Europe very well," she said, indignantly.

"The big cities, where the life is purely cosmopolitan— yes, I daresay," he answered, allowing his scorn to come into his voice. "That is not fundamental European civilisation, though. You must look for that elsewhere."

"Where?"

"Albania," he said, really at random.

"Albania? I thought that was just a wild savage little country," she said in surprise.

"It is small, and it is wild, but you will find what you are looking for there, if you allow yourself to see it," he said, getting up. "And do get over the idea that *size* has any value or merit. It is the enemy of most of the best things in the world—it is the enemy of the good life."

He bowed and walked out of the restaurant car, leaving her seated at the table, looking after him.

2

BACK in his sleeper, Nils sat looking out of the window, watching the panorama of the plain of Lombardy sweeping by, the tall slender lines of poplars, like rows of green quill pens, swinging round at sharp angles as the train passed them. The fields were tidier, better tilled than fourteen years ago—one had to hand it to Mussolini for that, he admitted. Gradually the irritation that he had felt at the end of his conversation with Mrs. Thurston subsided, and he began to wonder why he had been irritated at all. Even if she belonged—as she did—to a class and a type that he disliked and despised, it was not her fault that she had betrayed her characteristics so thoroughly: he had manœuvred her into lunching with him, and had forced her to talk. Yes, he had been unreasonable and boorish again, thought Nils remorsefully. He lit a cheroot, and went on thinking about her.

He felt that in some odd way they had got onto terms, not of intimacy, exactly, but of truthfulness. That sometimes happened in trains, he knew, who spent so much of his life in trains. That was common enough; but what was really odd was his impression of the way their conversation had followed, not the obvious surface lines which it might have been expected to take, but the subterranean ones of her secret preoccupation or need. That the need existed had been guess-work at first on his part, but she had confirmed the guess by pursuing something, he wasn't sure what, in their talk; coming back, time after time, and even when arguing, to, as it were, look for something or contest something. What *was* she looking for? What was the source of her misery? Had her husband, whom he was convinced that she had loved—the mine-owner—gone sour on her in some way? Had she had a child and lost it? She was too young for a child to have gone sour on her—that was a tragedy of the forties, and he would be surprised if she had seen thirty yet. But if her husband had just plain died, there should not have been this cynical discontented misery—the simple loss of a beloved mate had usually something tranquillising about it, setting the mourner in a sort of withdrawn calm. She was not calm, and not withdrawn; in spite of her lack of interest, she lived very much in the market-place. That was the pitiful thing about her—somehow she was essentially unplaced. Nils found himself feeling a pity that surprised him for this strange woman, and above all for her spiritual homelessness.

The train ran into Venice across the lagoon, paused for some minutes, and ran out again. Nils watched from his window, as they returned to the mainland, the tracery of spire and dome etched on the silver sky above the silver water. He noted too, with angry disgust, the shallow flat domes of the huge petrol and oil containers, built into the landward shore of the lagoon, in apparently endless numbers. "That's it—stick them down within half a mile of Venice, and then curse your enemies for vandals if a stray bomb hits St. Mark's," he said sourly to himself.

Now as they swung eastwards along the coast, Murano, Burano, and Torcello stood up, small isolated etchings in blue ink over grey-blue water; to the north, from the window of the corridor, he could see the distant mountains sweeping down towards the sea. As the train neared Trieste he rose and stood in the corridor to look at them; now they were close enough for their distinctive colour to be visible, the cold pearly tone of the limestone, and beside the track the small brilliant lime-loving flowers appeared—grape-hyacinths, scillas, minute irises, and silver-leaved starry little objects, pink or white or yellow. Nils didn't know what they were, but his heart rose in him at the sight. Always, as he

27

approached Trieste, he experienced the same excitement from the first sight of the Karst, the great limestone ranges which run down from the Karawanken almost to the borders of Greece; this was the first touch of South-East Europe; the breath of Slavdom blew off the limestone, and from the valleys and plains beyond streamed out the sense of antiquity that enfolds all lands still partly Eastern. Beyond those white ranges, he reflected happily, lay the Old Testament.

He and Mrs. Thurston dined together after Trieste, as the train climbed up into the silver-white hills. Francesco and his dining-car had gone, a Yugo-Slav head-steward reigned in his stead; the menu was in Yugo-Slav and rather poor French. The new steward, however, also knew Nils of old, and greeted him with warmth; moreover he reacted to Mrs. Thurston's appearance exactly as the previous one had done, and urged her to take an aperitif.

"What are all these things?" she asked Nils, as the man poured out a string of names.

"Have some slivovitz—it's the most happy-making drink there is," Nils said; and he spoke in fluent guttural accents to the steward, who bowed appreciatively. Mrs. Thurston may have supposed that he was merely ordering the drinks; in fact he was telling the man that they were not to be hurried, and might wish to sit through both services.

"What language are you talking to him?" she asked, getting the malachite cigarette-case out of that huge bag, and fitting a cigarette into the be-diamonded holder. She did this in an easy unaffected way, this time, and spoke with a sort of friendly interest such as she had not so far shown. Nils was pleased.

"Serbo-Croat," he said, lighting her cigarette for her. "You don't speak it?" (He had taken that risk with some confidence.)

"No."

He lit a cigarette for himself, and then, the slivovitz arriving, raised his glass to her. "Prost!" he said.

"Here's how!" she responded, raising hers.

"What," Nils asked, indicating the flamboyant golden initials on the black bag, which, as before, was propped against the window, "does the G. stand for?"

She looked faintly surprised. "Gloire," she said.

"Like Gloire de Dijon?"

"Yes," she answered, smiling a little. "Silly, isn't it?"

Nils actually thought it was.

"Parents have very bizarre ideas about names," he said noncommittally. "Did your mother call you that to celebrate some event, or did she guess in your cradle that you would end up glorious?"

"Neither. She read it in a book. I used to be fearfully ashamed of it when I was small, but now I've got sort of accustomed to it," the owner of the name said.

"Later on of course they will be able to call you Old Glory," he said, grinning.

"Oh, cut it out! I had plenty of that at school," she said energetically.

"Would you call your own daughter by such a name?" he enquired. "I mean, people sometimes learn, and sometimes they do not."

"Definitely I shouldn't, if I had a daughter. That much I have learned."

"No daughter? That is a pity," he said, looking at her deliberately. She had come to the restaurant car tonight without a hat, so that the pretty shape of her small head was clearly visible, and the full beauty of that peculiar dark-gold hair. It was a very strange colour; like honey, he decided, when the bees have been sent with half-filled combs to the heather—not the blackish green of true heather honey, but a golden-green. As she met his glance with a rather mocking little smile, he went on—"A son, perhaps?"

29

"No. I've no children," she said shortly.

Well, there was that established. But she didn't seem resentful of his questions. He looked out of the window—up a side valley a great blunt-headed peak showed creamy in the evening sunshine.

"There is some splendid climbing in these mountains," he said. "Have you ever climbed here?"

"No."

"But you do climb, don't you?"

"Now why should you think that?"

"I'll tell you afterwards. But you are a mountaineer?" he persisted.

"Yes, I have climbed a good bit, as a matter of fact," she said slowly, with a curious hesitancy, "but I don't see why you should have supposed that *I* climbed."

He was puzzled by her stress on the "*I*"—she spoke as if it was natural that he should have supposed that someone else did.

"I supposed it for a very simple reason. You walk like a mountaineer."

"But you haven't seen me walk."

"Oh yes I have. I saw you walking down the corridor to breakfast this morning, and by the way you balanced yourself, when the train swayed—and even in those ludicrous shoes of yours!—I could tell that you were a ski-runner or a mountaineer, or both. But I thought, a mountaineer."

She laughed—but Nils had a curious impression that his explanation had relieved her in some way.

"You drew a lot of conclusions from my back view walking along a train!" she said, with mockery—"my ancestry, and that I climb. Are you sure you aren't a detective as well as a factory inspector?"

"No—I am not. I am simply a little observant. And as I climb myself, I am familiar with climbers' ways. Where have you climbed? In the White Mountains? The Rockies?"

"No, in the Alps, mostly—a little in the Pyrenees."

30

"Do you know the North *arête* of the Grivola?"

A strange look, happy and also visionary, came into her eyes when he asked that.

"No—but I've always wanted to do it. It is the most lovely line, isn't it?"

"It is. The purest curve in the world! Have you climbed in the Graians at all?"

"No—only looked at them from the south side of Mont Blanc."

"Oh—have you been up by the Brenva? Or by the Col de l'Innominata?"

"Neither—I'm not a tiger, at all! I meant from small things like the Aiguille Noire de Peuterèt or the Trelatête. Oh," she said with sudden eagerness, "do you know the ridge walk from the Col du Géant along and down to the Col des Grandes Jorasses? It is such fun; like walking along the roof-tree of a house, a lot of the way—but you have literally one foot in Italy and one foot in France, because the frontier runs along there! And if you drop your matchbox, it only stops six thousand feet down."

She spoke with real enthusiasm, at last, and it added unimaginably to the beauty of her face. He looked at her in wonder. So she had known happiness and natural eagerness; that aspect was part of her too, as much as her misery and disaffection with life.

"Yes, I have done it once," he said. "But I don't call that a 'small thing.' You must have a good head."

"Oh, my head's all right," she said simply.

They had emptied their glasses, and the steward was hovering over them to ask if he should serve the soup. Nils told him No, to bring some more slivovitz; it was very agreeable sitting there, with his companion in this happy mood, while the thin spring woods, the clear rushing waters and the pale mountains of Slovenia swam past, glowing in the evening light. Mrs. Thurston raised her delicate brows when the second round of drinks came.

31

"Isn't it very strong? You aren't trying to make me tight, are you?"

"No, only to make you happy!" he said, smiling very directly at her.

Her bright look was suddenly dimmed.

"Making anyone happy is a large order," she said.

"I know it. But mountaineers are a happy race. They know joy as others do not know it. Cold, hungry, exhausted, in danger, they still have some secret spring of satisfaction," he pronounced, "and they carry it with them down to the cities and the plains."

Her eyes became far-away as he spoke, looking past him from the train window to the visible mountains without. "Oh, I guess they do," she said, without shifting her gaze.

Nils pursued her mood.

> "The heights of granite and the grassy steep
> My spirit in a magic fortress keep
> Where in the silence, singing waters start,"

he quoted.

She brought her eyes back to him.

"What's that?"

"A poem."

"Do you know the rest?"

"No—just those lines stuck in my head."

"I don't wonder. They're true all right. Who wrote it? Do you know?"

"A girl," he said. "A girl who climbed, and was always homesick for the mountains when she was not among them."

"An English girl?"

"Yes. But it is a long time since she was a girl. She will be a middle-aged woman by now."

"Do you know her?"

"I did, when she climbed. It's years since I saw her."

"What was her name?"

"Glanfield—Miss Glanfield."

32

She frowned a very little.

"I seem to know the name, but I don't know why. I don't think I met her climbing," she said, with an obvious effort of memory.

"Oh, you wouldn't. I believe she stopped climbing years ago."

"Why?—if she loved it?"

"She married," Nils said. "But now you must eat something," he said as the steward appeared. "Here is the menu."

It was curious how at that, at the business of choosing her food, back came all the artificiality and exactingness which had become her second nature. She questioned each dish, with an air of dissatisfaction—would the trout be fresh, would the risotto not be oily?

Nils at length gibed at her openly—"What a fantastic fuss you make about a little food!"

"Fantastic? I don't see why. I like food to be nice."

"So do most people. If you were arranging a dinner for friends with fine palates, in a good restaurant, your fuss would be reasonable, laudable. But just for yourself, in a dining-car on a train, where all the food is edible and none is delicious, why bother? Why bother yourself, and why bother the waiter?"

"The waiter doesn't mind," she said, rather half-heartedly.

"No—he likes it; because of your clothes, and your pearls and your rings! But it is a false pleasure; and it wastes his time—and yours."

"I don't mind wasting my time—there's nothing much to do in restaurant cars anyway."

"In *this* restaurant car, you might be talking to me!— which gives me a real, not a false pleasure," he said, rather to his own surprise. He realised that this evening, that was true.

She smiled, a little unwillingly.

"You like scolding, I suppose?" she said.

He laughed. "No—though I do it so much. You seem to

33

provoke that, somehow. But I like it more when we just talk."

She looked at him as if puzzled.

"You are very odd," she said.

"In what way?"

"Oh, I don't know. Things that everyone else takes for granted, you are so serious about—and preach sermons on. Like food and machinery and civilisation."

"Aren't food and machinery and civilisation important things?" he asked, amused.

"Oh yes—only most people just leave them alone! Anyway they aren't very interesting." Her expression brushed them aside. Then it changed in some subtle way—not so much to interest as in the direction of something sly, almost cajoling.

"Tell me more about Albania," she said, putting her elbows on the table.

"Are you going to Albania?"

"Not directly—I don't suppose so. I think I'm going to Istanbul."

"Don't you know?" he teased.

The weary discontented look came into her face again.

"It doesn't much matter where one goes," she said; with a curious dead bitterness. "But tell me about Albania—why you think it so worth seeing."

"First, it is very beautiful," Nils began. He was rather pleased that his remark about Albania had stuck. "The mountains are so beautiful, and the great lakes, Scutari and Ochrida; and just now, the nightingales are singing in the woods all day and all night. Then the people are handsome, and have a special charm which is recognised all over the Balkans; and in the country—which is most of Albania except Tirana and Durazzo and Scutari—every one is in fancy dress! That is very unusual and delightful today."

"Don't they wear costumes in the towns?"

"Less. But in Scutari, yes—a lovely costume, with aprons and embroidered shawls or veils. And on the Sunday after

34

the Ascension—that is about three weeks from now—all the peasants come in to Mass from the country round about, in their most glorious dresses. That is the time to see Scutari."

"Are they very religious, then? I thought they went in a lot for murdering and brigandage and all that."

"Not now—not much. The King has made great reforms, and the Gendarmerie run by the British really does keep order. That is a wonderful thing, what a few men, who know how to rule and have the unselfish tradition of ruling, can do with a backward people! But religion—yes. Even before the reforms, when there was much murder, religion was a part of their life, a most important part. In Albania, still, it is as it was all over Europe in the Middle Ages, the Age of Faith. Among the Moslems it is something the same. And it gives a great form to their way of living, savage as it would seem to you."

"Oh, are some of them Moslems still?"

"Yes, indeed—as in parts of Yugo-Slavia. Burrel is Moslem, but Mirdita and parts of Mati are Christian—Roman Catholic. Franciscans, the priests are mostly. Devoted men. At Torosh there is a great church, and a mitred Abbot. That is another thing to see—High Mass on Whit-Sunday in the church at Torosh. Again, all the people come from miles around in costumes of very great beauty, and fill the church with the glory of their clothes and of their conscious devotion. It is one of the most splendid sights left in the world."

"Can one stay there? Is there a hotel?" she asked, casually. Nils laughed.

"My dear young lady, no! Not in Torosh."

"Where do people stay, then?"

"In tents, if they have them. If not, they sleep in the open. One does not find any of your cosmopolitan 'confort moderne' in Albania, thank God! If one travels, one takes a tent and a camp-bed, and food and cooking vessels, and sleeps where one pleases, under the stars. Actually at Torosh, those who know Prince Lek-Gionaj can sometimes stay with him."

35

"But how do you cart all the doings around? You'd need a lorry!" she said, wide-eyed.

He laughed again.

"A lorry would not be much good to you," he said, "for there is no road for wheeled traffic to Torosh. There are only two real metalled roads in all Albania."

"How does one get about, then, with all these beds and things?"

"With a horse-caravan, of course—and men to lead them."

"But it's like Africa!" she ejaculated.

"Really it is more like Asia," he said. "You see there life as it is described in the Old Testament. And it has great beauty and power."

"Virtue, I suppose, too?" she said mockingly—"women using their hands."

"Exactly that," he said gravely, looking full at her. "There one does see, still in its untouched vigor and purity, the life that has been fundamental to European civilisation, that still is fundamental to it—peasant life alongside the life of the aristocratic landholder, the fellowship of the soil. And that is important to see, because it is the source of the inner strength of man, instead of its destroyer, as the life of the city is."

She frowned a little over this pronouncement.

"You're mad about cities!" she said, and pondered for some time. "But—all that you've just said, about the spirit and the life of the soil," she went on presently. "You said the aristocratic landholder was part of it. I thought the landed aristocracy were considered an anachronism everywhere, nowadays. Don't you believe in equality?"

"As you use the word, no!" he said. "Not even in the equality of opportunity. The State must attempt to provide that, of course, as a moral obligation, and to satisfy men's consciences. But neither I, nor the Albanians, nor anyone who knows anything about breeding animals believes in equality, if he uses his mind."

36

"What on earth has stock-raising got to do with it? It's a political and social question, surely?"

"Do you think the man in the Argentine who pays four thousand guineas—that is twenty thousand two hundred dollars—for a Scottish yearling bull really believes that all bulls are equal?" he asked, looking at her with a sort of bland quizzicality. "If he does, why does he not breed from any old bull, instead of paying that fantastic price and having the creature brought thousands of miles across the ocean?"

She laughed, a little unwillingly.

"He's paying for pedigree stock, of course, to improve his strain. But we were talking about human beings."

"I beg your pardon, we were, and are, talking about equality," he retorted, "a thing Nature does not know. But let us talk about human beings. Do you really think that the offspring of two drink-sodden slum parents, say a Bowery bum and a Bowery broad, however carefully you bring them up, are likely to be equal physically and mentally to the children of the fifth generation of substantial Vermont farming stock, or some of the Montenegrin or Albanian mountaineers?"

"Of course not—no. But we want to eliminate bums."

"Admirable. But you have not eliminated them—not only so, but the modern trend is to increase rapidly and steadily the class from which they chiefly spring, what Rebecca West calls 'the mindless, traditionless, possessionless urban proletariat.' And you pretend that they are the equals of these others. That is a doctrinaire falsehood, and the stock-breeder knows it."

"You really *believe* in aristocracy then?"

"Certainly. I do not see how a sensible man, who has been in contact with it, can do otherwise. This is unfashionable today, but we live in a very credulous and a very ignorant age and moreover a whole hemisphere, which for nearly a century has been out of contact with aristocracy, is beginning to tell the world that it would be better without it! That is not true, any more than mental and physical equality is a reality; but those who have never seen aristocracy, and therefore know no better, believe it; and also those seize greedily on this false creed who have most to gain by it, the urban proletariat who, having neither traditions nor possessions, wish to exalt themselves by bringing all men down to their own level. And since they are many, and have the franchise, and governments want votes, they are encouraged in this dangerous folly both by catch-penny statesmen and by the Press."

She laughed a little.

"You *are* a reactionary! But tell me, what's the use of the aristocracy anyway? What good do they do? Most of the ones I meet are just play-boys."

"I said the aristocratic *landholder*, remember. As for the ones you meet—I had better not say what I think about the people you probably habitually meet! But I think they are not all aristocrats, I think they have very little connection with the land, I think South Americans and transatlantic millionaires figure largely among them, *dépaysés* urban internationals, also mindless and traditionless,—though not possessionless. To me, such people are the wealthy equivalent of bums!"

She laughed aloud at the earnest, almost savage way in which he brought out the last words.

"My God, you're not so far out!" she said.

"Wait a moment—I wish to answer your question." The steward was clearing the table and bringing coffee; Nils spoke to him in Serbo-Croat, asking some question, and in a moment small glasses were brought, and a special bottle from which the steward filled them, carefully.

"What's this?" she asked, sipping.

"Another sort of slivovitz—better. It is much better, this, than any brandy you would get on the train."

"It's delicious," she said, truthfully. "All right—go ahead!"

38

"One should always see events, or classes, to some extent in the light of the past, from the historical angle," he said, choosing a slender cigar from a box which the steward brought—he nipped it carefully and lit it. "Peasants do this," he went on, "because the memory, the history, is preserved among them—whereas in the towns, in a couple of generations it is lost. But it is foolish to judge in ignorance of all this—and among educated people, like you, unpardonable."

"I'm not all that educated. Go on."

"In those countries, you see, which have had a Middle Ages, the landed aristocracy in the Middle Ages performed several useful functions. They protected the peasantry round about, at a period when the State could afford no such protection; they put down highway robbery in their domains, punished the evil-doers, decided disputes, and generally acted as law-givers—most of them held regular courts of justice; also they raised troops to defend their country in time of war, and armed and mounted them at their own expense. In fact they acted as the judiciary, the police, and the army for the mediaeval state."

"That's interesting," she said thoughtfully, her chin on her hand. "I didn't know all that." Her eyes were distant—Nils guessed that she was thinking of her mine-owning husband, who had spent so much on cottage bathrooms and pit-head baths. "But that's the past—that's all over now," she said.

"Nearly all—not quite. If you went to Albania you would see something of the same sort left. But to speak of the landed aristocracy as it is commonly spoken of today, with contempt, as though the 'Old School Tie' "—he spat out the words savagely—"were something shameful; to assume, as the yellow press assumes, that all members of the aristocracy are just restaurant play-boys, like the modern rich of the towns, is to condemn oneself as ignorant, as ungrateful, and as ungracious. And do not forget"—he too leaned an elbow on the table and held a minatory forefinger out towards her —"that the very blood of these people still carries the inher-

39

itance of responsibility for others, of leadership, and their minds and hearts the tradition of it. These things are not nothing; they are a great enrichment to any society, to any nation; to turn one's back on them is to be as foolish as a man who should eliminate all the pedigree bulls from his ranch, or the blood stallions from his stud. Look at Spain!—because of all the good blood she lost in the Inquisition. A second-class power, which was a great nation."

"Yes, I suppose Spain is that, now," she said.

"And the 'classless society'," he pursued, again spitting the words out contemptuously, "is not only crassly ugly, it is suicidal, and also it is false. There is no classless society, not anywhere in the world. Russia comes nearest to it, but even in Russia there are distinctions. Do the masses ride in cars? No—they ride in trams, or trudge along the pavement. Who then rides in those smart Russian-built limousines of which Moscow is full? The Commissars, the 'spetsi', or experts, technicians as we should say, the opera-singers and the ballerinas, the new aristocracy of Russia."

"State service and art aren't a bad basis for an aristocracy," she interjected.

"Not at all bad—you are right. Great things may come out of Russia. The point is that even there, is not this *sacré* equality. In America also you have class differences, in actual fact, but there wealth takes the place of rank. I think it is a poor exchange."

"Why?—apart from its being less picturesque?"

"Surely you can hardly ask that question seriously?" he said, leaning back and staring at her. "Very well, I will tell you why. The millionaire who rises from being a corner-boy has no traditions save those of corner-boys. It is true that from the safety of his achieved millions he may endow a university to give others the education he missed himself, or a hospital because his ancient mother died of cancer; but how many of them feel a general obligation to serve their country, to go into politics or the public service?"

40

"Mighty few," she said. "But——"

He swept her aside and went on.

"Whereas the hereditary aristocracy of Europe—and this is particularly so in my own country, Sweden, and in England, and also in Hungary—have the tradition of responsibility and of public service. And this affects a society in many ways. It gives stability and strength, it gives experienced leadership, and it gives an example. Look!" he said, dramatically,—"I shall give you one small instance, one comparison; you can say it is trifling, but trifles can be very indicative of tendencies of great importance. In the United States, the little girls in shops and streets, the typists, imitate the clothes, the dresses—of whom?"

"Film-stars, mostly," she said, carelessly.

"Of course. And to imitate them, they study their pictures in the papers. And what do they see? They see them lounging half-naked at Palm Beach, they see them drinking cocktails by bathing pools, they see them with their last husband or their next husband or their latest lover. But in England, for example, whom do such girls imitate? They imitate the clothes and dress of the younger peeresses, or the Royal Duchesses, like the Duchess of Kent. And how do they see *them* portrayed? With their children round them, or visiting a hospital or opening a school, or inspecting Girl Guides. Performing some public service—always service! Do you think this is without effect on the girls who see? I tell you, such things get in through the pores of the skin, and are of great effect. They colour the whole social outlook of a country, in both ways. In the one nation, the thoughtless and uneducated—and not only they!—admire and respect wealth and success; nothing else is held up to their admiration; in the other, where wealth and success are in fact despised, they admire and respect rank and tradition, the tradition of service. Which do you think shall do most for the moral standards of a nation?"

"That's probably true enough," she admitted, "though I'd

41

never thought of it that way before; but Americans don't like rank being a fixed thing—they like every man to have the same chance."

"And have they not, in England? That is the great strength of English society, the fluidity of rank. If a man performs great public services he is made a peer, and so brings new blood into the aristocracy. When I was at Oxford—yes, I was there—I had my punctures mended at a little cycle shop in Long Wall Street, and boarded my little dog there— Mr. Morris, the owner, who mended my punctures with his own hands, was glad enough to get five shillings a week for her keep. Now he is Lord Nuffield, and sits in the House of Lords, and wears the ermine."

"That's only one."

"Nonsense! There are many. Look at the Archbishop of Canterbury—he was a son of the manse, and went first to the village school. Look at Lord Weir! Look at all the Wills and Coats peerages! Almost all these were first working-men or tradesmen, and now are noblemen. In a republic they would get no reward but their wealth; in a monarchical democracy they get an intangible reward, indeed, rank— but a very potent one. Their rank carries with it the tradition of obligation, of service, of responsibility; and so potent is this tradition that with very few exceptions, in one generation or at the most two, they feel and behave as do the old aristocracy, and their children acquire the same ideas of service and gentle behaviour." He looked back at her and smiled quizzically. "A gentleman is not a bad thing," he said.

Some thought darkened her eyes and twisted her mouth.

"Of course not," she said impatiently. "But we—Americans—don't like privilege. You can twist it all round as much as you like, but there *is* something in equality."

"There is something," he agreed gravely—"but one wants to be quite clear which forms of equality are real and possible, and which are not. There can be, and should be, absolute equality before the law. That is vital—and in Sweden and in England, where judgeships are not political appointments, and judges are incorruptible, that exists—as most oddly, it does not exist in America. In England you cannot pack a jury or buy a judge, and the rich man or the political boss has no better chance before the law than the poor man. The Sacco and Vanzetti trial could not have happened in England, or anywhere in Scandinavia."

"People harp so on Sacco and Vanzetti," she said petulantly. "It was only one case."

"Yes. But it shocked the conscience of the world. Quite humble people, here in the Balkans, heard of it with horror and dismay. You see they had taken the American claims to equality and liberty at their face value; but this one case tore down their simple illusions, because the injustice to two poor men was too manifest, too plain. So they began to wonder, and to ask of those who returned—and they found out the truth about American equality before the law, that often it is really just words, like an advertisement. They do not understand about advertising, here."

"Were you ever in the States?" she asked abruptly.

"Oh yes—many times, and for long periods," he said. "That is why I know about equality over there. But look— shall we go on considering what forms of equality are real and possible? Because there is a second one, very important —indeed I should have put it first."

"What's that?"

"The absolute equality of the human soul before God. That *is* a reality."

She looked at him in surprise, as if to see if he were serious.

"I don't see what that has to do with equality here on earth," she said at last, slowly.

"It does not surprise me that you do not," he said—"for it is a truth, a concept, that has been largely lost sight of in communities which concentrate on the theory of social equality. But, first, it is literally and indisputably true, as

43

true as man's physical nakedness at birth and death; and secondly, where it is realised and felt—as it is here in Europe —as an actual part of man's daily life, it has a profound effect on the social structure. It removes, almost completely, any sensitiveness about social inequality; for the peasant who is profoundly conscious of his relation to God, and knows that it is identical with the relation to God of his local Count or Prince, does not worry unduly about his relation to his social superiors. 'We are all men,' he says happily. 'We are all God's children, and He is our Father.' And resting in that security, that fundamental and complete equality, he gladly and gracefully touches his hat to the landholder, or kisses his hand. What does it matter? All souls have equal value, and God is our loving Father. Why then not kiss the Durchlaucht's hand? It is the custom, and it is pretty and gracious; it is a part of good manners; and the human soul at ease, as European souls are at ease, likes and enjoys the grace of good manners. You will not find here that edgy hypersensitive uneasiness which seeks to prove that 'I am as good as the next man' by discourtesy, by refusing the polite salutation, by the gruff reply to a civil request." He smiled at her. "You know of what I am thinking," he said.

She sat in silence, frowning a little.

"Yes, I do know," she said at last. "I love the politeness in Europe when I come back. But—Americans don't like to be servile."

"And must courtesy be servile? The peer is polite as well as the peasant, remember. Is that servility?"

"No—of course it isn't. And we don't think it servile when it's the peer." She paused and frowned again. "But you fox me by suggesting that *God* has anything to do with it."

"God has to do with everything," Nils said gravely. "It is the loss of the sense of God, in daily life, that causes such unhappiness in America, in spite of all its many religions."

"Do you call America unhappy, then?" she asked, her eyes

44

very wide. "Why, they think the world of happiness. 'Life, Liberty, and the pursuit of Happiness'—it's in the Declaration of Independence."

"I know. Most strange, that seems to us."

"Why?" she asked rather defiantly.

"Don't think I am trying to provoke you," he said gently, "or to make fun of what you revere for the sake of making fun of it. It is much too important for that. This is a question of a true or a false conception of life. That phrase about men's rights—not their duties, you remark—is at the root of so many misconceptions, because it is in itself a misconception. Learning can be pursued, and overtaken; virtue too"— he smiled—"and truth. But happiness, the Blue Bird—that has always eluded those who pursue it, and mankind has always known that it does, and must. Here, we know this; the veriest peasant, whom you so despise for his 'low standard of living' knows better than to pursue happiness directly. What can we think, what can you expect us to think of a nation which inscribes so irrational an aim practically in its constitution? Listen—" as he saw her face darken with vexation—"it was said long ago 'The good man is happy though crucified.' Is that what the Declaration of Independence means?"

"No," she said shortly,—"it means what it says, that people have a right to try to be happy."

"And you think they are happier there than here?"

"I—yes, I think so. They have more chances of it, anyway —more leisure, more freedom, and much more comfort."

"Ah!" He pounced on the word. "Comfort, yes. *Things* again! Shall I tell you what those words have really come to mean? 'Life, Liberty, and the pursuit of Comfort.' But happiness has escaped their grasp, to judge by all the usual signs."

"What signs do you judge by?" she asked, fitting another cigarette into her holder. He lit it for her.

"I judge by a people's conversation, and their current

45

writing, and the faces of the old," he said. "In America I find few evidences of happiness in any of these. And your own young writers make no secret of the national unhappiness. One of your poets said to me over there, only a few weeks ago—'I don't get it. You're all living on a volcano, and yet every place I go in Europe, I see such happy faces.' I asked him, to see what he would say, what you asked me a moment ago—did he, then, think Americans unhappy? And I thought his answer so important that I wrote it down." Nils pulled a small note-book out of his pocket, saying—"I have a very bad memory,"—and turned the leaves.

"Ah, here it is." He read—" 'We are a most terribly unhappy people. Spiritually, emotionally and sexually, we have lost our way; politically we never really knew it. We do not know what we want, nor where we are going. So we just grasp desperately at the things we *can* get—wealth, comfort, amusement; we have built up a great structure of material luxury to keep out the empty spaces of the spirit, as our forefathers built stockades round their communities to keep out the perils of the wilderness. We keep the radio going all the time to distract our empty hearts. We console ourselves with clever mechanical gadgets as a homesick child consoles itself, desperately, with toys. But in fact we are the most unhappy nation on earth. Most of us don't realise it, and would die sooner than admit it; but we are, and you have only to read us to see it. Our art—which is almost all writing—gives us away, as Art always does give away the truth. It is our very unhappiness which gives us this obsession about happiness. You don't have it, over there —the obsession, I mean—because you have the thing itself.' "

He closed the little book, and replaced it in his pocket. "That was an American speaking," he said, and sat back and took a sip from his glass.

To his immense surprise, she put both her hands up to her head in a gesture of real desperation; and spoke in a high-pitched tone, pouring out her words in a flood.

"I don't get it either! I don't see why you have to pick on America, and go for our gadgets just because we want to be happy, and like comfort and clean ways and cars and victrolas! Everyone in Europe isn't so happy, anyway! Why can't you let America alone? It lets you alone."

He saw that she had had more than she could take—the discussion of unhappiness, or something, had got under her skin. He pondered making some soothing reply, and turning the conversation. He *had* preached at her, unpardonably, anyhow. Then he looked at her again. Her white hands still held her white forehead, the scarlet-tipped fingers interlacing across her dark gold hair. No, he thought; this is desperately serious, and for some reason it is serious for her; to try to make her understand is really more important than her being hurt and angry. I will try.

But first he took up the bottle and refilled her glass and his own.

"Put down your hands," he said simply—"and drink some of that. So—" as she did as she was told. "Now, I will try to tell you."

"For almost the whole world today," he began slowly, "the great problem is how to combine mechanisation on the scale on which we now have it, with the good life. Human life has run on on much the same lines for four thousand years—sowing and reaping, spinning and weaving, cooking and eating food; loving and marriage, birth and death, the pursuit of knowledge, the creation of beauty, the service and adoration of God. And till the nineteenth century it has run at much the same tempo, the same pace. The one great shake-up before that was the discovery of the printing-press, which made it possible to disseminate ideas much more widely and more rapidly than before. That, we have to some extent assimilated; man has adjusted himself to literacy, up to a point.

"But since the beginning of the nineteenth century have come also the steam engine and the internal combustion

47

engine, the telegraph, the telephone, and the wireless; and these have altered the tempo of human life, and made it at once immensely more rapid, and infinitely more noisy than ever before. At the same time the invention of machinery and the flooding of the world with mass-produced goods have modified many aspects of human life: for instance man's sense of dependence on the soil and the weather—which reminds him daily of his dependence upon God; and also the workman's intelligent knowledge of what he is making, and his pleasure and pride in the work of his hands. Pleasure is of God—and any loss of pleasure is in itself a loss of part of man's dignity, and of that happiness which comes unsought. All this is having spiritual and psychological and nervous results, and mankind must adjust itself to the new conditions, or perish. We have not yet had time to measure these results fully; what we do already see is that cancer, crime, and nervous maladies are on the increase, in less than three generations.

"This is the great modern problem for the whole world," Nils went on—"this process of adjustment, this question of how to combine mechanisation with the good life, the healthy mind in a healthy body. And here in Europe, because we are ancient nations, habituated to thought and valuers of tradition, we realise instinctively that mechanisation may not be an unmixed blessing, and that if the adjustment to it is too rapid, it may spell disaster. It is not yet certain that it may not spell disaster anyhow. I, who inspect factories all over the world, know what the turning from being a field worker into being a factory hand does to a man! and so in Europe, where the process of swamping the individual life by the mechanised life has not yet gone too far, we wish to control it, to put on the brake. We are, some of us, very vividly aware of what is at stake, of what we are in danger of losing, and so we are on our guard. We feel that we must defend ourselves from false gods."

The moderation of his tone, and the breadth of his statement, had calmed her down—he had seen that while he spoke. But at his last words she raised her eyebrows.

"False gods! Isn't that rather strong?" she said. "Even in America we don't worship showers and ice-boxes yet."

"Are you sure? I am not sure," said Nils, with that funny Nordic simplicity of his. "If I saw and heard, in America, the same emphasis laid on purity of administration, on business integrity, on scholarship and thoroughness, and on the graces of humility and modesty as I see and hear laid on them here in Europe, I should think that you worshipped those things! But I do not! The resounding claims, in America, are not made for things such as these, but for central heating and Pullman trains and labour-saving appliances and cars for all. It *looks* as if those were what America most values, most aspires to. 'Wheresoever a man's treasure is, there will his heart be also.' Tell me, where is America's treasure?"

"Oh, how would *I* know? But I still don't see that you can prove that there's any harm in gadgets."

"Not yet—I tell you, there has not been time to prove that definitely. It is the importance which is attached to them that we feel to be certainly injurious."

"Why? What has it got to do with Europe, anyway? Why can't you let us alone?" Her voice was petulant again.

"That is what *we* ask," Nils said, smiling. "Do you constantly find European publicists talking and writing about 'the European Way of Life,' or about raising the standard of living in America, or about the 'backward nations' of the United States?"

He paused and looked at her; she laughed, a little unwillingly.

"It is America which will not let the world alone," Nils pursued—"which holds up its way of life as the ideal for every nation, and seeks to impose its own standards of living—which many people think ridiculously and unwholesomely high—on others, partly of course in the search for markets.

If it were openly stated that it *was* just a search for markets, that would be one thing, but it is not; by a tremendous propaganda campaign this materialistic conception is held up as an ideal, as somehow part of liberty, and above all, as a form of happiness. To search for markets is legitimate, but to make a virtue of so doing is not. Most of all it is a crime to dress up salesmanship in the garments of philanthropy, and to try to drag spiritual values into advertising. Those are false gods indeed, debasing ones—and we who see their falsity have the duty to protect ourselves from them. That is the one unforgivable sin, the sin against the light."

She sat drumming her fingers on the table; her expression was half-disconcerted, half-resentful. It reminded him of her dissatisfied face at breakfast, and an impulse came to Nils to ask her about herself. He did not usually yield readily to impulses, and now he argued with himself that it was getting late; that his strictures had clearly upset her; that if she was not tired anyhow, she must certainly be tired of *him*— that as she was going to Istanbul, there was all tomorrow, and he had far better leave it for tonight. But the impulse did not yield to argument; she sat silent, frowning at the table, her pretty profile reflected in the window against the darkening landscape outside; he continued to sit watching her, and suddenly he said—

"Let us leave the nations, and their happiness. You— forgive me, but why are *you* so unhappy?"

Up went her eyebrows; her whole face went on the defensive.

"Why in the world should you think I am?" Her voice was colder even than at breakfast.

But Nils, having yielded to his impulse, went ahead with it like a tank.

"Oh, your face! When I first saw it, more than the beauty, I saw the misery! And you are not one of those who cannot be happy, for when we spoke of mountains and of climbing, there was joy in your face, as in the face of a bride."

50

The defensive expression lessened, but for a long time she sat silent, looking rather bleakly at her hands. Nils waited—he had shot his bolt, but he was surprised to find with what anxiety he was waiting to see if she would answer him.

"When I climbed mountains, I was a bride," she said at last. She reached for her bag—Nils gave her one of his cigarettes and lit it for her. Blowing out smoke—

"Yes," she said rather tonelessly. "You're quite right—I was happy then. Incredibly happy. But it's all over now, and there isn't anything left that's worth bothering about."

"Why is it all over—please?" Nils asked.

"I should have thought you'd have known," she said, with rather dreary surprise. "He was killed climbing. Oh, I don't grudge that on the mountains," she said with a sudden furious energy—"but I do on the men who left him to die! I hate all men, I think, now. Damn them, damn them!"

"I am sorry. I did not know." Nils spoke without any awkwardness, only with complete sincerity and simplicity. "I am glad that you do not hold it against the mountains," he said then.

"Do you know why I don't?" she said, putting her elbows on the table and leaning towards him, with a directness as complete as his own. "It is because of something I heard him say once—it was in a speech at a mountaineering dinner, and I think he must have been a little bit tight, or he wouldn't have said so entirely what he really felt. He said—'Of all the gifts that the mountains hold for us—and to some of us they give so much that if they should exact the uttermost in return, we think ourselves still in their debt—of all those gifts' . . . and so on. I knew that was true for him, before he said it—but I've never forgotten those words. It could have been true for me too, in time—it was getting to be true. But now all that's finished with."

"What was the great gift, the greatest of all?" Nils asked. He wanted to keep her talking naturally; to probe farther into her tragedy, directly, was impossible.

51

"Friendship," she said slowly. "But you know I don't believe that was true, although he said it then, and he did adore his friends, and they meant the world to him. But I believe mountains meant more to him than any human being could."

"Yes—that can be so. I believe that is true of me—so far," Nils said.

"Are they like religion to you, too?" she asked. "They were to him."

"Not quite. God, who made them, is still above them. But they are one of the supreme expressions of God," he said, "and they evoke—I know it—the great religious feelings of adoration and faithful service. For one feels that to climb them is somehow to serve them."

"Oh, he felt that!" she said, her face alight.

"Of course. Mountaineers do. You should go on climbing," he said. "You need the religious sense."

"I guess I do," she said, and fell silent again. Nils left her alone, wondering what line her mind was following. Presently—"Are there mountains in Albania?" she asked.

"Indeed yes—it is nearly all mountains. Not like the Alps; there is nothing much over nine thousand feet, but there is some fine climbing on the limestone, and it all waits to be explored, from the climber's point of view." He was glad that the conversation had moved back to this degree of normality.

"How does one get to Albania?" she asked then.

"By a number of ways. From Italy, by boat from Bari; or if one is going from London one leaves this train that we are on at Zagreb, goes down to Susak, and so by steamer to Kotor or Durazzo. For you, if you went from Istanbul," said Nils practically, "you would take a steamer to the Piraeus, and then get another boat from Corinth up to Valona or Durazzo."

"I see." She sat pondering. "And all those tents and ponies and things, to hike around with—can one buy them there?"

52

"No. One can buy very little in Albania. But General Stanley, the Head of the Gendarmerie, can usually arrange all that—or one of the Legations. The Gendarmerie have plenty of tents and camp-beds, because they must rely on them for all their tours of inspection."

"That *is* extraordinary—in Europe, today," she said. "But it sounds nice."

"It is nice," Nils said, smiling at her. "You should really go."

"Oh well." She smiled back at him, and rose. "Thanks for all the drinks," she said. "Goodnight."

"Goodnight." Nils too had risen, and bowed. "We meet at breakfast, I hope," he said—"as today."

She smiled again, with sudden brilliance.

"Maybe," she said, and left the empty dining-car.

3

UNDRESSING in his sleeper, swaying to the rocking movement of the train, Nils racked his brains, trying to remember
about the accident to Mrs. Thurston's husband. Thurston—
Thurston—the name was vaguely familiar, but in what connection he could not for the life of him remember. Nils had
never belonged to the regular trade-union of English and
international climbers, who met one another every summer
in Zermatt, Chamonix, Courmayeur or Grindelwald, knew
all one another's names, ages, and notable expeditions, and
were *au fait* with all climbing gossip—a busy man, constantly
travelling, he had spent his brief leaves climbing and ski-ing,
but he was out of touch, and always had been, with that
climbers' world; his only real friend among English climbers
had been, years ago when they were both young, the ardent
and delightful Miss Glanfield. And long since he had lost
touch with her. He had heard that she had become a rather
well-known writer, or thought he had; but Nils had no
time for reading novels.

He opened the window at the top, drew down the blind
again, switched off the ceiling light and got into bed and
lay, his hands clasped behind his head, staring at the white
reflection of the pillows on the shining reddish panelling,
and chasing his recollections of the name Thurston through
his memory. Killed climbing—"the men who left him to die"
she had said. Oh *yes!* There had been that international expedition to the Himalayas, and a story—a story with rather a
strong smell—about a climber and some porters being left up
on a high camp, when bad weather came on; and the climber
and some of the porters had died. He had been in China at

the time, and seen few European papers, but—it was coming back now—the man who had died was an Englishman. Thurston—no, he couldn't actually pin the name to it, but that was almost certainly it. Not quick of him, not to have guessed sooner, only he was bad at names, and his memory was so overloaded as it was with the myriad names he *had* to remember, in his job.

As people do, he went back over his conversations with Mrs. Thurston in the light of this fresh knowledge. That was why she had said "I don't see why you should have supposed that *I* did," when he spoke of climbing; she had expected him to know that her husband climbed, and no doubt the accident had made banner headlines when it happened. He tried to remember how long ago it was—about five years, at a rough guess. Poor woman, he thought —no child, her husband lost in agonising circumstances. No wonder there was misery in her face. It all added up; given her upbringing and surroundings, her reactions were just about what might have been foreseen. A pity, Nils said to himself, soberly—a great pity, for she might have been otherwise. Mountaineering would have gone on teaching her its timeless lessons of patient continuance in well-doing, of endurance, and above all of worship and of joy. She had the capacity for joy, and she had the capacity for feeling—her sudden violent outburst in defence of American institutions had shown that. Funny how her very speech went American when she felt that America was assailed! But probably it was too late to do anything about it— certainly one could not cure a woman of a mortal sickness like that by a few conversations in a train. If one could have taken her to the Alps, now, for a month, and let her climb and climb, lipsticks and mirrors left behind, getting her nails scratched and broken on the rough surfaces of rocks, and her face tanned by sun and new snow!—and all the time, resting on sunny summits, stretched after the descent by tumbling streams in flowery pastures, have pumped into her hope and faith, and another view of life and of the world—then indeed one might have hoped to help her a little. Poor creature—pretty creature! Or if she would really go and take a look at the true life of a country like Hungary, or Yugo-Slavia, or Albania. Curious how she had kept on about Albania. But she won't, Nils thought, switching off the light; people never do those things. He turned on his side, thinking with pleasure, in spite of his gloomy meditations, of how he would see her at breakfast in the morning, and fell asleep.

He was aroused some hours later by the train stopping at a station; the absence of motion, cries outside, light through the chinks of the shutter do so arouse even the most hardened traveller when an express stops at night. He glanced at his watch—just after twelve; it must be Zagreb. He lay sleepily, listening to the usual noise of voices upraised without, sounding louder in the night; steps in the corridor, the banging of doors. How long they had been there he had no idea. Still sleepy, he resisted for some time the normal impulse to raise the blind and look out, to verify for himself what station it was, but at last he gave way to it, and turning on his elbow, not only raised the blind, but put the window right down and stuck his head out, to get a breath of the night air. Even in the station it had a fresh tang in it. Yes, it was Zagreb all right—there was the big notice, both in Cyrillic and in Roman letters. He glanced casually up and down the platform. To his right, outside the coach behind his, porters and officials were fussing round a pile of immense trunks and boxes, all alike of white hide with green painted bands round them. A millionarish lot of baggage, Nils thought idly—and then, as the porters moved, he saw two women standing just beyond the pile. One, small and neat, he had never seen before, but there was no mistaking the other. Tall, graceful, Parisian, a mink coat over her arm, that ridiculous bag in her hand, Mrs. Thurston was standing on Zagreb platform in the middle of the night, beside—

undoubtedly—what Francesco had called the "mountain" of her luggage. Nils gaped at her.

The whistle blew—slowly the long train gathered motion and pulled out of the station. Nils drew in his head, rearranged the window and blind, and went back to bed. So she *was* going to give Albania the once-over, was she? "If I were English," he said to himself aloud, in that tongue, "I should say that I should eat my hat!" Then he laughed, and turned out the light. But it was some time before he went to sleep. He was wondering very much what Mrs. Thurston would make of Albania, and still more, whether he would ever see her again.

4

THE Durazzo boat was steaming steadily down from Ragusa towards the entrance of the Bocche di Cattaro, and in one of its small, brightly-cretonned staterooms Mrs. Thurston sat on the bed, arranging her face and hair before the little mirror on the wall. She had not unpacked anything because she was only going as far as Cattaro; but this Yugoslav steamship company had the agreeable habit of providing passengers with staterooms even for a day trip. At Cattaro she was to spend the night in an allegedly very good hotel, the Slavia, and next day Warren Langdon was picking her up in his car and taking her down to Albania, driving her over the famous Mt. Lovcen road. All these arrangements she had made by an exchange of long and expensive telegrams with Warren Langdon at the American Legation at Tirana; her maid had been despatched to Venice, with a proportion of the larger green and white trunks, to sit at the Lido and await orders.

Gloire Thurston had gone ahead with all this on rather a blind impulse; she was not a person who had the habit of looking much within. She had been lonely and fed-up, and there was no one she much wanted to see in Istanbul; Albania sounded different from anything she had ever seen, so different as perhaps to be a little amusing—so she had just decided to go there. Luckily she knew Warren Langdon well, and he had fixed everything for her. But now that she was actually on her way she began to wonder a little whether she had been mad to do anything so bizarre on the recommendation of a chance-met stranger in the train. It was a chilly, grey, blustery day; from the little window she could see, through travelling showers of rain, the mountains of the coast, blue-black and menacing—altogether a prospect to prompt doubts of a reckless enterprise. Gloire did not want to doubt, did not want to think why she had set out for Albania, did not in fact want to think at all. She wanted a drink, and any distraction that the boat might offer; pulling an artful turban instead of her hat over her close hair, and putting on her coat, she went off in search of both.

The drink she got easily enough. Seating herself in the saloon, she drawled "Slivovitz" at a steward, who promptly brought it. Distraction looked less likely. She surveyed her fellow-passengers. There were not many, and most of them were short, blondish men and women, with thick figures and unfashionable clothes, talking a sibilant tongue she could not recognise; they were Czechs, only Mrs. Thurston didn't know it. But presently a woman came in who attracted her attention. She had a good figure, but slouched distressingly; she carried a large despatch case. She was well and even cleverly dressed, in a dark brown and cream imprimé, with a well-cut brown coat, and expensive brown shoes and gloves. But she did not create in the least a fashionable impression—her coat was creased and wanted brushing, so did her shoes; her hat, small, neat, and smart as it was, was worn at the wrong angle, and the hair below it was vaguely unfashionable. All this aroused a certain interest in Mrs. Thurston's mind, which had nothing else to occupy it at the moment, as the woman sat down at a small table close by. Since she understood what to buy and wear together evidently rather unusually well, why on earth didn't she put her things on properly and hold herself decently? This was the sort of problem which really intrigued her, and she looked at the rather uncared-for face. It was square and firm, with fine blue eyes, unplucked eyebrows, and a neat short nose; the complexion naturally good, clear and slightly tanned—an intelligent face; when the woman, no doubt feeling Gloire's glance, raised her eyes suddenly and looked at her, it was a blue glance, keen and incisive. Gloire felt that she would like to talk to her. She was certainly English, and there was no one else who looked in the least conversible on this ghastly boat. There was no ash-tray on the stranger's table—when she lit a cigarette Mrs. Thurston leant over and put one down on it.

For the second time the woman looked up, with that blue, brilliant glance, and a half smile.

"Oh, thank you," she said, and put her match in it.

"Revoltingly cold, isn't it?" Mrs. Thurston said.

"Yes. That's the bora," said the lady.

"What's the bora?"

"The north wind. It's always horribly cold with it."

"Do you know this coast, then?" Mrs. Thurston asked.

"A good deal of it—pretty well."

"Do you know Cattaro?"

"Yes—darling place."

"What's the hotel like?"

"Well, which are you going to? The Slavia is very much all right if it's open but the other is quite quite awful," said the lady rapidly.

"I'm going to the Slavia," said Mrs. Thurston.

"Oh, is it open already? Oh, well, then you'll be perfectly all right." She looked at Mrs. Thurston as if she was trying to see her and couldn't, and then added—"There's quite good bathing—it has its own beach."

"I shan't do much bathing this weather," Gloire drawled—"and I'm only stopping one night."

"Oh really? Oh, what a pity!" said the lady. "Oh well, do go into the town—it's so lovely—and see San Metodo and that other little church, the very early one, with the picture of Our Lady on the iconostasis, that they say is a portrait by S. Luke. It certainly looks as if it might be—it has much more character than most of those iconographic paintings, and it is very ancient, obviously."

Gloire was a little overwhelmed by all this information, so rapidly poured out. She was quite unequal to discussing iconographic paintings, whatever they might be. She made some vague reply, and then said, amiably—"Have a drink."

The lady looked at her empty glass, this time as if she did see it, and said, "What are you drinking? Slivovitz? Good. Yes, I'd love one."

The steward, hovering round the curtained door of a sort of galley, was after the manner of stewards keeping an eye on Mrs. Thurston—a movement of her head, and over he came.

She said "Slivovitz" again, and held up two fingers. As the man moved away the lady drew her chair over to Mrs. Thurston's table.

"You're going up Mt. Lovcen tomorrow, and driving back, I suppose?" she asked.

"No, I'm going right over, and down to Scutari. You're not stopping at Cattaro?"

"No, I'm going on to Durazzo."

Gloire was a little surprised. The Englishwoman, too, was going to Albania! Gloire felt as if a little of her thunder was being stolen.

"Is there a good hotel there?" she asked—it was the question that always sprang, automatically, to her lips about any fresh place.

"No—both are quite frightful, I believe, but I'm not going to them. I'm staying with friends," said the lady.

"Do you know Albania well?"

"No—not at all. It's my first visit."

"Mine too," said Gloire. She wasn't sure that she liked this new acquaintance very much, but she was definitely curious now about more than her appearance. Who were her friends in Albania? Next to no one had friends in Albania. Who was she, anyway?

This last query was promptly answered. The steward summoned them to lunch. It was the ingenuous and frugal

61

habit of the steamship authorities, having conned over the passengers' passports, to write out each person's name on a small slip of cardboard, and stick it into a sort of slot made for the purpose on the embroidered linen cases in which everyone's napkin was placed. So the lady in brown and Gloire, ushered by the steward to seats side by side, were each able to read the other's name, embedded in red cross-stitch. "Mrs. S. Hanbury" read Gloire, silently; as she raised her eyes they met those of her neighbour.

"Now we know!" the lady said, smiling, and Gloire felt that she liked her better.

They were not left to pursue their acquaintance in peace. Opposite them an English couple took their seats, a pursy elderly man and a stout chattering little woman. The few tentative approaches which Gloire and Mrs. Hanbury had made to each other's journeys were swamped in a flood of direct questions and personal experiences poured out in suburban accents.

Mrs. Potts—for her napkin-case also revealed her identity —didn't care much for the food on these boats, nor for the accommodation; clean enough, but only cold water. She wasn't sure that she cared much for Dalmatia anyhow; she hoped Greece would be more interesting. They hadn't found Ragusa very interesting, had they, Tom? Tom, consuming the despised food, made no sign of either agreement or disagreement. Where had they come from? Gloire said that she had been at Split. The little woman asked Mrs. Hanbury if she hadn't found it rough, coming down from Split? Mrs. Hanbury said she had not come from Split.

"Oh, you're not together then? Sorry—I thought you were. Have you been in Ragusa too, then? I didn't see you about."

"No—I was in Cavtat," said Mrs. Hanbury repressively.

This moved the little woman to transports of excitement. "In Savtat? Were you reelly? Did you meet Susan Glanfield? They say she's staying in Savtat," she said eagerly. "You know, the writer."

Mrs. Hanbury looked steadily for a moment at the little woman. "No, I didn't meet her," she said blandly. She went on with her lunch; Gloire thought she looked rather amused about something. But she did not think about it, because she was pondering where she had heard the name Glanfield recently—quite recently. Oh yes—he—the man in the train—had quoted that poem; that was by a Miss Glanfield, a girl who climbed. But she had not connected her at the time with Susan Glanfield. Of course she had read her books. But it might not be the same.

At Gloire's suggestion, she and Mrs. Hanbury had their coffee on deck; both recognised their common desire to escape from their fellow-travellers. "God, what a ghastly woman!" Gloire said, when they were settled in two chairs.

"The suburban middle-class is the most dreadful of all modern social products," said Mrs. Hanbury, rapidly, as usual. "They have neither the country virtues of wisdom and solidity, nor the quick wits of the town. They are neither gentle nor simple, they have no interests. Doctors say that the women in the suburbs get all sorts of neuroses from sheer boredom."

"Do *you* think country-people have so many virtues?" Gloire asked—she was rather struck by meeting this echo of the Swede's theories.

"Oh, surely—isn't it well recognised?" Mrs. Hanbury replied.

It was pleasant on deck—they were within the Bocche now, and in shelter, so that the wind was much less strong; there were gleams of sun on the hills, turning them from cold blue to a warm cream; and now and then the small towns on the shore were caught by the bright rays and illuminated, so that they stood out sharp and clear, like little pictures. Gloire practically never asked questions about anything but hotels; but Mrs. Hanbury, without being asked, told her the names of the places they passed, and any facts of interest about them, and Gloire listened passively and quite contentedly—it passed the time, and Mrs. Hanbury had a very agreeable voice. She seemed to know a lot—probably that was why she was so careless about her clothes. But as they moved deeper and ever deeper into the long fiord, even Gloire began to be impressed; the mountains grew higher and more bare, crowded in closer and closer above the water; the steamer nosed its way between them, on and on—there seemed no end to this voyage. When at last Mrs. Hanbury pointed ahead to a cluster of roofs, overhung by a steep grey shoulder of rock, and said "There's Cattaro," Gloire felt that Cattaro lay at the very end of the world. It looked sinister. She said so to Mrs. Hanbury.

"Oh, no—it's a lovely little place, and there's a lot that's worth seeing," Mrs. Hanbury declared. "You might go round the walls this evening, and do the churches tomorrow morning before you start."

"Do they talk any known language? Or how does one find out where things are?"

"Well no—that is rather the trouble; they only talk Serbian, mostly. It is not like Ragusa or Split. Unless you could get hold of George," said Mrs. Hanbury. "Yes, you must get hold of George," she said, suddenly energetic, sitting up, and opening her handbag. "George will probably meet the boat anyhow," she said, scribbling on a card—"and he does speak English—of a sort." She smiled as she said that, with a rather delightful look of interior relish, as if she enjoyed thinking of George's English.

"Who is George?" Gloire asked, half bored and half amused at being thus organised by another stranger.

"George is Cook's local representative. I forget what his other name is, or how he came to learn English. But it's quite adequate, and he's a tower of strength; he knows where everything is, and adores showing people round. You treat him as a friend, and then give him a tip! There," she said, taking up her despatch case from the deck beside her, and slipping the card into an envelope—"Give that to

64

George; if he isn't at the boat, tell the porter at the Slavia to send for him."

But George was at the boat. When the steamer had worked her way alongside the quay, on which stood a small crowd, for the most part rather garishly dressed in peasanty clothes, Gloire went down the gangway alone, looking hopefully for the uniform of a porter from the Slavia, while Mrs. Hanbury stood above at the rail, not far from the two English passengers. Gloire felt a little forlorn—she could see no sign of a porter; she was to be left alone, it seemed, at the end of the world, among a strange crowd of swarthy people of an alien race, speaking a strange tongue. She stood waiting, while her luggage came ashore, and a thin stream of local passengers, carrying bundles, passed up the gangway. Suddenly she heard Mrs. Hanbury's voice, upraised from above—"There he is!—there's George, there, in the straw hat. George! George! That lady has a note for you—will you look after her?"

A small thickset man in a blue pin-stripe suit and a boater, at this identified himself as George by taking off the hat, bowing and calling back at the pitch of powerful lungs:

"Yes, sure, Miss Glanfield! Oh, pleased to see you, Miss Glanfield! But why don't you get off and come to Cattaro again, eh? Where do you go, now?"

"I'm going to Albania this time, George. I'll come back soon—next year, I expect."

"That's right—come back—soon as you can. When do you write us another book, eh, Miss Glanfield? All right. Goodbye; I look after the lady." And he came pushing through the crowd towards Gloire, who during this interchange of greetings stood fascinated, watching now her new acquaintance, Mrs. Hanbury, so suddenly metamorphosed into Susan Glanfield, the novelist, and now the faces of the suburban couple. On the woman's, incredulity, indignation, and finally a sort of eager triumph appeared in succession—

Gloire saw her turn and begin to move towards Mrs. Hanbury, who, waving, fled.

"Poor devil—*what* a trip she'll have!" Gloire thought to herself, for once grinning as honestly as a monkey. "Anyway it was true—you can't meet yourself, I guess." And she turned to greet George, holding out Mrs. Hanbury's envelope.

George proved to be all that Mrs. Hanbury had said. He took the note and put it in his pocket, shook hands, and asked for her luggage. Mrs. Thurston's luggage was as usual almost painfully obvious—the green and white boxes had already attracted a curious and admiring crowd. But George had bad news for her—the Slavia was not yet open. No, not for another fortnight. She would have to go to the Serbia, in the town.

"Is it good?" Gloire asked gloomily—she thought she remembered that Mrs. Hanbury had said something disparaging about it.

"Oh, all *right,* quite all *right,*" George replied cheerfully; "anyway it's the only one. Come, we take your stuff and fix a room, and then have a look round, yes?"

"That will be perfect," Gloire said, with a faint mechanical smile—she was automatically beginning to put the charm machinery in motion on George, on whom all depended. The green and white luggage was piled onto a hand-cart, drawn and pushed by two wild-looking youths with little round brimless hats or caps, like pill-boxes, stuck, as if gummed, to the side of their heads, and embroidered shirts; the splendid strength of their loins and thighs showed through the thin cheap cloth of their European trousers—the strong springy movement of their insteps and ankles seemed unhindered by their cheap and broken European shoes. Gloire and George followed them through an arched gateway in an immensely high and thick wall, and found themselves in a sort of open square, from which streets branched off—but they were the smallest streets Gloire had

66

ever seen, not more than wide enough to allow the passage of the hand-cart.

"No cars inside the wall," George proclaimed; "streets are too narrow. No horse-carts either. It's a small city; we don't need them."

Gloire smiled again, this time unmechanically; she wondered if her Scand, Larsen, knew Cattaro? It would be right up his alley, she thought—a whole town arranged to dispense with any traffic larger than a wheel-barrow!

The hotel, when they reached it, was a large, gaunt, unprepossessing-looking building; Gloire waited on a sort of small terrace, flanked by oleanders and bay-trees in tubs, while George, by shouts, summoned a dark wild-haired woman in a long skirt and a black and white spotted apron. They disappeared into the interior; the young men and the luggage followed; Gloire lit a cigarette and looked at the cracked paint on the window-shutters, the unpolished brass door-knobs, the torn lace curtains in the lower windows, with distaste and misgiving. She shrugged her shoulders a little—it was only for one night, anyway. But how was she to let Warren Langdon know where she was? He would have left Tirana by now, and she had no idea where he would be spending the night. She had better telegraph to Tirana and tell them to forward it.

George reappeared. "I got you a fine room, Mrs. Thurston. Running water, a fine bed; very nice. You be all right. Now, shall we see Cattaro, eh?"

"Won't you have a drink first?" Gloire said.

George would. They sat at one of the little tables, whose paint was disfigured by spots of rust wearing through it; George ordered in a strange tongue, vermouth for himself, slivovitz for Mrs. Thurston.

"Does anyone speak English or Italian in this hotel?" Gloire asked.

"No, Mrs. Thurston—sorry, no. Mrs. Miskitch, she speaks German."

67

"Oh well, that's all right—I speak a bit of German. Who is she?"

"She's the proprietress, Mrs. Thurston; this is her,"—as the wild-haired woman reappeared with the glasses on a cheap tin tray. "Mrs. Miskitch, here Mrs. Thurston."

Gloire bowed and spoke a few words in German. Mrs. Miskitch seemed to understand, though she looked dour and made none of the conventional hotel remarks about hoping the visitor would be comfortable. This was perhaps as well, Gloire thought, since she was convinced that she would not be comfortable in the least and knew herself for a bad liar.

After their drinks they went sight-seeing. George duly suggested the walls, but Gloire, after one look at the way in which they shot almost vertically skywards up that cliff of rock above the town said no, not the walls. They visited various churches, including the one with the portrait of Our Lady. Without, its dome gave it practically the shape of a haycock, and it was really not much larger; within, the gloom and mystery were cool and soothing, though Gloire was too ignorant to be much impressed by the small wooden panel which was S. Luke's alleged portrait; George illuminated it for her with a stump of a candle from his pocket. After they left each building he would say, briskly, —"Now we see so-and-so; Miss Glanfield say we must see this," and hustled her off to another church; Miss Glanfield must have got a lot onto that card, Gloire thought. What an odd person, to take so much trouble to make a total stranger see a place thoroughly. An enthusiast, she supposed, with a shrug. Or another missionary, like the man in the train. How very odd if she were really his Miss Glanfield, the mountaineering friend of his youth.

But Gloire was much more struck by the town itself than by any of the churches which George dutifully showed her. The buildings were high and thoroughly urban, in extraordinary contrast to the narrow streets, hardly more than paved passages, in which they stood. And it all looked very poor. There was nothing but the cheapest manufactured trash visible in the shop windows—cheap textiles, cheap belts and shoes, cheap unfashionable men's hats, cheap cosmetics. Only the food shops, with their cheeses and sausages and wicker-bound stone jars of vermouth and slivovitz looked at all appetising.

It all looked so dead-alive, too. Men, strong and athletic-looking, like the youths who had dragged her luggage to the hotel, sat about in the squares, talking or smoking, but doing nothing else; women, hatless or with handkerchiefs on their heads, stood at doors or in knots at the street corners, gossiping and idle. Gloire did not realise that this was that slower tempo of life of which Larsen had spoken; work, and hard work too, was in fact done in Cattaro, but it was not done all the time, and now, in the evening, the little city was at leisure. And not spending any of its leisure rushing home by train or bus, because it *was* at home; nor in hastening to the cinema or some place of amusement, because in the first place there was none, and in the second, the citizens of Cattaro were still sufficiently amused by leisure itself, and by the age-old pleasures of talk and gossip with neighbours and friends. Gloire for her part felt it all very depressing—it was "small-town" to a degree; it held nothing of the things she valued. Stares of course followed her, but she felt that they were not, as in the great cities where she was at home, a tribute to the perfection of her appearance, but just the stare of the savage for the stranger —any stranger. She remembered how in Paris her French and Viennese friends used to refer to anything raw or backward or uncivilised as "Balkaan"—well, this is it, she thought; now I know what they meant; Cattaro is Balkaan all right.

Long before George had come to an end of the sights he wished her to see, Gloire cried off, and suggested more drinks. They had these at a café looking out onto the big square near the city gate. Gloire asked, in her flat drawl, why the streets were so narrow.

"Lack of space, Mrs. Thurston. There is so little room here between the hills and the water, and anyway we had to get the houses inside of the walls, for security."

Gloire was vaguely alienated by this.

"The shops aren't very good, are they?" she said.

"No, Mrs. Thurston, they ain't. Not like the shops on Regent Street or Fifth Avenue."

"Oh, do you know the States?" she asked. "Is that where you learnt English?"

"Yes, Mrs. Thurston,—New York and London; that's where I was. New York is fine. London is fine too. Rich. But our shops, now; they are poor, and poor stuff in them; because we are a poor country, Mrs. Thurston. We haven't much industries. If we could get capital we might start some industries. But capital ain't easy to get. That's why our Tourismo is so important to us. Miss Glanfield, she's a good friend to Yugo-Slavia; her books double our British and American Tourismo, and British and American tourists, they pay best. Not always bargaining, like Germans and Czechs."

"Why do you want industries?" Gloire asked. She was thinking of the man in the train, and his strictures on industrial life. Was this comic little man, George, going to give him the lie?

His answer surprised her.

"We want *arms*, Mrs. Thurston—arms and planes and ships, but we can't make them ourselves. If we had a steel industry we could; we got the iron and we got the coal, but we've not got the industry. Not like the Czechs—look at the Czechs! They got the Skoda works; they can make arms, all they want, and sell to other people—to you in England, even. We can't make them, and we're too poor to buy all we need."

"But what do you want arms for?" Gloire asked, again vaguely irritated—the little man was so desperately in

70

earnest, in his cheap suit, with the perspiration shining on his dark excited face; she was a little repelled.

He stared at her for a moment, at her question, as if he were looking at some unrecognisable animal. So that Swede had stared at her once or twice in the train—Gloire felt her colour rising. But George was answering her politely enough; more politely than the Swede.

"Italy, Mrs. Thurston," he said. He jerked his arm out behind him. "There sits Italy just across the water, coveting our country and our ports, so she can make the Adriatic an Italian lake! A lot she take already. Trieste, Pola, Fiume —those all belong to our people; Slovenes mostly. Zara is ours, but she take that. She publish books—maybe you buy some in Split or Dubrovnik, they shove them in the Italian book-shops—like 'L'Italianità del Littorale Adriatica'; got up splendid, with fine pictures. People buy them for the pictures, and believe all that rubbish. Because the God-damned Venetians were all down here way back, we don't, we Slavs, want them here now. We threw them out. But that's the claim they make."

"But that's just books, about culture and all that. They don't make that claim seriously, surely?" Gloire asked, as usual slightly incredulous. She had in fact bought and read the handsome volume on the Italian-ness of the Adriatic Littoral, in Split.

"You bet they make it seriously, Mrs. Thurston. You bet they mean to do it, when they think they've got everybody used to the idea. You say you're going down to Albania—you see what you find when you get there! Italians in everything. They run the Army there now, training them they call it. Training!"—George, regrettably, leaned aside and spat. "The British, they *do* train people," he pursued. "They make a swell job of the Albanian Gendarmerie. But now the Italians try to make the Albanians throw them out of that. Who runs the Albanian air-service? The Ala Littoria. Who's developing the copper-mines? An Italian company.

71

Oh, they want Albania all right; once they get those two ports, Valona and Durazzo, they can bottle up their damned Adriatic Lake; and even if we have a bit of a merchant fleet, they can stand over us." George leaned back in his chair, breathing heavily; he mopped his brown forehead with a gaudy silk handkerchief and gulped down his slivovitz. "The British are a grand people," said George, "but they don't notice much. Not till it happens to them. Reckon they're such gentlemen, they don't know what scabs some other nations can be. I like them a lot, but Jeese, do they drive me mad, being so blind?"

In the Hotel Serbia at Cattaro, that night, Gloire Thurston had a really violent reaction against the impulse which had sent her on this wild-goose chase to look at Albania. It is curious how irrationally some places seem to us evil and intimidating—but if they do and one is alone, the effect can be almost overwhelming. Gloire was nearly overwhelmed by the Hotel Serbia. All those ideas she had had, coming down the final lap of the Bocche on the boat, about Cattaro being the last place in the world, came back to her as, shrinkingly, she unpacked the minimum, and laid it out on sheets of tissue paper on the unsavoury toilet table—the drawers, with their refuse of old hairpins, stale powder, and loose wisps of hair, she shut again with a shudder. God! it was ghastly, she thought, as she put on a wrapper over her nightgown and got into the horrible bed, arranging a scarf on the untempting pillow. She lit a cigarette and lay back, staring up at the unshielded bulb which hung from the fly-blown ceiling. What a fool she had been to let herself in for this.

Why had she come? Well obviously, because of that man in the train, the Swede, Larsen or whatever his name was; but why should she have paid so much attention to what he said? She frowned at the ceiling, over this unusual exercise of examining her own motives. Really, because he had talked to her so oddly. He had seemed in some curious way to *know* about her, even before he asked. How peculiar

72

of him to ask, too! But then he was very peculiar. Only, in spite of the strange views he had on things, she had had the feeling that he really knew something that might help her—if anything could help her, ever again. It was queer, that—it had just kept on coming over her. Because really! —any other man, she would have told where he got off for saying half, a quarter, to her of what the Swede had said. And the only direct advice he had given her, actually, was to go on climbing, and to go to Albania. And she had been mad enough to come, and now look where she was!—and probably Albania would be worse. Oh well, Warren would be here tomorrow, and would take her to the Legation for a bit, where it would be clean and she could get a bath, anyway.

She got out of bed, switched off the light, ran back, and lying down in the dark, tried to sleep. Outside, irrationally and inexplicably a bird began to sing—at midnight. Gloire listened, and realised that it was a nightingale. A nightingale in a city—how insane! Larsen had said they sang all day and all night in Albania. Well damn Larsen anyway, letting her in for this.

Aoh! That was something crawling! She felt for her torch, ran to the door, switched on the light, and threw back the bed-clothes. Was that a scuttling flat form? How revolting! Shivering with chill and disgust she got into bed again, and pulled up the repellent bed-clothes. She would leave the light on for a bit; then she might catch the brute if he came back. She lit another cigarette and again lay staring upwards.

That Swede—his notions were quite mad. Look at this appalling room, and that awful toilet! Plumbing was a good thing, anyway, and she wished to God he could see *this* place! But though she fought with him in her thoughts, there persisted that odd idea—that he had known what was wrong with her, that he knew something that could have helped her. What was wrong with her? For the first time

Gloire consciously asked herself that question. Oh, she didn't know, except that she minded so awfully about Tony still, and so hated a world in which such a horror could have happened to him. She shut her eyes, to shut out the unbearable vision of Tony up in that little tent, with his broken ankle, and the blizzard screaming outside, and help not coming and not coming—then opened them again. She saw Tony now as she remembered him, with his eyeglass and his little fair moustache, trudging up to a hut, bent slightly under his rücksack; saw him on steep rocks, clambering like a great cat, swift, deliberate, sure; saw him, in old tweeds, going into one of his cottages of which he was so proud, talking with easy courtesy to the miner's wife, making little jokes—and the woman so at ease with him, bluntly friendly, civilly direct about repairs or anything. What had that man said about souls at ease liking the forms of courtesy? Well that was true, anyway. And Tony was like those landholders the man talked of; he did have the tradition of obligation. She hadn't been able to understand it, when she first went to England; she had chafed under it, as under all those other traditions which governed his life; she hadn't been able to see the point of it all. Somehow that Swede had made her see the point better than she ever had—tying it all into history that way made it make more sense. But she didn't *want* to go on thinking about Tony, she thought, moving restlessly—usually she managed not to. Damn the Swede, churning all this up.

Without warning, thunder crashed violently overhead; a great clap, and then a long rolling peal, reverberating among the mountains—as it died away she heard the nightingale again, singing louder than ever, as if in rivalry; and then another and another tuned up. Idiotic birds! And where were they? The Serbia was in the very heart of the town. She got up and went to the window, threw open the venetian shutters, and leaned over the sill. The air was strangely sweet. The nightingales were still singing like

74

mad, but somehow now their city song was less insane, it was even comforting. Where the devil were they? It was too dark to see. They couldn't be sitting on chimney-pots, like starlings!

A flash of lightning answered her question. To her right, over a wall, a large ilex-tree stood in a courtyard, silhouetted in the fierce light against a tall house with pointed windows and a beautiful balustraded balcony. Blinking, Gloire just registered the astonishing beauty of that sudden picture. She waited while the thunder rolled and echoed for the vision to come again. It did—and this time, her eyes focussed in advance, she saw it more clearly—the exotic shapes of the windows, the rich carving of the balustrade, and the dark glitter of the great tree in which the nightingales, rapt and lyrical, carolled against all Heaven's artillery. Something melted and broke in her, at that—while she still leaned from the window, down came the rain, heavy, steady, healing—a loosening of tension; and with it, to her astonishment, her own tears fell. God, you are an ass! Gloire adjured herself—she went back, switched off the light, and groped her way to bed. In a few minutes, lulled by the heavy swish of the falling rain, she fell asleep.

5

GLOIRE'S mood of revolt against her expedition had lessened by the next morning, and she drank her coffee on the little terrace outside the hotel in bright sun and tolerable spirits. George reappeared, and took her round some rather indifferent antique shops. But before she left she had another panic. Eleven-thirty came, noon came, and there was no sign of Warren Langdon. Gloire walked down several times to the city gate, in case he should not know where to look for her—George pattered beside her, constantly urging her "not to worry, Mrs. Thurston. Everyone here know the Slavia, it's shut; everyone here know where you are." But in spite of this, by 12.30 Gloire was almost desperate. Stay another night in that hotel she would not, and yet if Warren didn't come, where could she go?

At a quarter to one, in despair, she had lunch—this too she ate on the terrace under the oleanders, and it was as good as last night's dinner had been bad; delicious fish, faultlessly fresh, with some aromatic herb sauce, and an excellent salad. And while she was eating it, up the steps came Warren Langdon, in his seersucker suit, fanning himself with his Panama, and emitting gloomy apologies. He had slept at Scutari, on purpose to be in good time, and had taken the lower road, by Budua, to be earlier still; but the road had been pretty well washed out by last night's storm and it was all they could do to get through. Now they would have to hustle to make Scutari tonight, as they would have to go right over Mount Lovcen. Gloire said she wanted to go over Lovcen anyway, and hadn't he better have some lunch, as it was right here? So Warren Langdon finished the fish and gulped down some wine, while George mobilised the youths and the hand-cart, and carried Gloire's luggage off to the car. And a few minutes later Gloire sank, with a sense of returning to civilisation, into the deep back seat of the Cadillac; Warren stepped in after her, and the linen dust rug was spread over their knees by the chauffeur. This, Gloire felt, was much more like. Albania, seen this way, might after all not be so bad.

The Mount Lovcen road is, as Warren Langdon said, really quite a phenomenon. Immediately behind Cattaro it rises from sea-level to close on five thousand feet in thirty-two hairpin bends, looped to and fro across the face of what is practically a precipice. It is superbly engineered, but the Cadillac was a long car, and at most of the bends it had to take two bites. Gloire's sense of luxury and safety lessened considerably as Cyril, the White Russian chauffeur, repeatedly backed his machine to the very lip of the road to make the turn; backed it moreover not at a cautious creep, but with a vigorous rush that sent the gravel spurting from under the broad tires. "Can't you make him take these curves more slowly?" Gloire was at length driven to protest. Mr. Langdon, who was smoking a cigarette in a long, stained ivory holder, merely laughed his deep laugh.

"Oh, Cyril knows this road," he said. "And it's no use talking to him. He just has his own ideas."

Warren Langdon was a long, lean New Englander, with a deeply-lined face, sunken eyes, and the curiously tragic expression that is characteristic of so many Bostonians, at once sensitive and impotent, but with a certain gauche charm—also typical of his kind. He had a soft low voice, very musical—the sort of voice that the English associate, if at all, with the South, but which is in fact very characteristic of old New England families; he was well-informed to the point of being learned, another New England trait which is little recognised abroad—he spoke French quite faultlessly. His gloomy expression was the outward and

77

visible sign of a profound and rather helpless disillusionment—with life, and with the personality and prospects in this world and the next of Warren Langdon; these however he had by now—he was fifty-six—so fully accepted that he was far from being a gloomy companion; a rather acidly philosophical outlook caused him to take the slings and arrows, great or small, of fortune with considerable calm. Unless they affected other people; then he was deeply, overtly, and musically concerned. He had known Gloire from a child. Gloire always suspected him of having been at one time in love with her mother; she further guessed that he had not married her because, though immensely rich— Gloire's grandfather had made sanitary fittings—she was a Middle-Westerner, and would not have gone down in Warren's Bostonian circle. As a girl Gloire had spent enough time in the comfortable Langdon house at Wenham, Mass., to realise how rigid a control the normal Bostonian's family and circle exercises on his private life, especially where his marriage is concerned. When Warren did eventually marry a Newburyport girl, poor, pretty, inbred, nervous and intense, his family, Gloire was sure, had been delighted. But the prettiness had not lasted, the intensity presently ceased to mask a certain lack of intelligence, the nervousness intensified; Gloire had been deeply relieved to learn that Melanie Langdon didn't like Albania and had "stayed home" after their last leave. His sister was keeping house for him. Gloire remembered Miss Anne from Wenham days, tall, formidable, with pince-nez and gold chains and a warm heart; as definite and certain about life as her brother was hesitant. Miss Anne almost certainly disapproved of her, Gloire; but her rectitude and good manners had, and always would, prevent that disapproval from manifesting itself in any obvious way.

Just above the last of the hairpin bends, where the road flattened out a little and turned inland, they ran into thick mist, white, cold, and clammy. "Oh, con*twist* it!" Warren cried, disappointed as a boy. "Now you'll not get the view! I did so want you to get the view." Gloire had wanted to get the view too, but there was nothing to be done about it; they drove on to Cettinje, the small derelict ex-capital of Montenegro; in the mist its pink and white houses, its former ministries and palace looked more derelict than ever. Then they began to descend, into country warmer and richer than the white sea-face of the range up which they had come; they emerged from the mist that shrouded Lovcen's head, and the afternoon sun shone brilliantly on tumbling streams in steep valleys, with a wealth of shrubby growth between the rocks—among the pale green foliage of wild pomegranates, pale and vivid as green flames, the red flames of the flowers burned, astonishingly. Far below, through flatter land, a river wound, shining; further still was the silver gleam of a great lake—Scutari, Warren told her. He talked a good deal, telling her much that was worth hearing of Montenegro's past and Yugo-Slavia's present. But Gloire did not pay much attention. She was beginning to get sleepy, after her broken night, and now and again drowsed off.

It was a long drive. Presently she found herself getting hungry as well as sleepy—the sight of men eating bread at a little inn by the roadside made her sharply aware of the fact. She glanced at the watch on her wrist—it was six o'clock, more than five hours since they had eaten.

"Warren, have you any food?" she asked him, interrupting a long précis of recent Yugoslav internal politics.

"Why, my dear, no—I'm afraid I haven't," Warren replied. "You're not hungry, are you?"

"Yes, starving. Haven't you some chocolate, or something?"

"Why no—isn't that too bad? I'm most terribly sorry." Warren was melodiously desolated. "I figured we'd get in to Scutari in time for dinner. It's those darned floods made me so late."

"Well can't we stop and get something to eat, some-where?"

Warren looked troubled. "I don't think you'll get much to eat anywhere before Scutari," he said doubtfully; he leaned forward and consulted the chauffeur in Russian. The result was negative. "He says Scutari's the first place," Warren said resignedly, sitting back again.

"Oh rubbish, Warren! There are these little *estaminet* places right along the road—look, there's one now."

"Yeah, but you wouldn't get anything there you could eat."

"I'd get bread," said Gloire vigorously—opposition was stimulating her appetite.

"And since when did you start eating bread, Gloire? What about your figure?" he teased her.

"Oh, cut it out, Warren. I tell you I'm hungry! If you haven't brought a basket, or chocolate, or anything, I *must* eat bread. Tell him to stop at the next little pub place we come to, and get me a loaf.

Mr. Langdon did as he was told, but without result. Cyril nodded, but merely stepped on the accelerator and made the car bound forward over the road, which had now de-teriorated considerably; they shot past several inns, where the sight of men cutting away at long loaves exasperated Gloire.

"Warren! He's not stopping—he's going right on. Make him stop."

Warren laughed gloomily.

"My dear, if Cyril doesn't mean to stop he *won't* stop," he said. "He's that kind of a man. He just can't believe you want to eat bread."

"I can't think why you keep him, then," Gloire said angrily. "I wouldn't keep a chauffeur who wouldn't obey orders."

"He's the best mechanic between Belgrade and Athens—in fact you might pretty well say he's the only one," Warren

80

replied pacifically. "I have to keep him. I'm terribly sorry I forgot to bring some food, Gloire—it's my fault."

Gloire closed her eyes without replying, and sulked in silence.

The reason for Cyril's reluctance to stop presently became apparent. After consulting a large turnip watch of florid gold and enamel, in the Empire style, he leaned back in his seat, and still travelling at the same relentless speed, addressed his employer. It was now 6.30—the Albanian-Yugo-Slav frontier, beyond Podgoritza, closed for the night at 7.30; they would not anything like make it; would it not be a good plan to stop in Podgoritza, find the magistrate, and get him to telephone to the frontier post and arrange for them to be let through? Warren agreed. Gloire, when the new move was communicated to her, stared incredulously.

"But haven't you a *laisser-passer?*"

"Sure I have—but that won't help at these little places. You're in the Balkans here. No, it's a darn good idea."

Soon after seven they swung into Podgoritza, over the river bridge, and proceeded to seek out the magistrate. Gloire had by this time two urgent determinations, not one: to buy bread and if possible also chocolate, and to find a lavatory. Really Warren was *too* inhumanly vague, she thought. They passed a largish hotel, and Gloire suggested stopping there for bread; but Cyril had his own ideas. They pulled up in a square, filled with the evening crowd; without a word to her the two men jumped out, one on each side, and vanished in the multitude. Unable to ask her way, furious, Gloire sat while the crowd condensed round the Cadillac, full of delighted curiosity. Before she had decided what to do, a tall man in a hideous Homburg hat stepped up to the window, and addressed her, to her immense relief, in American.

"Say, you got a swell car—damn fine. Yank car, hey? You a Yank?"

81

"Yes!" said Gloire, feeling unspeakably un-European.

"Ah, fine. Shake!" said the man, thrusting a dingy paw through the window. "You know Omaha, Nebraska? I drive a taxi in Omaha six years."

"Yes, it's a grand place," said Gloire desperately, shaking hands with him. "Look—I want to buy some chocolate—can you tell me where to go?"

"I buy you some fine chocolate—you give me the dinara and I get it pronto," said her new friend.

"No, I want to stretch my legs," said Gloire, scrambling out. "If you could mind the car, and tell me where, I'll go." In her mind she was wondering if she would have time to get to that hotel, and back.

However, she was again frustrated. The repatriated Slav from Omaha, Nebraska, was not going to lose a second of the company of this fascinating stranger; he detailed a companion to mount guard over the car, and led Gloire off, extolling the glories of America, and telling her how "up-state" Podgoritza was. Podgoritza *was* pretty up-state, at that, Gloire thought; however in a small shop, much to her surprise, she found quantities of a French chocolate made in Lyons. She bought six slabs—Heaven knew when she would get any more in this God-forsaken country—opened one and tried it. Still more to her surprise it was excellent.

But it was impossible to shake off her new friend, so she went back to the car just as Warren Langdon also returned to it, a long loaf escaping from a sheet of yellow paper under his arm. He was accompanied by Cyril, for whom Gloire was beginning to conceive a positive detestation.

"We've found out where the Prefecture is—come on in, let's go," Warren said. Gloire was swept off again. Well, I have some chocolate, anyway, she thought.

The Prefecture was situated in a street which at first seemed full of promise. Along one side stretched a row of yellow-washed houses, of which it was the largest; on the other lay some derelict buildings, among what Gloire would have called waste lots, liberally besprinkled with bushes. The moment Warren Langdon and Cyril had disappeared into the Prefecture she nipped out of the car and began to prospect. But she had reckoned without the inveterate curiosity of the Balkans. She had not noticed that there were many—or indeed any—children playing in that street, but suddenly she was surrounded by a mob of them, as she picked her way over loose bits of masonry towards the bushes—they swarmed round her, smiling, laughing, shouting, fingering her clothes. Desperate, Gloire took a high line. She left the waste lots, walked down the street, and turned at random into a shop. There were three women and a man in it. "Sbogom!"—God be with you—said Gloire; it was one of her two newly-acquired words of Serbo-Croat. Then, with a brilliant smile, she took the man by the shoulders, pushed him to the door, pushed him out, and shut the door on him. Turning to the women again—"Molim," she said, which is the Serbo-Croat for "please"—and then by a diagrammatic gesture explained what she wanted. The women were quick—laughing, delighted, they applauded her; one of them led her out through the back of the shop and down a flowery garden to a little shed, overhung by some creeper in bloom; when she emerged, triumphant and unspeakably thankful, the woman handed her a blossom—with a sort of exasperated delight, Gloire saw that it was a passion-flower.

She sat quiet and contented now in the car, munching her chocolate and great lumps of bread which she pulled off the end of Warren's loaf. When he returned they drove off; leaving the town, they roared along a straight road in the gathering dusk. They were down in the flat country now, with the Lake of Scutari away to their right—once or twice, when the road rose over a piece of higher ground, they could see it for a moment, a metallic sheet of tea-rose pink, catching the glow from the west. At such moments, silhouetted against the water, across the flat lacustrian plain, great plants stood up, like black candelabra three feet high—

83

asphodels, Warren told her they were; now in seed, but three weeks ago they had been a sheet of pale pink, the colour of apple-blossom. Some echo from her rather inadequate education rang in Gloire's head at the word asphodel —things Tony had read to her came back too; the hereditary classical magic of Hellas, from which Europe can never escape, laid hold on her in that twilight hour, in that strange land—and a small thrill of exaltation ran through her. The dead walked through fields of asphodel—that much she remembered, and it was sufficient. They *would*, of course, walk through pink candelabra, faultless in shape, beside shadowed waters that yet glowed with a pale rose—perhaps Tony walked there now. Vaguely, she felt him possibly near.

There was a longish pause at the frontier. Dark wild-looking men in uniform, with lanterns, scrutinised their papers, themselves; Warren got out and talked to them. Yes, the message from Podgoritza had come—and they were really the right people? And the lady was English, an English passport? They gutturally exclaimed the Albanian equivalent of "Tiens!" But at last the long barrier of pole and wire was swung back, and the Cadillac was allowed to proceed.

Gloire never forgot that drive from the frontier to Scutari. Though she did not fully realise it at the time, it was the first instalment, so to speak, of the fulfilment of the Swede's promise to her. It was by now dark, and their headlights lit up the road ahead of them with long wavering beams, piercing a deep blackness. In this blackness, suddenly, small lights shone—hundreds of them, red, and the size of large marbles. Even Cyril slowed down. Gloire leaned forward, puzzled by this phenomenon; and now saw curved shapes in pairs above the little red lights—they were approaching a flock of goats, being driven home from pasture on the lake shore. The drovers came in sight at length, as the animals surged past the car—wild figures, in a strange magpie dress of black and white, with dark wild faces, grinning or scowling in the glare of the headlights. This happened over and over again; the road was full of droves of goats and goat-herds. And each time Gloire leaned forward to look, and each time when they had passed, sat back with a curious little rush of excitement. These were splendid faces and figures that loomed up out of the dark, wild, *Balkaan,* as they were; this was a splendid place, holding splendid scenes—she had never in her life seen anything so dramatic as this Albanian night, starred with the red eyes of strong-smelling animals. Splendid things should happen here. A deep satisfaction, greatly to her own surprise, held her; and she was still under its spell when they pulled up out-side Colonel Robinson's house in Scutari, where she was to spend the night.

Colonel Robinson, of the Albanian Gendarmerie, was a tall gaunt Englishman of about fifty, with rather ferocious moustaches and a very quiet lazy voice; his wife, fortu-nately, had taken to Albania like a duck to water; she was Scotch, a large comfortable woman, who had turned her tumble-down villa in Scutari into a comfortable well-run Scottish home, but yet found time to plunge herself into welfare work in the town—she had first created, and now ran, a children's clinic and a school of hygiene for Albanian women, raising the money God knew how. She was quite unperturbed by the arrival of her guests at 9.30 P.M.—she hustled Gloire upstairs to a small clean room, very un-luxurious, but with hot water on the wash-stand, and fetched her, unasked, a whisky and soda to drink while she washed—"You'll digest your dinner better if you take it a bit in advance," she said. Gloire's whole being applauded this sentiment. Refreshed, she went downstairs and consumed an excellent dinner—but by now her head was ringing with fatigue, eye-strain after the long drive, and alcohol on an empty stomach; she hardly heard a word of Warren's highly local conversation with Colonel Robinson, and the moment the meal was over she thankfully accepted Mrs. Robinson's

85

sensible suggestion that she might like to go to bed at once. Snuggling between clean sheets, she fell asleep immediately.

There was only one spare room at the Robinsons', and Warren Langdon slept at the Excelsior, the local hotel. He came round to breakfast next morning bubbling with secret enjoyment, and over coffee he told them the cause. While he was dressing a note had been brought to his room from an Albanian merchant, a man of substance and an old and trusted source of information, begging the favour of an interview in private. "So when I'd shaved," Warren drawled, "I had the old buzzard up." The old buzzard, with a most pronounced *visage de circonstance*, had explained that he felt Mr. Langdon ought to know that great events were toward. Today, Sunday, was the twelfth centenary of the foundation of the Church of S.——, in the town, and for this celebration Bishop X., of the Franciscan Order, had come to Scutari to celebrate High Mass and to preach. But this was merely a blind for a high diplomatic intrigue. An English lady had also arrived in Scutari last night, by car, very late; she was a cousin of Mr. Anthony Eden's, and she had come on a secret mission to meet the Bishop and discuss the future of the Catholic religion in Albania, and other important matters.

"What a thrill!" said Gloire, who after a superb nine-hours' sleep felt well, wide awake, and unusually interested in everything. "Who is she, and where is she staying?"

Warren laughed.

"She's right here!" he said. "*You're* the lady!"

"Nonsense, Warren. Why, you brought me in yourself."

It took considerable explanation on Warren's part, with corroboration from Colonel Robinson, to convince Gloire that in Albania there was nothing particularly unusual in such mistakes. The English lady had really come, both she and her passport had been seen in Podgoritza and at the frontier—it was a mere nothing that the well-disposed Albanian had failed to register the fact that she had come, so

86

to speak, in Warren's own pocket; and the making her a
cousin of Mr. Eden was a typical primitive exaggeration.
Mr. Eden's was one of the few English names known in
Albania; and any wealthy Englishwoman was naturally
supposed to be his relative, in a country where practically
all the notable families were related to one another.

All Gloire found to say was "Gosh!—how lunatic."

"Oh, something like that is always happening," said
Colonel Robinson. "Robina, you remember that wretched
woman who came to stay at the Excelsior some years back,
and got the huge bill? What's this her name was?"

Lloyd, Mrs. Robinson said—Mrs. George Lloyd. But by a
very natural confusion the management of the Excelsior had
assumed that she was Mrs. Lloyd George, and had charged
her accordingly.

"Anyhow, the least you can do, I feel, is to go and hear
the Bishop preach at High Mass," Colonel Robinson told
Gloire. "And you will see some lovely costumes."

Gloire was quite willing to do this—the costumes in
Scutari were one of the things the Swede had told her
about, so to High Mass they went. The large church was
crowded to the doors; the women sat on one side of the
aisle, the men on the other; they went up to the front
where Gloire, separated from Mr. Langdon and Colonel
Robinson, found herself surrounded by a cloud, a foam
of white veils. It was like being at church with hundreds
of brides, she thought. She was vaguely aware, as the
women stood and knelt, of full dark trousers or short stiff
black skirts standing out from the wearer like a bell, wide-
sleeved silken shirts or bodices, and gaily-striped woven
aprons; but what impressed her were the veils. The women
of Scutari, on festive occasions, cover their heads with short
veils, falling to the waist or below at the back, of some
filmy white stuff, chiffon, lawn, or muslin, most delicately
embroidered—the one immediately in front of Gloire was
as fine as a cobweb, and "worth mints," her appraising eye

told her; under it she could see the gleam of pearls from the embroidered fillet round the woman's forehead. And when they knelt, she was struck by the beauty and devoutness of the white folds, falling so soft and yet so severe from the bent heads, so that each woman looked like a mediaeval Madonna in some noble religious painting. Well, the Swede had been right about the costumes, anyway. It was fantastic to sit in a whole churchful of people in fancy dress.

After Mass they strolled about the town. It was all less Balkan than Gloire had expected, but she was struck by the contrast between this rather handsome modern city and the beautiful and archaic costumes which, Mass over, filled the streets as if with flowers or butterflies. Now she could see the beauty of the woven aprons, and the richness of those pearl-sewn bands round the forehead, more clearly; and here too she saw the poorer women, who instead of the veils wore hand-woven red and white striped shawls over their heads. Ravishing!

Colonel Robinson, as they turned into a side street, pointed to the wall at the corner and said—"Seen that, Langdon? That's the latest."

Gloire and Warren Langdon both looked where he pointed. On the wall, in black letters on a small panel of white paint, the name of the street had been neatly inscribed: Rruga Kolonel Herbert; but this had been crossed through with a heavy black brush, and above it was another panel with the words: Rruga Generale Graziani.

"The bastards!" Warren ejaculated. "They've done that in Tirana too."

"Oh yes, it's going on all over the place. It's all part of the same scheme, and we're sitting down under it, as usual!" said Colonel Robinson bitterly.

"Who was Colonel Herbert?" Gloire asked.

"The best friend Albania ever had—Aubrey Herbert," said Warren, with a warmth so unusual to him that Gloire looked at him in surprise. "They wanted him for King instead of William of Wied, but he wouldn't take it. He'd have made them a grand King, too. I'm not much on Kings; but this was a country that needed a King, if ever country did."

"But they've got a King now, haven't they?" Gloire asked vaguely. Warren looked quizzically at her.

"My dear, yes; so much even England and America knows!—Albania has a King."

"Well, what's he like?"

"Oh, Zog's all right," said Warren, but without quite the enthusiasm he had shown for Colonel Herbert—he pronounced it Zahg.

"He's really doing pretty well, you know, Langdon," Colonel Robinson observed, "considering the pressure that's put on him, and the total lack of support he gets from anywhere outside." The two men drifted off into Albanian politics, but Gloire soon stopped listening; it was too technical for her. She was thinking of what George had said, sitting outside the café in Cattaro—was it really only the day before yesterday?—about Italy. "You see what you see when you get down into Albania," he had said; well, she hadn't been in Albania twenty-four hours yet, and already she had seen that highly significant alteration of the name of the street.

She reverted to the subject when she and Warren, after lunch, were driving on down to Tirana.

"Why do the Italians want to get a foot in here? If they really do?"

"You bet your life they really do!" It was funny how Warren Langdon, the career diplomat, echoed almost the very words of George, the Slav courier. "As to *why* they want it—and they want the country, not merely a footing in it—there's a whole complex of reasons. Do you really want to hear, Gloire?" he asked, turning to look at her with a certain incredulity.

"As a matter of fact, I do," she said, rather vexed. It was odd, but she did.

"O.K., my dear. You shall. Well, it's partly this infernal idea of empire and expansion," Warren said—"but there's more to it than that. Strategically, this coast is pretty important to Italy. It's only around forty-seven miles across the Straits from the Bay of Valona to Otranto, and Valona is a superb natural harbour. A hostile fleet in there could hurt Italy a lot. Then there's flat ground for airfields all down the coastal plain here, from the Drin—we'll cross it in an hour or so—to the Vijosa. So far only one has been made—the one at Tirana, which the Ala Littoria operates. But this coast in hostile hands could be a real menace to Italy."

"But Albania could never threaten Italy—it's so tiny and behind-hand," Gloire said.

"Quite right, my dear. But what lies in there?" Warren gesticulated inland at the blue shapes of mountains rising on their left. "Yugo-Slavia," he said with emphasis. "Italy is always looking over Albania's shoulder at Yugo-Slavia."

"Why should Italy and the Jugs be so afraid of one another?" Gloire asked, thinking of George again.

"That's a long story too, but it all hangs together. After the World War Yugo-Slavia got—well, some people think she got a bit more than her share," Warren pronounced. "Anyway she got most of the old kingdom of Montenegro, where we were yesterday—with Cattaro, which is another swell harbour, and she got the Dalmatian coast right up to Fiume. That is a potential menace to Italy too. But what made the Italians so sore was that under the Pact of London—the secret treaty made in 1915, under which Italy came into the war—they had been promised the hinterland of Trieste, and Fiume, and a whole strip of the Dalmatian coast, as well as Valona and quite a bit of land round it."

"Who promised it to her?"

"Britain, France, and Russia."

90

"But was it theirs to give away?" Gloire was wide-eyed. Warren laughed.

"Well, no, maybe it wasn't. But it had all belonged to either Austria-Hungary or Turkey, and both were enemies, so they reckoned it a fair deal to divide it up. Those were the bad old days," Warren pursued, "and I guess the British aren't very proud of the Pact of London! Anyway the mere existence of it rotted up every attempt to settle the Adriatic question at the Peace Conference, especially where Albania was concerned. These poor toads have old Woodrow Wilson to thank, as a matter of fact, that they weren't just divided up and handed over in three bits to Greece, Yugo-Slavia, and Italy. He put his foot down."

"Well, so what happened?"

"Another little private war between Albania and Italy, in 1919 or 1920—I guess it was 1920. The Albanians tried to throw the Italians out, and the Italians tried to dig in. But they couldn't make the grade, then. Their troops in Albania were rotten with malaria, and the reinforcements in Italy were rotten with Communism—they didn't want any more fighting, and the whole Italian nation, for once, recognised an unjust cause when they saw it. The troops refused to go and fight, the stevedores refused to load the ships, the railwaymen refused to handle the trains. The whole thing broke down, and the Italians had to withdraw." Warren fitted another cigarette in his stained holder, lit it, and proceeded with his exposition.

"But fifteen years of Fascism have cured all that," he went on, blowing out smoke. "No Italians think for themselves any more, or question the rightness of the Government's actions. And the Government is getting going again. They want this country and they mean to get it."

Will the Albanians like that?"

"Like hell they won't! The people spit on the ground when they hear the word Italian!"

"Then why does the Government do things like changing

91

the street names? And is it true that they're going to throw out the British officers from the Gendarmerie, and put in Italians?"

Warren turned round and looked sharply at her.

"Who told you that? Mrs. Robinson?"

"No. I heard it in Cattaro, as a matter of fact."

Warren blew out more smoke. "Ill news travels fast," he said. "Don't talk about it here, Gloire. I'm afraid it may happen, but it will be a disaster for the country if it does. They've done a superb job, these Gendarmerie officers."

"Yes, but Warren, if they have, why throw them out?"

Warren didn't answer at once. They were bowling along through flat green country, rather marshy; hills rose on their left, blue, and dark with the shadows of clouds—to the right the flat greenness spread away to the horizon, beyond which, invisible, lay the Adriatic. Among the reedy marsh were small patches of grassland, on which stood tall pointed wicker erections, like huge baskets ten feet high—they were full of hay. The road was very bad—Cyril swung the car continually to avoid holes in which you could have buried a dog. Now and again they passed small houses, very tumble-down, and thatched with rushes, with projecting eaves which made them look almost like the huts in a kaffir kraal. The whole effect was of a poor, very backward country.

"There's no simple answer to your question," Warren said at last. "Nothing is simple out here. That's the trouble with our people back home—they want everything to be too simple; black and white, right and wrong. Italy could do a lot for this country, and for herself at the same time, if she had an unselfish tradition, as the Dutch and the British have. This place is the gateway to the Balkans; and Italy wants to boss the Balkans—if she doesn't, Russia or Yugo-Slavia will. It's understandable enough, whether it's laudable or not. Besides, the Italians are great road-makers. That would do this country a lot of good. What it needs before all things is communications. Look at this road! Oungh!" Cyril had failed to avoid one of the grave-like holes, and they bounced in their seats. Gloire laughed and straightened her hat.

"There's copper in those mountains, masses of it," Warren went on, again waving his long clever hand at them—"if there were roads, you could get it out, and it would be worth mining. That would make this country rich."

"But what's that got to do with throwing the British out of the Gendarmerie?"

"Quite a bit. It's another reason for the Italian interest in this place—they can do with plenty of copper!—and it is another reason for Albanian pliancy to Italian wishes. No one else has built them airfields or offered to make them a fine set of roads. Italy can—and does—pose as the friend of Albania; her only friend."

"But doesn't the Government see what she's really after?"

"Maybe they do. But even if they do, it's a choice of evils. There are other smash-and-grabbers to right and left of this wretched little state."

"Who?"

"The Greeks to the South; the Yugo-Slavs to the North. I told you—after the war it was only old Woodrow that saved Albania from being carved up in three bits. The Yugos only just didn't get the whole of the North down to the Drin."

"Where's that?"

"Well, it's right here, as a matter of fact," Warren answered. During the last few minutes a river, grey and rapid, had approached the road on a gradual slant from the left, and now ran beside it.

"Here you are," Warren said, as the car, with a hollow sound, ran onto a long slender bridge—"this is the Drin."

"But—we've been in Albania for miles and miles," Gloire protested. "All that stretch yesterday before Scutari, and all the way we've come this afternoon."

"Just the same, this was the line the Yugos wanted, and

93

damn nearly got," Warren told her. "And in the South, the Greeks damn nearly got the whole country pretty well up to Valona."

"But I can't see why such ideas were ever considered."

"Believe you me, they were—and if there were another war, and Greece and Yugo-Slavia fought on the winning side, they'd be considered again," said Warren, with a sort of sour energy. 'Reward your friends' is a great motto! The Greeks are great hands at propaganda, much better at it than these poor little people. They say they're disunited anyway, with their three religions—Roman, Moslem, Ortho-dox; and it's darned easy to call them down because of their feuds—I know that. And the British and American publics tend to think that since there's only a million Al-banians anyway, they're too small to matter. God rot and damn," said Warren with surprising sudden anger, "the whole cursed conception of *size*! As if size has anything to do with it!"

Gloire was startled. Warren, the American diplomat, was echoing Larsen now, as he had echoed George not long before. Funny how everyone who knew these countries seemed to have much the same ideas about them.

"Did you ever meet a man called Larsen?" she asked Warren suddenly.

"Why, I don't recollect that I did," Warren answered, turning to her in surprise at this sudden change of subject. "What is he? A diplomat?"

"No, he's in the International Labour Office. I just thought you might have," said Gloire carelessly, rather regretting her impulsive question.

"He a boy-friend of yours?" Warren enquired, turning his deep-set eyes on her with a sort of gloomy amusement.

"Oh God, no!" Gloire replied. She shifted back onto the former subject. "*Are* the Albanians very disunited, actu-ally?"

"No. It's true that they have three religions—Roman in

94

the North, Moslem in the centre, and Greek Church—Orthodox—in the South, but——"

"Why?" Gloire interrupted.

"Well, there are perfectly good historical reasons for that," Warren said, brushing the question aside. "And it's quite true that they did have the most ruinous blood-feuds—till Zahg had the guts to make it illegal to carry arms, and the Gendarmerie more or less enforced the law. And they are politically immature—well, so is the U.S.A.! It's so easy to misrepresent all that, and you bet your life it has been done, *and* thoroughly! But the point is," said Warren, again with that surprising energy, "that they're a distinct race, with perfectly individual traditions. The Albanian colonies right through Greece have never been absorbed—they've never even bothered to learn Greek; they've taught the Greeks to speak Albanian! Same goes for the Kastriote colony in Southern Italy. And since they were freed from the Turks—they revolted against them fifty-two times, by the way; that's an average of a revolt every eight years for four centuries—their national consciousness has gotten the bit between its teeth, and believe you me, it's come to stay. No one will ever be able to make Bismarck's damfool mistake about the Albanians again. They don't want to be under the Jugs or Greeks or Italians—they want to be themselves."

"Of course. Why shouldn't they?" said Gloire carelessly. She was peering out of the window of the car. "Warren, what on earth is that bird?" she said.

Warren leaned across and peered too. On the telephone wire beside the road sat a bird with a longish tail, brilliantly coloured in black, coral-red, and vivid jade-green, bright and glowing as enamel.

"That's a bee-eater," said Warren, sitting back. "Place is full of them."

"It's exquisite," said Gloire, also sitting back. "Wouldn't it be heaven in a hat?"

95

Warren looked rather sourly at her. He didn't know quite what to make of Gloire at the moment—now apparently interested in Albania, now vague and vain as of old, as he had always known her.

"What did you want to come to Albania for, anyway?" he asked her suddenly. "You haven't told me that yet. I wouldn't have thought it was at all your cup of tea."

"I thought I'd like to see something a bit different," she said, with elaborate casualness.

"Well, I guess you will," he said rather grimly.

Gloire's face took on a curious little air of satisfaction. "I guess I will, all right," she said.

6

WARREN LANGDON, for some time after their arrival in Tirana, continued to wonder what had prompted Gloire to come to Albania. His reaction to her proposed visit had been the same as that of most people who knew her, at the prospect: pleasure at the idea of having someone so decorative about, tinged—usually rather strongly tinged—with anxiety as to how she would behave. Ever since she grew up Gloire had generally had one or more admirers hanging around—the worst type of continental Duke or Count, or else quite impossible South Americans. (Warren did not find it easy to extend the Good Neighbour policy to individual Latin-American gigolos when they were actively engaged in compromising Gloire, of whom in his vague and helpless way he was rather fond.) Also he had had to take Anne into account. Miss Anne, always generous with disapproval of everything and everyone which did not conform to Beacon Street standards, could not have disapproved more than she did of Gloire; since her marriage she had never heard her name mentioned without wondering aloud how in the Name of Fortune that girl could have captured that attractive well-bred Captain Thurston. Warren always agreed that Tony Thurston had been "darn nice"—like many high-class Americans he used the lower forms of his native speech out of a rather pleasing affectation—and his mere presence, his tough unsubtle British husbandliness had sufficed to keep the Argentines and Dukes at arm's length. But since her husband's death, Warren had gathered that Gloire was "worse than ever," as Miss Anne put it. He had asked her why she had come to

97

Albania, but what he really wondered was for *whom* she had come.

However, no one obvious appeared—no Counts or Dukes sprang up out the ground, and Warren and Miss Anne set themselves, conscientiously but rather depressedly, to entertain their guest. Diplomatic societies are usually small, but in Tirana the society was even smaller than elsewhere, few legations having a staff larger than three, of whom one was usually the archivist; Military and Naval Attachés belonged to and lived in Rome, and appeared at rare intervals for a sort of pastoral visit. The other resources of Tirana were slender in the extreme. There was no theatre or opera, and only one hotel worth mentioning, the Ritz—which bore but a slight resemblance to the Ritzes of other capitals. In fact a Moslem Monarch, and some beautiful but inaccessible scenery was about all! Diplomatic life in Tirana, Warren said, was much more like Jane Austen than Harold Nicolson—it literally did consist largely, as far as he and Miss Anne were concerned, in taking tea and reading aloud.

However, he did his best. One could go for picnics—that is to say, one could go for two picnics, to Kruja, and to the old castle of Petrella, up in the hills towards Elbasan—those being the two directions in which there were roads. And one could go to Durazzo, to which there was also a road, and visit at the British Legation. And Gloire could meet the Corps, such as it was. Warren anticipated, with a sort of dismal relish, introducing such a bird of paradise into the modest flock of sparrows of the local society. But he was sure Gloire would very soon become bored, and then to *désennuyer* herself she would begin to behave frightfully, and there would be a whole lot of trouble with Anne.

At first, however, his fears were not realised. Gloire did dazzle the local society, certainly, but it obviously enjoyed being dazzled, especially the male half. Nor did she seem anywhere near as bored as usual. The fact was that Gloire, actuated still by the impulse given her by Larsen, was for the first time in her life looking at a capital with some other motive than seeing what amusement or sensation she, Gloire, could personally extract from it. She constantly asked to be "shown everything"; and everything did not bear the usual Gloire construction of restaurants and cocktail-bars—of which in any case there were next to none in Tirana. She asked to see hospitals and schools!—and Miss Anne, with grudging and incredulous approval, faithfully took her to view them. Gloire was rather struck by those institutions, as a matter of fact; the admirable and up-to-date equipment introduced under the "Zahg" régime was startling in a capital which was in many respects so "small-town" and so rag-time.

For Tirana in 1936 was rather a rag-time capital. Large parts of it consisted of small ramshackle wooden houses, "shacks" Gloire called them, or of stone ones, behind high walls and almost windowless on the street side; there was of course the Mosque, old and beautiful; on the outskirts were the modern and rather attractive villas of the diplomatic corps and the official and business communities. Finally there was the Whitehall of Tirana, a broad street with the various newly-erected ministries, as gaily-coloured as Neapolitan ices, stretching away from a large square in which it had once been intended to have a sheet of ornamental water. But though the hollow for this had been dug out, funds ran short before it could be cemented and filled; and Nature, abhorring a vacuum, had stepped in and taken the place in hand. A dense growth of bushes, wild hollyhocks, long grass, and acanthus now filled it, in which goats browsed. Nature crept up to the very edge of Whitehall, too. Sitting one day in the Cadillac, waiting for Warren outside the Ministry of the Interior, Gloire was fascinated to observe a small flock of brown and white sheep emerge from the bushes behind the Ministry of Education, nip

99

smartly across the roadway, and disappear into the under-growth behind the Ministry for War.

Confronted with such scenes, Gloire's rather facile contempt tended to get the upper hand. She had always despised the badly-dressed, the insignificant, the people who didn't know what restaurants to go to, and whom the maîtres d'hôtel in the right restaurants did not instantly recognise and fawn upon. She was too ignorant to recognise the measure of achievement which Tirana represented, the distance which the little capital of a little nation had already travelled in its twenty-five years, or less, of independence—a distance as great as from the Old Testament to the twentieth century. She had no idea of how close the Old Testament lay to the very outskirts of the city.

It was in one of these moods of contempt that she asked Warren, one day when she had been in Tirana nearly a week, whether he really liked being there? They were sitting out in the long open-fronted garden room at the back of the house, where the Langdons had their meals in warm weather; the dining-table stood at one end, at the other was an assemblage of garden-chairs and swing seats, flanked by small tables for drinks and ash-trays. Warren had a genius for comfort. Miss Anne, on the other hand, sat always in an uncompromising high-backed chair, and the small table beside it seldom carried anything more adapted to relaxation than her work-box, gold thimble, and gold scissors. She did smoke, on principle—one cigarette after lunch, one after tea, and two after dinner; before dinner she drank one cocktail; they were her deliberate compromise with the modern world, and a part of the companionship which she felt it a duty to extend to her brother in Melanie's absence.

Warren turned round in his chaise-longue, at Gloire's question and looked at her from under his grey eyebrows. How distinguished he is, she thought idly. She had a momentary absurd wish that Larsen could see Warren.

"Yes, I like being here a lot," he replied, slowly.

"Why on earth? It's such a hick town," said Gloire, discontentedly.

"I like the Albanians terribly," Warren said.

"Now Warren, you can't possibly like all those ghastly men, the Cabinet or whatever they were, in the frock-coats, that we met at that luncheon yesterday. Their top-hats! I can't think where on earth they got them.

Warren laughed.

"Why my dear, I grant you their top-hats are pretty comic, and they're no beauties themselves, in that dress. But they're mighty nice men, all the same. I don't suppose it has ever occurred to you," said Warren, taking a sip at his John Collins, "that the transition to modern ways is always a little comic, but you can take it from me that it is. People can hardly put a foot wrong with traditional dress, just because it *is* traditional—it's as effortlessly beautiful and right as the fur on a sable or the coat on a horse. But modern dress requires a great deal of skill and a great deal of experience—as well as a lot of money—if it's to come off." He looked at her as she sat in one of the linen swings, in her sleeveless white shark-skin frock, the skirt so short that it showed the knees of her long silken legs, with her faultless hair and face, and the heavy bizarre gold necklace and bracelets that she wore—the latest dress-makers' fad extended even to jewellery.

"You *do* bring it off, my dear," he guyed her indulgently; "but then you devote pretty well all of your time to it, don't you? And a whole heap of money. Your friends in the top-hats can't do that—they're running a country, in very difficult circumstances, on a minute exchequer. But they're great people."

"Great in what way?" Gloire asked.

"Why, they're plucky and exceedingly intelligent—much more intelligent than you would ever find out, because they haven't the Western tradition of talking to women about things; they still feel orientally about women, that you should just pet and flatter them. The Turks are still that way too, Melanie tells me," Warren put in parenthetically—"she got pretty mad with them when we were in Ankara."

"Did the Turks *pet* Melanie?" Gloire asked, with delighted incredulity, thinking of that gaunt face and figure, rigid with nerves.

Warren laughed.

"No, I guess not—just flattered her. But they wouldn't talk politics with her, and that made her mad. She thought them all fools. But they aren't fools, any more than these boys here are."

Warren, in his leisurely way, pursued his exposition. Warren was like that—ask him a question, and he would go on carefully answering it for hours. Very restful, Gloire found it. You didn't have to listen unless you wanted to.

"They're somehow nearer to reality than we are," Warren was saying.

"Just how do you mean?" Gloire interrupted.

"Why, they're still familiar with the plumb bedrock conditions of life, the soil, and the weather and all that, that we've gotten sort of air-conditioned away from, with our artificial temperatures and our refrigerator-cars bringing us fruit and vegetables from sub-tropical climates at all seasons." He smiled. "When we were talking politics, after luncheon yesterday, old Vrioni, the Minister of Finance, was pointing out that if the Cabinet stood up to the Italians about—well, about something or other—they would get a particular sort of reaction, and he finished off by saying—'Tease the donkey, but take the kick.' I like people who still use those country proverbs so naturally. And then they have a very distinctive quality, among all these Slavs down here."

"Who are they actually—what race I mean? You say they aren't Slavs—I thought everyone down here was Slav, that wasn't Greeks or Turks."

"Well, I won't say you're a disgrace, Gloire, because

102

pretty well everyone is the same way! But that's no credit to the world! The Albanians," Warren pronounced, "are just about the oldest race in Europe. They're Thraco-Illyrians; the one living remnant of the very first Aryan immigrants to this little continent. That's pretty interesting, to me. They were right through the Balkans at first; in the fourth century B.C., the kingdom of Illyria stretched from Trieste right down to the Gulf of Arta—that's below Corfu—under a pretty good King they had: Bardhyllus—which means White Star."

"Well, what became of it? If they had such a great kingdom, why did it fade out?"

"Oh, other nations came up—history's just one long see-saw! First the Greeks, then the Romans. Rome was a terrible leveller," said Warren. "It took a couple of centuries but Rome finally annexed Illyria, and what's more, she annexed if for just the same reasons that Italy wants to annex Albania today—because for security purposes she wanted the ports of Valona and Durazzo—Durazzo was called Dyrrhachium then."

Gloire was shocked.

"How absolutely bloody—I mean, to think of this annexation business going on and on for two thousand years."

"Well, that's the way it was. The King then was called Gentius—he was taken to Rome. He invented gentians; anyway they were called after him. If you know what a gentian is, beside the liqueur," said Warren, looking quizzically at her.

"Don't be an owl, Warren—I know the liqueur *and* the flowers," said Gloire without heat. "The liqueur's lousy," she added.

"You're right! It was under the Romans this place got Christianized," Warren went on. "St. Paul came and preached at Durazzo, and all round about."

"Did he really?" Gloire asked, but without much enthusiasm; she was more interested in Gentius than in St.

103

Paul. She and Tony had picked gentians together, on morains and high pastures.

"Sure. He says himself—'Round about into Illyricum, I have fully preached the Gospel of Christ.' He's one of the favourite local saints."

Gloire was rather impressed by this. It was queer to think that St. Paul, a person in the Bible, whom one knew about, had travelled and preached, perhaps, in this very place where she now was.

"I wonder if he spoke Illyrian," she speculated.

"Thraco-Illyrian," Warren corrected her. "No, I guess St. Paul used an interpreter," he pursued.

"I should think that would be terribly damping, when you were preaching away like mad, to have to wait while somebody else translated, and not know if he was getting it right," said Gloire, pushing the floor with her sandalled toe, and setting the swing seat in motion. "Get me another drink, Warren dear—there's a lamb."

Warren hoisted his great length up out of the chair, mixed her a drink, and brought it to her.

"Thanks," Gloire said. "Well, go on," she said, after taking a sip. "What happened after the Romans?"

"Oh, one damned thing—or damned nation—after another. When the Empire broke up, all these infernal races came pouring in. The Celts were the first, I guess. They didn't amount to much; they pushed right on, North-west, to populate Gaul and Britain and Ireland—leaving their kilts behind them!" said Warren, a smile deepening the lines on his face. "Then it was Goths, Huns, Avars, Serbs, Croats, and what-have-you—a whole procession, none of them very permanent, either. But about the seventh century the Bulgars appeared, and I be damned if the Normans didn't come here too!"

"The *Nor*mans? What on earth did they come for?" Gloire enquired, drinking and swinging. The Normans were a relief—vaguely, she knew about the Normans.

"On a Crusade. Robert Guiscard took Durazzo fifteen years after the Norman Conquest. It was the Normans," Warren pursued reflectively, "who invented the name Albania, but I haven't an idea why.

"And here's a funny thing," he went on—"you were asking in the car the other day why some of the Albanians were Orthodox, not Roman Catholics. Well, history knows all the answers! When another lot of Crusaders attacked Constantinople in 1204, and took it, the damned Venetians took a hand, and helped——"

"Why the damned Venetians? surely it was O.K. for them to fight the Turks?" Gloire put in.

"The Turks weren't in Constantinople in 1204, my poor benighted child," drawled Warren, "it was still the old Byzantine Empire. The Turks only took Constant in 1453."

"Oh, sorry—my error. Go on," said Gloire, quite unabashed.

"Well, the Venetians helped, as I say, so they were given all this coast as a nice little *pourboire*," said Warren sourly. "'Reward your friends' was going strong, even then. But a guy called Michael Comnenus gathered the folks together, the Albanian Minute-Men, threw the Italians out, and set up a state in Southern Albania. It was around then that the South Albanians turned Orthodox—Comnenus was Orthodox himself. And I daresay by that time the Albanians were beginning to think that Roman Catholicism wasn't so hot, since the Crusaders and the Venetians were both Romans."

Gloire laughed. She was rather amused to see how familiar Warren was with all this, so that he talked about it as matter-of-factly as if it had all happened last week.

"Go on," she said briefly.

"Oh well, there you are—Bulgars, Serbs; Venetians, Serbs; Bulgars again, right down the centuries. It's an endless story, and wretchedly the same right along. But the point is," said Warren, putting down his glass and turning round

105

to stare at her with great intensity from under his grizzled eyebrows, "that these Albanians went right on fighting and resisting the whole enduring time, never giving in, never being absorbed. That's why I say they're so individual. A tough people!" said Warren, and took a long pull at his drink.

Gloire was struck by his enthusiasm. Warren's enthusiasms were rather rare; he was too diffident and too disillusioned to kindle easily.

"They sound pretty tough, I must say," she said. "It's funny they've never got anywhere, except way back in prehistoric times, under the White Star Line!"

"It isn't really funny," Warren retorted. "And if all that, what I've been telling you, wasn't enough, the God-damned Turks had to come and just sit on the country for four hundred years, like they did in the rest of the Balkans. Stagnation, that was; no education, no improvements; just barracks and taxation. The Turks quite plainly *froze* the Balkans for four centuries—that's why the whole Balkan outfit is so mediaeval today. And remember they were only cleared out of here in 1912."

"As late as that? I didn't realise," said Gloire. "But I thought the Turks were frightfully go-ahead now."

"So they are. But that's only since Atatürk—he was smart enough to see that if they were to get anywhere in the modern world, they had to go all modern."

"Was Atatürk an Albanian? Someone once told me so," Gloire asked idly.

"No. But most of the best men in the Young Turk outfit, before Atatürk, were. Enver Bey, Talaat Bey, Djavid Bey—all Albanians."

"You're pretty partisan, aren't you?" said Gloire coolly.

"A bit, maybe I am. Not altogether. Everyone who knows these people feels the same. Why, even Anne likes them now," Warren said.

Gloire laughed. If Miss Anne had stamped Albania with

the mark of Beacon Street approval, there was nothing more to be said!

She had been curious, from the moment she arrived in Tirana, to see whether she would meet Miss Glanfield again. But for some time there was no sign of her. However, the very next day, at lunch, Miss Anne said—

"Warren, the Carruthers have asked us to luncheon on Saturday. I suppose we should go? It's rather short notice."

"Yes, surely—we're not engaged elsewhere, are we?"

"No. They have a British writer staying with them," Miss Anne pursued. Gloire pricked up her ears.

"Who's that?" Warren enquired, devouring his grilled Bari lobster.

"Susan Glanfield."

"Oh—that lady! Yes, I'd certainly like to meet her," said Warren. "She's quite a writer. I shall be able to tell her where she gets off about the Yugos, too."

"Now Warren, I beg that you won't be argumentative," said Miss Anne repressively. "You know that Lady Carruthers would dislike that extremely."

"So she would!" replied Warren, with a glint at Gloire. "I'll try to behave, Anne."

But Gloire had another idea in her head, which she was determined to put into execution as soon as possible. "Take a look at Albania," Larsen had said. Well, she had taken a look at the capital and its immediate environs, she had been for one of the two picnics, she was about to see Durazzo. But she wanted to get right out into the country and look at the people—to go to the place, whatever its name was— with the Abbot and the great church, of which Larsen had spoken.

And as she and Warren sat in the garden room after lunch she electrified him by saying suddenly—

"Warren, I want to go up-country. Will you fix it?"

Warren was obviously horrified by this request.

"Go up-country?" he echoed. "Why, my dear, you'd hate

107

that! It's practically impossible, anyway. There are no hotels, you know."

"I know there aren't. But you can take a pony train, and tents and beds and things, can't you? General Stanley must have everything. And I suppose he could fit one out with an interpreter and a guide, couldn't he?"

"Why," said Warren doubtfully—"maybe he could. But it would be terribly rough and uncomfortable. It wouldn't suit you at all. Whatever gave you that idea?"

"I just want to go," said Gloire stubbornly. "I want to see the country and the people. You can't see them properly here."

"Well"—Warren was uncomfortably thinking, more or less aloud. "Yes, I suppose we could make a trip down to Valona—maybe we might go on to Butrinto and see the excavations. Though the mosquitoes down at Butrinto are just nobody's business, Carruthers says. But we could take mosquito-bars, I guess."

"You don't have to come," said Gloire.

"My dear, you can't go alone."

"Oh Warren, don't be so New England! Of course I can go alone. Anyway I don't want to see excavations. I want to go right up-country."

"But there's nothing to see up-country, as you call it—just mountains and wild, wild places," Warren protested. "There's no place to go."

"Yes there is. There's that place with an Abbot, and a big church, and a kind of prince living somewhere close by, that one stays with," said Gloire obstinately.

Warren looked at her with an enquiring gaze. Who on earth had been putting that into her head?

"Oh, you mean Torosh," he said. "But that's a hell of a trip! And just anyone can't go and stay with Lek-Gionaj—you have to be invited."

"Well, people get invited, don't they? Anyhow I don't have to stay with him—I can camp," said Gloire firmly. "But

108

that's where I'm going, Warren, and if you won't fix it with General Stanley, I will." Gloire had met the General and considered, not altogether mistakenly, that she had done rather well with him.

Warren Langdon groaned practically aloud. He knew how remorseless and even unscrupulous Gloire could be in getting her own way about anything she happened to want. But it was not perfectly simple for him, as an American diplomat, to go to the British head of the Gendarmerie and ask quite a large favour of him for one of his, Langdon's, guests.

He knew, as Gloire did not, how much was involved. It was not merely a case of being lent beds and tents, as Gloire blithely assumed, and being "fixed up" with a guide and an interpreter—though even to procure these took some arranging, and it was not nothing to ask a man for the loan of his camp-bed! Warren knew that General Stanley would be reluctant to have a woman who was totally ignorant of the language, life, and customs of the place wandering about High Albania without sending one of his own officers to look after her; and that meant the question of chaperonage—especially in the case of someone who looked like Gloire!—and would also involve a gendarmerie escort every yard of the way, since for reasons of discipline as much as of security, gendarmerie officers never travelled without one. A lot of official time and man-power, and a certain amount of official money would have to be spent on Gloire's whim—for he could not believe that it was more than one of her usual frivolous whims.

However, he also knew from past experience that to oppose Gloire would only make her more obstinate, so he said pacifically—

"No, don't you worry. I'll talk to the General about it. I daresay we can get it fixed up."

"Do, Warren. That will be angelic of you," said Gloire cajolingly.

"Who's been telling you about Torosh, anyway?" Warren unwisely asked her.

"Never you mind." Gloire dropped the cajoling manner abruptly. "You get it fixed, Warren my angel—and do it quickly, won't you? I want to be at Torosh by Whitsun," said Gloire, lighting another cigarette. "But remember, if you don't get going, *I* shall," she added, and got up, and walked off to her room.

Oh, damn the little girl! Warren thought. What an obstinate, selfish, tiresome little cuss she was—and always had been. If only that nice husband of hers hadn't been killed, he might have beaten some sense into her; British husbands did, he understood. But that thought brought a sudden relief. Gloire was, after all, a British national with a British passport. That would make it a shade less embarrassing to bother the General on her account. Then a sudden suspicion flashed into Warren's mind. Could there be some man in High Albania whom she wanted to see? No, that was impossible. There just wasn't anyone; Gloire couldn't know any Albanian men, and the only foreigner there this year was his mad compatriot, old Dr. Emmeline Crowninshield, who as usual was wandering around with her "health unit" —a pony team loaded up with medicines, and an Albanian servant who, so the story went, acted impartially as groom, anaesthetist, hospital orderly, and lady's-maid. But if there wasn't some man, why in tunket should Gloire want to go off camping in the wilds? Warren shook his handsome grey head—it was an insoluble puzzle.

In spite of Gloire's threat, Warren did not hurry himself over asking the General about her proposed trip—he decided to discuss it with Sir Arthur Carruthers when he saw him on Saturday; they were on excellent terms, and he could "sound out" the Englishman about General Stanley. He continued to wonder about Gloire. She wasn't running true to form—all this visiting schools and hospitals was very unlike her, and she was quieter, somehow.

110

The drive from Tirana to Durazzo used to take rather over an hour, though it is barely thirty miles; this was due to the extremely poor character of the road. If there were two cars making the trip, they had to travel at least three miles apart, to allow the clouds of white dust which rose from the untarmacked surface to blow out across the fields and settle on the roadside vegetation—it was considered rather bad form to pass another car on the Durazzo-Tirana road. Warren explained all this to Gloire as they drove out to the British Legation luncheon; Miss Anne opined that it was evidently to be a largish affair, for there were several other cars before and behind them. Warren cursed aloud as a large Isotta-Fraschini shot past, blotting out everything in a white cloud.

"Warren! Who is that?" Miss Anne enquired indignantly.

"My dear, you don't have to ask! It's the Italian, of course —the S.O.B.!" muttered Warren vindictively. When the dust had settled he pointed out to Gloire the airfield and buildings of the Ala Littoria, on the outskirts of the town; and beyond the level flat in which Tirana lies, perched on a spur of the hills, the rugged outline of Kruja, Scanderbeg's mediaeval fortress. The road presently crossed a low stony ridge, before dropping again to a flat straight stretch, running between the sea on one side and a large sheet of water on the other, flanked by a healthy swamp—that was the lagoon, Warren said, turning round from the front seat to impart this information. "The road's built on a causeway— at one time Durazzo was an island. That's it—right ahead." Gloire saw in the distance a long hump-backed hill standing out against the sea; at its foot lay a modern-looking town, and more ancient buildings were piled up on the slope, tier above tier of pinkish-brown tiled roofs, with the sharp minarets of a mosque dominating all, in the clear midday light. Close at hand the slopes of the ridge which they were crossing were planted with orchards of fruit-trees, well grown and carefully tended.

111

Warren drew Miss Anne's attention to them. "Looking pretty good, aren't they?"

"Do they grow much fruit here?" Gloire asked idly.

"Not as much as they should. It's a perfect climate for it —not for citrous stuff, of course, but apples and pears. Greece grows them intensively, and makes a packet out of it, and they could do just the same here."

"Why don't they then?"

"The usual reason—lack of capital, and of education. If I had twenty-five million dollars," said Warren, "I would loan it to Albania at one per cent, on condition that it was used for fruit-growing, under expert supervision, and in ten years I would have this country one big garden, and humming like a hive."

As they drew level with the lagoon, Gloire's attention was caught by a fleet of immense white birds, slowly moving up it before the wind—above them a cloud of sea-birds wheeled and cried.

"Warren, what on earth are those birds? They're too big to be swans," she asked.

"Pelicans," responded her host promptly. "The lagoon's full of them."

In Durazzo they drove for a few moments along broad streets between large white buildings, characterised by that modern featurelessness which, except in America, so seldom succeeds; Miss Anne commented on them. "They call it functional, but to me it's just vacant," she concluded. Then they turned right and crept through narrow streets where only one car could pass, between ancient untidy houses with shutters at the windows, or high walls from which creepers hung—after a pause, while the cars before them emptied, they turned into a lane as narrow as any, and drew up before a small door in a blank wall—a gaily-uniformed dragoman bowed and saluted as he opened the door of the car.

"What an extraordinary place!" Gloire murmured.

"It certainly is," said Miss Anne. "How Lady Carruthers

112

puts up with it I can't think. Why, there's barely plumbing! And all the rooms are so inconveniently placed. I should hate to live here."

The British Legation at Durazzo was an extraordinary place. On the seaward side of the town the immense walls of the Venetian fortifications still stand (or stood before the Italian bombardment in 1939) and the Legation was built partly on, partly in the actual wall. Visitors passed through the street door into a small courtyard, with oleanders in tubs and a fig-tree growing against the wall, and climbed a steep outside staircase to a second door, which led into the house proper—the kitchens and store-rooms were on a level with the courtyard, hollowed out, like caverns, in the massy thickness of the wall itself. Gloire and the Langdons now climbed this stair, and were ushered by a second liveried servant through a long narrow room with a table set for luncheon, and out onto a paved terrace, shaded by an awning—as they stepped out, the blue of sea and sky, and the southern midday glare hit them from under the awning, like an almost palpable blow.

It was a large party. They were greeted by Sir Arthur, tall, tidy, with a scholarly precision of manner, and by his wife, equally tall and giving an impression of being less scholarly and socially more competent. There were introductions—to the Greeks, the Spaniards, the French, the Yugo-Slavs, and one or two Albanian Ministers and their wives. And finally to Miss Glanfield. She met the Langdons first—as Gloire approached she greeted her with a look of amusement.

"Did you have a ghastly trip down with those shattering people—after George gave you away?" Gloire asked at once.

Miss Glanfield smiled.

"Well actually, yes," she said. "Only when we got out from the Bocche again it got quite rough, and they were sick, thank goodness."

"Oh, do you two know one another, then?" Lady Carruthers enquired.

"Yes, we were on the boat together from Ragusa to Cattaro," said Miss Glanfield. She turned back to Gloire.

"Tell me, how did you get on with George? Did he show you San Metodo? And were you comfortable at the Slavia?"

"I wasn't at the Slavia—the wretched place was shut. I was at the Serbia, and it was frightful," said Gloire. "But George was grand. He showed me everything."

"He's a touching creature, really," said Miss Glanfield; "so passionately patriotic, so aware of his country's failings, and so set on remedying them in quite the wrongest possible way."

"What way?"

"Now we can't have our two precious strangers talking to one another all the time," said Lady Carruthers firmly, coming up with an Albanian in tow. "You've no idea how valuable you are here! Miss Glanfield, Mr. Frasheri wants to talk to you. And Count de Tourville wants to talk to you," she said to Gloire. It was evident that he did—it was evident that all the men present did, to some extent. Warren, leaning against the railing of the terrace drinking a cocktail, cool and loosely elegant in his seersucker suit, watched with some amusement the impact of the two new women on the local society. The men of course all eyed Gloire, as men everywhere always did, with a sort of covetous and fascinated pleasure. The women observed her with doubt, envy, and a grudging admiration; at Miss Glanfield, on the other hand, they looked with curiosity and slight awe, faintly tinged with patronage because she held herself carelessly, because her hair was unfashionable, and because she was not more imposingly dressed. She looked an agreeable woman, Warren thought—she was talking very fast and with immense animation in French to M. Frasheri, and M. Frasheri seemed to be liking it.

One of the good things about the Carruthers, Warren al-

114

ways maintained, was that unlike most British Ministers and Ambassadors, they served two rounds of drinks before meals. Over his second cocktail his host came up to talk to him, and Warren seized this opportunity to speak about Gloire's trip.

"How very decorative your guest is!" said Sir Arthur, glancing at her tolerantly through his tortoise-shell spectacles. "Is she one of the Yorkshire Thurstons?"

"Well, her husband was," replied Warren—"he was killed climbing in the Himalayas."

"Oh yes, of course—I remember. A shocking business," said Sir Arthur. "Terrible for her."

"Yes, I guess it was—I think she was pretty fond of him," said Warren. "By the way," he said, leaning a little towards his host and lowering his voice—"I wanted to talk to you about her—about a plan she has."

"Oh really? What sort of plan?" asked Sir Arthur—his voice was perfectly non-committal, but Warren's hypersensitive perceptions told him that the Englishman had gone on the defensive at the mere idea of being consulted about Gloire.

"Why, she has taken the idea into her head that she wants to see more of the country, and get around," said Warren, immediately rendered irresolute by his realisation of the Englishman's attitude.

"Oh yes. Very nice. Well, you could take her down to Elbasan and Valona—even to Butrinto, if you don't mind the mosquitoes, couldn't you? The excavations there are well worth seeing."

"That wasn't quite what Mrs. Thurston had in mind," said Warren feebly. He took a pull on his resolution. "What she really wants to do is to go up to Torosh," he said desperately, "and see the costumes, and all that."

"That's rather an undertaking, isn't it?" said Sir Arthur equably. "Has she got all her kit? She'll need a tent, of course, and a camp-bed and flea-bag and so forth for that

115

trip—even if it could be arranged," he added rather cautiously.

"That's what I wanted to consult you about," said Warren uncomfortably. "Do you think the General would be willing to arrange it for her? I know it's quite a business."

"It is, as a matter of fact," said Sir Arthur. "I've no idea if he would feel he could spare one of his officers to take her just now. She couldn't go alone, of course; and then"— he glanced at Gloire—"she would really have to take some other woman along, wouldn't she? And it's not easy to find anyone. If she's going to be here some time, I should be inclined to wait a little—she might make friends with someone who would care to go with her. Though very few women seem to want to—it's pretty rough up there."

"The trouble is, she wants to be there at Whitsuntide," said Warren desperately.

"Oh well, ask the General," said Sir Arthur. "He always gives you a straight answer! Well, Madam, and how are you?" he said, turning to the French Minister's wife, who approached at that moment.

Discomfited, Warren moved away and set down his glass. That was that. He had been accustomed to find the Englishman most helpful about such minor problems, but this time he, Warren, had evidently opened his mouth too wide. With perfect courtesy, but with complete decision, Sir Arthur had said No. Well, he supposed he would have to try it on with the General himself.

In this uncomfortable frame of mind he was pleased, at luncheon, to find himself placed next to Miss Glanfield. The dining-room at the Legation was really not a room at all, it was a long broad passage leading from the drawing-room and Sir Arthur's study at one end of the house to the bedrooms at the other, with high windows on the landward side. Since it was so narrow, the table had to be long and narrow too. Warren and Miss Glanfield sat facing the windows—Gloire was immediately opposite. Warren did not

116

really agree with Miss Anne about the house; he thought it had great charm, and that the terrace, the view, and the romantic situation, perched on the city wall, fully compensated for the inconveniences. Turning to Miss Glanfield, he opened by asking if she did not think it extraordinarily attractive?

"Oh yes indeed—it has so much character; so much more dignified and amusing than those Lutyens-ey super-villas that the Office of Works has stuck down all over the Balkans," Miss Glanfield replied rapidly. "It's inconvenient, of course—but then convenience isn't everything."

Warren laughed at her description of the Balkan Legations, which he felt to be justified.

"And how do you like Albania?" he pursued.

"The very little that I've seen of it I like extremely," she answered. "Of course I've only been here a few days. But I find them extraordinarily attractive people. That man I was talking to before lunch, for example, M. Frasheri—he's so intelligent, and full of a sort of direct ardour for his country, and an honesty about its failings that I find enormously engaging."

Warren was increasingly pleased with his companion. He liked the way in which, when you offered her a subject, she took it up and carried it on, gave you of her best on it, instead of letting it drop with a dull thud after a single banal sentence of reply.

"You don't get put off by their being so small-town and unsophisticated?" he asked, thinking of Gloire's strictures—M. Frasheri was wearing a frock-coat.

"Good Heavens no! How could they possibly be expected to be anything else in the time? And all that is quite unimportant."

"I agree," he said. "I find them mighty nice too. I'm glad you like them so well. Will Albania wean you from your devotion to the Yugo-Slavs, do you think?" he asked, turning to gaze rather quizzically at her.

In return, he got that blue stare.

"Do I need weaning from my devotion to the Yugo-Slavs?"

Evidently Miss Glanfield was very capable of self-defence.

"Don't get mad at me," Warren hastened to placate her. "I had better tell you right away that I'm an Albanian fan, heart and soul, and you have the name of being the champion of Yugo-Slavia. You're such a redoubtable champion, I was hoping to enlist some of your sympathy for these people here."

"I think that may happen without anyone's help," said Miss Glanfield quietly, but with a certain emphasis. "But perhaps I should tell you, Mr. Langdon, that my interest in these countries isn't political at all. I'm much more interested in their economic and social conditions—I don't dabble in politics." She gave him a small smile. "So now we both know where we are," she said.

"The social and economic conditions in this country could do with some looking into," Warren observed, "and some outside help."

"I expect so—I hope to see something of all that," Miss Glanfield replied. "Even in this short time it strikes me that the place is full of undeveloped possibilities. Fruit-growing, for example; it's obviously an ideal place for that if it could be done scientifically, and the marketing were properly organised, with careful grading and a recognised standard adhered to."

The American was so delighted with this manifestation of sympathy for his favourite project that he hit the table a resounding bang, making the glasses dance; everyone looked up; Miss Anne peered apprehensively down the table through her pince-nez; Lady Carruthers laughed.

"Lady Carruthers, I *beg* your pardon." He turned to his companion. "Miss Glanfield, Ma'am, you're a wonderful woman! I've been preaching fruit-growing in this country

118

for years, and you come and tumble to it in only one week!"

"Oh well, I saw the orchards, and asked about it," said Miss Glanfield deprecatingly. "It's rather obvious, really, if one knows anything about agriculture."

"Yes, but how many women do know anything about agriculture?"

"Well, quite a lot of Englishwomen do, as a matter of fact. You see the soil is still an intimate friend, with us, although we're so heavily industrialised—it's very curious."

Warren was charmed. He went on happily talking, his discomfiture over Gloire's trip quite forgotten. Gloire across the narrow table was near enough to observe what was going on. She was rather intrigued at Miss Glanfield's particular brand of attack. There was the beautiful, rather caressing voice, and there was a sort of impersonal cajolery. Miss Glanfield talked on any subject with ardour and interest, but it was ardour and interest in the subject, not for the person talked to; there was absolutely no hint of coquetry, which she was still quite good-looking enough to employ. And yet it worked! To Gloire this was quite a new technique, but it clearly appealed to Warren; and on the terrace, after lunch, she saw it appealing to the Greek Minister, to another Albanian beside M. Frasheri, and to Mr. Hickson, a small neat man who seemed to be on the Legation staff. As a matter of fact she found that it even appealed a little to her when, just before they left, she again found herself talking to the Englishwoman. They dwelt on the horrors of the Serbia, on George, and on the sights of Cattaro—Miss Glanfield was determined to find out what she had seen, was sympathetic over the horrors, and laughed a great deal. She had a direct, infectious, ready laugh, whose spontaneity was unexpected in a person of her age.

Warren for his part watched them together with interest. He expected there to be a certain latent animosity between two women, both in their own way outstanding, but so

119

totally opposed; instead, there seemed to be if anything a certain sympathy.

Driving home in the car—"That's a mighty nice woman," he observed generally.

"She's a little *exaltée*," Miss Anne remarked.

Gloire said nothing. In her heart she was inclined to agree with them both. Miss Anne as usual had put her finger on it—*exaltée* was the word for Miss Glanfield.

7

WARREN LANGDON had very little appetite for his task of tackling General Stanley about Gloire's trip. More than once he thought of telling her quite definitely that it was impossible. But it was as difficult, and usually as futile to tell Gloire that anything she wanted was impossible as to tell it to a spoilt child: which, by heck, is just what she is! —Warren growled to himself. Also, he had long entertained a sort of indulgent affection for Gloire, to which pity had added itself since her husband's death; it was this, as much as anything else, which took him round to the General's villa next morning before lunch.

The General was at home—in fact he was sitting having a drink with one of his Colonels in the small untidy garden, bare in the middle and tangled round the edges, which surrounded his residence—a camp-bed and a tent lay airing in the sun on the sparse weedy grass which did duty for a lawn. The General was a bachelor, and his establishment looked it.

He greeted his visitor cheerfully, and shouted to his servant for another glass; the Colonel made some excuse and took his leave. When they were alone Warren, rather hesitantly, unfolded his errand.

As Sir Arthur had foretold, the General gave a straight answer, without any hesitation at all.

"I'm so sorry, but no can do just now," he said at once. "As a matter of fact, I can't spare the men. Miss Glanfield is going at the end of the week, with the Robinsons—it's in his district, and he was about due to make a round in any case. And—er—I don't think they know one another; anyhow one can't very well put a stranger into a party of this kind—close quarters and all that; mightn't work, might it?"

"You know Mrs. Thurston is British too," said Warren.

"Yes, yes; of course—but it isn't quite the same thing," said the General a little testily. "The Government here is anxious that Miss Glanfield should be given all facilities—I'm terribly sorry, my dear fellow, but you see how it is. Of course, if she happened to be a friend of Miss Glanfield's it would have been different; they might have joined up then. But as it is, I'm afraid it's no go."

So that had been the reason for Sir Arthur's unhelpfulness, Warren reflected gloomily, as Cyril whirled him homewards through the dusty untidy streets. It was quite understandable, he admitted; and Gloire didn't look in the least the sort of person who would be anything but an encumbrance on such a trip.

Luncheon was waiting when he got home—Gloire, idly glorious in flowered beach pyjamas, at which Miss Anne glanced with restrained disapproval, sat between them.

"The Carruthers are being very energetic about Miss Glanfield," Miss Anne pronounced. "They've sent cards for a cocktail party on Tuesday. Do we have to go, do you think? All that way again, twice in a week?"

"Why, I should say we might as well," Warren answered. "How about you, Gloire?"

"Oh yes, let's go," Gloire drawled. "I like that funny house."

"I like Miss Glanfield," said Warren. "Yes, let's go, Anne."

Miss Anne always retired to her room on Sundays after lunch, with such issues of the "Christian Science Monitor" as had recently percolated to Tirana; Warren and Gloire moved to the farther end of the garden-room, and when the servants had brought coffee and cleared the table, Warren rather timorously reported his mission to the General and its result. Gloire, as he had expected, was indignant and hurt.

"How lousy!" she exclaimed. "Really, how unspeakably lousy of him!"

"Why Gloire, you can't really be surprised. It means taking an officer and goodness knows how many men off their ordinary duties, just to cart you around. You can't expect it. It's quite different for Miss Glanfield—the Government want her to go, so she can write it all up. You can't do that."

"I don't suppose she'd have minded me going along," said Gloire mutinously, pushing the floor with her foot and swinging to and fro.

"Now, Gloire, I do beg that you will leave it alone," said Warren, instantly alarmed. "I've risked, and gotten, two rebuffs, trying to give you what you wanted. You must realise that you can't always have things just the way you wish them. It's time you grew up," said Warren, for once exasperated into frankness of speech, "and learned that your whims don't just rule the world!"

To his dismay, Gloire burst into tears.

"It wasn't a whim," she sobbed out. "It was something else. I *wanted* to go! Oh damn! damn!" She sprang off the swing seat, and whirled away to her room.

It was another hot, glorious and glittering day when they drove over to Durazzo for the Carruthers' cocktail. Miss Anne as usual insisted on starting excessively early. At the further end of the causeway, just short of the town, where the road still ran between low banks, topped with straggling hedges wreathed in purple vetch and a still deeper purple clematis, they saw two people emerging from the swampy ground by the lagoon; they were wading half-way up to their knees in water, but presently they scrambled up the bank onto the road and stood there; the man shook his feet, one after the other, like a wet cat; his companion was a woman, for she unkilted her skirt, which had been held above her knees by a belt, and let it fall to a normal length.

"Gracious! Who on earth can that be?" exclaimed Miss

123

Anne—as the car approached the couple the occupants recognised Miss Glanfield and Mr. Hickson.

"Mercy! What a sight she is!" Miss Anne exclaimed again. "And she'll be terribly late."

"We'd better give them a lift," said Warren; with some trouble he forced Cyril to stop.

Miss Glanfield came straight to the car. She was rather a sight. Her stockings were stained with mud and water; her linen dress was creased where she had kilted it up, and splashed with mud, as indeed was her face; she carried a rather damp bunch of wild flowers, in which long trailing sprays of the purple clematis were conspicuous—in spite of this, she was somehow radiant, with her tanned face and brilliant eyes and smile.

"Want a lift?" Warren enquired.

"Oh, that *would* be lovely. But you're in all your glory, and we're in a most terrible mess," said Miss Glanfield.

"No, come along in. Hickson, you have my seat," said Warren, getting out; he let down the two small seats, and he and Miss Glanfield sat on them.

"That *is* good of you. I'm afraid we're a little bit late," said Miss Glanfield. "We've been birding."

"You've been *what?*" Miss Anne asked.

"Looking at birds. The marsh is an incredible place for birds," said Miss Glanfield, "and Mr. Hickson knows where to find all the nests. We found a black tern's nest, and a short-toed lark's."

Gloire looked at her in astonished amusement. This was not at all her idea of a well-known writer—neither her muddy and dishevelled appearance, nor her eager pleasure, as unaffected as a schoolboy's, in the nests of short-toed larks. She didn't know whether she really thought it tiresome, or rather nice.

"You've got terribly wet," said Miss Anne. "Aren't you afraid of taking cold?"

"On this hot day?—oh goodness no. The pelicans," Miss

124

Glanfield went on, turning to Warren, "are too enchanting!
Did you know that they *sail*? I didn't."

"I certainly did not."

"Well, they do. There were a lot of them, thirty or forty,
sitting on a bank by the water, so we stalked them—that's
how I got so fearfully muddy," said Miss Glanfield frankly.
"And when we were quite close they saw us, and lumbered
off down the bank and paddled a little way out, and then
they turned their backs to the wind and spread their wings
a little, like a swan does when he's angry, and just sailed
away up the lagoon, like an armada!"

"Miss Glanfield is a close observer," put in Mr. Hickson,
who had hitherto remained perfectly silent—"I had never
noticed before that they sail instead of paddling."

"What's that you're carrying?" Warren enquired.

"Flowers, Mr. Langdon—don't you see?"

"They look like weeds to me," said Warren.

"Oh no—look at this delicious clematis—it's obviously
montana, only purple instead of white. I'm going to try to
strike some cuttings, though it's pretty hopeless while
they're in bloom."

At the Legation—indeed some distance short of it where
they were held up by previous arrivals—Miss Glanfield
sprang out.

"Will you excuse me if I go on ahead? I must change like
lightning." She slammed the car door and hastened off, followed by Mr. Hickson.

"I call that a most peculiar woman," said Miss Anne.

"Why?" Gloire asked, for some reason roused to opposition by her tone.

"Well at her age, to go paddling around in a swamp after
birds, and getting late for a party that's given for her,
seems to me very peculiar," said Miss Anne imperturbably.

"She's an enthusiast, Anne," said Warren. "You're allergic
to enthusiasts."

"Why no Warren—not for a cause; you cannot say that of

me," said Miss Anne. "But to be so enthusiastic just over birds and a whole lot of muddy weeds seems to me strange in a middle-aged woman."

"It is unusual—but I don't know but what I rather like it," Warren said.

Gloire had been seriously upset, both by the failure of her plan to go up to Torosh, and by Warren's straight words to her. It was a long time since anyone had criticised her so openly, except for the strange Swede in the train; indeed but for him, no one had done it since Tony died—a thought which had produced a fresh burst of tears when she was alone in her room. She had had a *real* reason for wanting to go—the only person, since Tony died, who had seemed to know what was good for her, had told her to do that thing; and now she was to be prevented from doing it. An obscure sense of genuine frustration, of something serious to her being hindered, had made her weep very bitterly that Sunday afternoon. She had tried out the idea of appealing to Miss Glanfield, but in the end she had turned it down. It really wasn't the sort of thing one *could* do—Warren would be maddened. Now, this afternoon, meeting her like that, all muddy and dirty and late, a little absurd, had somehow given Gloire the idea that after all it might be worth while, possibly, to try it on. People who were not afraid of being absurd themselves might understand absurdity in others, might be absurdly kind. Still undecided, she climbed the narrow stairs into the Legation.

In a surprisingly short time Miss Glanfield reappeared, full of apologies, and looking rather nice. Though she held herself so badly she moved well, with both strength and grace; Gloire, remembering Larsen, wondered again if she were *his* Miss Glanfield. I could ask her that, anyway, she thought.

But in the end she did ask her the other thing. Three or four cocktails just gave that reckless edge to her mood that made it seem possible. Most of the company were out on the

126

terrace, and Gloire, seeing Miss Anne making discreet faces at Warren to indicate that the time was come to leave, and also seeing Miss Glanfield standing by the railing, for a moment alone, went straight up to her, and said with a sort of desperation—

"Miss Glanfield—Mrs. Hanbury—I hear you are going up to Torosh end of this week. I—I wanted most terribly to go there. But they say I can't, because you've got Colonel Robinson and all the gendarmes. And I wondered if you would mind frightfully if I came too? I don't think I should be much trouble. And it's absolutely my only chance of getting there for Whitsun."

Miss Glanfield looked at her. She was obviously very much surprised by this request. After a moment she said—

"Why do you want to be there at Whitsun?"

"Because a man called Larsen told me to."

"Larsen?" Miss Glanfield sounded puzzled and surprised.

"Yes—a mountaineer."

"Not *Nils* Larsen?"

"Yes."

"Oh, do you know him? I used to, ages ago."

"No, I don't really know him," said Gloire. "I just met him on the train. We talked, and he somehow made an impression on me. He told me to come and look at Albania, so I should understand European civilisation—so I just got off the train at Zagreb and came," said Gloire, desperately frank.

Miss Glanfield, to her immense relief, laughed her rather noticeable laugh.

"How like him! Well good for you! Was that your only reason for coming?"

"Yes. I just cabled to Warren from Split and said I wanted to come."

"One always wonders why people come to Albania," said Miss Glanfield. "I wondered why you were coming on the boat."

127

"So did I!" said Gloire. They both laughed.

"He told me I should see Torosh just at Whitsun," Gloire pursued, encouraged, "because of the costumes then, and the service."

"Yes, that is largely what I came for," said Miss Glanfield. "I've been wanting to see that for twenty-five years—rather longer than you! And I wanted to see the Carruthers and the Robinsons—they're all very old friends. But it's amusing that you should have run into Nils Larsen, and that he should have sent you here."

"He told me a bit of a poem of yours, too," said Gloire, driven on by a slight discouragement at Miss Glanfield's remark about the Robinsons, which might have been intended to freeze her out.

"Oh did he? What poem?" Miss Glanfield asked, without much warmth.

"Something about granite heights keeping you in a magic fortress, and water singing in the silence," said Gloire—rather falteringly, for her.

Miss Glanfield said nothing for a moment or two. She turned away and looked out over the bay, up the line of the shore to where the small bare outline of the little hill stood up behind the town. Then she turned back to Gloire.

"Do you climb?" she asked abruptly. "Did you climb with your husband?"

"Yes, I did a good bit—two seasons in the Alps, and two short goes in the Pyrenees, at Whitsun." Gloire was moved by the directness of the question. A ridiculous little thought darted into her mind, warming her strangely—if she lets me come, I shall be able to talk to her about Tony. No one has ever allowed me to talk about Tony. His friends didn't like me, and no one else understood.

"Well, I think you ought to come," said Miss Glanfield at length, in a decided tone. "I'll see the General about it— I'm sure we can arrange it. What kit have you got—to wear, I mean?"

128

"I've got shorts," said Gloire, delighted.

"Oh, you can't wear shorts," said Miss Glanfield. "That's impossible here. Haven't you got any trousers?"

"I may have a pair of slacks—anyhow I'm sure I can fix that," said Gloire, with unwonted eagerness. "Mrs. Hanbury, it's terribly good of you!"

"Not a bit. You won't be able to borrow slacks from your hostess, I fancy," said Miss Glanfield, with what was practically a grin.

"And how not! Mrs. Hanbury—Miss Glanfield—oh, which do I call you?" said Gloire.

"Mrs. Hanbury, of course. The other's a trade name."

"Well, I don't know how to thank you, anyway. This means a lot to me. It is most frightfully good of you to let me come along."

"Oh, nonsense. I think perhaps we shall have fun together. Have you any Kletterschuhe? We might conceivably get a little rock-climbing."

"Oh no, I haven't," Gloire almost wailed.

"Oh well, never mind. Bring some sand shoes or tennis shoes—you'll want those to walk in anyhow, on these hot rocky paths. You've met the Robinsons, haven't you?"

"Yes, they put me up in Scutari. She's grand," said Gloire, remembering that whisky-and-soda.

"She is. And she speaks Albanian well, so we shall be able to talk to the women," said Miss Glanfield.

"Oh, is she coming too?"

"Yes rather. Well now," said Miss Glanfield briskly, "I'd better go aboard the General and get all this settled. He's not gone, has he? Oh no, there he is. We start on Saturday morning at 4 A.M. from here. I expect you'll have to sleep here—I'll talk to the Carruthers about it. I dare say they have a bed. The Robinsons meet us at Rësheni. Can you ride?" the writer finally asked.

"Oh Lord yes!"

"Good. Well goodbye, my dear child. I'll ring you up

129

when everything's been arranged, but I'm sure it will be all right."

"Oh, thank you," said Gloire. "You really are——'

But Miss Glanfield was already threading her way purposefully through the throng in General Stanley's direction, and in a moment Miss Anne came up and swept Gloire off to make their adieux to her hostess.

In the car going home—"Well, Gloire, you had quite an innings with our authoress," Warren observed. "Do you like her?"

"Yes, she's nice," Gloire replied. She choked back an impulse to come clean to Warren and have done with it; it would be easier as well as more prudent to do it when they were alone, and let him cope with Miss Anne's disapproval.

However, she told him as soon as they got in, when Miss Anne had gone upstairs.

"Warren, you may as well hear right away. I'm going on that trip after all. I told Miss Glanfield I wanted to go to Torosh, and she's taking me along. She's fixing it all up with the General."

"Well, I be darned!" Warren ejaculated. "Aren't you the limit?"

"No really, Warren dear, it's all right. There's no need for you to be lousy about it. I don't think she minds and I *do* mind."

"What beats me is *why* you want to go all that much," Warren said, fanning himself with his hat.

"It beats me, rather," Gloire said, with a funny little smile. "But I just do. Now look, Warren, stop disapproving and tell me where I can get some slacks, because Miss G. says I have to have them."

Miss Glanfield's host and hostess were not very encouraging when she informed them that she had agreed to include Gloire in the trip to Torosh. She referred to her as "the Thurston child."

130

"You're really incurably maternal and soft-hearted, Susan," Sir Arthur said. "Child, indeed! She's a spoilt hard-boiled little never-mind-what, if ever I saw one. And that ridiculous name! Imagine going on as an adult, calling oneself Gloire!"

"Yes, it's an asinine name. I believe she had an asinine mother. She may be an asinine person herself—in fact in lots of ways I'm sure she is."

"Then why in the world do you let her force her way in, Susan? It's really ridiculous," Helen Carruthers said.

"I think she may have another side. After all, she does climb—or did," said Miss Glanfield slowly.

"Really, Susan, you are too absurd, the way you always assume that climbers are *ipso facto* repositories of all the virtues," said Sir Arthur.

"Well Arthur, you must admit that mountaineering is one of the few respectable hobbies left in the world," Miss Glanfield replied. "There's no money in it, and it doesn't advertise itself—except for the few unutterables who write themselves up, and they're so few that they hardly count. On the whole, nasty people just don't climb."

"That's all very negative."

"Yes, Arthur. I'm not going to throw my positive pearls before cynics like you."

"Now she's called me a swine, Helen!" Sir Arthur complained. "What a guest!"

"Has she got a flea-bag and all the doings?" Lady Carruthers enquired practically.

"Not a thing. But General Stanley says that one of his fantastic Colonels has everything, including a tent as big as a Methodist Chapel, and he's going to impound all that for her," said Miss Glanfield tranquilly. "Oh and Helen, I'm frightfully sorry, but really she ought to sleep here Friday night, so as to be on the spot. Can you bear it? Is there a bed?"

Sir Arthur groaned aloud.

131

"Well otherwise Arthur, I shall have to leave at 2 A.M. instead of at 4, to go to Tirana and pick her up—and either you or Stefan will have to get me coffee," said Miss Glanfield.

"No, of course she can have a bed. Don't be absurd, Arthur," said Lady Carruthers. "She won't eat you. Let's go and have coffee."

"My dear, I feel that's just what she might do, at any moment," said Sir Arthur, getting up and opening the door.

"I think you're an absolute toad, Arthur," said Miss Glanfield, as they went out onto the terrace. "I think she's very pretty, and very spoilt, and very miserable, and you ought to be merciful, not so hideously censorious."

"My dear Susan, in our service the quality of mercy is strained to breaking-point all the time," said Sir Arthur. "Sugar?"

Miss Glanfield would have had some difficulty in explaining exactly why she had agreed to take Mrs. Thurston up to Torosh. It is always difficult to explain our habitual actions, just because they are habitual; and this was in fact the sort of thing she did almost automatically. She had a profound belief in education, and in the educational value of all such experiences as travel affords; she had an almost passionate love of knowledge, the more accurate and detailed the better, for its own sake; she adored accumulating small bright nuggets of fact, which she gloated over secretly as a magpie gloats over his useless and miscellaneous hoard. It *really* made her happy to find the nest of the short-toed lark, and to see black terns at close range; it made her blissfully happy to find and identify new flowers. (But she had to identify them—consequently she travelled about with a large accumulation of bulky botanical tomes.) It made her feel both expanded and enriched to see churches like S. Method's, or to look at S. Luke's alleged portrait of Our Lady. And

132

because she felt all these things herself, with a simplicity which was undoubtedly curious in a mature writer she assumed that other people must feel them too; if it gave her pleasure and did her good to look at iconographic paintings, it must do the same for people like Gloire Thurston. So, in an almost missionary spirit, she directed Gloire—and many like her—to churches, pictures, bird sanctuaries, museums and Roman remains, regardless of the fact that what meant so much to her might mean little or nothing to others. And of course when she did happen on a genuine desire to go somewhere and see something, she naturally and unthinkingly aided and abetted it.

But in Mrs. Thurston's case, there was more to it than that. The younger woman's appearance and manner proclaimed her as belonging to a class of people whom Miss Glanfield sedulously avoided, because they bored her and she disapproved of them—their mode of existence seemed to her strangely and perniciously futile. She had organised Gloire's sight-seeing at Cattaro, on the boat, quite automatically—she would, without thought, have done the same for the devil himself, if she had happened to meet him on a boat off the Dalmatian coast. But to include such a person in an expedition on which she set as much store as she did on the journey to Torosh was another matter. She had been immensely surprised by Gloire's request; she recognised a certain urgency behind it, and, though less acutely than Larsen, she was vaguely aware of some hidden wretchedness in this pretty, ultra-fashionable creature. Miss Glanfield of course expected ultra-fashionable cosmopolitan people to be wretched, because she would have been wretched herself leading their life; but, unlike Larsen, she had been familiar with Tony Thurston's tragic story; she had known him, and she was quite prepared to assume that his widow, however futile, must have known desolation. Why that should be linked with this desire to see Torosh she had no idea—Gloire's few remarks about Larsen were peculiar and intriguing, but did not really throw much light on it. But plainly the urgency was there; and her natural impulse to mercy and pity caused her to say yes.

Nor did she regret her impulse. Having the girl along would alter the character of the trip, but would not necessarily spoil it; if she had done a couple of seasons in the Alps with Tony Thurston she would certainly be able to keep up, which was the main thing. And Larsen had wished her to go. Memories, strangely operative still, came up out of the past at his name. He must have had some good reason for sending her—and she, Susan Glanfield, was not going to oppose, even now, the wishes of Nils Larsen, whom she had not seen for twenty years.

8

"I STILL don't see quite why Susan had to insist on this
girl's coming too," Colonel Robinson said rather gloomily to
his wife on the Saturday morning, as they stood stamping
their feet to get the chill and stiffness out of them, after the
long drive down from Scutari to Rësheni. Rësheni, in the
valley of the Lesser Fani, was to be the starting-point of
the expedition; a small side-road led to it, off the main
Durazzo-Scutari highway; this came to an abrupt end
among green meadows and a group of houses, a few yards
from where they stood—the meadows sloped gently down to
a belt of wood, beyond which lay the river. It was seven
o'clock; the hidden sun was just beginning to spread a glow
behind the hills to the east, and the air was still keen. The
team of men and ponies which was to carry the gear of the
expedition had already assembled, and the luggage was
being disposed on the various pack-animals; a little apart
stood three ponies with saddles and bridles for the women
to ride. There was a man to each pony, and a picturesque
group they made. The North Albanian mountaineer goes
about his daily business in tight-fitting white trousers with
a serpentine black band down the leg, a full-sleeved white
shirt closed tight at the wrist in a long close-fitting cuff—
very formal and elegant, and a short-sleeved black cloth
jacket cut square and full, hanging loose to the waist; the
wide sleeves terminate half-way to the elbow, and the whole
is trimmed with large black bobbles, and a line of black
fringe across the back. (The passion of South-East Europe
for the swinging pride of tassels and fringes has almost certainly some significance which anthropologists and psychol-

135

ogists have not yet explored.) A black cummerbund supports the High Albanian's trousers—but looks perpetually as if it will fail to do so; his bare feet are encased in open raw-hide sandals, usually with the hair still on them; on his head, for the most part, he wears a high round flat-topped cap of white wool, which is neither knit nor woven, but beaten and shrunk with some mordant, first in a bowl and then on a block, till it takes on the consistency of a thick felt. Most of the pony-men at Rësheni were so dressed, but a few, instead of the black-banded trousers, wore full white linen ones, and a linen tunic to the knee, with a sleeveless homespun zouave, embroidered round the neck and arm-holes, instead of the tasselled black jacket. One man, older than the rest and so short as to be almost stunted, who escorted one of the riding ponies, wore not the white cap but the head-cloth, swathed in thick folds across the forehead and draped under the chin—it produced a very Arab effect. Among the pony-team, either observing or directing operations, stood not less than seven gendarmes, very trim and smart in their green uniforms. It was something of an event when Colonel Robinson went on one of his rounds of inspection, and the Lieutenant from down the valley, and the one from Ndërfanden across the river, had both turned out to meet him with their men.

General Stanley had done Miss Glanfield and Mrs. Thurston rather well in the matter of equipment. He had not only provided tents and camp-beds, but he had sent these up to Rësheni the previous day under the escort of Fran, his personal orderly, who bore the rank of Sergeant; Fran was to accompany the two ladies and wait upon them in every way throughout the expedition. This was a relief to Colonel Robinson, who knew what a weary business pitching tents and erecting camp-beds, and even cooking supper, can be to amateurs after a long day's march. He and his wife, on the drive down, had been rather anxiously discussing the probable capabilities of the said two ama-

136

teurs. Miss Glanfield had been a school friend of Mrs. Robinson's and he knew her much less well than his wife, though he called her Susan and counted her as a friend; but friends are one thing and companions on a rather rough and exacting expedition another. Robina had succeeded in reassuring him as to Miss Glanfield, but Gloire's appearance had filled him with dismay at the prospect of her company. Hence his grumble.

"Susan said in her letter that Mrs. Thurston had some special reason for wanting to come," said Robina pacifically.

"H'm. Well, I hope she doesn't think she can strike up flirtations with handsome Albanian men," said Colonel Robinson, whose mind, after twenty-four hours of Gloire, ran on much the same lines as Warren Langdon's, after some twenty-four years of her. "Because there's nothing doing. They're absolutely death on that. It's curious, no one would ever guess how much more rigid their social code is than that of most so-called civilised countries. And there are no foreigners up there this year, if that's what she's after," he pursued. "There's nobody but old Dr. Crownin-shield. She won't do her much good!"

"Oh, where is she? Shall we run into her? I do hope so—she's such fun," said Robina.

"She was in Mati last week, taking a baby case—I haven't heard of her since. But this damn girl," he went on—"I do feel she'll be totally out of key up here. And how will she keep up? She doesn't look as if she could walk ten yards."

"Her husband was a mountaineer—you know, the one that got left behind on the top of the Himalayas, and died," said his wife. "She climbed with him, Susan said, so she must be able to walk."

Colonel Robinson grunted. He was still unappeased. A simple, practical, and normally rather unimaginative man, when he gave his mind to a subject he mastered it thoroughly, and his heart was apt, silently, to follow his mind. Both had now been given for some years to Albania and

137

the Albanians; he knew them well, he liked them and respected them; he was well aware of their backwardness and defects, and like the parent of a backward child, he disliked exposing them to an unsympathetic gaze. But he was also very much alive to their virtues, none of them at all easily expressible in modern terms of mass values. He knew them for a people either not exposed to, or oblivious of, economic pressure, non-starters in the race for wealth and self-advertisement; self-sufficing in their uneconomic world of older, more enduring, and more imponderable values. He could make Miss Glanfield see all that, indeed she would probably see it without any making—but not that wretched little cosmopolite. Also he was vexed at having this trip spoilt, as he gloomily expected it to be. It was very seldom that Robina could manage to get away to accompany him on one of his journeys, or indeed that they felt they could afford the extra expense.

He looked across now at the group round the pack-animals.

"They seem to be getting into a bit of a muddle," he observed. "We must have those loads right, or we shall be wasting time the whole day. I'd better go and see—" and he strode across.

Left to herself, Mrs. Robinson sat down on a heap of logs under one of the houses, and gave herself up to happiness. She too was an extremely simple and practical person, but she had more capacity for living in the present than her Dick. This jaunt was a holiday and a treat—well-earned, she could honestly feel; and besides Dick there would be her dear, her brilliant Susan, who in spite of wealth and fame was always so faithful and affectionate to her less glittering friends. She was not going to let the presence of one foolish little fashionable spoil all that. She pulled off her unbecoming felt hat, leaned her solid figure back against the rough wall, and watched Dick among his men. How jolly they were, tugging and wrestling with the loads with such cheerful and unskilful zeal, and turning faces bright with affection and respect on her tall husband. In that clear but muted light, without shadows still, the group had real beauty: the black and white figures, the ponies, the vivid grass; Robina Robinson could not describe beauty as Susan could, but she could feel it, and she sighed with pleasure. The air was sweet, after the city smells of Scutari; and now women came out of the houses and talked to her. What a good thing that it was a Saturday, they said; "Never start an undertaking or a journey on a Tuesday—evil will follow," they said, mouthing out the familiar proverb with country relish.

From down the narrow road came the hoot of a horn, and a white cloud of dust approached. Mrs. Robinson got up, and was standing by the roadside when the Legation car from Durazzo, with its small Union Jack fluttering from the wing, drew up.

Both she and Colonel Robinson surveyed its passengers appraisingly as they got out; it was important that they should have the right kit for riding and walking. Miss Glanfield passed easily. Her wide knitted beach-trousers of dark blue were tucked at the ankle into white cotton socks under low-heeled white canvas shoes; a dark-blue blazer, belted, with an enamel mug hanging from the belt, a white shirt, a soft felt hat, and a haversack completed her costume; it was practical, dignified, and harmonious into the bargain. Mrs. Thurston's was rather less satisfactory. She had somehow raised a pair of grey flannel trousers, but with them she wore a very gaudy cotton shirt and a foolish little pale-blue linen jacket; her shoes were rubber-soled, thank goodness, but had idiotic open-work toes; she wore no hat at all. Dark glasses of enormous size, with white rims, added to her general resemblance to a film-star at Miami.

Colonel Robinson turned promptly to the business in hand.

"Now Susan, what luggage have you and Mrs. Thurston got? We've got all your sleeping gear loaded—we just want your personal stuff."

Porfiri, the Legation chauffeur, was already extracting their luggage from the boot. Fran stepped up and was formally presented by Colonel Robinson, a small neatly-made man, very smart in his uniform; he had an alert, intelligent, sensitive face and a splendid set of very white teeth, which flashed when he smiled. He and another gendarme bore the luggage across to the waiting ponies. Colonel Robinson went with them; the three women repaired to Mrs. Robinson's heap of logs and sat down.

"I expect you could do with some coffee," said Mrs. Robinson, extracting a thermos from a large leather case slung on a strap.

Gloire and Miss Glanfield, after a three-hours drive and a start at 4 A.M., found that they could do with it very well indeed, and with the rich home-made cake that accompanied it. Munching contentedly, they watched the group of men adjusting the loads on the ponies.

"I like the black bands on their trousers," Miss Glanfield observed.

"You know what that is, don't you?" said Mrs. Robinson. "That—and the black jackets—is in mourning for Scanderbeg."

Miss Glanfield, who knew all about Scanderbeg, said—"Is it really? Still? Robina, how enchanting!"—but Gloire, who did not, felt impelled to admit her ignorance and ask who Scanderbeg was.

"Hasn't your learned uncle told you that yet?" Mrs. Robinson asked.

Gloire raised her plucked eyebrows, which somehow looked more artificial than ever in that wild valley, under the rough wall of that primitive house.

"My uncle?"

"Mr. Langdon, I mean. Isn't he your uncle?"

"Oh God, no."

"Oh, I'm sorry. Well never mind. Scanderbeg—since he hasn't told you. Scanderbeg's real name was George Kastrioti; he was one of the four sons of John Kastrioti of Kruja, who were sent as hostages to Constantinople; the Sultan took a great fancy to him and made him ruler of a Sanjak. He was such a good strategist, and won so many victories for the Turks that they gave him the title of Scanderbeg, which means Prince Alexander, because they said he was as great a commander as Alexander the Great."

"How pretty," said Miss Glanfield. "I didn't know that that was how he came by his name, Robina."

"But if he fought for the Turks, why do these people mourn for him?" Gloire very naturally wanted to know.

"Oh, because when he got the chance he came back—he made a wonderful seven-day march from Nish—and ousted the Pasha from Kruja; and he threw the Turks out and became the independent ruler of Albania and Epirus. He was that for twenty-three years, fighting the Turks, alone, the whole time. He was a Catholic, and all South-East Europe looked on him as the one successful champion of the Christian faith; when he died, and the Sultan heard it, he said: "Asia and Europe are mine at last! Woe to Christendom! She has lost her sword and shield!""

"When was all this?" Gloire asked.

"In the fifteenth century. The Turks returned then, of course—and the country sank back again. But Scanderbeg's reign made an enormous difference to the Albanians," said Mrs. Robinson earnestly, "because it gave them the memory of freedom from Turkish rule as an actual possibility, and so it kept up the sense of national independence. And being the people they are, they recognized and seized on that; and in their daily lives, and their ordinary dress, they commemorate it."

"Do the white caps mean anything?" Gloire asked.

"Oh yes, rather. They used to wear red tarbushes, like the

141

Turks—but Zog forbade that and said they must be white, to emphasize the end of Turkish influence."

"They *are* rather wonderful, Robina," Miss Glanfield said, looking across at the group of men. "It's a glorious story, and a glorious attitude to it."

"You've no idea how fine they are, till you come to live among them. I do like them so," said Mrs. Robinson with great simplicity.

"Why are some of the Scanderbeg stripes broad and some narrow?" asked Gloire, who was still watching the men round the ponies.

"That shows which tribe or clan a man belongs to, like the different tartans in the Highlands. When feuds were still going on it was extremely important to know at sight what clan a stranger came from, whether he was a friend or an enemy."

"I should have thought it a bit unwise to advertise oneself like that," said Gloire, half jokingly. "Didn't they ever change trousers if they were going into enemy country?"

Mrs. Robinson stared at her for a moment.

"No. That would never occur to an Albanian," she said quietly. Oh dear, she thought—I hope she won't go and say that sort of thing to Dick. And she too began to have her doubts as to whether after all the pleasure of the expedition would be able to surmount Mrs. Thurston's presence.

"I want to know more about the clans and how they are organised, Robina," Miss Glanfield rather hastily put in. "Will you tell us?"

"You'd better ask Dick that—he puts things better than I do."

"What a mass of gendarmes," Miss Glanfield pursued. "Are they all coming with us?"

"Oh no." Mrs. Robinson explained about the gendarmes. "The Lieutenant from Ndërfanden will escort us so far—he's come out of his district to meet us, to show respect—

and then he will send two of his men on with us to the half-way point between here and the next post, where another couple will meet us and take over; and so it will go on all the way."

Gloire thought this very amusing. The loading had at last been completed, and the pack-animals began to move off in single file towards the wood; one of them had a foal at foot, leggy, furry, and awkward; it gambolled beside its mother as she moved sedately forward.

"Gracious! That little thing isn't coming too, is it?"

"Oh yes; it's still being suckled. It can't be left," said Mrs. Robinson, getting up as her husband approached. "Are we to ride at once, Dick?"

"Yes, you'd better—we shall be fording the Fani in a minute or two."

The three women examined their mounts as they approached them. Mrs. Robinson's was the largest of the three, a mouse-coloured pot-bellied creature; its drooping head and dejected ears gave little promise of staying power. Miss Glanfield's was black, neatly built and spirited; Gloire had a bay. They mounted; stirrup-leathers were adjusted, and they rode off, Fran and Colonel Robinson walking alongside. Gloire's pony-boy, the stumpy elderly man in the head-cloth, insisted on leading the bay pony; she asked Colonel Robinson to tell him that she knew how to ride and would rather handle her pony herself. Colonel Robinson did so, and the little man, rather discomfited, let go of the bridle; Fran called out some remark in Albanian which was greeted by the others with laughter.

"What's the joke?" Gloire enquired of Mrs. Robinson, who was just behind her.

"Fran's making fun of your poor little man. He said—'Don't measure your importance by your morning shadow.' It's one of their favourite proverbs."

Gloire found herself laughing too; the sun was up now, and their shadows stretched out across the bright grass of the meadow. It struck her suddenly as odd that she should be amused by what was after all a very elementary form of joke. If one of her set had made it in London or Paris she would probably have told him not to be obvious. But then in London or Paris one was almost never out when the morning sun cast long shadows on grass wet with dew. Gloire stuck her heels into her pony's ribs and trotted on ahead of the others, in high spirits. This was fun. After all her set-backs, she was really on her way to Torosh, where the Swede had bade her go; and the sun was shining and the air was delicious. Goody! said Gloire to herself, as she trotted forward into High Albania.

Behind her, the atmosphere was less cheerful, and comment unfavourable.

"What a fantastic get-up," Colonel Robinson said, eyeing the unconscious Gloire's back with disfavour, as she disappeared into the wood.

Miss Glanfield hustled her pony alongside him.

"Look here, Dick—and Robina—I am most frightfully sorry about this. I couldn't explain properly in my letter, I wrote in such a hurry; but I had to let her come. I do hope she won't be too much of a nuisance."

"Why?" asked Colonel Robinson, ignoring the pious hope.

"Well"—Miss Glanfield hesitated. "I think it's really important to her to come, in some way that I don't quite understand myself. But her whole heart was set on seeing Torosh at Whitsun."

"How on earth had she heard of it?"

"Someone whose opinion she values—and I value too—told her to."

"Good Gad, don't tell me you and she have any friends in common!" ejaculated the Colonel.

"Now Dick, don't be petty! Yes, we have—one! But look, darlings, I do apologise enormously," said Miss Glanfield, leaning from the black pony to lay her hand on his arm. "I wouldn't have done it if it hadn't seemed really im-

144

portant to. She's had a rotten time, losing that terribly nice husband—who I should say was the one respectable influence she's ever had in her trivial little life. Look on it as a work of mercy," said Miss Glanfield earnestly.

"You'd talk round the devil himself, Susan," the Colonel grunted.

"Susan dear, you mustn't stroke him here," said Robina tranquilly; "it will shock these people."

"Will it now? How enchanting," said Miss Glanfield again, quite unperturbed, removing her hand from the Colonel's arm.

Ahead of them, the subject of their conversation rode into the wood. The air here struck damp and cool, and had a toadstool-y smell—small oaks sprang from knobby mossy roots. And here the nightingales began—that were to be for Gloire Thurston one of the abiding things about this expedition. From every side came their bubbling reiterated voices, so that the whole shady place rang with sound, of an astonishing volume. Even as Larsen had foretold. A dreamy calm expression came over her delicate face, a sense of peace and fulfillment filled her. Lovely. Here was lost Joy again at last! How right the Swede had been, she thought, for the first time with full conviction.

Beyond the wood the path emerged onto the flat stony margin of the river; the shallow rippling water stretched away for a hundred yards or more to the further bank, which was masked in willow scrub; beyond its silvery green rose the high blue of hills. Here the rest of the caravan had paused; the foal was seizing the opportunity for a snack. When Colonel Robinson emerged from the wood, a little ceremony took place. The Lieutenant from down the valley and his two men stepped forward, and made a formal farewell; they recited in unison something that sounded like verse, and ended by giving the Albanian salute—bringing the right hand stiffly to rest over the heart, and then cutting it away smartly. Colonel Robinson gave the same

145

salute in return, and they marched briskly off through the wood.

The whole cavalcade now plunged into the stream; the water was up to their knees. Colonel Robinson hallooed to his wife to send her pony back for him; the Ndërfanden Lieutenant was carried over on the back of one of his men, and Gloire's little fellow hoisted Fran on his back and brought him across in triumph. There was a lot of shouting, splashing, and laughter over the crossing; everyone seemed to feel that fording rivers and getting wet to the knees was fine fun. This mood chimed with Gloire's; she felt that if she lived out here in the country, she might come to like the Albanians as much as Mrs. Robinson did. These wild-faced laughing men were much more engaging than the politicians in the top-hats at Tirana.

While they waited for Colonel Robinson Miss Glanfield dismounted and began to gather flowers along the river-bank. Suddenly she raised a doleful cry.

"Oh, goodness, what an idiot I am!"

"What's amiss?" Mrs. Robinson enquired.

"I've left my vasculum behind. How could I be such a fool?"

Gloire had no idea what a vasculum was. Nor, it seemed, was Mrs. Robinson any better informed.

"Your *what*, Susan?"

"My flower-tin. Now all these will fade before I can press them."

"If you can wait till lunch, I can give you the cake-tin," said the resourceful Robina. "We can eat the cake, or put it in something else."

"Oh, marvellous, Robina."

When Colonel Robinson arrived they continued on their way; first across a flat valley floor, where the soil was dark and rich—there was however little cultivation except a few strips; it was mostly pasture, and rather rushy at that. Miss Glanfield observed that it wanted draining.

146

"Yes," Colonel Robinson agreed with a sort of groan.

"But why don't they do it, Dick? It's such a waste of this good ground."

"Not interested," he said. "It's very hard to make them take any serious interest in agriculture."

"But why not?"

"It just isn't in their tradition—partly because much of the soil is so poor, I suppose. They're a bit more enterprising in the South. They like stock-raising well enough—you'll see some splendid sheep and goats up at Lek-Gionaj's, or over in Kossovo, if you go there; but of course in sheep they go in for milk rather than wool."

Their path left the valley and climbed an easy slope on the further side, bare and open; the sun was now fairly hot, and Mrs. Robinson's mouse-coloured pony began to show signs of distress. The good-natured woman got off to relieve it, and walked; Gloire and Miss Glanfield presently got off and walked too, less for their ponies' sake than for their own—neither had ridden for some months, and the small saddles were making them very sore. Here and there they came on patches of cultivation, little more than scratchings in the earth; Miss Glanfield was struck by the contrast between this country and Bulgaria, where, as she pointed out to Colonel Robinson, the tillage was both intensive and skilful. He agreed that, yes, the Bulgars were like that— "though their soil is better than this. But they're born gardeners; gardeners and *chocolatiers*; those are their two forms of national genius."

"What's the national genius of the Albanians?" Gloire enquired. She had no tactless intention, but her flat careless drawl made her question sound ironic to Colonel Robinson's hostile and sensitive ear.

"It's rather early days to say that yet," he said defensively. "When a country has only been free from foreign despotism for twenty-four years, one hardly knows what they may become."

147

"Weaving is one of their skills—and embroidery," said Mrs. Robinson. "All the clothes these men wear"—she gestured ahead at the caravan—"are hand-woven. And some of the lawn they weave is exquisitely fine. The women weave their own silk, too, for their best shirts and tunics. You'll see them at Torosh."

"Like Gandhi," said Gloire. "But it can't compete nowadays, can it?"

Nobody answered her. Perhaps it couldn't compete. Or perhaps that native skill could be turned to a use at once commercial and artistic, as in the hereditary weaving families of Lyons and Broussa. That was what Colonel Robinson, who spent much of his time pondering this particular problem, was thinking—but he was not going to say so to the "damn girl."

Towards noon, when fatigue and heat were beginning to gain on the party, mulberry-trees and more cultivation betokened the presence of a larger village, and presently they came to the first houses of Ndërfanden. At a crossways in the centre was a pleasant spot—a pool under a great rock, lapping on one side against the wall of a house, and overhung by a large poplar-tree; water splashed from a spout. Here they halted for lunch.

"Can we drink this?" Miss Glanfield asked, pointing to the spout. She was thirsty.

"Not without asking—*never* without asking," Robina replied. "I'll find out." She spoke to Fran, who enquired of a passing woman, and then turned and nodded. "Yes, this is good water."

"How does one ask if it's good in Albanian?" Miss Glanfield enquired.

"Asht ujë mirë—Is this water good," Mrs. Robinson responded.

"Which word is which?"

"Asht—is, ujë—water, mirë—good."

"Asht ooiy miray—asht ooiy miray." Miss Glanfield
148

mouthed the alien syllables over, memorising them. Suddenly she turned with a startled expression to Mrs. Robinson, who was unpacking the lunch with Fran's help.

"Robina!"

"Yes, what?"

"But that's quite extraordinary!"

"What's extraordinary?"

"*Ooiy*. Look—you have some Gaelic, or had. *Uisge*—water in Gaelic; *Ooiy*, water in Albanian. It must be the same root."

"So it must," said Mrs. Robinson tranquilly, giving Fran the tin-opener. "How very funny—in all these years I never thought of that."

"Never thought of what?" said Colonel Robinson, coming up.

He was told.

"Yes, I daresay that is it," he said. "After all the Celts left the kilt and the plaid here too, and these people have lots of traits in common with the Highlanders. Look at the clan system, here in High Albania itself."

"Oh yes, Dick, I wanted to ask you about that. Tell us now, for goodness' sake, while we're sitting in comfort."

"Oh well, there isn't an enormous lot to tell," said Colonel Robinson deprecatingly, taking a sandwich from a packet which Fran offered him. "Only people talk a pack of nonsense about it. The Germans, for instance, always write of Albanian Chiefs as 'feudal.' They're not feudal in the least, any more than Highland Chieftains were feudal. They didn't, and don't, hold land from the King in exchange for military services, or for dues in money or in kind, as feudal lords did, because to begin with till very recently there wasn't a King to hold it from. And the lesser families don't hold land from the chief; they own their own land. There are the hereditary great families, like the Lek-Gionajs, whom I hope you'll see; but they have emerged in the course of time."

"When did they emerge? I mean how long have they been ruling families?"

"Not ruling, Susan—great, I said. Well, that varies. Mirdita and Mati, where we're going, is the one district which preserved its autonomy and its great family all through the Turkish occupation."

"Which family is that?"

"The Lek-Gionajs."

Gloire pricked up her ears. Larsen had spoken of Lek-Gionaj. She listened with more attention than usual as Colonel Robinson went on—

"It's rather complicated, the whole tribal or clan system, but it boils down to something like this. The smallest unit is the *fisse*, or family—that is to say people having a common male ancestor, who mayn't intermarry. They are grouped in *bairaks*—*bairak* means standard, really—and the *bairaktar*, or standard-bearer, is the hereditary chief and military leader of that group, which usually means a particular valley or district. Some of the very large tribes have several bairaks and bairaktars—Mirdita is divided into five bairaks. Each bairak is ruled by a council of elders presided over by the bairaktar—he's half a magistrate and half a sort of hereditary mayor."

"Then is Lek-Gionaj a bairaktar?" enquired Gloire.

"No—he's much more than that. He's the hereditary chief of the whole of Mirdita."

"A sort of prince, in fact?"

"Well, you might say that he corresponds to a small German or Austrian princely family—the Fürst, who is never royal; but they don't use that title here. A much closer parallel is with the Scottish hereditary chieftain who bears no title at all, like the Mackintosh or the Macleod—or the head of Clan Cameron, who is just called Lochiel."

"But Dick, you say the baktiar——"

"Bairak," from Colonel Robinson.

"Oh yes—bairak. Well, you say it is ruled by a sort of

council with the—I can't get that word right!—it's so like
bactrian camel!"

"Bairaktar," said Colonel Robinson patiently, but amused.

"Yes!—well, with him presiding. But what sort of law
do they administer? Turkish law? Albanian law? Or the
Code Napoléon, or what?"

"My dear Susan, why on earth should they have the
Code Napoléon?"

"Well, they have gold francs and napoleons as coinage,
so I thought they might have the Code Napoléon. Anyhow, everyone seems to have that when they start having
modern laws at all. Why, the Turks have gone in for the
Code Napoléon now," said Miss Glanfield serenely.

"Well, the Malissori—the mountain tribesmen—haven't
gone in for it yet," said Colonel Robinson, laughing. "Up
till quite recently, the only law they really recognised was
one quite of their own, the law of Lek Dukhagin."

"What was that?"

"You mean who was that, though you don't know it.
Lek was a member of the Dukhagin family; he lived in the
fourteenth century, and was a sort of Solon." He nodded at
Gloire with a friendly grin. "I don't mean in the American
sense! Presumably Lek merely gathered up and arranged
tribal law and custom as it existed in his day," Colonel
Robinson went on, "but his canon, as they call it, had and
still has an extraordinary authority. There is no going
against 'Lek said it,' which is forever quoted in the mountains; the Ten Commandments or Catholic law are simply
non-starters if they conflict with the Canon of Lek—and so
was Turkish Law, the Sheriat, in the days when it tried to
compete. And yet, you know, it has never been written
down—it was purely an oral tradition, and still is."

"It is fascinating," said Miss Glanfield thoughtfully.

"It is. It's a whole mediaeval way of life, preserved, like
an insect in amber, in the fantastic isolation in which these
people have lived."

"Extraordinary," Miss Glanfield said. "It's so wonderful, because it really gives us a chance to see the kind of way we lived ourselves in mediaeval times. Because that is implicit in what we are now—only we tend so to lose sight of it."

Gloire pricked up her ears again. Hadn't the Swede said something like that, when he was defending aristocracy in the light of history?

"Anyhow, what was Lek's famous law like? By the way— Lek, Lex—is there any connection?" Miss Glanfield asked, her mind, thirsting as usual for information, darting in two directions at once.

"I really don't know. If it's a coincidence, it's certainly an odd one," said Colonel Robinson. "Never thought of it myself, I must admit."

"Well, never mind," Miss Glanfield said. "It just struck me. What was Lek's law, or canon?"

"Rather odd and primitive. It was immensely detailed— I couldn't possibly tell you more than a fraction of it. But, in general, there were only two main punishments: fines, and the burning of property. There was no imprisonment, because there were no prisons. I imagine that Lek, who was evidently a most intelligent and highly practical person, realised that any attempt to enforce imprisonment would only have led to armed raids on prisons, and so to worse disorders than ever. And there was no death penalty."

"Really? How very advanced. The death penalty was so prevalent in the Middle Ages, even for trivial offenses," said Miss Glanfield. "Was there no death penalty even for murder?"

"No. Murder was punished by a fine. Killing in defence of honour—blood-taking, it was called, was punished by having your house burnt out. It was nothing out of the way for a man to have been burnt out four times for shooting in defence of honour."

"But"—Gloire's eyebrows were raised again—"surely killing is murder, whether it's in defence of honour or not?"

"Public opinion didn't hold that view with regard to duelling, even in the most highly civilised European countries; and in France and Italy, doesn't hold it today," Colonel Robinson said rather coldly. Gloire subsided—nor it did; she knew Italy well enough to know that.

"What was killing in defence of honour usually for?" Miss Glanfield asked.

"A number of things. For adultery, as in the rest of Europe —or for abduction of a girl. Adultery was—is—very rare; the Malissori are as rigidly chaste as the Irish. But Lek was really quite sound. Without any impartial authority, the death penalty would only have started a fresh blood-feud, and the Turks didn't provide any such authority. Lek wanted to check feuds; he realised they were sapping the manhood of the country, just like the Corsican vendettas. He did invent the *Besa*, by which all offences could be compounded by a fine except an injury to a stranger while under your roof. Only blood could wipe that out, and that's why Albania is the safest place in Europe for travellers."

"But he didn't succeed, did he? Surely feuds went on till quite recent times?"

"No, he didn't succeed. But——"

Mrs. Robinson broke in at this point.

"Dick dear, once you start on feuds, there's no end to it. And we ought to be getting on soon, oughtn't we? It's a long way still to Shpali. Susan, will this do for your flowers?" She held out a large flat oval short-cake tin, still ornamented with tartan paper.

"Oh yes, splendid!"

"But how will you carry it?"

"Oh, ah—yes; how can I?" Miss Glanfield was fishing her flowers out of the pool in which she had immersed them during lunch.

"Fran could punch two holes in one side, and put a string through, I daresay," said Mrs. Robinson.

"Could he? That would be ideal, Robina."

Fran could and did, while they smoked a hasty cigarette; he returned with the tin, Miss Glanfield put her flowers in it, and on Colonel Robinson's instructions gave it to her pony-boy. By the time all this was done the caravan had moved off again, and was already out of sight. The second stage of the day's march had begun.

9

WHEN the riding party got under way again Gloire and
Miss Glanfield walked—Mrs. Robinson, after a short spell
on the mouse-coloured pony, changed over to Miss Glanfield's; her own mount was again showing signs of distress,
panting, pausing, and stumbling.

"What's wrong with that animal?" Colonel Robinson
asked, looking back—he was walking ahead with Gloire.

Mrs. Robinson, who had been holding a lively conversation on the subject of the pony with Fran and the three
pony-men, heaved herself into the black pony's saddle before replying.

"Poor Mirash—they say he has the breath weakness."

"What's that?" Miss Glanfield asked.

"Some sort of consumption, I should think."

"Ridiculous to send an animal like that," Colonel Robinson grunted. "Sure you don't mind walking, Susan?"

"No, I like it, Dick."

The road now wound uphill a good deal more steeply
than before; it was also very hot, and they were grateful
when the track plunged into a wood, which like that by the
Lesser Fani rang with nightingales. The road—to give it its
courtesy title—was here a good deal more roadlike than the
single-pony track on which they had so far travelled; it
was at least six feet wide, and fairly smooth—it would
almost have been possible to drive a Baby Austin along it.
At the moment, Colonel Robinson said to Gloire, they were
on the main direct route from Ndërfanden to Scutari. "We're
climbing to the Malsi ridge now; then we go along it for a
bit, and drop down into the valley to Shpali. That's

where we spend the night." Colonel Robinson was dutifully endeavouring to make himself agreeable to Susan Glanfield's unwanted guest.

Gloire for her part was also anxious to make herself agreeable to Colonel Robinson. Carelessly egotistical as she was, she was not really obtuse; she had realised from the outset that she was being allowed to come on this expedition as a favour, and in the last few hours she had also realised that the relations between Miss Glanfield and the Robinsons were pretty close, so that the presence of a stranger could hardly fail to be a restraint. So, without real humility, but as a practical measure, she was doing her best.

It was not brilliantly successful. Without in the least meaning to be tiresome, she produced a comment on the track.

"It's extraordinary that this should be a main road, isn't it? I mean, one wonders why they don't have real roads, like other people."

Her usual flat careless drawling tone again gave her words, to Colonel Robinson, a critical note which she had not intended.

"One doesn't wonder if one knows the reason," he said rather shortly. "Here in the North, not to have roads was a matter of settled policy for the Malissori. Where there were roads the Turks came in strength, and the country was Ottomanised and corrupted, and local institutions interfered with; where there weren't, the Turks either didn't come, or came in such small numbers that they could easily be dealt with."

"I see," said Gloire. "But now——"

"In four hundred years a settled policy becomes a national habit," he went on, brushing her interpolation aside. "The Turks haven't been gone twenty-five years yet, remember, and this country is fearfully poor. It can't do everything at once."

"The Italians want to build roads for them, don't they?"

the hapless Gloire pursued—she vaguely remembered Warren's having said this, but for the moment had unluckily forgotten what she had heard about Italian policy towards the gendarmerie.

Colonel Robinson stared at her for a moment.

"I daresay," he said, and stopped.

"Susan!" he called back. (He couldn't stand much more of this.) "Come along here. We'll be getting a good view in a minute."

Miss Glanfield strode forward and joined them. Sure enough, in a few moments the track emerged from the wood, and flattened out on the summit of a narrow ridge; on their right they looked down into a deep wooded valley, with a grey river tumbling in the bottom of it, and much higher mountains than any they had yet seen rising beyond; to their left they looked away over lower hills to the flat country, golden and indistinguishable in the afternoon sun, a blaze of indefinite glory. The air up here was strong; Gloire and Miss Glanfield both breathed deep.

"Goodness, it *is* lovely, Dick. What a glorious place."

"Yes, it's pretty good," said the Colonel, appeased.

The track wound along the ridge just below the crest, which rose on their left, for the most part of bare coarse reddish soil, from which large paler blocks projected at intervals. But these were not the only feature of that barren ridge. Out from the ground here and there sprang great tufts of huge silvery leaves, as thick as velvet—from the centre of one or two of them rose even more silvery furry flower-heads, still tightly in bud, so that their clubby immature branches looked like silver coral. There were others too —groups of graceful plants with shallow dark-purple flowers, rising on very slender stalks from flat rosettes of wrinkled dark-green leaves; and near these, arranged by Nature with the most skilful art, big tufts of some low-growing plant with minute leaves and large wide-open flowers of a very strong and vivid rose-pink. Miss Glanfield exclaimed,

157

and sprang up the bank; she did not at once pick anything, but stooped, looked, examined; then she unclasped a knife from where it hung at her belt, opened it, cut a clubbed stem of buds from the centre of one of the silvery plants, and to Gloire's surprise and horror, proceeded to break it to bits, examining each piece with great care.

"Something rare?" Colonel Robinson enquired.

"Not rare, I don't think. I'm practically certain it's *Verbascum olympicum*. But it's interesting to see it growing where it belongs."

"It turns into a great candelabra sort of thing later on," the Colonel volunteered.

"Yes, with rather small yellow flowers."

"That's right. Robina calls it a mullein."

"She's quite right," said Miss Glanfield, smiling.

"What's the purple thing? It's frightfully attractive," said Gloire.

"Another verbascum—*phoeniceum*. They have them in gardens at home; our nurserymen have bred them into all sorts of pinks and creams, but I imagine this purple is the type. What frightful fun to find them!" said Miss Glanfield.

"And this little pink chap?" the Colonel enquired, catching this botanical infection, in the way the most uninstructed people often do—specialised knowledge of concrete things is curiously alluring.

"A phlox, I *think*, but I can't be sure. I must have that," said Miss Glanfield, picking a few small sprays. "Where's that man with my tin?"

The man, with Mrs. Robinson, Fran, and the other two ponies appeared almost immediately; Miss Glanfield took the tin, installed the new specimens in it, and they proceeded on their way. The flowers gave everyone an interest and an occupation. Both Gloire and Colonel Robinson started to pick whatever caught their attention, and bring it to Miss Glanfield—a maroon and white vetch, a very furry

158

sulphur-yellow clover, a kind of hawkweed—and Miss Glanfield either gave a running commentary on what it probably
was, or exclaimed that, oh, that was lovely! That was *quite*
new to her.

The pony-men were deeply interested; so was Fran; Mrs.
Robinson called from her pony to say that they were asking
if the lady was a doctor?—because if so, she must be about
to cure some very strange disease, for most of these herbs
were of no ordinary medical value whatever!

But Miss Glanfield's ranging eye did not confine itself to
flowers. The track was now much harder and stonier than
down in the wood, and the largest stones had been flung
off it and lay in a narrow border along the valley side—
mostly thin flattish shards of the pale rock, looking for all
the world like broken pieces of coarse crockery. Scanning
these as she walked along, Miss Glanfield suddenly stooped
and picked something up; she turned it in her hands, and
gave a startled exclamation.

"What have you got now?" Colonel Robinson asked with
tolerant amusement.

"A skull, of all things!"

"Nonsense! Here, let me see."

She handed it to him. A skull it was, beyond any doubt—
the jaw and nasal bones had come away, but there was the
flat shallow bowl of the cranium, with the serrated lines of
the joins.

"How very peculiar," Mrs. Robinson observed. "Are there
any other bits?"

They grubbed and poked among the shard-like stones, but
nothing else came to light.

"Do you suppose it's modern?" Gloire enquired.

"I've no idea. I shall send it to the British Museum when
I get home, and find out," said Miss Glanfield, as with an
expression of intense satisfaction she stowed away the object in her haversack.

"I *do* like that," she observed as they again walked on—

159

"to find a human skull lying by the roadside, just like that!"

Colonel Robinson burst out laughing.

"Really, Susan, you have most peculiar tastes! Why on earth do you like it?"

"Because I like the feeling of being in a place where people are killed quickly, in the open, and perhaps not even buried—just left lying about."

"Curiouser and curiouser! I can't see why you should like that."

"Oh, don't you? Don't you like people to be rather brief and casual about life and death? I do. We make such a hideous business of it all; being ill in nursing-homes, with rapacious matrons and cold-blooded nurses, and flowers, and friends coming to see you! Such a fuss. When it's time to die, die!—and quickly, and as naturally as possible. If people were left in their homes they would die in half the time, with their own reverent loving incompetent people about them—and it would be much nicer, and save no end of money!"

Colonel Robinson laughed again, but his wife protested.

"I think that's very unjust, Susan. Nursing-homes and hospitals do wonderful work."

"Yes, I suppose they do, Robina. I don't mind people going to nursing-homes to be cured—that's sensible. But I do disapprove of the modern attitude that you can't do the simplest thing, like dying or being born, in your own house. Why, good God, women go into nursing-homes to have their *babies* now!"

"But isn't that a good thing?" enquired Gloire, who was indoctrinated with American ideas on the subject.

"I don't think so. I think it's a most pernicious thing."

"Oh, why?"

"Because it's artificial and unnatural. Babies ought to be born in the same room as their fathers and grandfathers—but anyhow in their own homes, where they belong, among people to whom they are personally important, to whom

160

they mean the future," Miss Glanfield pronounced with her usual rapidity and decision.

"But people's homes are so unhygienic," Gloire objected. "In the States, no one dreams of having a baby at home. They all go into hospitals—the doctors prefer it."

"I know. And the baby is swept away from its mother and put in a hygienic cot in an air-conditioned ward with fifty other babies, and nurses in masks—*in masks!*—feed it on processed milk, and its wretched father, for the first three weeks of its life, can only peer at it through a glass pane in the door! I know!" said Miss Glanfield. "But how you can expect a baby produced like that to turn into a normal human being, or its parents to be real human parents, I cannot see."

"You ought to be an Albanian," said Colonel Robinson.

"Are the birth conditions here frightful?"

"Pretty bad, especially up-country. They're getting better, but very slowly. That old Dr. Crowninshield has done a bit to improve matters, and so has Robina, as a matter of fact."

"I know." She dropped back a pace or two and walked beside Mrs. Robinson, laying her hand on the pony's sweating quarters.

"Look, Robina, I want to get this clear—I don't want you to think I'm crying down all you've done, because I think it's splendid. I'm sure it's frightfully important that people should be as hygienic as they can *in their own homes,* but not this ghastly brave new world idea! Birth is part of life— rather a vital part, really," she smiled. "And if you divorce birth from the normal home life and routine you are creating a false attitude towards it—in the parents, in the other children, and in some mysterious way in the infant itself, I really believe. You may think this nonsense, but I don't think it's an accident that later on these hospital-born, nurse-fed children, at bedtime, instead of shouting for their Mummy to come and tell them a story or sing them a hymn, as ours do, hustle her out of the room so that they can

161

switch on their private radio and listen to 'Steve and the Redskins', or whatever the bedtime programme is on their particular net-work! That may be modern and it may be hygienic, but it isn't how you make human beings, or people who are going to be any good at adult relationships." Now she turned to Gloire, who like Colonel Robinson had fallen back to listen.

"I had a great argument with one of your gynaecologists, the last time that I was in the States," she said. "He took the line that if by 'hospitalising' births you could reduce infantile mortality by ten or even five per cent, it was worth doing. I said 'No—it was better to have ninety or even eighty-five per cent of fully developed human beings, than a hundred per cent of incomplete ones.' We didn't agree!" She laughed.

"Well, that's one point of view," said Colonel Robinson.

About half a mile further on the track divided; the rather large one on which they had been travelling since they left Ndërfanden dipped down to the left, and a much smaller one branched off to the right. This was their road to Shpali. It kept level for a few hundred yards, still holding the crest of the ridge; at the point where it began to drop they came on two gendarmes, who stood at the salute as Colonel Robinson approached.

Another little ceremony was gone through. The two newcomers, who were the Shpali gendarmes, recited their little verse—a sort of oath of loyalty, Mrs. Robinson explained, to their ruler and officers. They fell in behind Colonel Robinson, the Ndërfanden gendarmes stepped forward, saluted, recited the oath in their turn, wheeled round, and though only two in number, marched off on their return journey as smartly and impressively as a whole regiment. The pack-animals had not waited for this performance, and were again out of sight; escorted by the two new gendarmes, the walking party set forward again.

Downhill, steeply, the track plunged through a wood of

162

high trees. A spring bubbled temptingly from under a bank —Gloire went to it to drink.

"Here, wait!" Colonel Robinson called to her—"it may not be good."

"But I'm thirsty."

"I can't help it." He spoke to the two Shpali gendarmes. "Sorry, Mrs. Thurston, but this one isn't good. We'll come to a good spring in about half an hour."

It was that or more before they reached the second spring, where a shallow wooden spout fed the clear water into a hollowed tree-trunk. Colonel Robinson ordained a halt— they had a good stretch still to Shpali, he said, and another subsidiary ridge to cross. When the gendarmes and the pony-men drank themselves, after watering the animals, Colonel Robinson drew Miss Glanfield's attention to a curious little ritual. Each man pulled a minute piece of rag from somewhere about his person, and placed it on a dead branch by the spring—the gendarmes unravelled a thread from the edge of their puttees for the purpose.

"Yes, I see. What's that for? Is this a sacred spring, like in Ireland, and are the rags votive offerings?"

"No, nothing so devout. It's pure hygiene." He grinned at Gloire. "They always say you should never drink from a strange spring without placing a rag or a thread of your clothing close by, so that you may be saved from an illness that a change in water might cause. They're very sensitive to water."

"But the rag can't make any difference to the water—if it's strange, it's strange," Gloire objected.

"Well, they think it does: if you leave something of your own by the spring, it makes it a sort of neighbour, I suppose."

"It's a nice idea, anyway," said Gloire, anxious to be amiable—indeed as they lay resting on the ground by the spring both Robina and Miss Glanfield were aware of the general improvement in the tone, the feeling of the party.

For one thing they were all experiencing the delicious lassitude of natural healthy fatigue after prolonged exercise in the open air. People who normally lead ultra-civilised and rather artificial lives are peculiarly susceptible to this, and the effect is increased when the actual exercise is part of a return to more natural conditions—really prolonged effort, eating little, wondering when you will come to water; and when too the modern organism is subjected once again to the great natural rhythm of the day: chill at morning, noon-day heat, the cool of evening—and to the necessity, by one's own bodily exertions, of reaching a particular spot by nightfall. By Miss Glanfield all this was expected, and always delightful when it came; she lay saying little, for once, thinking how good it was, and comparing it in her mind with other rests by other springs, in Spain, in Anatolia, in Italy, in the White Mountains and the Tatra. To Gloire it was quite unexpected—that she should feel so actively content and happy when she was hot and sticky all over, and her hair must certainly be a mess, and her face worse, and all the muscles of her thighs and buttocks were sore from what riding she had done, was a considerable surprise. But she too had one thing to compare it with—rests by Alpine streams, coming down with Tony after some stiff climb, and flowers in the grass, the guides making little jokes, and the glorious sense of achievement, this same idle all-permeating happiness, this sense that life was good. Good in quite a different way to the vague muzzy feeling that everything was really more or less O.K., and the people one was with not so lousy as one had thought, that overtook one after a number of cocktails in the Ritz Bar—any Ritz Bar. Her present frame of mind owed nothing to White Ladies or Old-Fashioneds.

She said something of this to Miss Glanfield a little later, when they had reached the valley, crossed another river by a rickety wooden bridge supported on stone piers, and were climbing the lesser ridge on the further side; tired as she

164

was—and except for Colonel Robinson they were all a little tired, for they had been riding and walking for eight hours —she felt the strong lift of the muscles in her legs with conscious pleasure, as they breasted the new slope.

"This reminds me of the end of a climbing day, a bit," Gloire began, breathing easily through her strong young lungs. "I mean, it doesn't look like it—there are no pines, only these green trees, and all the nightingales; aren't they fantastic? But it feels the same."

Miss Glanfield looked at her with interest and approval. So perhaps she had been right after all, and there was another side to Mrs. Thurston. She made some sympathetic and encouraging response, while her mind ran on, thinking about the pretty creature at her side. The day had brought her to feel a rather heavy sense of responsibility for her. She had not realised in advance how much the Robinsons were going to mind this importation of hers. Miss Glanfield's careless generosity, which had turned out so well for Gloire, did not spring from a real love of humanity, but from her uncalculating and simple desire to make everyone happy, and still more to furnish everyone within reach with the sort of experience which she personally valued. There was actually something egocentric about this simplicity, like a child's passionate absorption in its own toys; otherwise she might have stopped to think about how the inclusion of Gloire Thurston in the trip to Torosh might affect the Robinsons. But she had not stopped to think. Now, too late, she realised what she had done, and decided that she must take the burden of the girl as far as possible on her own shoulders.

They talked for some time about the Alps, Miss Glanfield asking what climbs she had done, and Gloire rehearsing them—with obvious pleasure, but with that characteristic drawling vagueness of hers about times and routes. When pressed, she proved to remember quite clearly; it was a sort of affectation, Miss Glanfield decided, or the *poco curante* attitude of her generation which made her talk like that. She was not to know that Gloire was in fact struggling with a desperate embarrassment; she wanted to talk openly of Tony, whose life and death were implicit between them in every word they spoke—and this very embarrassment, and her effort to screw herself up to the point of speech, made her affected as she had not been when she spoke of climbing to Nils Larsen. Miss Glanfield of course realised the unspoken presence of the dead man between them, and if she had really been a lover of humanity she would probably have guessed at Mrs. Thurston's need, and helped her; but, as has been said, she was not—she felt, and was, sympathetic and friendly, but no more, and it was insufficient. Gloire fell back presently from the too difficult attempt, and turned to something else. She had enjoyed even this rather superficial talk about climbing with the writer, and her faint sense of disappointment was quite untinged with criticism; she was so wholly without moral sophistication herself that it never occurred to her to feel anything lacking in the older woman's treatment of her, since she had nothing better, or even as good, to compare it with; indeed her growing liking made her interested beyond her wont in the other's views, and she reverted to the conversation up on the ridge.

"I never heard anyone before say all those things about not having babies in nursing-homes," she began, swinging along beside Miss Glanfield with a stride as easy as hers. She does walk well, the writer thought; they had topped the lesser ridge now, and were descending rather steeply into another valley by a rough path—she noticed how Mrs. Thurston loosened her knees for the descent, and her skilful easy swing on the inner heel at each angle of the path. She was a beautiful walker, anyhow.

"Do you really believe," Gloire continued, "that it can affect the *baby*, being kept from its mother and air-conditioned and all that, just for those first three weeks?"

"I think it very probable. One can't measure how sensitive a new-born infant is to impression, but the whole trend of modern psychology is to suggest that the first months and even weeks of a child's life are enormously important. There's no possible doubt, of course, that there is a quite different emotional link, lasting right into maturity, between a breast-fed child and its mother and a bottle-fed one; and since that is undoubtedly so, I think the other is probably true too. Certainly the indirect effect, through the parents' attitude, can't fail to affect the child—and anyone who takes the trouble to use his eyes can see for himself that it does," said Miss Glanfield.

"Did you ever talk to Mr. Larsen about this?" Gloire surprised her by asking.

"Good Heavens, no! I haven't seen Mr. Larsen for twenty years at least. But why?"

"I just thought you might have. He hates all gadgets, and he's pretty anti-American too."

Miss Glanfield wheeled sharply round to her, and spoke brusquely, if good-naturedly.

"My dear child, for goodness' sake don't start that line," she said. "Surely you've lived long enough in Europe to know that we all talk perfectly cheerfully about one another, and criticise the institutions even of nations we're devoted to, and nobody minds. The English don't think Dr. Renier anty-"—she pronounced it as Americans do—"British because he wrote that very amusing book 'The English— are they Human?'—we all loved it, and thought him very clever. And if one criticises or makes fun of certain aspects of their national life to Hungarians or Spaniards or Austrians or Chinese, they don't at once tax one with being *anti* their country—they laugh and argue. The only people in the world who make that particular fuss are the Americans, and considering the wealth and power of the U.S., it's really too absurd—and madly boring."

"I'm sorry," said Gloire. "I know we—they—are that way. It's a kind of bad habit, I guess."

"A *frightful* habit!" said Miss Glanfield, smiling. "Tell me, how American are you, actually?"

"Only half. My father was British. But I have always been over there a lot, and I was brought up in a kind of American way, with my mother making several marriages," said Gloire with great simplicity.

Miss Glanfield laughed.

"I see. Well, don't get me wrong! I'm not really anti-American at all, only anti-mechanisation—because I think that mechanisation, pushed beyond a certain point, is bad. It's the great problem of this century, I feel, for the whole world: how to adjust human life to the mechanisation we have already acquired, at what point to limit it for the future, and above all, how to prevent its impact on more primitive nations, like this country here, from producing the results that it has produced elsewhere."

"You mean in America?"

"America, and other countries. People tend to instance America when this is being discussed, because mechanisation has been pushed further there than anywhere else, and for longer, so that we are beginning to see the results on the human species—and also because the Americans themselves attach such a fantastic importance to their baths and plumbing and gadgets of all sorts. They talk as if people could hardly be human beings without all that; we in Europe are beginning to wonder if people can be human beings *with* it! But it is really a problem for the whole world, and each nation has got to solve it somehow."

"But you think the results on the human species are bad?" Gloire persisted. Larsen, the Swede, was almost present to her, so vividly did the writer's words recall his.

"If it goes too far, yes. I think electric light in cottages, and plenty of hot water, is good for everybody, from the African kraal to the Swiss chalet—where they have it anyhow! The Swiss, as usual, have made this adjustment, so far, better than any other nation."

168

"Could you tell me what values you think people lose by gadgets? And how they lose them, exactly?" Gloire enquired. She was wondering when Miss Glanfield, whose mind seemed to run so much on the same lines as the Swede's, was going to use the word "virtue."

She did not use it then—nor did she answer at once. Their path had reached the valley, and emerged from the musical greenery of the scrub which clothed the slope; meadows stretched before them, with a few small houses tucked under a wooded hillside; beyond the meadows a river raced past, singing its strong loud song, and curved round a rocky knoll on which stood a grove of immense ash-trees. The air was very still, and fragrant with the smell of wood smoke; the voices of children rang from the water-side; in the evening light the scene had a simple beauty, homely and very tranquillising. Miss Glanfield turned to her companion.

"How do you feel, now at this moment?" she asked. "Don't you feel different to what you usually feel at about 6.30—when you are pulling up your socks, as we all are, to go off to some cocktail party?"

"My God, yes! I feel absolutely grand," said Gloire, stretching her arms and inhaling. "And terribly hungry."

"So do I. But don't you think there may be some connection? You realise what we've been doing, don't you? We've been travelling today as people have travelled for the last five thousand years."

Gloire gaped at her.

"Have we? I suppose we have," she said slowly.

The others were close behind them, and at this point they too came out of the wood, a straggling little procession; Mrs. Robinson was riding, and the Colonel walked at her side. Miss Glanfield pointed to them.

"The Flight into Egypt was like that," she said—"the Woman riding, the man walking beside her. And that is how St. Augustine travelled from Rome to Britain, and

169

Marco Polo from Venice to Peking, and Virgil to Mantua and Dante to Verona."

"Well, so what?" said Gloire, but without derisive intention.

"So, apart from the fact that you've walked and ridden till you're stiff, today, you feel differently from if you had been travelling in a stream-lined air-conditioned Pullman. You haven't come nearly so far, but you've seen more, felt more, and learned infinitely more about the country you've been passing through. And the fact that you've been travelling as man has always travelled has done something to you—unless you're quite abnormal."

"Yes, but exactly what?"

They were interrupted.

"Well, here we are," said Colonel Robinson, coming up to them. "This is Shpali. We camp over there—" he pointed towards the grove of ash-trees. "I think our fellows are there already. Come along."

Sure enough the caravan had halted in the ash-grove, and the animals had been unloaded and were already grazing the deep grass under the trees; the foal was being suckled by its mother. On their way to the grove they passed a small white building with a projecting flag-pole and an oval metal shield over the door; some gendarmes were drawn up by it, and there was more saluting and reciting. Colonel Robinson came with them as far as the grove, checked over the bundles on the ground, gave some hasty orders, and then excused himself. "I must go and see my chaps. Fran will see to everything. Robina, you say where you want the tents. I shan't be long," and he strode off.

There ensued the usual slightly confused pause which always accompanies arrival at a camp on the first days of an expedition, before everyone has got into their regular routine. There was everything to be done, and except for Fran, no one quite knew where to begin. Fran however did know. He unrolled bundles of bedding and tents, sorted them out,

170

and erected them—General Stanley's small and workmanlike Mummery for Miss Glanfield, and that tent which had been likened to a Methodist chapel for Mrs. Thurston. The three women sat on the grass and watched. Now that the exertion was over, and their goal reached, they all realised that they were pretty tired—indeed it soon became clear that Mrs. Robinson was rather overtired. Gloire roused herself, went and retrieved her green-and-white suitcase from the heap of luggage, and produced a bottle of vermouth; they drank, smoked, and felt better. Miss Glanfield brought out her flower-press—several sheets of wire netting with layers of lint between, held in place by webbing straps; in this she placed her flowers, flattening out the leaves, spreading the petals, and arranging the stalks. Colonel Robinson now reappeared.

"We haven't any drinks, have we?" he asked his wife. "Oh yes, you've got some vermouth—splendid."

"It's Mrs. Thurston's vermouth," said Robina.

"Oh, but do have some," said Gloire.

"Mind if I take it away? I'd like to give these fellows a drink," said the Colonel.

"Not a bit," said Gloire, wondering how long her vermouth would last at this rate, but glad to have done the right thing for once.

"What about your fire?" said the Colonel to his wife— "Fran will be needing it for supper. Better get it going, hadn't you?"

"I'll get the wood," said Gloire, springing up. "You sit still," she said to Mrs. Robinson, who was beginning rather painfully to heave herself to her feet.

"Sure you can manage?" asked Miss Glanfield, rather rhetorically, Gloire felt—she was still intent on her flowers.

"Sure."

She moved rapidly here and there through the grove, gathering fallen boughs; the teamsters were occupied in the same way—they grinned and made cheerful remarks as they

171

passed her. She collected dried grass from the rocky slope above the river, laid her fire neatly, and set the grass alight —soon she had a fine fire going. Fran, flashing his splendid teeth at her, set covered pots in the edge of the blaze; he made some remark which she couldn't understand.

"Fran says you're a very good fire-maker," said Mrs. Robinson.

"Quite the boy scout! Asht mirë?" she said to Fran.

Gloire was enjoying herself. After a long day—it was now nearly seven, and she had been up and about since three— she was delighted to feel still so fresh and strong. She went on collecting wood, but as she walked about she was aware of the beauty of her surroundings. The ash-trees were immensely lofty, tall as English elms, and beautifully grouped: the tents, the hobbled ponies grazing, the camp-fires and the men in their strange dress made up a striking scene. She thought, as she passed to and fro, of what Miss Glanfield had been saying just as they arrived. Gloire was in a much more receptive mood now than she had been when she talked with the Swede in the train. The ideas presented by Larsen had then been absolutely novel to her, and as uncomfortable as they were novel; but the leaven had been working ever since, helped on by additions from George, from Warren Langdon, and finally, today, by her pleasure in the trip itself. Yes, it was all pretty good, this, she thought, pausing for a moment in her labours—there might be something, there might be quite a bit in what Miss Glanfield said. If she and the Swede both said it, there almost had to be.

Presently Miss Glanfield joined her.

"Well done you!" she said. "How nice to have a young energetic person in the party, to do all the hard work! But I'm sure you've got enough now—come and look at the chapel."

Gloire had noticed a small ruined stone structure in a little clearing at the edge of the trees, where the ground fell away steeply to the river, but her uninstructed eye had not recognized it for a church. Half the roof had fallen in; on the other half the rafters remained; but it had a minute shallow semicircular bulge in the solid stone wall at one end, which Miss Glanfield pointed out to her as the apse—a crumbling wall of unmortared stones enclosed it. Very small, it was, rough and simple, with a curious grace and pathos in both its simplicity and its decay, under the delicate protecting greenery of the immense trees.

"Not very like our St. Paul's, is it?" Miss Glanfield said.

"But why should it be?"

"It's St. Paul's Church—Shpali means St. Paul's. They say he preached here," said Miss Glanfield with a happy look. "I wonder if he was here at Whitsuntide too?"

This reminded Gloire of the main purpose, for her, of the expedition.

"Do you know how far it is on to Torosh?" she asked. "And what time High Mass will be?"

"No, I don't. Are you a Catholic?" Miss Glanfield asked.

"Oh no. But we have to get there in time for High Mass, haven't we?" said Gloire—"I mean to see the people and the costumes, and be at the service."

"Yes, we ought to. We'll find out at supper."

But they did not find out much. Sitting, some on stools and some on the wooden boxes in which the main stores were carried, round the little folding table, they presently ate an excellent meal of Fran's preparing—soup brought ready made in bottles by the Robinsons and a vast omelet with kidneys in it, for which Fran had raised the materials in Shpali. Over it Gloire put her questions to Colonel Robinson. Torosh was some three and a half hours' walk on from Shpali, and there was a terrifically steep pull up to it, he said—he supposed High Mass would be at eleven.

"Oh, nonsense, Dick. You're thinking of England. It's always at 10.30 in Scutari, if it isn't at ten."

"Well, ask Fran, then."

But Fran did not know; nor did the two Shpali gendarmes, who stood at a small distance, rifle in hand, mounting guard over the party.

"Well, if it's at 10.30, I suppose we start at seven," said Gloire hopefully.

"That's about it—seven or sevenish. Get up at 5.30, breakfast at six," said the Colonel carelessly. "I'll tell Fran. We must turn in early, with two early starts, today and tomorrow."

No one disagreed with this. The food was making them sleepy again, and aware of their fatigue. They sat smoking after their meal, watching Fran's endeavour to blow up the Lilo on which Mrs. Robinson intended to sleep—the Robinsons, hardened to camping, had not bothered with tents. The Lilo's pump had been forgotten, and Fran, kneeling on the ground, blew with his shapely mouth; the pony-men strolled over to watch. One of them made a remark which caused Fran to relax his efforts and burst into laughter—Mrs. Robinson laughed too.

"Now what's the joke?" Miss Glanfield enquired.

"They say Fran ought to do that to my pony, the one with 'the breath weakness', and put some air into it," said Robina, still laughing.

"Dick, what are these trees? Not ordinary ashes, are they? The leaves are so much finer, more like a mountain ash," said Miss Glanfield, tilting herself back on her stool to gaze overhead, where the foliage made a delicate feathery pattern against the pale sky and the first stars.

"My dear Susan, I haven't an idea—I'm no botanist. We call them ash-trees," said Colonel Robinson.

"The leaves are more like rowans, now I come to think of it," said Robina. "I'm sorry we're such ignoramuses, Susan."

"I can send a bit to Kew when I get home," said Miss Glanfield, "it doesn't matter—they're lovely, anyhow."

They were. Even Gloire felt that when, having unpacked,

174

undressed, and washed in the folding canvas wash-basin on four legs with which her magnificent tent was provided, she went to empty out the water. Having done so, and put back the unusual vessel, she stood for a moment at the tent door. Close by, Mrs. Robinson was heaving and chuckling on the Lilo, which Fran had blown up too hard, and was being rebuked by her husband, rolled up in his sleeping-bag on the ground beside her, and already half asleep. Beyond, the little chapel glimmered palely in the light from the two immense fires which the teamsters had made—Gloire stepped round the corner of the tent so that she could see them. They lay or sat round them, the black and white of their dress, and their very defined features, emphasised in the rich fierce light, which added to their romantic splendour. What people!—what a place! Oh, she had been right to come; and she had not been mistaken in her first reaction on the lake road to Scutari. Splendid things must happen here. She glanced upwards. It was dark now, and against the blackness of the sky the foliage on which Miss Glanfield had commented, lit up by the firelight to a golden green, etched a most delicate tracery, through which stars burned here and there; it was like an embroidered canopy supported by the vast columns of the trees. The nightingales were singing their heads off; the river sang its strong untamed song in its rocky bed. Gloire breathed deep. The peace, the natural glory of the place, struck deeply into her. As she turned back, reluctantly, into her tent, which smelt canvasy, looped up the door, and got into her camp-bed, she was aware of a feeling which she had not known for years. She wanted someone, some person, to share all this with, and to relate it to in her mind afterwards. Inevitably, her thoughts turned to Larsen. He would understand. Quite consciously, at that moment, she wished he was there—and her last thought, before she fell asleep, was that she wished she knew where to find him, so that she might write (in her large uneducated hand) and tell him about it.

10

THE cold waked Gloire at half-past three. It was, or
seemed, extreme, and after some time spent in hopeful
snugglings, she got up to look for something more to put on
her bed. Being up, she decided to take one of those little
nocturnal walks; there were some bushes down on a slope
beyond the grove to which she had walked with Miss Glanfield and Mrs. Robinson the night before.

Dawn was barely breaking as she stepped out of the tent
—she could just make out a magpie group of huddled forms
round the embers of the camp-fires. The grass was damp
and cool under her bare feet; the nightingales were still
singing like mad—she found time to wonder when they
stopped to eat, for they seemed to sing the clock round. The
bushes, in the dim light, loomed large and ghostly; as she
returned, a movement at the top of the slope caught her
eye. Their body-guard, the two gendarmes, were standing
stiffly at the salute for the passage of the lady in her nightgown. Gloire giggled as she went back to bed.

Although Fran called them to time at 5.30, had breakfast
ready sharp at six, and began taking down the tents the
moment they were out of them, the start was late. The loads
were recalcitrant, and though the men tugged and hauled,
or stood, their fine bony faces puzzled, intent, and eager,
load after load slipped lopsidedly. Gloire was in a frenzy.
At length Colonel Robinson said resignedly that he would
see to it, and the women had better start. Gloire's hopes
rose, though it was already twenty minutes past seven, but
they were soon dashed again. As they started down the
track towards the river it became clear that Mrs. Robinson,

who insisted on walking because of the sick pony, was still tired, and she went very slowly indeed. If that was how she walked downhill, Gloire fumed to herself, what would she be like on the pull up which Colonel Robinson had foretold?

"We're going to be late," she murmured desperately to Miss Glanfield.

"I'm afraid so."

"Well, I shall go on ahead," said Gloire, determinedly.

"Yes, do; why not?" said Miss Glanfield tranquilly.

Gloire edged away from the party, and round a corner, bore ahead with her splendid stride. She looked at her watch again. It was 7.30. She would probably be late if High Mass was at 10.30; and supposing it was at 10? Well, she *would* make it, whatever the others did, she thought, setting her mouth; she didn't know the way, but she would manage somehow. She swung on down to the bridge.

This was a charming erection, though Gloire did not pause to admire it. Two dry-stone ramps and a central pier carried the wooden superstructure high above the sparkling water, the floor was of wooden planking five feet wide; there were no handrails. Gloire's hasty feet sounded hollow on the planks as she crossed, and strode off along the further bank.

But she had reckoned without the vigilance of the gendarmerie. Soon, pattering with peasant lightness, even in their heavy soldierly boots, the body-guard from Shpali overhauled her. She could not understand a word they said, but the two neat figures kept at her side. Presently however they began to stop, at ever more frequent intervals, to point behind them, and to address her with increasing urgency—the word *Coronelle* emerged clearly and constantly from the stream of unfamiliar syllables. Gloire could not imagine what a Coronelle was; she smiled and walked on. But this would not do—they plucked, very respectfully, at her sleeve, saying "Coronelle" again, and pointing first backwards, and

177

then at themselves. Gloire at length guessed that they wished to return to the Coronelle—it might be the caravan, she supposed, which was now in sight and looking quite wreathlike as it wound down the path to the bridge. She indicated to them by signs that they should return. No, that would not do either; they shook their heads respectfully but violently at the suggestion. Oh, damn the men, and their scruples! She was wasting precious minutes over this nonsense. She reverted, in this extremity, to her Podgoritza technique. She took one gendarme by the shoulders, turned him round, and pushed him back along the path by which they had come, firmly repeating "Coronelle," since that seemed to be the operative word; then she returned to the other, tucked her arm through his, pointed forward and said "Torosh!" This worked. They hesitated for a moment, then nodded and broke into laughter—one went back towards the caravan and Gloire with her single escort resumed her march at a round pace.

The track followed the river, which flowed as usual in a stony bed twice its own breadth; the hills were now practically bare, like the top of the Malsi ridge, and pock-marked with some dark shrubby vegetation which gave off a strong aromatic scent as the sun got higher and the heat increased. But presently there was a fresh delay. They came to another of the neat buildings with the metal shield and the flagpole, and Gloire's heart sank, for outside it, saluting, stood two fresh gendarmes, evidently waiting to take over the party for the next lap. However, her little bodyguard was quick and helpful. She heard the words "Coronelle" and "Torosh" in a spate of talk, and then with commendable speed one of the fresh escort stepped out beside her, while the other stood at the salute. And on they went.

Gloire in her brief mountaineering days had gained the reputation of being "a mover" among Tony Thurston's climbing friends, whatever else they might have had to say about her; but never in her life had she moved to such purpose as she did on that Whitsunday morning on the road to Torosh. After another mile or so along the valley the track started to climb the shoulder of one of the pock-marked hills, first diagonally, then in a series of zig-zags; the sun was hot on their backs, the rough surface of the track was hot under their feet; the gendarme was soon streaming with perspiration, Gloire's heart was pounding and her face almost purple; but her lungs held good, and she could still rejoice in the strong lift of her muscles at each stride. She could do it—even this appalling "pull up." Once or twice the gendarme suggested that she should stop and rest, but she shook her head; finally, to convince him, she held out her wristwatch, pointed to the hour of ten, and said "Torosh!" very firmly, crossing herself as she did so. The gendarme looked puzzled but nodded and went on. However, the idea which Gloire had tried to suggest germinated gradually in his mind. Almost at the top of the hill up which they had climbed from the valley they came to a spring, by which a stunted pine cast a patch of shade—here the gendarme stopped, politely took Gloire's wrist, pointed to 10.30 on her watch, said "Torosh" and crossed himself in his turn. Then he pointed to the spring.

"Good-oh," said Gloire. It was now a quarter to ten. In that case she would have a drink. "Asht ujë mirë?" she asked, pronouncing the words carefully.

The Albanian was delighted at this sign of intelligence, and when they had both drunk, and were sitting for a moment in the shade, he went on trying to make conversation.

"Fresc," he said, pointing vaguely at the ground—Gloire didn't quite get it. Then he pointed at the open-work toes of her canvas shoes and said "Fresc" again, and now Gloire realised that *Fresc* meant cool, and agreed that yes, her shoes and the shade were both *fresc*.

It is a fact, and a rather curious one, that on great enterprises undertaken for some serious purpose, such as pilgrimages, the small and trivial incidents of the way build

179

up into an essential part of the whole experience, especially in retrospect, but also at the time. And on this journey of Gloire Thurston's to Torosh—which was really a pilgrimage, however little she realised it—all the delays and difficulties, this fierce climb, these absurd attempts to communicate with her guide became, ultimately, inextricably interwoven in her mind and memory with what she did eventually find at Torosh. Indeed, though it was long before she realised it, they typified with a peculiar aptness her rather fumbling search for she did not quite know what—knowing only that it was something important, and that she needed it.

The Abbey Church at Torosh stands on a shelf above a narrow ravine, among those pale black-spotted hills; up the small valley behind it, where the ground is less steep, lie terraced gardens and plots of cultivation, and above these again the slopes of the main range, pines and pasture, rise higher and higher till they culminate in the long bare pinnacled ridge of Mali Shënjt, the Mountain of the Saint. It is a wild landscape, bare and rather harsh, but without the austerity of Spain—various, individual, free, and above all full of light: light flung back from the pale desiccated lower slopes, from the sparse pastures, and from the bare silvery rock of the mountain summits. Climbing up out of the valley, as Gloire had done, the whole panorama breaks upon the traveller at once, as he tops the ridge—the broad irregular trough in the hills running for several miles up to the col at its head, with the white ridge of Mali Shënjt overlooking it on one side, and the more wooded mountains above Mati on the other; while after a few steps more, almost beneath his feet, his astonished gaze is arrested by the sudden and wholly unawaited spectacle of the great Church, standing massive and imposing on a flat gravelled space, with its rococo belfry towering above the loggiaed porch, and the ecclesiastical buildings spreading away, tall, square-set, and severe, from its eastern end. It is so large, so florid, so wholly unexpected in those wild surroundings that it creates a quite startling impression. Where, one asks, is the congregation to fill such a building?—for except for a few small houses among the terraces the great valley spreads away, apparently empty save for rough pasture, forest, and bare high-lying scree and rock. But a congregation there is, as Gloire Thurston was soon to see, come on foot by narrow stony tracks from the hills and valleys for miles around, where their modest dwellings are tucked away out of sight in the gulleys and ravines, near water and what little fertile soil the land affords.

And both church and congregation are at once the work and the monument of a very wonderful body of men, the Franciscans of High Albania. Throughout the dark and discouraging period of Turkish rule, the Franciscan Order took the Albanian mountaineers under its wing, and saw to it, decade after decade, century after century, that in these remote, lonely, and uncomfortable fastnesses the faithful, such as they were, should be ministered to, converts made, and the tide of Islamism stemmed. Many, perhaps most, of these devoted priests were of Albanian blood, members of the Albanian colonies in Calabria and Apulia, whose forbears fled there at the advent of the Turks. It is one of the most romantic and least-known stories in the long, romantic, and gallant history of Roman Catholicism, this of the Franciscans in Albania. They shared the fortunes and misfortunes of their wild flocks; like Lek Dukhagin and many others they sought, and like them failed, to check the ever-prevalent blood-feuds; they adhered—being of like blood—so far as their faith permitted to the customs of their splendid if primitive parishioners, to whom they had to act not only as priests and pastors, but as doctors, official scribes, and private letter-writers,—since they alone, under Turkish auspices, had the privilege of literacy. Whether they approved or disapproved, they faithfully recorded the strange and traditional decisions of the Clan Council, the *Pleknija*—decisions much more often based on *Adet*, or Custom, than

181

on Catholic doctrine. And there to this day they still are, working, praying, celebrating Mass, exhorting, healing, teaching, in an unimaginable spiritual and intellectual isolation, but wholly patient, wholly devoted, wholly absorbed in their lonely task.

It was only a few minutes after Gloire and her guide left the cool, the *fresc* shade of the pine-tree by the little spring that they came over the crest of the hill and saw first the great stretch of the valley and the high grey peaks above it, glittering, dark pines and all, under the strong sun, and then, immediately below them, the imposing architectural mass of the great church. Gloire was for going down at once, but her guide would not have this; he led her, rather unwilling, to another of those little cabins of the gendarmerie, where a corporal and two of his men insisted on giving her Turkish coffee in minute cups, and cigarettes which they rolled for her themselves out of their fine hairy tobacco, licking the paper along the join with a flick of the tongue as neat as a cat's, and twisting up the ends. Gloire was learning things; she disliked the idea of putting what the corporal had licked into her own reddened mouth, but she smoked several of his cigarettes with a perfectly good grace, and gave them her own State Express. They brought out an accordion from the cupboard in which they kept their files, and begged her to play it; Gloire could not play the accordion, but her guide could, and did, and the men sang some wild song; they indicated that she should sing, and Gloire obliged. But she had her eye on her watch, and presently she broke up this ingenuous party and set off down the steep zig-zags. It was Whitsunday, and after all, after everything, she was about to hear High Mass in the Abbey Church at Torosh. She was still very hot; her clothes stuck to her everywhere, but she, who cared so intensely for her own comfort, for once did not mind. More remarkable still, she had not even powdered her nose in the gendarmerie post, nor did she do so now; as damp and shiny as

182

any of the congregation, she passed with her guide through the doors into the cool dimness within, and knelt down. They were quite at the back; she knelt on the left, among the women; her gendarme joined the throng of men on the right.

It was indeed a throng. The great church was full. There were no seats; the worshippers knelt on the uneven stone floor; and the space left between the two sexes was not a straight line, but serpentined up towards the High Altar. As her eyes grew accustomed to the dim light after the blazing sunshine outside she began to look about her. Mass had begun, and up at the far end, among the lights and incense, several splendidly-robed figures moved to and fro; there was chanting. Gloire was more interested in the congregation. When they stood, she saw a charming thing. All the small children were ranged at the chancel rails, like a long particoloured wreath in which white predominated:— little white tunics for the boys, little coloured tunics for the girls, little white trousers for both. The women around her were all dressed in the full white trousers and white tunics reaching almost to the ankle, with velvet jackets in dark reds and plummy purples and deep greens, and aprons of brilliant many-coloured silks, their heads for the most part tied in black fringed shawls. So much she could see—not more, for the church was very dark where she stood, down by the door. And the smell was almost overpowering. (That she was accustomed to in Italy.) But as the service proceeded she became aware of something more impressive even than the splendour and strangeness of this galaxy of magnificent costumes and of vivid, severe, and handsome faces, nearly all stamped with a sort of haughty dignity. This was not at all like a fashionable congregation in St. Peter's, attending some famous religious ceremony, with its rather off-hand conforming to ecclesiastical convention by kneelings, risings, and crossings—all carried out almost mechanically in the intervals of shrewd observation of one's

183

neighbours and whispered comments. There was none of that here—except among the children at the altar rail, who shoved and nudged as children will, at all times and in all places. Nor was there any of the rather self-conscious devoutness and concentrated piety of a well-trained Anglican congregation in London. Here was something much bigger, more primitive and yet more fundamental, more compelling. The congregation was chanting in unison, but the men answering the women and the women the men, in an immense antiphonal volume of sound that carried a profound assurance. And more than this—something in that whole concourse of mountain people was being drawn, irresistibly, towards one part of the great church—towards the altar and the Celebrant; and was being held there in a tension like that which holds a chord in music—inevitable, inescapable, profound. There was no outward sign of this at all—the splendid faces remained aloof, impassive, withdrawn—but it was there, and Gloire Thurston, the dissatisfied spoiled ultra-modern product of two continents and many capitals, was aware of it, and could not escape it. It was so immense, and to her somehow so frightening in its immensity that she was almost relieved when the service ended, the organ crashed, and the congregation, she and her gendarme among them, streamed out again into the intense blazing sunshine, which was more normal, more bearable than that invisible blazing intensity within.

Outside, the sexes still kept apart, at first. The women remained in the porch, or gathered in the shade just outside it, on the north side of the church; the men grouped themselves on the steps at the foot of the tower, sat on the low wall overhanging the ravine, or spread about over the open space; the children chattered and ran, gay and free, but the little boys kept with the men, the little girls with the women. It was evidently a social occasion—the women talked with great liveliness, the men, their rifles on their knees, chewed the meat of weightier discourse with shrewd

184

grins but without laughter. Old and young, they were alike fine to look at; the men, not tall, slightly and sparely built, with dark faces, much weathered; fine in the bone, expressive even in repose; their loose flowing trousers gave a sort of magnificence, as of regal robes, to their easy attitudes.

But Gloire was more interested, for once, in the women. Out here in the brilliant light she could see them properly, note the exquisite detail of their brilliant woven silk aprons, and the fringed shawls or scarves which bound these round their waists, below the sombre richness of their velvet jackets. Some of the younger ones were heavily hung with ornaments, strings of gold or silver coins round their necks, heavy bracelets on their wrists. But what impressed her most of all was the effect—quite unsought—of their attitudes and grouping: the hierophantic gravity of that great cluster of white tunics, like the bells of vast campanulas, in the shadow of the church wall, and the stern fall of their black-fringed head-dresses. No ballet—and Gloire, who loved ballet, had seen many—had ever equalled this mountain congregation, talking pleasantly outside the church door on a feast-day, for formal grace and severe beauty. She noticed especially how still they stood—the bells of the campanulas hardly moved, the hands very little, though the faces and voices were now vivid with animation.

Presently there was a general movement outwards onto the great gravel square, where everyone stood looking up the hillside. Gloire looked too, and saw the caravan winding down the zig-zags; in a few moments she was joined by Mrs. Robinson and Miss Glanfield. They exchanged questions and answers—yes, she had been in time; yes, the service had been fine. (Gloire had neither the desire nor the capacity to express what the service had been like.) They walked about, admiring the dresses; Mrs. Robinson talked to some of the women. Presently Colonel Robinson joined them.

"Well, it's all fixed, so far," he said, taking off his felt hat and mopping his forehead. "Lek-Gionaj's gone home, but he left word that he wished us to lunch with him. And the Abbot wants us to take coffee with him, so we'd better go round to the Presbytery now. I could do with some coffee, I must say. Phew!—it is hot." He turned to Gloire. "Well, how did you get on? I gather you walked two of my chaps pretty well off their legs."

"We got on fine," said Gloire. "I think your chaps are sweet. They gave me coffee and played the accordion to me, and sang."

"Did they, by Jove! Where was all this?"

"Up there in the hut."

"My splendid Post! She calls it 'the hut'!" said Colonel Robinson, who was in high good-humour. "Whatever time did you get here, then?"

"About five to ten."

"Good God! And you didn't leave Shpali till half-past seven! Well, that beats all records," said the Colonel.

A young priest was waiting at the door of the Abbot's lodging, and led them through bare whitewashed passages into his reception-room. This was a large apartment, but little less bare than the passages—the Abbot sat in an arm-chair behind a large plain deal table, with two kitchen chairs, one on each side of him, for his assistant priests; the guests sat on a row of kitchen chairs opposite. On the wall behind the Abbot was tacked a large square of plain cheap black stuff, in the centre of which hung a small piece of bright rug or carpet, making a background for a large cru-cifix; on the table stood a carafe of water and a bowl of flowers. There was nothing else in the room at all—the roughly-boarded floor was bare. Gloire, who was familiar with the holy parlours of ecclesiastical dignitaries in Italy, was rather painfully struck by the poverty and austerity of this one.

However the Abbot took his poverty lightly, and was not in the least austere himself. He was a big cheerful ugly man, wearing that expression of discreet wisdom and tempered geniality which the Roman Church so usually impresses on the faces of her more responsible sons; he also looked, and was, highly intelligent and serenely practical. Coffee was served almost at once, more of the sweet thick Turkish stuff, accompanied by glasses of cold water. The conversation began in Albanian, but presently at Miss Glanfield's instance switched to Italian, which she and Gloire could both understand. It was all about the district—the two administrators, the civil and the ecclesiastical, discussed affairs of importance to both. Yes, Tirana was still remitting the taxes up here; that was essential, the Abbot said; the poverty was bitter, though the harvest prospects were better than last year. The attendance at the schools was on the whole encouraging; the Colonel would have heard that they had had two pupils accepted by the college in Scutari. There had been quite a good attendance at the weaving classes organised by that English lady—(all who know Albania will know to whom the Abbot referred)—and the articles they had made last year had brought in a helpful little amount of extra money to the district. Ah, the Government should give her more support, the Abbot said; that was the sort of thing the country needed, to turn the native skill of the women to account in producing for export articles which they could make in their own homes, without neglecting their families. But the Government of course had many other preoccupations. "Ah well," said the Abbot, with a fine smile and an accepting gesture of the hands—"she will have her reward. As we say here: 'Do a good deed and plunge it in the sea; if the fish don't recognise it, God will'."

"We need so much help here," he said, turning to Miss Glanfield, who had interjected a question now and then. "We need European help, ideas, education. We have been in subjection to Asiatics for so long that we have Asiatic standards ourselves, in all but morals. But they are good

187

people, these; they have great potentialities. I am glad—"
he bowed, and it was like a pontifical pronouncement, so
great was the dignity of the office superimposed on the
natural dignity of the man—"I am glad that you are come
among us. I hope you like my people."

"Father, I like them enormously," said Miss Glanfield,
with her spontaneous earnestness and flashing that blue
glance.

"I hear you are going to Lek-Gionaj," the Abbot pursued,
now to the Colonel. "Ah yes—the daughter-in-law is ill, I
learn; her child is newly born, and something has turned
amiss."

"We're only going to lunch," said the Colonel.

"So? I thought you were to stay."

When they had left the Abbot, and were setting off again
—"So that's why it's only lunch," Colonel Robinson said to
his wife.

"Yes, he must hate not putting us up," said Robina.

"Why should he hate it? We're such a mass," said Gloire.

"They're fantastically hospitable, these people," replied
the Colonel. "They can't bear to fail in hospitality, because
to fail in hospitality is to fail in honour. There are innumer-
able stories—true ones—of people at feud with another lot,
and their enemy coming, all unwitting, to their house at
night, and being recognised, and yet entertained with perfect courtesy."

"My goodness, we have got something to learn from
them," said Miss Glanfield, "whatever the Abbot may say
about their needing to learn from us."

"We have indeed. There's one particularly typical story,"
the Colonel went on, "of a mountaineer who was found
guilty of murder and sentenced—by the Turks—to be hanged.
The Turkish officer said to him, after the verdict—'Have
you ever before been in such a terrible situation as you are
today?' The Albanian thought for a bit, and then he said—
'Yes—I was once.' 'When was that?' 'When strangers

188

knocked at my door, expecting hospitality, and I had nothing to give them. Then I was indeed shamed'."

"Oh, lovely!" exclaimed Miss Glanfield. "And when you think of our careful cutler-counting, and the nicely-adjusted invitations of calculating dowagers! By comparison, we're revolting."

"I think cutler-counters are revolting by any standards," said the Colonel.

The residence—for house is hardly the word—of Gjergj Lek-Gionaj, hereditary Kapidan or Prince of his clan, stood boldly on one of the projecting spurs running down from Mali Shënjt, commanding the valley below and the track up to the pass at its head; the slopes round it were of that characteristic formation of decomposing rock, flecked with a sparse dark growth of stunted pines and juniper. The house had recently been added to and in part rebuilt, and its flattish spreading tiled roof and gleaming whitewash concealed the massiveness of the structure and gave it, from a distance, a deceptive resemblance to a large country villa in Southern Italy. But this was no villa. On all sides but one, where the ground dropped steeply to the valley, the upper slope was revetted into a wall of mortared stone at least twelve feet high, surmounted by a stockade of oak palings the size and thickness of railway sleepers; the only approach was by a sloping ramp, leading up to a solid oak gate in this stockade. The house itself, whose walls were four or five feet thick, was built round three sides of a square, forming a sort of courtyard—the fourth side was partially closed by a slatted wooden building, isolated from the rest. In this courtyard, into which the caravan filed with its usual deliberation, there was a feature which at once caught Miss Glanfield's eye. On the courtyard walls of ancient houses and castles in England the mellow stone or brick often holds rings, fastened by staples driven deep into the masonry, to which the horses of travellers used to be tied—in this Albanian courtyard the masonry held in great

189

numbers, not rings but iron hooks, whose use immediately became apparent, for the gendarmes and the pony-men at once hung their rifles on them by the slings! Miss Glanfield, naturally, was charmed by this.

The Prince and Princess—it is the nearest English equivalent for their position—met their guests in the courtyard; Lek-Gionaj greeted them first, and then with Colonel Robinson proceeded to deal with the disposal of the baggage and the men and animals of the caravan, including the gendarmerie escort; his wife, who had stood with folded hands and in perfect silence, now stepped forward and did her part, the welcoming of the women guests. Mrs. Robinson translated her little speech. She said:

"You are welcome, very welcome. The house and everything in it is yours. But here we are in the mountains, and I fear that you will suffer—indeed I fear that you will suffer much."

Mrs. Robinson having made some suitable response, Mme. Lek-Gionaj led them indoors, and up a broad stone staircase to a vast room, as large as two billiard-rooms, in which a long table was set for a meal—a welcome sight, for it was now 1.30, and they had breakfasted at 5.30. Besides the table the room contained immense numbers of small high-backed wooden chairs of cheap modern make, a huge brass samovar, a wireless-set which did not go, a brass bedstead in one corner, and some bright Kelim rugs; on the walls were two pictures, an oleograph of the Holy Family and an enlarged and expressionless photograph of Lek-Gionaj's father. The three windows were set so high and deep in the thickness of the wall that it was impossible to see out of them; they were heavily barred with iron scrollwork.

"Can we wash?" Gloire asked at once.

Yes, this could be arranged. Out on the landing at the head of the stairs, a large china basin was set on a chest, and filled with cold water from a copper jug; there was also produced a small pink-and-white bath-towel in that raised pattern which became fashionable about 1925, and, reposing in a cut-glass ash-tray, a cake, of all things, of Morny soap. With these rather primitive arrangements they managed to wash. Their hostess had left them for the moment, but a tall manservant in particularly splendid costume, with spectacular narrow moustachios curled round and as it were appliquéd on his tanned cheeks, attended them throughout, and when the washing was over, with a low bow flung open the door of another useful apartment.

Miss Glanfield went first, and came out as usual full of learned comment.

"But it's a *garde-robe*, pure and simple!" she said delightedly to Mrs. Robinson, as Gloire passed in. "And at last I understand why *garde-robes* in mediaeval castles are always in a turret—to get two windows and a cross-draught, to carry off the smell. Not that it does carry it off much; but still I see the idea. This doesn't seem to be in a turret; it's just in an angle of the wall, I fancy—I must look at it from outside. But it has the two windows."

Gloire, who knew nothing and couldn't have cared less about mediaeval *garde-robes*, was distinctly disimpressed by the sanitary arrangements of the Lek-Gionaj home. A hole in a stone floor and two small unglazed windows was not her idea of plumbing at all—the only thing which amused her was being bowed in and bowed out again by, practically, Rudolf Valentino in person. She said so to Miss Glanfield, who laughed.

"It's very good for you," she said. "We're all much too fussy about smells. Smells don't do people any harm—only real sewer gas. *Bad* plumbing is death; no plumbing just smells, but it's perfectly healthy."

"It's incredible," said Gloire with finality.

The sufferings foretold by Mme. Lek-Gionaj now began. The travellers returned to the enormous room, where they were soon joined by Colonel Robinson and Lek-Gionaj;

they were all extremely hungry, and the laid table raised eager hopes of food. But the Albanian tradition of hospitality includes no idea of time, so a long pause often ensues. (Also during this interval the meal is very often, in fact usually, being caught, killed, and cooked—all of which takes time.)

A long, a very long pause ensued on this occasion. Lek-Gionaj, attended by Pieter, his eldest son, sat on two of the upright wooden chairs opposite Colonel Robinson, and talked to him; Mme. Lek-Gionaj, attended by two of her daughters, a beautiful girl of seventeen called Lisa, and Marte, a gay little creature of about nine, sat opposite Mrs. Robinson, Miss Glanfield, and Gloire, and conversed with them; Rudolf Valentino handed round minute glasses of raki, the aniseed-flavoured liqueur of those regions, and a metal dish of flat squares of a rather hard sour white cheese. Each guest was supplied with a fork with which to spear the cheese; the dish was black with a thousand flies—spearing a piece, one blew on it to remove them before popping it hastily into one's mouth. Gloire didn't much like the cheese and thought the flies revolting, but she was so hungry that she took a piece whenever the dish came round, and so tired and thirsty that she emptied her little glass of raki as often as the servant filled it.

But the worst discomfort of that long wait was caused by the chairs. These, as has been said, were upright, with spoke backs and wooden seats of the most uncompromising sort. The three Englishwomen had spent some hours of the previous day in the saddle, for the first time in many months, and anyone who has ridden knows the effect of such unwonted exercise on that part of the human frame which sits on chairs. The hard wooden seats became a torture as time went on—the three foreigners sat forward, sat back, sat sideways, leaned their elbows on their knees, in their efforts to reduce the pain of their posteriors; but in vain.

And all the time, of course, they were perforce keeping

up, through Mrs. Robinson, a polite conversation with their hostess. This was a rather one-sided affair—left to themselves, the ladies of the Lek-Gionaj household seemed to think it enough to sit in an attitude of polite attention, holding their hands out in front of them with the fingers interlaced, assiduously twiddling their thumbs. This ended by positively obsessing Gloire and Miss Glanfield. Mme. Lek-Gionaj twiddled her massive thumbs, Lisa twiddled hers, and Marte, as little as a doll, twiddled her tiny ones. Gloire, spying about, observed that in the men's party, where the conversation was a good deal more animated, Lek-Gionaj sat twiddling his, faithfully copied by his son Pieter; and when not pouring out raki or handing cheese, Rudolf Valentino stood by the wall near the door, and twiddled as vigorously as his masters.

Conversation through an interpreter has its drawbacks. There can be no nuances, no grace-notes, no subtle turns of phrase—it is a matter of question and answer, statement, and agreement or disagreement, as bald and categorical as a telegram about a cargo of beans. Miss Glanfield, fecund in comment and enquiry, kept it up nobly; but even she was at last daunted by the barrenness of this form of intercourse, coupled with the discomfort of the chairs. "I wish you could ask her when we're to have lunch," she said wistfully to Robina; "but I suppose you can't. Could you tell her that we had such a lovely walk, and started at six, do you think? Just casually?"

Robina laughed her fat laugh and told Mme. Lek-Gionaj that her guests were rather tired, as they were not used to walking.

"She says she knew you would suffer," she said in reply—"but you shall lie down after lunch."

"Yes, but my God, when will after lunch *be*?" Gloire exploded. "It's after half-past two now. *I* should like to ask her why she doesn't do something about these unspeakable flies," she went on, blowing at another piece of cheese on

193

her fork, and fanning the persistent insects off her face. "Couldn't they Flit them, or something?"

Mrs. Robinson laughed again. "Flies are part of it," she said, and after the manner of interpreters turned and told Mme. Lek-Gionaj how much her visitors admired the defunct wireless-set.

However a few minutes later Mme. Lek-Gionaj and her daughters rose and took their leave.

"That means lunch," said Mrs. Robinson.

"You don't mean to say she's going to *cook* it?" said Gloire in despair.

"No no—it's coming. That's why she's gone."

"But won't they have lunch?" Miss Glanfield enquired.

"Yes, but not with us. The women don't eat with the men in Albania, as a rule—only in the very modern official circles."

"Where do they eat then?"

"In their own rooms. By the way," said Mrs. Robinson, with a rather nervous eye on Gloire, "we're to spend a couple of nights here. It was a mistake in the message that we were only to lunch."

"Oh, how perfect," said Miss Glanfield with enthusiasm.

"Oh God!" said Gloire.

At this point, simultaneously, Lek-Gionaj rose and waved his guests towards the table, and Rudolf Valentino flung open the door and ushered in a stream of servants with dishes. The guests stepped forward and were about to sit down, when the door opened again, and in walked a little old lady, white-haired, rather bent, in a grey cashmere dress with pince-nez on a black cord, and a firm neatness of expression and hair-do that could hardly have emanated from anywhere but New England.

The Robinsons advanced upon her with delight.

"Dr. Crowninshield! How splendid! But what on earth are you doing here? We thought you were in Mati."

"Pieter's wife is pretty sick," said the little old lady, in accents which warmed Gloire's heart. "She has puerperal fever and breast ulcers, poor child. They sent for me, so I came along. I shall be here quite a time, I imagine. But how very agreeable to meet you."

There were introductions, of which the Robinsons took charge, to Gloire and Miss Glanfield, and then at last they sat down. Dr. Crowninshield was evidently on the happiest of terms with her hosts, and talked to them in Albanian with perfect ease and naturalness—the uncouth syllables pouring from that closely-formed New England mouth, under the pale New England eyes, the tight hair, and the pince-nez, were a phenomenon so startling that Gloire could not take her eyes off it.

The long-awaited meal was very good when it came. There was soup—a kind of Scotch broth, but much more strongly seasoned with herbs than is usual in Scotland, and with a sort of noodles in it instead of barley. Next came boiled lamb, swimming in broth; this was followed by roast lamb, a whole innocent on a vast platter. There were no vegetables; the meal was rather on the muttony side, as Miss Glanfield observed in an undertone to Gloire. However they enjoyed it; but after the fourth course they were more than satisfied—sleepiness began to gain on them, and it was with something like dismay that Gloire saw Valentino bringing in yet another dish.

"Not *more?*" she murmured to Mrs. Robinson.

"This is dessert," said Dr. Crowninshield, who had overheard. "It's very good, too. Is it getting you down? We eat rather largely in Albania."

"It's all lovely," said Gloire hastily—"only we seem to have eaten mountains, already."

Dr. Crowninshield laughed.

"You have to learn to take a very small portion of everything," she said. "But the dessert will be the last."

It was. It was a sort of sweet pancake, very thick, and quite as good as Dr. Crowninshield had foretold. And after it had been consumed, and been followed by *more* coffee, and *more* raki, Colonel Robinson, poked up by his wife and Miss Glanfield, indicated to their host that they had in fact made a very early start and would be glad to rest. At once, Lek-Gionaj said, and gave an order to Valentino.

Gloire and Miss Glanfield had innocently supposed that they would now be led off to bedrooms. But not at all. In Albania, in the mountains at any rate, though the duty of hospitality is interpreted with princely liberality in the matter of food and drink, accommodation is on simpler lines. Even in great houses, there is usually *one* guest-room—and this was it. Valentino, aided by his assistants proceeded to bring into the room four very large fat mattresses, stuffed with wool and upholstered in Turkey-red cotton, which he laid in the three vacant corners of the room and under one of the windows; at the head of each he placed a large red pillow, and over all he laid a Turkey-red quilt, with a clean sheet of crimson twill tacked to its under side and coming down over the top; he folded these back at one corner with the expertise and precision of a well-trained housemaid, and then stood and bowed invitingly towards his handiwork. The guests, led by the well-trained Robinsons, rose and left the table, the last of the plates and glasses were whisked away, Lek-Gionaj wished them a pleasant rest, and bowed himself out—and the four travellers and Dr. Crowninshield (who seemed to be *beata possidens* of the brass bedstead) were left to themselves. It was 4.30. Each chose a mattress, and lay down. The mattresses were heaven, deep and soft; so were the down pillows; but so were not the flies.

"My God!" Gloire exclaimed after a few uneasy moments—"what on earth does one do about these flies? They're sitting all over me."

"Put a handkerchief over your face," advised Dr. Crowninshield, who had already done so.

"But that will be so stuffy."

"You'll get accustomed to it."

Gloire did as she was told; Miss Glanfield silently followed her example. In a few minutes, flies or no flies, they were all five fast asleep.

11

DR. EMMELINE CROWNINSHIELD, in her brief appearance at lunch, had inspired Miss Glanfield with the liveliest curiosity. This was not unreasonable. A little white-haired old lady in long skirts, wearing the very aspect of a lifelong inhabitant of some small New England township, who proves to be a qualified physician and surgeon, would be something of a portent, met anywhere—but to find such a one wandering about High Albania, talking the language with mastery and on terms of intimacy and affection with the local inhabitants, was really startling. She fell asleep wondering what had brought the old lady to Albania, and above all what had prompted her to stay there to exercise her skill—and waking after about an hour and a half of rather stuffy dozing, she instantly began to ponder all this again. Her curiosity moved her to pull the handkerchief off her face, turn over on her red mattress, and gaze at the small figure on the brass bedstead, quietly reposing under a red quilt like her own.

The penetrating effect of the human stare apparently operates even through a handkerchief, for after a few moments there was a stir under the opposite quilt and the bandanna was twitched off, revealing the neatly-arranged white hair under the hair-net, and the stone-pale, tight-lipped, lined old face, pince-nez and all. For a long moment the two women looked at one another in silence across the bare stretch of floor, a prolonged and somehow communicative gaze. Then they both smiled, still in silence. Miss Glanfield had a strong feeling, at that moment, that she and this small improbable stranger had somehow achieved, mysteriously, an effective contact in that silent interchange. Normally she was wont to be sceptical about such direct apprehensions, and to discount them at the time; but on this occasion she acted on her impression. Feeling under her red pillow for her cigarette-case she slid out from under the quilt and in her socks tiptoed across the floor to the old woman's bed. Dr. Crowninshield put out a neat little claw and patted it, and Miss Glanfield obeyed the gesture and sat down.

"I'm sure you're wondering what I'm doing here," said the American at once, in a whisper.

"I am," Miss Glanfield whispered back, lighting a cigarette. "Passionately," she added, half-smiling.

"Well, I daresay I'll tell you sometime. But just now you tell *me* something, while we're quiet. What's been amiss with that attractive child, and why is she here?"

Miss Glanfield was instantly struck by the implications of one small word in that final sentence, packed as it was with implications—the word "been." Involuntarily she glanced across to the mattress in the opposite corner, where a long low outline and another handkerchief represented all that could, for the moment, be seen of Gloire. Been? Was she cured already, in the little old woman's opinion? or was it just American phrasing.

"I don't know—what's been wrong with her, I mean. She lost her husband some years ago. She's here because she wanted to come, and I brought her," whispered Miss Glanfield, blowing smoke at the clouds of flies.

"Unh-huh," was Dr. Crowninshield's non-committal response.

"Why do you say 'been wrong with her'?" the writer pursued—broadly speaking no conversation, however bizarre, could be too bizarre for her, or find her unprepared to respond. In fact she was delighted with the strange swiftness of the old woman's insight. She was undoubtedly a witch! "Do you think she's over it, whatever it was?"

199

"I think she's *dans la bonne voie.*"

"You wouldn't have said that a week ago, if you'd seen her then," said Miss Glanfield rapidly.

"Maybe not. I do say it now. Maybe you've done her good. I surmise you could do her a lot of good, if you do little enough about it," said the American surprisingly.

"I've not done much so far but get her here."

"Well, she'll want more of you than that. But not as much as you might very conceivably give her."

"Oh, how on earth?" Miss Glanfield, still unperturbed, was delighted by the significant and unexpected quality of Dr. Crowninshield's utterances. This was Delphi in person.

"You might overwhelm her with your ideas—make her accept something that was ultimately bad for her, because it came from you, and she likes you; try to make her live on your level, which isn't her level. I guess you often do that to folks. I read you, you know," said Dr. Crowninshield, smiling, with a very keen fine glance.

"Oh, but do go on!"

"You're pretty nice!" said the old lady—"I guess you don't mind my criticisms a bit!"

"It's fascinating! But I shall try to remember. What else?"

"I fancy that's about all. I'm sorry for her. If nothing comes between you, you may help her a whole lot, if you aren't too energetic with her."

"What could come between us? I'm just trying to think."

"I don't know. But remember that in any conflict, you'd break her and her little arts like a butterfly on a wheel."

This final pronouncement from Delphi did upset Miss Glanfield.

"Oh really, Dr. Crowninshield, I don't think I should! I'm sorry for her too. After all, I arranged for her to come on this trip."

"My dear, you just wouldn't know you were doing a thing! But she'd get broken, just the same."

200

"That's horrible," said Miss Glanfield thoughtfully. "Am I horrible?" she asked, looking very directly at the old woman.

"No. You're a fine person. But you're big, and potent—you're like a turbine in a drawing-room, among her sort of folks. And if you touch a turbine in the wrong place, you get frizzled."

"Oh dear!" said Miss Glanfield, frowning with thought, her indeterminate eyebrows drawn down level above those very blue eyes. "This is frightful. My husband always says things like that, but I don't pay very much attention to him —one doesn't you know. And I have a clever, excessively lethargic friend who always tells me my energy is so tiring. But I always tell *her* how fearfully enervating her laziness is, to people like me! Surely the lazy ones aren't the only people to get consideration?"

Dr. Crowninshield, at this, laughed aloud, a little dry crackling New England laugh. They had both raised their whispers practically to the normal tone of speech by this time, so absorbed were they in their most peculiar interchange; but Dr. Crowninshield's laughter brought it to an abrupt end. Three recumbent figures stirred under three red quilts, three handkerchiefs were pulled off three faces— the others had woken up.

"What's the time?" Colonel Robinson asked.

"Six," said Miss Glanfield, looking at her watch.

Gloire sat up and stretched her arms in a lovely lazy graceful gesture, and patted her mouth to cover a tiny yawn.

"What time do the flies go to bed?" she enquired, flicking her bandanna at them as the skilful crack of a whip.

"After dark," said Mrs. Robinson, also sitting up, and beginning to comb out her hair. Gloire did this too—but whereas the Colonel's wife would have reminded the cultured onlooker forcibly of the more dismal type of Ricketts woman at her toilet, Mrs. Thurston looked like something

201

off a Grecian urn. The Colonel threw aside his quilt, stuck his feet over the edge of the mattress, and began to put on his shoes. Miss Glanfield from her coign of vantage on Dr. Crowninshield's brass bed surveyed them with delight— it was such an unwonted scene of mixed domesticity. So this was Albanian country-house life! Charming.

Rudolf Valentino now entered, bearing a tray with tiny cups of Turkish coffee, which he handed round to each bed. When he gave Dr. Crowninshield her cup he said something to her in Albanian.

"What happens now?" Gloire asked, lighting a cigarette and setting to work on her face with a piece of cotton-wool and some fluid out of a small bottle.

"You go and see the animals," said Dr. Crowninshield. "The Lek-Gionajs will be ready when you are, he says."

"I've seen the animals at least eight times," said the Colonel, putting his now shod feet back on the mattress, and starting on his coffee.

The animals proved to be so spectacular as to be worth seeing nine times, Miss Glanfield thought. When they went downstairs, parting from Dr. Crowninshield, who returned to her patient, they were led out to a bare open space in a hollow below the house, occupied by a large enclosure of wooden uprights, rather like the split-chestnut fencing seen in the southern counties in England, but stouter, and over six feet high. About it at a distance of some forty yards stood a ring of tall stout poles, and on the slopes above, overlooking the hollow, were several open-fronted wooden shelters with heaps of blankets. Mme. Lek-Gionaj, translated by Mrs. Robinson, explained the uses of all these things to her newest visitors. To the poles round the central fold the dogs were tied at night, so that when the wolves came prowling down the shepherds could safely shoot at the marauders without fear of injuring the dogs; the shepherds slept in the open-fronted shelters, so that they could fire at

202

the wolves as they lay, when the barking of the dogs aroused them.

"But do wolves really come here?" Gloire asked incredulously.

"Oh yes—constantly."

Folds and shelters were alike empty, and Gloire asked where the animals were? For answer, Mrs. Robinson pointed up the mountainside. Above the dark pine woods, the pinnacles of Mali Shënjt were glowing golden in the last sunshine, though where they stood was already in shadow; the head of the valley and the upper slopes were bathed in a flood of rich light. And down from these sun-bathed upper slopes into the blue lake of shadow below two rivers were pouring, a white river and a brown river, gathering small tributaries as they flowed from branching gullies and isolated clearings—a brown river of goats, a white river of sheep. Shouts and the barking of dogs accompanied their flow, and were borne to the onlookers on the still mountain air.

"Heavens! What masses! Are they all coming here?"

Yes, they were—and presently first the white and then the brown torrent debouched into the hollow, and like a river expanding into a lake, spread all over it. Miss Glanfield now saw what she had not noticed at first, that a division ran across the main fold, dividing it in two—the entrance was just by the division, and a man standing in it, with a stick and incredible skill, divided the sheep from the goats, as the surging flood bore down upon him, turning them into their several quarters. Baa-ing, bleating, they rushed at him, the sheep jumping, the goats galloping flat—but he made no mistakes; the sheep and lambs poured into one fold, the goats into the other. The kids to Miss Glanfield's surprise were excluded, and remained bleating desolately outside. As usual she asked the reason for this.

"They'll milk the goats in the morning, so the kids have

203

to be kept apart from their mothers during the night," Mrs. Robinson told her.

"But where will they go?"

"You'll see—in the little fold."

She did see, presently. When the flowing river slackened and all the sheep and goats were disposed in the folds, two solid floors of brown and white, shoving and pushing noisily round the water-troughs and food-racks, the shepherd who had so skilfully organised their disposition went and opened a gate into the smaller fold at one side, and the dogs, barking, hustled the kids into it. Along with them went three old rams, with curling horns and fleeces that swept the ground.

"What in the world are the old tups doing in there, Robina?" Miss Glanfield asked.

"Oh, they act as sort of nurses to the kids—show them how to eat and drink, and make them feel at home," Mrs. Robinson replied. And indeed, the elderly rams proceeded quietly to the smaller drinking and food-troughs provided for the kids, who presently stopped bleating so piercingly after their mothers, and followed this sensible example.

"How very amusing!" said Miss Glanfield. "But why rams?"

Mrs. Robinson applied to Mme. Lek-Gionaj.

"She says billies aren't reliable; they might knock the kids about," she said—"and of course if it was sheep or nannies there would be a riot. But rams make splendid foster-mothers."

For some reason this use of the rams particularly charmed Miss Glanfield—but indeed the whole scene charmed her. She glanced round the darkling hollow—at the troop of shepherds with their wild faces and bizarre dress, at the horde of sheep-dogs, almost as savage as the wolves at whom, apparently, they were wont to bark, at the enormous wealth of animals now safely folded against Nature's still potent enemies. Mrs. Robinson, to whom she mentioned the riches such flocks must represent in a pastoral community, in return quoted the Albanian proverb—"God grant me not crops in my fields if I do not have my cup of milk."

Finally, she looked at the Lek-Gionajs themselves, standing among their flocks and herds and servants as Abraham and Sarah might have stood of old on the plains of Palestine. Lek-Gionaj was a short man, thick-set; it was hard to see much of Abraham in the semi-European dress which he affected—an old-fashioned Norfolk suit with pleated back and patch pockets, knee-stockings, and stout black laced shoes, most oddly combined with a collarless shirt, gauged to the neck, and an immensely broad cummerbund of striped black and silver silk which, embracing the bottom of his neat waistcoat, fastened in front with a huge silver buckle set with turquoises, at least eight inches across. Yet there was something patriarchal about him; the quiet, substantial satisfaction with which he stood, feet apart, surveying his fleecy, vocal, visible wealth—a satisfaction which the sight of packets of gilt-edged securities in a safe can never quite afford—and the tone of friendly interest and calm unquestioned authority with which he spoke to his men.

In Mme. Lek-Gionaj, on the other hand, it was easy to see Sarah, or the wife of any patriarch. She was a massive woman, much taller than her husband and immensely broad in the beam, with a large, broad-browed, big-mouthed face, firm and solid as an early Epstein sculpture. Her face in repose was so expressionless as to be almost sulky, but gave a great sense of latent power. Her huge frame was splendidly clothed. Full white linen trousers tapered down from her vast hips to quite small feet, and over them, bell-like, hung the skirts of her white linen tunic, which was most delicately pleated and embroidered on the bosom; over this was a jacket of deep purple velvet, and a brilliantly striped silk apron fell to her knees, held in place by another silk shawl, embroidered this time and tied round the waist. Over all she wore a sleeveless coat of white woollen homespun, reaching in front only a few inches beyond the armholes, which were surrounded by a band of embroidery in vivid reds and greens—there was more of this embroidery on the hips and round the neck and hem. It was of an Oriental magnificence, this dress, and the stern impassive countenance was almost oriental too. Her head-dress was as stern as her face. A fringed shawl of black silk was folded squarely across that great sculptured forehead and bound above the ears—it fell in a black cascade of fringe down to the middle of that vast white coat at the back—in front, a great plait of bronze-dark hair was somehow drawn up through the black folds, and lay across her head like a coronal. She wore no jewellery, and indeed her natural splendour needed none. Calmly, silent except when addressed, she stood watching her flocks, her husband, and her off-spring—for Marte and Lisa had accompanied them down to the fold, and Pieter stood with his father. Oh yes, so indeed might Sarah have stood, Miss Glanfield thought, or that great matron of whom King Solomon sang, or the notable woman who entertained the prophet Elijah. This was what womanhood meant in a simpler, earlier world. It was impossible to conceive of coquetry, or the competitive spirit, or ruinous extravagance in the pursuit of fashion so much as entering into the conception of that great creature, traditionally garbed, traditionally occupied in secular duties and responsibilities.

It occurred to her to wonder what Mrs. Thurston was making of this scene, and of their hostess, and she turned to where she stood. Graceful, slight as a wand beside that enormous matriarchal bulk, in her grey flannel trousers and her little linen jacket, with her plucked eyebrows and scarlet mouth and nails, it was now Gloire who looked exotic, strange, among that group of Albanian women; though her dress was dim beside theirs in actual colour, their severe and archaic outlines made her somehow gaudy; she was smoking and looked a little bored, but not discontented.

Dr. Crowninshield's words came back into Miss Glanfield's mind. Strange old woman—little New England witch! How odd all that had been. She must think more about it. But she had said Gloire would want something from her—a lot, but not too much—and the writer moved over to Mrs. Thurston to share her impressions, and asked her if she did not think Sarah, in the tents of Abraham, must have looked rather like their hostess?

Gloire bestowed a glance on Mme. Lek-Gionaj.

"She looks more like Mrs. Noah to me," she replied briefly.

Miss Glanfield stifled a laugh. Mme. Lek-Gionaj did look uncommonly like that stalwart figure, striped in red and yellow, who used to preside over the wooden animals on the nursery floor in the days of her youth.

"But how do you mean?" Gloire went on—she was quite ready to listen to Miss Glanfield's ideas, whatever they were.

Miss Glanfield said a little of what she meant as they strolled up towards the house—of the timelessness of women like that, and of their lives and outlook; of the minute fraction of the human race, taken as a whole, which lived for amusement and self-expression, or at least felt a certain degree of amusement and self-expression to be not only allowable but almost a duty. Gloire listened, and for once did not argue or raise objections, but what she thought of these ideas it was impossible to tell—all Miss Glanfield could be sure of was that the younger woman was certainly peculiarly receptive at the moment to anything she chose to say. She looked often at Mrs. Thurston, pondering how far Dr. Crowninshield's theory was correct, as they walked round the house, admiring the new portion which had been built on a few years before—breaking off, characteristically, to nip round the end to try to identify the *garde-robe* from outside. In this she was successful; she came back triumphant and breathed into Robina's ear that it *was* in the angle of the old building, as she had guessed.

The new building had a fine doorway in delicate close-

207

grained pale grey stone, with six names carved across the
lintel—of course Miss Glanfield had to know whose they
were. Mme. Lek-Gionaj obliged—those of her husband and
her five sons. Gloire was outraged.

"For gracious' sake! Mrs. Robinson, do ask her why her
name, and Marte's and Lisa's aren't carved up there too?"

Mrs. Robinson did as she was asked. The result was un-
forgettable. The great woman stood there, and for once
a gleam of feeling, an expression of amusement, almost
of mockery, appeared on her harsh magnificent face.
"Daughters?" she said, and struck the palms of her two
hands, one across the other, with the gesture of one who
wipes off dirt. In that instant it was clear to the three
foreign women that at least the germs of feminism lay
hidden in that gigantic bosom.

To the left of this entrance another door, less ornate,
opened direct from the courtyard into a great room, as
large or larger than that on the floor above where they had
eaten and slept—here the men employed about the establishment lived, and here the visiting gendarmes and teamsters were housed. The visitors looked in. Except for a number of coarse bright rugs on the floor, the room was quite
bare; the pack-saddles of the pony-team were piled up in
one corner, and in another on a raised platform quilts and
bedding, neatly folded, lay under a vast coloured sheet;
out in the centre of the room, under the light of the high-
set scroll-barred windows, the teamsters and gendarmes,
seated on the floor, were brewing coffee over a small char-
coal stove, smoking and chatting.

"No, they don't want chairs because they never sit up to
a table, even for meals," Colonel Robinson said in answer
to a question from Gloire; "they eat out of a huge dish, or
dishes, set on the floor. The Prince himself only installed
those chairs upstairs a little while ago; the last time I was
here there weren't any."

"I wish he hadn't!" said Gloire.

208

"Yes, we used to sit on cushions and divan things when I've been here before," said Mrs. Robinson—"it was heavenly."

"And you say all the men sleep there?" Miss Glanfield pursued.

"All but thirteen, who sleep fully armed on the floor of Lek-Gionaj's bedroom," said the Colonel.

"But what on earth for?" Gloire was wide-eyed.

"A body-guard," said the Colonel carelessly. "Last time we were up here together there were shots in the night— do you remember, Robina?—and in the morning they showed us the bullet holes in the wall."

"How fantastic!" said Gloire.

"Does that sort of thing never happen in Chicago?" the Colonel asked, turning a sarcastic eye on her.

"Oh rubbish, Dick," Mrs. Robinson intervened. "Look, you talk to the Prince, will you?—we're going to see the kitchen with Madame."

The kitchen in the Lek-Gionaj mansion was, exceptionally, on the ground floor—as a rule in Albania the animals, poultry and farm implements occupy the bottom level of the house, and the kitchen, sleeping rooms and guest-room are upstairs; but the Lek-Gionajs had stables for their animals for winter use, and therefore a ground-floor kitchen. It was another very large room, like a great cavern, faintly lit by a paraffin lamp hanging from the ceiling, and the last of the daylight which crept in through the barred windows. A wood fire burned on a wide open hearth; above it hung a great copper pot in which water bubbled: permanent hot water, Mrs. Robinson murmured to Gloire—the pot was kept there day and night; a metal coffee-pot stood in the ashes—coffee too was on tap night and day to be ready to serve to any chance guest. On the floor in front of the fire a woman knelt, arranging a freshly-skinned lamb on a spit; presently she took it up and placed the spit in front of the flames. Under the window were shelves, on which stood

various cooking utensils, and silver-washed copper bowls
of *kous*, the sour milk of the whole Balkan region; very
large flat trays or dishes of this same silvered copper, some
of them worked in beautiful designs, were ranged against
the walls—it was from these, placed on the floor, that meals
were eaten, Mrs. Robinson explained.

As their eyes grew more accustomed to the dim light
Gloire and Miss Glanfield noticed other details. The walls
were covered with metal vessels of various sorts, ladles,
knives, spoons and tongs; from the smoke-blackened rafters
hung quantities of dried gourds, which aroused Miss Glanfield's interest—they contained beans, pulse and lentils, Mrs.
Robinson told her, and also dried seeds for sowing. On one
wall hung a guitar. As there were neither presses nor tables,
obviously everything had to lean or hang, and did. The
place seemed full of a crowd of women, occupied in various
ways—one, kneeling on the floor, was rolling out pastry on
one of the metal trays; another, also kneeling, was chop-
ping up herbs on a smaller dish; Mme. Lek-Gionaj ran an
expert and masterful eye over each. Again Miss Glanfield
was reminded of the Old Testament—there was a primitive
austerity and yet abundance about the whole scene which
was strongly reminiscent of the great Biblical narratives.

Through an inner door there now appeared a queer little
procession; Lisa and an older woman carrying a cradle,
which they set down near the hearth. This was Pieter's
baby; it had been taken up to its mother to be suckled—
they were allowed to look at it, Mme. Lek-Gionaj towering over them, a strange look of satisfaction and—almost—
amusement on her impassive face. Even Miss Glanfield was
rather disconcerted by that cradle. Not that it was not
beautiful—it was, very; elegantly and plainly shaped of
wood, long and very narrow, it was decorated with fine lines
of gold on a dark-brown ground. But across the opening of
the wooden hood a stiff piece of towelling was tightly
stretched, excluding not only light from the infant's eyes,

but obviously practically all air as well. When the older woman had unfastened the towelling they saw the little mite, heavily swaddled; its minute head lay on a very hard pillow, below it was merely hay under a piece of linen cloth; such freedom of movement as its garments left to it was still further reduced by a plaited woollen cord with which the cradle was lapped round and round, so that it should not fall out.

"But why do they hump the cradle up and downstairs?" Gloire very pertinently enquired. "Why not just take the baby out and carry it up?"

"Oh, you *can't* persuade them to do that, it's hopeless," said Mrs. Robinson distressfully. "They will keep the baby in the cradle all the time, even when they're nursing it. Usually, when the mother is well, she kneels on the floor by the cradle and nurses the child that way. That's why there's such a fearful amount of breast ulcers—the breasts never get properly emptied, of course, unless the child is held close to them."

"But Robina, I really don't see how it can breathe properly behind this thing," said Miss Glanfield, fingering the thick homespun web. "However long do they keep it in the cradle?"

"Oh, if there isn't another baby, for ages and ages," Mrs. Robinson replied—"till it's two or more; long after its feet are sticking out over the end, often."

"Well, I must say that seems very mistaken," said Miss Glanfield seriously.

"Oh, don't talk about it, Susan! I've been wrestling with this for years," said poor Mrs. Robinson, her cheerful face full of distress. "The only thing one can say is, I suppose it has some eugenic value—only the very strong babies survive. Perhaps that's why they are such an exceptionally tough, healthy race."

Dismayed, they watched the elderly woman close the bright-eyed morsel of humanity up again, tying the web

211

of cloth tightly across the wooden hood, while Mme. Lek-Gionaj, still with that inscrutable expression of amused satisfaction, stood looking on. Into this antique scene, at that moment, stepped the neat little figure of Dr. Crowninshield, carrying a silvered tray heaped with steaming cloths and an enamel can with a lid. Expertly, and as one familiar with the house, she emptied the contents of the enamel can out through the door into the courtyard, reached down a gourd from where it hung at the side of the hearth, dipped it into the copper pot, and refilled the can—then tipping the cloths into it she replaced the lid, and taking down a hook from a nail on the wall, she hung the can by its metal ring over the fire.

"Sterilising under difficulties!" she observed to Miss Glanfield, with a thin-lipped smile. "No, she's not much better," she replied to an enquiry from Mrs. Robinson—"I've just been fomenting her. I had that miserable baby out of the cradle for her to nurse this time, anyway!" Then, courteously but authoritatively, she gave her orders to Mme. Lek-Gionaj in Albanian. The young mother was to have broth—broth and nothing else—no bread, and no milk, for her supper; Lisa was to sit with her, all the time—Lisa's supper could be taken up to her; if she complained of pain, Lisa was to send for her, Dr. Crowninshield, at once. And Lisa was not to talk to her. "Not one small word! Have you understood?" the little old lady said menacingly to Lisa. "She must sleep—if she does not sleep she may die," she said with great emphasis to Mme. Lek-Gionaj.

The massive woman looked at her with calm recognition of her authority and knowledge.

"It shall be as you order. The young women of today," she added, with a faint air of contempt, "have no strength. I have borne eleven children, and I nursed them on meat, not broth!"

"God looked on you with favour," returned the old American unhesitatingly; "His ways are not to be ques-

212

tioned. But I ask you to seek out a foster-mother near by, whom we can call in in need; it may be that Pieter's wife will not be able to nurse this child. She is very gravely ill. But if we spare her and she recovers she also may bear Pieter many children."

Of this conversation Mrs. Robinson rehearsed the substance to Miss Glanfield as they went upstairs, leaving Mme. Lek-Gionaj among her hench-women in the kitchen. Dr. Crowninshield came with them, and seated herself rather wearily on the side of the brass bed. The rest of the party had been looking forward to relaxing again on those delicious mattresses, but alas, they had been removed. Disconsolately they seated themselves once more on the wooden chairs. The ceiling lamp had been lit, and its harsh glare was reflected back from the red and green tartan American cloth which covered the table; flies whirled round it in a cloud. Rudolf Valentino brought in first more coffee, then raki and cheese; there was no sign of the Lek-Gionajs for the moment. Gloire asked when supper would be?

Around ten, Dr. Crowninshield told her.

Gloire looked at her wrist-watch. "My God! And it's only half-past eight now."

"She told you you would suffer," the Colonel mocked.

"Well, I am suffering. Too right, she was." She shifted on her chair, and finally—"I shall suffer as little as possible, anyway," she said, and lay down flat on her back on the bare floor, pulling a garment out of her suitcase and propping up her head with it. From this position she turned on Miss Glanfield. Gloire was tired; she was slightly overwrought by all the crowding impressions of the day, beginning with her forced march to Torosh and the service there, and closing with the sight of that helpless imprisoned baby; the prospect of a long hungry wait for supper, the flies and the general discomfort rasped her nerves and temper. "You may say what you like about modern inventions, but

213

honestly, I think this set-up here is absolutely ghastly," she burst out. "Wretched little babies being half-smothered, and their mothers made sick by their miserable old ideas! And treating women that way—not allowing them to eat with guests or the men, and leaving the girls' names out of that inscription! I call it frightful. Why should women be kept down like that?"

"I don't think anyone defends their treatment of infants," Miss Glanfield said equably.

From her seat on the brass bedstead, Dr. Crowninshield took a hand.

"You speak of the women being kept down," she said—"but that's a complete misconception. A married woman here has enormous authority and power—but she doesn't worry about the outward appearances of it. When I see people like Mme. Lek-Gionaj running some fifty women and more men, with her children and grandchildren growing up around her in willing obedience, and affection, and respect, and her husband relying on her for wisdom and counsel, whether she eats with the guests or not seems a small thing! I often compare her in my mind with the professional women and business girls back home, who are so proud of their 'economic independence'—living alone or with a woman friend in some little apartment, and I think that they have nothing on her. They are puttering around at some little artificial job; she is building men and women."

Poor Gloire was silenced by this little homily from her country-woman; she was always getting a homily from one or other of them, Miss Glanfield reflected, half amused, half sadly. She herself now put in a question.

"Dr. Crowninshield, how do the girls here get educated? The upper-class ones like the Lek-Gionajs—and the others too? Have a cigarette," she added, jumping up and taking her case over to the old woman.

Dr. Crowninshield took the cigarette, while the Colonel mumbled an apology.

214

"Thank you, my dear. In old days," the American said, "the girls of the great families used to get sent to some other noble house, and the young men too, to learn manners and household duties and so on—I guess even the Albanian mammas found it easier to cope with other women's daughters than with their own! But there's less of that now. The most important education they get is the education of the hearth—I mean at home; and that goes for all classes."

"Why the hearth?"

"Because that is the centre of it all. There they learn to cook, and spin, and mind the baby"—Gloire snorted, but Dr. Crowninshield ignored her—"and sort seeds, and do the hundred and one daily jobs—feed the silk-worms, and all the rest of it. And it's round the hearth in the evenings that the children learn the qualities that lead them to real manhood and womanhood—listening to the old tales and stories. The older people select the stories so wisely, and relate them so beautifully that they would stir any heart, I guess," the old woman said earnestly. "I know they do mine. It's at the hearth that the concepts of honour and courage and hospitality and respect for women have gotten such binding force. When the mental life of a nation is built up, primarily, at the family fireside, and based on affection, and not interfered with by much in the way of outside influences, it may stay pretty primitive, but it's very stable and very pure. Of course, that kind of an education has very great limitations; it doesn't go in for the arts or sciences, or fit people much for a commercial life. But it does equip them mighty well for the life they're mostly going to lead."

"I shouldn't call that an education at all," Gloire observed.

"It really boils down to this, does it, that education here has consisted in a sort of personal edition of domestic science, and folklore, and in character-training?" Miss Glanfield asked.

"That's right," said Dr. Crowninshield.

215

But Colonel Robinson did not agree.

"Not character-training in the sense that most of us use the word, Dr. Emmeline, surely?" he objected. "I've never heard an Albanian so much as use the word 'character.' I don't think they consider it. Tradition, yes; character in our sense, no. They say a person is or isn't honest, but that's about as far as it goes—and if he *is* honest, they tend to think he won't get very far, because he'll be out-witted!"

Dr. Crowninshield laughed.

"Why, in a sense you're right, Colonel—yes," she admitted. "But I'm talking about the mountain people, who are after all in a great majority; you're thinking about the towns. There's plenty of corruption there." She turned to Miss Glanfield. "They tell a story here, and declare it really happened, and fairly recently at that. A Ministerial post fell vacant and candidates who applied were asked three questions:

Have you ever been in prison?
How many people have you killed?
How much money have you laid by?

If the answers were 'never' or 'none,' there just wasn't a chance of the candidate being considered for the post."

Miss Glanfield laughed.

"But that's really a heritage from the Turks, surely?" Mrs. Robinson put in.

"Of course it is. Turkish corruption—before Mustapha Kemal Atatürk—was an international byword," said Dr. Crowninshield; "and it infected these people here. And then there's the cruel poverty, and the pressure of debt. Do you know"—again she turned to Miss Glanfield—"what the *normal* rate on loans is today in this country? Twenty per cent!"

"Plus bribes to officials to get anything done," Colonel Robinson contributed. "No wonder they think that money is happiness."

216

Miss Glanfield was horrified and said so.

"What is the solution?" she asked at length.

"An incorruptible administration is the first need," the Colonel answered her, without the least hesitation. "And for that they'll really need foreign help."

"British help," Dr. Crowninshield interjected; "the Italians are no use; they're corrupt themselves."

"Thank you, Ma'am. Actually," the Colonel pursued, turning to Miss Glanfield, "I believe Dr. Crowninshield is right. Why our little show has been rather a success is simply because we really have kept it pretty clean. If we hear of a man in the gendarmerie taking even the smallest bribe he gets fired at once. The people have come to realise that, and they appreciate it very much."

"What do you consider the ideal form of government for Albania?" Miss Glanfield asked, looking from Dr. Crowninshield to Colonel Robinson.

"A Constitutional Monarchy," came from the Englishman and the American woman simultaneously.

Miss Glanfield was surprised by this, and so was Gloire. But it was the writer who spoke.

"Will you tell me why?"

Colonel Robinson answered her.

"The whole Albanian outlook places so much emphasis on the individual personality that in their political life, as it develops, personalities, for a long time, will count for much more than any ideological theories of government. They're most blessedly free here from ideologies at present. For Albania a monarchy is by far the most suitable form of government, provided they get the right monarch. But he must be a real Bairaktar."

"Do you agree?" Miss Glanfield asked Dr. Crowninshield.

"I certainly do."

"You don't want them to be a Republic?"

"I certainly do not." The old woman spoke with considerable emphasis.

217

"Maybe I'd better explain," she went on. "In theory, as an American, I believe in Republics; but for Europe I definitely feel that monarchies are best. I've lived in Europe quite a while—since 1900—and I feel I know what I'm talking about."

"I don't feel that it's by any means proved that monarchy isn't the best form of government anyhow," said Miss Glanfield, thoughtfully, lighting another cigarette, and taking a fresh glass of raki from Valentino. "After all, the monarchical system has worn pretty well. It's been going on now for about four thousand years, and some of the finest flowers of the human spirit have been produced under it."

"But isn't it getting rather out of date, in the twentieth century?" Gloire asked. "I mean, isn't it rather obvious that Republics are the coming thing?"

"Well, is it?" Miss Glanfield riposted. "Republics are still in the experimental stage, aren't they?"

"Experimental stage! What on earth do you mean?"

"Simply that except for the brief episodes in Greece and Rome, there is only one Republic in the world which has passed its second century."

"Which is that?"

"Switzerland. That *has* been a success, unquestionably. But looked at historically you can only call them an experiment as yet, I would say. And just see what has happened to the four European countries which scrapped their monarchies after the last war:—Germany, Russia, Portugal, Spain. Today three are Dictatorships, and the fourth is well on the way to becoming one, if all one hears is true."

"But that's Europe," Gloire objected.

"My dear young lady," Dr. Crowninshield put in, "will you oblige me by looking at our own hemisphere for a moment. We have to face facts, however patriotic we may feel! Please compare political life and the administration of justice in the United States with that in Britain, or Norway,

218

or Sweden. I think you know the answer, but if you don't, you would do well to learn it."

"Oh, I'm glad you say that!" Miss Glanfield exclaimed. "I so often think—where is the best expression of human freedom to be found, I mean the most complete combination of liberty and order, and purity of administration? And there seems no possible doubt about the answer—in the monarchical democracies of Europe: Norway, Sweden, Denmark, Belgium, Holland—not to mention England."

"I agree with you," said Dr. Crowninshield. "The trouble is our people just don't know the facts about those places." She turned to Gloire. "I do know them—and the very words 'racket,' 'graft,' and 'party bosses' just don't exist there, let alone the things they stand for. It isn't an accident that all those words were coined across the Atlantic—and I guess it isn't an accident either that the one country in Europe where they really fit is republican France!"

Gloire was silent for a moment or two—she was digesting all this. At last—

"Why should that be?" she asked. "I mean, I expect all you say must be true—you've been into it; but what has monarchy to do with it?"

"I should say Miss Glanfield would explain that very well," Dr. Crowninshield said, looking at the writer.

Miss Glanfield was of course delighted to oblige.

"I think the practical value of monarchy today consists chiefly of two things," she said, more slowly than was her wont. "It gives a stability, a sense of continuity with the past, which is of value to a nation, as a sort of sheet-anchor; and then it gives a point, a focus, to that inescapable desire to serve or worship something greater than oneself. And now that in most countries (nearly all, except Poland and Hungary and Yugo-Slavia) religion has ceased to be a national concern and has become purely an individual one, there is a real need, hunger, for such a focus. People don't talk about it—they may not even be conscious of it; but it's there; and one proof that it *is* there is the highly conscious dictator-worship in the countries that have scrapped their monarchies."

"By Jove, I never thought of that. That's quite an idea," from the Colonel. "Carry on, Susan. I believe I've always thought all this, without knowing it, if you follow me."

Miss Glanfield smiled at him.

"You're like myriads of your countrymen so, Dick. Then of course monarchy hitches onto, in fact is an integral part of the aristocratic principle, with all that that stands for."

"Just what does that stand for, would you say?" Gloire asked. She was thinking of Larsen's words again.

"Service—responsibility. And the king hitches on to that because the monarchy is, in the old phrase, 'the fount of honour.' It's not nothing to a nation's outlook on life that its reward of service should be not wealth, but 'an honour.' Words mean something still. The papers talk nowadays of 'a barren honour,' meaning that there's no cash attached. But how can honour ever be barren? Honour brings its own lunch!" the Englishwoman pronounced, with great finality.

Dr. Crowninshield burst out laughing.

"Oh my dear, you're grand! And you're perfectly right. Do you remember the story in Herodotus, when Xerxes asked the Arcadian deserters, before the battle of Thermopylae, what the Greeks were doing? And got the answer—'They are holding the Olympic games, watching the athletics and the chariot races.' He asked what the prize was for which they contended, and was told it was a laurel wreath. And I guess you remember how mad Xerxes was when the son of Artabanus the Persian burst out—'Good Heavens, Mardonius, what manner of men are these against whom thou hast brought us to fight, who contend, not for money, but for honour!' I've always thought that a tremendous story. And I guess half France's terrible moral

220

sickness, and her fantastic concern with money and political power, the utter frivolity of her public men, is just because the principle of honour has been lost there. And I'm terribly afraid that to a great extent that goes for us too."

"Some nations can do without the dynastic principle, evidently," Miss Glanfield said politely. "The Swiss obviously can, and time may show that the Americans can too. But many nations just as obviously need it and want it. It's essential to the Yugo-Slavs, for instance—or really I should say the Serbs; and you tell me that it is for the Albanians too."

"Undoubtedly."

"But why," Gloire was beginning, when the door opened, and the stocky figure of their host appeared. Gloire got up and sat on one of the chairs; Dr. Crowninshield slipped off to see her patient; there was a fresh outburst of cheese and raki on the part of Valentino. Time had passed rapidly in their discussion; now, thinking up remarks and exchanging them through an interpreter it rather hung again; they were aware afresh of the hardness of those merciless chairs. It was a quarter to eleven—Gloire registered the fact by a surreptitious glance at her watch—when supper at last appeared and they drew up to the tartan oil-cloth.

Supper was rather a repetition of lunch. There was broth —with rice instead of noodles in it. There was the boiled lamb from lunch, cold; there was a freshly-roasted lamb hot—no doubt the one they had seen in the kitchen. A delicious novelty was wafer-like pastry with cheese in layers between—*burek*, the Robinsons said this was called. Miss Glanfield, dauntless as usual, thought up a number of questions for the Colonel to put to Lek-Gionaj; his answer to one of them she found extremely touching. "The Carruthers said they thought he talked German or Italian," she said—"do ask him, Dick, if he *really* doesn't? I should so much have liked to talk to him direct."

The Colonel passed this on, and a look of regretful resignation appeared on the Albanian's square shrewd face as he answered.

"He says—'No—my Father left me as he found me,'" the Colonel translated.

The meal was of course interminable; it went on till the guests were dropping with fatigue.

"Dick, it's half-past twelve; we really must go to bed," even Miss Glanfield was at last moved to protest.

"I don't see how *I* can suggest making a move, Susan."

"You must. Tell him the women are weak, or something. I shall die if I have to sit on this chair much longer," Miss Glanfield said firmly.

The Colonel still wavered, but Dr. Crowninshield intervened, and told their host that the women were weak, and had now been up and about for nineteen hours, which was more than they were accustomed to. Anyhow Lek-Gionaj rose, the red mattresses were brought in again, goodnights were exchanged, and he left his guests to themselves. The Colonel was excluded while the four women undressed, and was whistled in by his wife when they all lay under the red quilts.

"God, these damn flies are still at it!" Gloire exclaimed.

"They'll stop when I put out the lamp," said Colonel Robinson.

He was right. Presently a faint smoky aroma of paraffin filled the room, and very soon guests, flies, and all were silent and still.

12

MRS. THURSTON slept badly. Conflicting ideas surged to and fro in her mind, and she was just too sleepy either to sort them into order, or to banish them. Both Dr. Crownin-shield and Miss Glanfield seemed to feel that the life lived by Mme. Lek-Gionaj and her household had merits, and even beauties; but most of it filled Gloire with repugnance—the flies, the lack of plumbing, that wretched little baby; Mme. Lek-Gionaj's existence seemed strangely lacking in all that made feminine life as Gloire understood it agree-able. I *can't* see it!—she kept on saying to herself, as she turned to and fro on the red mattress.

External disturbances broke in on this internal conflict. Barely an hour after the lamp had been put out a thunder-storm rolled down the valley; fierce light flickered through the room, silhouetting the iron grilles sharply against squares of window suddenly a blinding blue, and bringing the samovar and the wireless-set into momentary gleaming prominence; thunder crashed overhead. And hardly had the storm passed and the moon again begun to cast scroll-marked squares of a more tranquil light on the floor than the barking of dogs began—at first faint and distant, but growing gradually nearer and louder as if some disturbing element were passing down the valley in the wake of the storm, rousing every homestead as it passed. Finally an absolute tornado of barking broke out quite close by; it was followed by a volley of shots, and then by a loud, desolate, and clamorous howling.

Gloire sat bolt upright.

"Goodness! What on earth is happening?"

"Only wolves," came briefly and tranquilly from the brass bedstead. "They'll go off pretty soon. I should go to sleep if I were you."

The barking and howling did eventually die down round the house, and the remoter sounds, receding into the distance up the valley, marked the return journey of the wolves. Gloire grinned a little to herself as she turned over for the twentieth time—wolves around the house were fun, anyway. And at last she did fall asleep.

Soon after six the party was aroused by the entry of Valentino with little cups of sweet coffee; then he brought in once more the china basin, the copper jar of cold water, the pink towel, and the Morny soap—Gloire watched between a yawn and a laugh as he set them on the floor of the hearth. She gulped down her coffee and attended to her face and hair; when Mrs. Robinson tactfully suggested to the Colonel that he should put his bandanna over his face while they dressed, she sprang up, washed, threw on her clothes, and set off downstairs. She felt fresh, restless, hungry, and greatly in need of the open air.

The front door was open and she went out into the courtyard. Here her attention was attracted by two men who were staggering from the direction of the kitchen, bearing between them an immense vessel blackened outside with smoke, burnished copper within; they carried it into the small wooden building which, standing alone, closed the courtyard to some extent on the fourth side. Gloire followed, idly curious to see what they were about.

The building was evidently the dairy, and on three sides was built entirely of narrow wooden slats like tile-battens, set an inch or so apart, so that the light entered freely; broad shelves ran right round the three open sides, and on them stood rows of very flat shallow vessels of some silvery metal which Gloire took to be pewter, but which was in fact copper washed with silver. The cauldron full of steaming milk had been deposited in the middle of the floor;

Mme. Lek-Gionaj, still wearing her magnificent costume of the day before, stood by it—seeing Gloire, she ordered one of the men to bring her a stool. On this Gloire seated herself, and watched the operations which the great woman now began. From the wall she reached down a gourd, round as a football, the stalk forming the handle; a small hole in the middle of the top was the only opening. With this, one would have thought, extremely awkward implement she proceeded to dip up the milk and pour it into the pans in a rather remarkable series of movements. Standing between the cauldron and the shelves she stooped, dipped, straightened up, and with a fully extended arm, by a bend of the hand and wrist tipped the milk into bowl after bowl —three, four, five; without spilling, without splashing. She only filled each bowl about half full, Gloire noticed; when nine or ten were done she moved a step, and stooped, dipped, rose, and poured as before. These movements had a deliberate and assured rhythm which impressed Gloire. Like all ski-runners, she knew about movement, its difficulty, its importance—as she sat there on the stool it struck her not only that Mme. Lek-Gionaj must have been doing this for years, in exactly the same series of motions, but that they were all part of a regular technique, as deliberate as the technique of Telemarks or Christys. Probably—it came to her with a sort of awe—others before her hostess had been doing this for centuries; the whole business was a traditional method of milk-pouring, carried out in the sequence and posture which endless experience had proved to be the best. No wonder she wore no apron, over all those glorious and unwashable clothes—she had no need of one, for she never seemed to spill a drop.

When all the bowls were half-full the Princess laid down her gourd, went out into the courtyard, and returned with a handful of small chips of wood; with these she made the round of the uneven hand-hammered bowls, pushing a sliver or two in under each of them till they stood steady and level—then, flinging the remaining chips out through the door with a bowler's vigour and accuracy, she took up the gourd and resumed her pouring, this time filling each bowl to the brim. Gloire watched, fascinated; she loved using her own body with skill, and would have liked to try her hand at pouring from that impossible gourd—but as she could not ask if she might she merely sat and looked on, smoking.

As the second pouring neared its end people began to flock into the dairy. Lisa and Marte appeared, and the household women—all with cups in their hands. The two men who had brought in the cauldron reappeared with a slatted wooden tray piled with square flat loaves of yellow maize bread, barely two inches thick; Mme. Lek-Gionaj sent one of them away again and from the tray held by the other broke pieces off the loaves, which she gave to her daughters and to the women, and then filled their cups with what was left of the milk in the cauldron. The second man now reappeared with a cup and another slab of bread; Mme. Lek-Gionaj filled the cup and gave it to Gloire, with a piece of the loaf—this was wheaten bread, evidently reserved for guests. Gloire was hungry, and the hot milk and saltless bread tasted delicious; perched on her stool, sipping and munching, she watched the rest of the household being given the first meal of the day. As their cups were filled the women and girls moved off, and others took their places; then it was the men's turn. They too came forward cup in hand; with them came Fran, the teamsters from the caravan, and the two gendarmes. All were fed, bowed their thanks, and moved off in their turn—Mme. Lek-Gionaj had a word for each, usually of a humorous nature, it seemed, for the dark faces broke into smiles, teeth flashed in laughter. Valentino appeared with several cups and took them away, filled, with a dish of the wheaten bread—doubtless to feed her companions, Gloire thought.

She looked round the dairy. The wooden ceiling was literally black with flies, and that mass of milk was unscreened, there was no sign of an ice-box to keep it in. Yet all those men and women, who presumably lived on it, and on the *kous* now setting in the bowls, looked perfectly healthy. Most extraordinary. Gloire was in fact strangely impressed by the scene she had just witnessed. "I can't see it," she had said in the night; now, in that dairy, she had seen—seen something, she felt wonderingly, of what Larsen had meant her to see.

But she ran away from her impression. Springing up with a smile and a nod to her hostess, she went out into the courtyard, and there encountered Miss Glanfield and Mrs. Robinson. Mme. Lek-Gionaj followed her, and greetings were exchanged—Mme. Lek-Gionaj's, as Mrs. Robinson subsequently told them, took the singular form of:

"Did you suffer?"

They decided to spend the day in an expedition up Mali Shënjt: Miss Glanfield could not see a mountain without wishing to go up it, and hoped for alpine flowers—Gloire was all for going up any mountain too. Since they were to leave next morning on their further journey they set off almost at once, in the rather faint hope that a return in the afternoon might produce the evening meal earlier than 11 P.M.; they took Fran, and Miss Glanfield's pony for the lunch—their gendarme escort of course accompanied them.

Mali Shënjt consists, as has been said, of a long ridge of mountain with pine-covered slopes rising to screes and open pastures, topped by a line of cliffs and pinnacles of bare rock. Their route led them by a good path through pine woods up to the pass at the head of the valley; there they turned left, and climbed over pastures and through more woods, till they came out above the tree-line on open slopes, half pasture and half screes fallen from the rocks above. As they climbed up over these, now in great heat, Colonel Robinson pointed out some small stone buildings

227

in a hollow by a stream—"That's where they come in summer."

"Who come?" Miss Glanfield asked.

"The Lek-Gionajs and the whole outfit, with the sheep and so on; they bring them up for the summer pasturing, and make cheese up here and hay lower down."

"Oh, just like the Senns in Switzerland," said Miss Glanfield, who was darting here and there, putting small bright flowers away in the short-cake tin.

"It would be rather fun to come up here then, wouldn't it?" Gloire observed, sniffing the keen mountain air like a dog, and looking round her with satisfaction.

"Shouldn't think it would suit you," the Colonel gibed; "it's luxury down at the house compared to what you'd get up here."

They lunched right on the top of the ridge; Miss Glanfield, who had given Fran her flower-press to bring along, spent most of the meal arranging her newest finds in it. Afterward she suggested to Gloire that they should look for a suitable piece of cliff and get some scrambling; the Robinsons found a patch of shade in which to snooze and settled down, the Colonel calling out that they ought to start back in an hour and a half, and not to do anything reckless—"We don't want any broken legs up here—damned awkward place for that sort of thing."

Gloire and Miss Glanfield kept along the crest for about half a mile, enjoying the vast view of tumbled country which extended in all directions, blue and white under the strong sun, till they reached a point where a big castle-like group of pinnacles jutted out from the main ridge. The rock looked pretty good, and they sat and examined possible routes up it. Having settled on a particular rib, they found a way down to its foot by a scree-filled gully, and then started to climb, Miss Glanfield leading. All went well for the first few minutes; the rocks were not difficult, and seemed fairly sound. But presently they reached a point

228

where a bulge above made it necessary to traverse to the left towards another gully, along a rather awkward ledge. It was not a dangerous place by mountaineering standards—the drop to the gully was only some thirty feet. Miss Glanfield moved carefully out along the ledge, testing each hand- and foot-hold—she reached with her left hand to a projecting leaf of rock, tried it, pulled on it, and then moved her left foot to a fresh hold; followed with her right, and cautiously transferring her right hand to the same hold, stretched out her left to feel for a further one. At that moment, with all her balance depending on one hand, the piece of rock came away in it, and before Gloire's horrified eyes her body swayed outwards, heeled over, and somersaulted down into the gully.

Gloire, who had been standing in a reasonably safe and comfortable position, watching the writer negotiating the traverse, turned quite sick; she found herself clutching the rock in front and felt her knees trembling under her; involuntarily she shut her eyes. Oh, but this wouldn't do, she thought, loosening her grip on the rock and trying to relax her muscles; she must pull herself together and go down. As she opened her eyes Miss Glanfield's voice called out—"Are you all right?"

"Yes" Gloire responded rather faintly; and now, looking down, she saw her companion lying on the rocks in the gully, with blood pouring down her forehead.

"Well, stay where you are a minute, and have a cigarette —it's beastly seeing anyone fall. When you feel quite steady come down. Do you think you can manage?"

"Yes, I'm sure I can," said Gloire more firmly, lighting a cigarette as she was told; she noticed with disgust that her hands were trembling. "Are you much hurt?" she called out.

"I don't know yet. I've cut my head. Damn this filthy blood!" Miss Glanfield also was trying to light a cigarette, and the blood was running down into her mouth.

Gloire, purely from shock, giggled. But the older woman's

229

composure restored her nerves—tossing away her cigarette, she started down the rib, circumspectly at first, then very fast; at the bottom she ran round to the foot of the further gully, scrambled up over the loose stones, and in a few minutes stood at Miss Glanfield's side. By this time the writer had shifted into a sitting position, and was rather ruefully examining her right leg, from which she had rolled up the blue trousers; there was a lacerated purplish patch half-way up it, from which a knob protruded horribly under the discoloured skin—Miss Glanfield prodded it gingerly with her thumb. Gloire felt sick again.

"I've broken the wretched thing, that's what I've done," the novelist said. "What an appalling bore!"

"What shall I do?" Gloire asked.

"Tie up this disgusting hole that bleeds, first," said Miss Glanfield, pulling a clean handkerchief out of her pocket, and taking the scarf from her neck. "Have a look at it, will you? It's up under my hair, I think."

Gloire dabbed away the blood with her own handkerchief, and gingerly pushed up the clotted hair; there was a large ugly wound in the scalp. She laid the clean handkerchief on it and tied it in position with the scarf.

"Good—thanks. Now you'd better go and tell the others. How furious Dick will be! If they bring the pony along here I expect I can ride it home."

"You're sure it's all right to leave you?" Gloire asked. —Miss Glanfield, in spite of her matter-of-factness, looked very white.

"Yes, perfectly. Tell Dick I'm sorry," Miss Glanfield called after her, as Gloire began to scramble down the gully.

When Mrs. Thurston, flushed and breathless, panted out her news to the Robinsons, the Colonel was at first incredulous. "How does she know she's broken her leg?"

"You can see the stump sticking up."

"Oh Lord."

"Susan would know, anyhow—she's done masses of First

230

Aid," said his wife. "But we must have a splint on it to get her down." She called to Fran and gave him some instructions; he promptly set off for the summer huts a little way below them, while Mrs. Robinson collected the pony. It had only a pack-saddle, but that would have to do.

"Let's send one of the chaps down for a pony with a proper saddle; it can come up and meet us on the pass," the Colonel suggested. This also was done, and without waiting for Fran the Robinsons and Gloire set off towards the gully. Gloire as she ran had marked down a small sheep- or goat-path across the screes, rather lower than the way she had come, and along this the little procession made its way. They were soon overtaken by Fran, bearing a small narrow board about three feet long, and a piece of clean coarse cheese-cloth. "What a sensible feller that is," the Colonel commented.

Gloire was worrying about how they were to get Miss Glanfield down the gully, which was steep, narrow, and full of loose rocks—the most awkward place imaginable in which to carry anyone; but when they reached the foot they saw that athletic and self-reliant woman making her way down it alone—on her back, walking on her hands and one foot, her injured leg stuck out in front of her, she had worked herself almost to the bottom.

While Mrs. Robinson padded the improvised splint with the Colonel's jacket and bound the leg to it with the cheese-cloth and everyone's handkerchiefs, Miss Glanfield apologised.

"I *am* sorry, Dick. A hand-hold came clean away. I had tested it, and it seemed perfectly good."

"You're the sufferer," said Colonel Robinson blandly. "But what licks me is how we're going to get you back to Rësheni. We can get an ambulance up there easily, of course."

"We must wait and see what Dr. Crowninshield says,"

231

said Mrs. Robinson. "What a mercy she's here. Now, Susan, how does that feel? Do you think you can manage like that?"

Miss Glanfield thought that she could—but in any case she had obviously got to. The Colonel and Fran carried her down the last few yards and she was somehow hoisted on to the pack-saddle; they set out, Fran leading the pony, and Mrs. Robinson, Gloire, and the Colonel taking it in turns to support the end of the broken leg. Some distance below the pass they met two of Lek-Gionaj's men and a saddled pony, and the transfer was made; Miss Glanfield proclaimed herself much more comfortable, but she was evidently in considerable pain, and they were all thankful when they mounted the ramp into Lek-Gionaj's courtyard, and the patient was lifted off and carried upstairs. Dr. Crowninshield came briskly in.

"Oh, so you are the casualty, are you?" she said coming over to the bed. "How far did you fall?"

"About seven yards," Gloire said.

"Un-huh. Well, first you'll have some of this," she said, pouring something into a medicine glass—"and then we'll have a look."

Most of the female members of the Lek-Gionaj family had come into the guest-room; Dr. Crowninshield, with good-natured firmness, turned out everyone but Mrs. Robinson, Gloire, and Zannell, her manservant, who brought in a large metal case of dressings and some enamelled trays. Quietly, expertly, with Zannell assisting, the old woman first attended to the head wound, shaving away the hair, disinfecting it, and putting in several stitches. "This will hurt, but I can't give you a local," she observed before doing so. "Oh well," said Miss Glanfield resignedly, and bore the stitches unflinchingly. Then it was the leg's turn. Yes, a broken tibia, Dr. Crowninshield pronounced—but she hardly spoke at all as she went about setting the limb, using a light splint, Zannell all the while assisting her with the silent expertness of a well-trained theatre sister. Finally she took a hypodermic from a smaller metal case, and prepared to give an injection.

"What's that?" Miss Glanfield asked.

"Anti-tetanus. I'm sorry, it will make you feel horribly. That's why I couldn't give you a local. But we have to do it with flesh wounds in this country. Zannell!" She and the Albanian raised the writer, gave her a lumbar injection, and then laid her down again.

"There!" Dr. Crowninshield said, dipping her hands in a basin of spirit held out by Zannell, and wiping them on a piece of gauze.

"Thank you very much," said Miss Glanfield, rather exhaustedly. She lay and closed her eyes—the shock, the ride down, and the rigid control she had exercised during the stitching and setting had pretty well worn her out.

"That's right—have a nap," said Dr. Crowninshield comfortably, and with a glance swept Mrs. Robinson and Gloire from the room.

"Well, how is she? And when can we take her down?" Robina said, when they were outside.

"She's been lucky," the old Doctor replied, lighting a cigarette. "If she fell thirty feet onto rocks—was it rocks?"—she turned to Gloire, who nodded—"Well, she was mighty lucky. She hasn't fractured her skull, and there's no sign of concussion yet; and that tibia is a reasonably straightforward break. I should say in about a month she might risk riding down to Rësheni, and get back to Durazzo by car."

"A month!—but my goodness, Dick has to be back in five days at the outside."

"So he may," the old lady said tranquilly—"but she can't go with him! We have to see if there is delayed concussion; there often is, with some people—and I want to start that leg right. Properly, of course, she should stay put for six weeks."

"But I must get back too," said Mrs. Robinson, much concerned.

"Well, you get right along back, my dear, whenever you want to. Zannell and I will look after her—she won't be our first patient."

"No, only that will mean such a fearful lot of extra work for you—her meals and everything; and she can't speak a word of Albanian, remember."

"I guess we'll manage," said the Doctor.

Here Gloire, who had been listening in silence, spoke.

"If it would be the least use I'll stay and help look after her," she said abruptly. "I could carry up her meals and all that, and do odds and ends." She spoke in her most casual manner. The old Doctor eyed her shrewdly.

"Why, that would be fine," she said. "That would be a lot of help."

Mrs. Robinson also looked at Mrs. Thurston, astonished and sceptical.

"But are you sure you'd want to? I mean, wouldn't you be miserable, with the flies, and no baths, and everything?" She was thinking that Gloire, uncomfortable and grumbling, might be more of a liability than an asset.

"No—I'd like to stay," said Gloire flatly. The picture of Mme. Lek-Gionaj in the dairy was in her mind as she spoke. There were other reasons too for a decision which surprised even herself, but uppermost was a desire to go on seeing what she had begun to see. "I'm not wedded to flies," she went on, "but I can put up with them for a month, I suppose."

"Well, that's settled then," said Dr. Crowninshield with finality. She gave Gloire's arm a little pat. "I'm glad—you'll help a lot. You can keep her company when I'm busy."

"How is Pieter's wife, by the way?" Robina asked.

"Badly," said Dr. Crowninshield briefly.

Colonel Robinson was as sceptical as his wife when he learned that Miss Glanfield would have to stay at Torosh for at least a month, and that Mrs. Thurston proposed to remain too. But Dr. Emmeline, who had somehow taken charge of the whole situation, seemed to have no doubts, and by the evening was already sending Gloire on errands downstairs, and telling her the Albanian word for this and that. Since the Robinsons had to return, it was evident that the sooner they left Torosh the better; the guest-room with five people in it was not much of a sick-room. Accordingly they set out next morning to return to Rësheni by another route. They took the gendarmes, Fran, and the caravan with them; Dr. Crowninshield was quite competent to organise fresh transport when the time came, and the Colonel undertook to leave word that an escort was to be furnished when required.

What with the tetanus injection and the sedatives with which the old Doctor plied her, Miss Glanfield was completely inert for the first forty-eight hours, and there was little Gloire could do for her but sit beside the mattress and keep the flies off while she dozed. On the second day, she asked Dr. Crowninshield if she could spare a few yards of medical gauze.

"What on earth for?"

"I thought I would make her a kind of mosquito-bar on a frame—just to go over her head and shoulders."

"Well, go ahead and make your frame, and I'll see if I have gauze enough for it."

Undeterred by this scepticism, Gloire went down into the valley, cut some willow-wands, indicated by signs to Lisa that she wanted string, and rather ingeniously constructed a frame like a small cape-cart hood, about three feet each way, with an arch in front to go over the body. The old Doctor set it over Miss Glanfield and then smiled dryly at Mrs. Thurston.

"Aren't you smart!" She rummaged in her metal case, and cut off a length of gauze. "There you are. Have you a needle?"

"Lisa will give me one, I guess," said Gloire, pleased and feeling at home in this New England atmosphere. She borrowed a needle and thread from Lisa, with whom she was coming to terms very happily by means of signs and smiles, and completed her frame. When it was set over Miss Glanfield, that lady proclaimed it perfect. It was the greatest boon to be able to lie and sleep, eat, or even smoke, protected from the ever-present flies.

After Colonel Robinson's departure the Prince and Pieter ceased eating with their visitors, so that the three women had the guest-room to themselves. Gloire proceeded to organise it according to her own ideas. She brought up hot water instead of cold in the copper jar, heated milk in the kitchen as required, and even brewed early morning tea in a jug.

By the fourth day Miss Glanfield was sufficiently re-covered to require conversation. She chatted a lot to Gloire, and after supper, when the old American was with them, steered the talk round to how she came to be doctoring in Albania, a subject on which she was still curious.

"Why, I always wanted to be a doctor," said the old woman, "from the time I was quite tiny—when other little girls were giving their dolls tea-parties, I had mine sick in bed, or else I was cutting them up! It worried my Mother terribly—she thought it morbid. And as a girl I was always reading every medical book I could lay my hands on. I decided when I was twenty that I would be a doctor, but of course over with us, in those days, that was considered just too bizarre for words. I had to wait till I was thirty to get my way."

"How did you manage it?" Miss Glanfield asked.

"God managed it for me—my dear Mother died," said the old lady calmly. "She considered my cutting up people even more morbid than the dolls. I just couldn't do it while she was alive; but as soon as she was dead I started right in." She spoke with a sort of determined relish. Both Miss Glan-

236

field and Gloire were startled by this unusual manifestation of filial piety.

"And where did you take your medical school? Harvard?" the writer asked.

"*No,*" said Dr. Crowninshield with tremendous emphasis. "Never at the place which refused to admit Sophia Jex-Blake as a student! She was my idol. No, I went to Edinburgh, as she did. That was in 1900, and I graduated, of course, in 1905."

"Oh, they had women medical students at Edinburgh as early as 1900, did they? I hadn't realised that."

"Yes indeed—there were quite a number around when I was there. Of course in those days we were taught in separate classes from the men, and had special wards set aside for our practical work—but we got our M.B., Ch.B., all right."

"And where did you start practising? And when did you come here, and why?" Miss Glanfield asked, with her customary eagerness. The old woman smiled.

"Why, naturally I thought of beginning back home, so I went over and started in the poorer parts of Boston." She paused, and began rolling herself one of the little Albanian cigarettes she had learned to smoke.

"And didn't it work?" Miss Glanfield enquired.

"Yes, it worked all right. But I found I just wasn't happy over there. I suppose I'd been in Europe too long."

Both Miss Glanfield and Gloire pricked up their ears at this.

"What was wrong with the poor old States?" Gloire enquired drolly.

"I was sort of conditioned out of the American Way of Life, I guess," the old woman answered.

"Was there too much prejudice?" Miss Glanfield asked.

"There was plenty!—but less than here. I got round that all right. No, I just felt I wanted to be where life was older. Anyway I came back."

"And how did you come to pitch on Albania to work in?" Miss Glanfield asked.

"Reading Miss Durham, primarily. While I was in Edinburgh I spent my vacations travelling—I went to Hungary, and I liked that, but I always preferred places that were wildish and off the beaten track, so I went to Greece and Serbia and Montenegro, and that had got me interested in the Balkans. Then just around the time that I came back to Europe Miss Durham's book on High Albania came out, and I read it at once—that would have been in 1909, I suppose—and it made me determined to see this place. So I came, and took a look around, and that decided me. In no other country I'd seen did the women and children need help so badly. I knew then, here was where I wanted to work, so I set to and got ready. I learned Albanian right away, and then I went back to England and took a course on children's ailments, and another at the Royal Free on gynaecology, and I put in some months on studying malaria and semi-tropical diseases; and then I got my gear together and came out here and started in. And here I've been ever since. So now you know it all!" she said, smiling very nicely at Miss Glanfield.

The writer was thinking that she wanted to know any amount more—the details of that beginning, the difficulties overcome. She looked with great liking and respect at the little figure sitting on the foot of her mattress, so small, so quiet, in which, for all her dry unemphatic speech, such a fervour for humanity burned; the New England neatness and precision in no whit affected by twenty years or more in these primitive surroundings. One of the best possible types, the good New Englander, she thought—durable and resistant as the native granite that juts out through the calm green of their pastures, just below the soil everywhere —a hint to the stranger of what to expect from the inhabitants.

"Did you never get discouraged or exasperated?" she asked.

"Both. Frequently. While the Turks were still here it was pretty hard going. But the need was just immense."

"What was your worst obstacle? Tradition?" asked Miss Glanfield, thinking of that cradle.

"Partly. I have a great respect for tradition, though. Poverty is their worst enemy."

"Ah yes. Are they stingy as well as poor?" Miss Glanfield asked. "I always think one of the worst troubles with any backward nation is their shrewd peasanty tight-fistedness and suspicion where money is concerned—it's what hampers the French so, oddly enough."

Dr. Crowninshield laughed.

"There's the Englishwoman speaking!" she exclaimed.

"Why the Englishwoman?" Gloire asked.

"Because the English are less mean about money than any nation on earth—I believe because they really *don't* care much about it."

"But we're not so rich," protested Miss Glanfield.

"Well yes, you are—anyway for a couple of centuries you were, richer than anyone else. But it's not a question of wealth, I guess, but of the attitude to wealth. Didn't someone once define a gentleman as a man who didn't care how he pronounced his words and never counted his change? Well, that's the British."

"No, we don't count our change much—but the curious thing is that our own peasantry, or what corresponds to peasants with us, don't either. They're really rather extravagant—they haven't the typical peasant attitude at all!"

"No, they have not. I think that's partly because the whole nation is more or less imbued with the gentleman tradition, and partly because of something that's just in the English blood, something sweet and spacious in it. What is much more peculiar," the old lady went on, "is why Amer-

239

ica, which has never had a peasantry at all, should have so much of that particular taint."

"You can't say Americans are mean," Gloire protested.

"No, Gloire, my dear, maybe not; but you can't say they're not money-conscious in a way the British are not. Money stands very high on our national priority list of values!—on the British it stands low. That's one reason why the debt question caused so much ill-feeling and misunderstanding. The war was won; there were a million Britishers killed as against 100,000 Americans; the British had lent freely to their Allies and borrowed quite as much for others as for themselves—and there was Uncle Sam shouting for his money! The British just couldn't understand that, and they despised America for it; our people were vaguely aware of their contempt, without understanding it either— and that just put an edge on the bitter feeling."

"It was all very unfortunate," said Miss Glanfield civilly. "Mind you, we should have liked to pay if it had been possible."

"My dear, you don't have to be diplomatic with me!" said Dr. Emmeline. "Of course you'd have liked to pay if we hadn't made it impossible with our tariffs, is what you mean —and you're quite right."

"If that's all true," Gloire said slowly, "mightn't it be partly because our huge mass of immigrants from Europe *have* been peasants? I mean, if there really is this feeling about money?"

"I think that's probably so, don't you?" Miss Glanfield said, looking at the Doctor.

"Maybe. The cause doesn't invalidate the effect."

The days slid by. Gloire found her time filled with small tasks. Every morning she stood in the dairy among the rest of the women with two cups, getting breakfast for herself and Miss Glanfield. The writer had to be given bed-baths, and after being coached for a day or two by the old Doctor, Gloire was able to undertake these. Besides washing Miss

Glanfield's person, she washed her clothes and handkerchiefs, and her own as well—this she did out of doors; Lisa was amused that she would not do them on a board at the stream, like everyone else, but insisted on using hot water, which she carried out from the kitchen. However they spread their launderings to dry on the same bushes, exchanging laughing comments; Gloire's brassière in particular aroused Lisa's curiosity and mirth. Carrying up water, emptying water, brewing tea, Gloire was forever in and out of the kitchen, and became quite familiar with the routine and work of the household—Marte coming in with a basketful of mulberry leaves and feeding the silk-worms, Lisa spinning wool, one of the older women weaving white homespun cloth at a hand loom, the constant preparation of food. The strangest thing about it all to Gloire was that the pattern of this archaic life was unrolled before her practically in silence, since she could not talk—to any purpose— with the participants; she moved through these scenes, but always a spectator. She said one day to Miss Glanfield that it was like living in a silent film.

"Do you mind?" the writer asked.

"No. It would be more fun if I could talk. I just have to watch more, to understand what's happening."

But the effect of this was to make her watch with much more attention than was her habit, so that the impact on her mind was sharper than usual. Going down late in the evening to warm the milk for Miss Glanfield's night-cap, she used to see what Dr. Crowninshield had called "the hearth school" in progress—Lisa, Marte, and some of the quite young girls sitting round the fire, while Mme. Lek-Gionaj held forth; the other women seated in the background, sewing or knitting, while the foster-mother, imported on Dr. Crowninshield's orders, squatted by the brown-and-gold cradle and suckled Pieter's first-born. Even without words, such a scene caught the imagination—the contrast between the deep tranquillity of occupation and attitude and the

241

eager attention on the dark faces in the firelight, the women in the background nodding approval at some familiar and expected episode. As for Mme. Lek-Gionaj, as a narrator she had obviously considerable powers; she used gestures sparingly but tellingly, and the inflections of her voice were a drama in themselves—Gloire used to linger, pulling her milk-vessel aside out of the hot ashes, merely to watch. All through these domestic scenes that great figure moved, calm, dominant, all-pervading—Gloire's eyes gradually came to convince her that Mme. Lek-Gionaj was indeed the mainspring of the whole mechanism of life in the Kapidan's house.

Though there was no fussy ostentation about it, there was order, too, and routine; and there was leisure. Gloire noticed that both men and women, in their spare time, were nearly always *making* something; the men carving a wooden spoon with an ornamental handle, or a distaff-top, or some tool for field-work—Lisa embroidering the front of a linen bodice or a shawl. They never seemed bored, though they had no newspapers to read, and if they had books, did not read them. But there was absolutely none of the sitting about yawning and painting one's nails and wondering what to do next with which Mrs. Thurston was so painfully familiar. Lisa, to her great entertainment, did stain her thumbnails with henna, and had a design in henna tattooed on the palms of her hands—a little sort of star or sun, with rays spreading from a circle and a tiny Greek cross in the center; when Gloire touched the other, uncoloured, nails enquiringly, Lisa laughed and shook her head and glanced meaningly in the direction of Mme. Lek-Gionaj, whose figure loomed in the distance—and Gloire understood that to colour more than the thumbnail was not approved of. But, unquestionably, Lisa was not bored; and to her surprise she found that she herself was not really bored either—she was too busy.

Poor Miss Glanfield, on the other hand, a fixture on her

red mattress under the gauze net, with nothing to read and no paper, even, to write on, was distressingly bored. She had a Balkan flower-book with her and spent her time at first identifying what she had already collected; but when that was done she had no resource but the society of Gloire and Dr. Crowninshield, who usually only spent the evenings with them. Miss Glanfield had not been so surprised as the Robinsons at Mrs. Thurston's decision to remain and look after her; but Dr. Crowninshield's words on the night of their arrival had inspired in her a rather unusual hesitancy in her dealings with Gloire. However the old Doctor's conviction that Gloire *had* a problem reinforced her own, and her natural kindliness (and the absence of any other occupation) made her really anxious to find out the source of that unhappiness.

She took her time over it. She talked to Gloire a great deal, getting onto easy terms with her, and observed with interest the way in which she was fitting herself into the Lek-Gionaj menage—through her she learned a good deal about it. She did not learn much from the silent visits which her hostess daily paid her, sitting massively smiling, regarding her with a wise examining air, and twiddling her thumbs. Lisa and Marte popped in at intervals, pretty and shy; one day Marte brought her a posy of flowers.

"Where did she get these, I wonder," the writer observed later to Gloire, examining the small objects, spread out on her red quilt. "I don't know this veronica, and she's only brought the flower, no radical leaves; if I had the whole plant, I could find out which it is."

"They went down to Mastrokol this morning to fetch silkworm cocoons," said Gloire, who had met the two girls and one of the women on their return and had watched the precious objects, wrapped in silk handkerchiefs, being fished out from inside their bodices, where they had been carried for warmth.

"Where is Mastrokol?"

243

"Down in the main valley, beyond Torosh. One of the married daughters lives there, and the cocoons came up by mule so far from Scutari; the girls went down with Maria to fetch them."

"I suppose that's too far to go and get another bit of this, root and all," said Miss Glanfield wistfully.

This gave Gloire an idea, and whenever she could she went off and collected a few flowers, complete with leaves and root, and brought them back to Miss Glanfield. To her rather amused irritation she was never left alone on these expeditions; sometimes one of the men about the place, more often Lisa or some woman was told off to accompany her. "It's no mortal use your kicking," Dr. Crowninshield told her when she protested—"Lek-Gionaj is responsible for you as his guest, and he wants no trouble; if anything happens to a guest it starts a far worse blood-feud than anything else could. Just make up your mind to it."

On one of these expeditions—fortunately when Lisa and old Maria were in attendance—disaster overtook Gloire's grey flannel trousers. They had gone up through the pine woods to the high pastures below the ridge of Mali Shënjt, and Gloire, scrambling up a boulder to secure a flower for Miss Glanfield, ripped a great piece out of the right leg, as well as splitting the seam. The trousers had been getting pretty part-worn anyhow, as Gloire truly said; they were cheap things concocted by a Tirana tailor in a hurry; on her rather discomfited return, with Lisa's apron tied over the gap, it was obvious that she must find something else to wear while they were repaired. Miss Glanfield's blue trousers were offered, but they were much too big. At this point Mme. Lek-Gionaj took a hand. Magisterially, with that remote amused expression, she took Gloire off to the women's quarters and there proceeded to fit her out with a complete Albanian dress—full white trousers, white embroidered tunic, a dark-green velvet jacket and a gaudy woven silk apron. She did this very carefully, holding various tunics

244

against her for the length; the green velvet jacket, con-
sideringly, she held beside Gloire's strange green-gold hair,
and then put her into it. There was no mirror—Gloire was
forced to admire herself as best she could in the top of
her flap-jack. She liked what she saw, and twirled around
gaily in front of Miss Glanfield and the old Doctor on her
return. Curiously, wearing the Albanian dress made her
feel increasingly at home in the Albanian household—the
women smiled at her as she went about among them. Even
when her grey trousers were mended she left them alone,
and flitted to and fro in her full white ones, her tunic, and
her pretty apron, thoroughly pleased with herself.

At last, one day when she and Gloire had been talking
about mountaineering, Miss Glanfield did what she had
failed to do on the walk to Shpali, and tackled, quite directly, the subject of Captain Thurston.

"I climbed once with your husband—did you know?" she
said to Gloire, who sat working at a piece of embroidery
which she was doing for Lisa.

The younger woman put down her work and looked
across at her with large eyes.

"No—did you really? When?"

"In 1914, early in July. We did the Nord-End of Monte
Rosa together. We were both in the Bétemps Hut one night;
I wanted to do the Nord-End and he was going to do the
Dufourspitze from the Grenz-glacier. But he had two
wretched guides—he was only a boy then——"

"Yes, he'd have been nineteen," Gloire interrupted.

"Oh, was he? Well, he looked even younger. Anyhow the
weather turned beastly in the night, snow was falling right
down to the hut in the morning, and his guides wouldn't
start. He was in absolute despair—it was his last day. I was
so sorry for him, I asked Christian if we couldn't take him
on our rope. You see, we had talked the evening before,
and I was tremendously struck by—well, by a sort of
religious quality in his feeling for mountains."

245

Gloire leant forward, her face transfigured by an intensity of expression such as Miss Glanfield had never seen on it, even in these last gay contented days.

"Oh, did you feel that? Even then? I mean so early on?"

"Yes, I did. That was why I was determined to take him. Christian wasn't keen—it was really a beast of a day, and it was taking a chance to try at all. Of course Christian knew that I could come down at least as fast as I went up, which is the vital thing," said Miss Glanfield with a sort of post-dated self-satisfaction which amused Gloire—"or that he and Knubel could sling me down!" she amended. "But I coaxed him—I told him what Antony had done; he'd had decent guides for the first three weeks, and had a terrific season—even traversed the Ober Gabelhorn from the Wellen-kuppe. So at last he agreed. Antony's guides were as thick as mud! I loved the tough way he paid them off, there and then, at four in the morning, and told them, in first-class Berner-Deutsch, that he hoped he'd never see them again, and that they would strangle themselves in their own rope getting down to Zermatt! The whole hut was laughing"—Miss Glanfield herself laughed at the recollection—"even the parties that weren't starting either."

"Fun!" Gloire said, her topaz eyes sparkling. "He could be most frightfully tough. Do go on. Did you manage it?"

"Oh yes, rather. The snow took off by the time we reached the foot of the rocks, and we had a grand climb. But it came on again coming down, and my nose got frost-bitten —I shall never forget Christian turning round, and coming back at me with a handful of snow, and plastering it all over my face, and rubbing it!" said Miss Glanfield with immense relish. "I thought he'd gone mad. After that we all tied handkerchiefs over our noses, and got down off the ridge out of the wind, and put brandy in our boots; and we ended up by making a new route down, because we didn't dare face the wind on the ridge again. But your husband was splendid—he was faster than I was," she said with charac-

246

teristic naïveté. "I remember Christian saying afterwards—
'Sie hatten recht, Fräulein. *Der* Junge wird ein berühmter
Bergsteiger sein.'"

Gloire's face dimmed at the last words.

"Well he did become a famous climber, but in the bloodi-
est possible way," she said bitterly. "He only made headlines when he was dead—and because of *how* he died. But"
—she made a visible effort—"can you tell me what he was
like, then? I mean, so very young? Was he shy? He was shy
later. How old were you, anyway?"

"I was twenty-four, and felt at least fifty!" said Miss Glanfield lightly. "No, he wasn't very shy, once we got started;
he was very courteous and formal at first—so amusing with
that baby face—and that made it all the funnier when he
came out with all those dialect oaths at his wretched
guides."

"You didn't keep up with him at all?" Gloire asked.

"Not really—no. You see the war came at once, and he
went out to France, of course, and I got married and worked
in London. He wrote to me once or twice—he couldn't
spell," said Miss Glanfield, smiling.

"He never could!" said Gloire, smiling too. "And that
was the last you saw of him?"

"No—I met him again once, oh, years later, at some Alpine dinner, when he made a most remarkable speech." She
paused, wondering whether she should mention that speech
to Gloire. "He said"—she went on—"and I so often thought
of it, afterwards—that however high a price the mountains
might exact from you, you would always remain in their
debt. That was true, you know, for people like him."

Gloire was looking in front of her.

"Oh, I know it was!" she said, turning now to Miss Glanfield. "I was there that night," she said almost wonderingly
—"we might have met then! But he knew so many climbers
that I didn't know. But"—and now bitterness and a sort of
despair came into her face and voice—"you know that wasn't

247

true for me! They hadn't given me enough—not to take away *that!*" she said, on a sudden sob. "If I'd had more climbing, with him, maybe I might have felt that way. But two seasons was so little. We were so happy," she said, with the utmost simplicity, feeling about for a handkerchief in her unaccustomed dress—failing to find it, she dabbed her eyes with the corner of her gay apron, as countrywomen the world over have dried their tears for generations.

The words and the gesture moved Miss Glanfield very much, but before she could speak, Gloire went on again. "I have so wanted to talk to you about him. I've never been able to talk to anyone about him. Everyone thought I was the wrong kind of wife for him; well maybe I was, but he was the right husband for me!" The flood-gates were opened at last, and the bitterness of years was pouring out. "They all thought I didn't care—but I *did* care. And if he'd lived, if we'd had more time, I'd have got different, I know I would. I did like some of his things—anyway I loved the mountaineering. I'd have got some good at that too."

"You did get good—I heard that much," said Miss Glanfield.

"Did you?" Gloire asked, with a sort of pathetic eagerness. "Did they say that?"

"Of course they did. You were very good, and very fast." Oh, how could one heal this piteous, resentful complex—loss, self-mistrust, and anger against "they," her husband's alien world—which Love, who can translate everything, had never had time to translate for her? That love had translated the meaning of mountains, had translated the ultra-English Tony Thurston himself, Susan Glanfield could not doubt. Pity moved in her, as it so easily did, almost unbearably.

But Gloire was going on again.

"You'll think this crazy, but someone has got to understand, some time, or I think *I'll* go crazy! And I've felt you would—or you might—ever since we picked you up by the

248

marsh that day. Can you see—it sounds selfish, but one is selfish, that's just one of those things—that I feel I've not only lost Tony, I've lost myself as well? I mean my chance of being different?"

"Yes, I do see that." She saw it quite burningly. "Oh Gloire dear, you can't think *how* I understand. You see, yourself is important too. And I'm sure he thought that, though probably he never said a word about it. He must have loved you so much."

At that, the younger woman burst into a passion of weeping. After the years of loss, of silence and deprivation, of cheap solaces and second-bests, in a loneliness she was too unskilled to break, this sudden fullness of comprehension was altogether too much for her. She sat sobbing, in that bare room, her honey-gold head bowed over a piece of Albanian embroidery, her tears falling fast on the lap of her Albanian dress. Miss Glanfield said nothing; she was putting out the strength of her soul for her in silence. No one has measured that strength, or its potency—only Pirandello has known and demonstrated that affection solves problems insoluble by reason or intelligence.

Mrs. Thurston's problem was not solved yet. She raised her head at last, and again dabbed her eyes with her apron. "I'm sorry," she said. "Look—I'd like to get this straight. It wasn't the mountains' fault—I don't feel that. It was those unspeakable men. They could have saved him if they'd had the guts. They didn't have them. Oh!" The tone of her voice was indescribable. "Are you surprised," she said, now in icy tones of hatred, "that I just don't feel the human race is worth bothering about, any more? People who could do that? Just leave him, to save their own skins?"

And that's how she's lived, Susan Glanfield thought, appalled by her voice—she's lived like that for years, with hatred in her heart. Poison—annihilation.

"Come over here," she said.

Very slowly Gloire came, and sat down on the red mat-

249

tress. Decisively, Miss Glanfield took her hand, and held it firmly.

"Listen," she said. "I do understand—all of it, I think. And it's natural in a way that you should feel like that. But you've got to stop, you know. That's not getting you anywhere—in fact it's moral suicide."

Gloire looked earnestly at her.

"Do *you* say that, too?" she asked.

"Of course. Who else does?"

"Mr. Larsen did."

"He would—naturally." (What in the world had passed between her and Nils Larsen in the train?) "And he's quite right. If you've just gone on hating the world at large, and trying to get all you can out of it and put nothing in, sort of scourging it—have you?" Gloire nodded. "Well, that's just hopeless."

"What can I do about it? I can't help feeling that way. I have tried, sometimes, and then it all comes back, and I get a sort of mad fit, and go and buy things, or have a terrific affair with someone—and then I feel beastlier than ever."

Oh, there you were! No tradition to steady her, no background of training and discipline; falling back on the cheapest, the flimsiest of material buttresses against despair, only to have them washed away, every time, by the tide of misery.

"Perhaps you can't feel otherwise, but you could make yourself *do* otherwise," she said, releasing Gloire's hand and lighting a cigarette. These flies have no sense of timing! she thought. "The only cure that I can think of—do you really want to hear?" she broke off.

"Yes—terribly."

"Well, I think it would be the exact opposite of what you've been doing—to set out to serve the human race, which has so misused you." (That was a fallacy, but it had to be accepted for the moment. It was not humanity as a whole which had injured Gloire, only a few men who found, in an emergency, that they were not as brave as they had thought.) "By trying to *do* it good, you would come to feel kindly towards it."

"Would I, I wonder?"

"I think you would. It always works with individuals."

"I don't see how I could serve it. What could I do?" Gloire asked.

"Anything would do—scrubbing floors in hospitals!" said Miss Glanfield vigorously. "But there's lots of time to think about that. At the moment you're serving humanity in the shape of one lady with a broken leg!"

Gloire laughed. "I like doing that," she said. "But——"

Dr. Crowninshield came in.

"How's Mrs. Pieter?" Miss Glanfield asked. Gloire got up and went to attend to her face.

"Better," the old Doctor said. "I believe she's going to pull through." She looked shrewdly at the others. "And what have you two been up to?" she asked.

"Oh, swapping lies—reminiscing about climbing," Miss Glanfield replied.

"H'm. 'Relate stories by day, you will go crazy'—that's what we say in Albania," said Dr. Crowninshield.

251

13

WARREN LANGDON was sitting in the garden-room at
Tirana, smoking and rather casually looking through the
monitoring of the Bari wireless one afternoon about three
weeks after Gloire had set off for Torosh; he was really
thinking about her, and wondering how she was getting on
up there. He and Miss Anne had been almost petrified with
astonishment when Colonel Robinson had rung up from
Lesh to report the accident, and informed them further that
Mrs. Thurston was staying on with the Lek-Gionajs to take
care of Miss Glanfield. "Well, I be darned!" Warren had
ejaculated. "Doesn't she want something sent after her—
clothes or something?" Warren was accustomed to Gloire
cabling all over the world to have something or other that
she wanted expressed or shipped or flown to wherever she
happened to be. "She didn't say so," the Colonel had replied. And hearing that Dr. Crowninshield was also there,
and that nothing seemed to need doing, Warren had relaxed,
still marvelling. It was pretty restful without Gloire, he
conceded to himself, but he wondered frequently how she
was making out.

The servant brought in a card. Warren took it from the
silver tray—M. Nils Larsen, he read. He turned it in his long
fingers, as if that would help him to place the name. No—
he didn't know anyone called Larsen, and yet he was sure
he had heard the name lately; it was lodged in that curious
upper limbo of the mind where the recent past, imper-
fectly attended to and therefore unpigeonholed, resides.
Not being an Englishman, Warren did not always have to
have a strong reason for seeing anyone; it was sufficient if

there was no reason for not seeing them. There was no earthly reason for not seeing Mr. Larsen, whoever he might be, and he told the servant to bring him in.

He rose to greet a tall man, heavily built and yet athletic-looking, with a pale, rather heavy, Scandinavian face, a brow of great intelligence, pale grey eyes, and a great mouth severe as a lawyer's. The stranger apologised civilly for disturbing him, and came to the point at once.

"You had, I believe, a Mrs. Thurston staying with you— so they tell me in the hotel; and that she is gone to the mountains, and there had an accident. I am come to enquire after her."

"No, it wasn't Mrs. Thurston who had the accident, it was the other one, Miss Glanfield. She broke her leg climbing some rocks up at Torosh, and Mrs. Thurston stayed on to look after her."

"Miss Glanfield? Pardon, but not Miss *Susan* Glanfield?"

"Susan's the name," Warren said, more and more intrigued by his visitor. "You know her too?"

"Yes—I did, years ago. But I did not know that she is here also."

"It was Miss Glanfield who very kindly took Mrs. Thurston along on the trip," Warren said, memories of his various embarrassments still lively. "She's a mighty nice woman."

"She should be. Young, she was very nice," Larsen said, with a simplicity which amused Warren. "I am sorry she is hurt. She was a very fine climber in old days."

"You a climber too? I suppose you were a friend of poor Tony Thurston's?" Warren asked; his visitor did not look at all likely to be a friend of Gloire's.

"No, I never knew him."

"Oh, so you're a friend of Gloire's, are you?" Warren pursued.

"Not a friend, no. I am interested in her," the stranger said surprisingly. "I should perhaps explain," he said gravely, without any cheap ingratiating smile. "I met Mrs.

253

Thurston in the train not long ago, and we talked much—about many things. I thought her unhappy, and her ideas false. I hope this does not offend you?"

"My dear man, I couldn't agree more," said Warren heartily; he was beginning to be delighted with this interruption to a hot dull afternoon. "She's pretty spoilt, is poor Gloire, and uncommonly futile in most of her ideas." He looked now keenly at his visitor from under his jutting eyebrows—the name Larsen popped up out of limbo, with where and when he had heard it: Gloire in the car, driving down from Cattaro—asking if he knew a man called Larsen, who was in the I.L.O. "Say, you didn't advise her to come to Albania, by any chance?"

"I did—yes. But I did not expect that she would," Larsen replied.

Warren laughed loudly.

"Oh, so you're the guy that caused all the trouble!" he said. "Did you tell her she had to go to Torosh at Whitsun, too?"

"I did this also—yes. Did it make trouble? I am sorry."

"Oh, nothing to worry over. She was just set on getting to Torosh, and it didn't happen to be convenient. But for Miss Glanfield, who's a most merciful person, she wouldn't have gone. But we couldn't make out why she was so keen on going there—Gloire's not much of a one for unsophisticated places and missing her comforts, as a rule. Now we know," Warren said, pushing a bell, and laughing again. "Have a drink? You like Old-Fashioneds?"

"Very much. Thank you." But Larsen picked on one word in Warren's remarks. His eyes, as deep-set as his host's, but pale where the other's were dark, regarded him earnestly. "Merciful—yes, she would now be that. She also thought, then, that Mrs. Thurston needed help?"

Warren's phrase, like so many of our phrases, had in fact sprung from an intuition below the level of his conscious mind. He was a little embarrassed at having it pinned down;

254

he had never thought whether Miss Glanfield was merciful or not—merely that she was intelligent and agreeable and "mighty nice."

"Oh, I wouldn't know that," he disclaimed. "I just know that she took her along when Gloire asked her to." He changed the subject. "Are you not in the I.L.O?"

"Yes."

Pretty interesting, Warren thought that must be. Was he investigating in Albania?

"No, here I am on leave. I was in Sofia—the chocolate and the tobacco factories. There is not much industry in Albania to investigate."

"No, thank God!" Warren exploded. "That's what makes these people what they are. But what they should do, of course, is to grow fruit."

Larsen was now as delighted as Mr. Langdon to meet such a kindred spirit. The deep-set grey eyes gazed earnestly into the deep-set brown ones.

"Oh, but how right you are! This is extraordinary."

"What's extraordinary?"

"That an American sees this—the perils of uncontrolled industrialism. For the whole Balkans, just now, this question is crucial."

"Some Americans see things," Warren said cheerfully. "But why do you say that this question of industrialisation is crucial for the Balkans right now? Do you think they consciously want their standard of living raised, at this moment?"

"That a little, yes; perhaps. But the real reason is other, I think. They have come to feel that only industrialised countries can have an efficient armaments industry, and they all want armaments industries, to be able to protect themselves from aggression, and to fight with a chance of winning. This is partly true, of course."

"I would say it was a hundred per cent true," Warren stated. "What's the catch in it?"

255

"That armaments alone are not enough, without the fighting spirit; just as the bravest army is ham-strung without modern equipment. That is the fallacy. There are countries which have some of the best-equipped armies in Europe, and armaments industries so large that they can export arms, even—but it does not follow that if it came to the point, they would fight."

"That's very interesting," Warren said. "But most of these fellows down here have the fighting spirit all right—a darn sight too much of it!"

"That is true," Larsen said. "And it connects with the other fallacy, that any of these small countries could resist an aggressor alone. Their only hope of *military* security would lie in co-operation, plus armaments. But they find co-operation much more difficult than anything else. And they do not see the fallacies, so the desire for industrialisation increases."

"Do you think it's inevitable, then?"

"To some extent. I think some improvement in their conditions even most desirable, if it could be so controlled that they would get the benefits of better economic conditions without the evils of industrialisation."

"But is that possible?" Langdon asked. "Industrialisation seems to me to run along the same old lines everywhere."

"But of course it is possible, Mr. Langdon. It is only that it has never been attempted, except in Hungary, a little. The industrial revolution occurred first in England, a small crowded island, and because the English are unimaginative and have little aesthetic consciousness, they made every possible mistake. England set a disastrous pattern for industrialisation, and all over the world, every country, so far, has followed that pattern—even your own America, with its vast spaces, and for all the lip-service done there to individualism."

"I'm glad you admit the British started it," Warren grinned.

256

"Yes, but they had this excuse—industrialisation was then a novelty, an experiment, and the consequences were not foreseen. Now they are known, so for other countries—you will pardon me—there is no such excuse. Britain is now trying to coax her people back onto the land; then why take them off it here? These people's houses are rough, but they are not slums, and there is no slum mentality—there are no bums and hobos in the Balkans. Everyone knows where he belongs."

"We have just aped the British right enough," Warren said. "But how would you apply all this, down here?"

"Create light industries, and disperse them, Mr. Langdon. Have *one* factory in each village, as they are beginning to do in Hungary: a sugar factory here, a starch factory there; a boot factory, a leather factory. Let the people get the economic benefits of factory wages, and yet enjoy the values of life in a small village, on the land."

"That would add to your freight charges."

"It would. But village workers could afford to take lower wages, because of their fields and gardens, their geese and pigs and cows; so your costs would not suffer in the end, if you could keep out the paid agitators, who cannot see that high wages alone do not mean prosperity. And if such a distribution of industry did shave a fraction off profits, is it not now time that the human race started to consider what production is *for*? Should we not think in terms of human well-being as well as in terms of shareholders? In terms of men and women? Would it not pay a State better to have a population of people like the mountaineers here, rather than of slum-dwellers? The English are now paying in taxation, and spending on social services, far more than the fraction of profits they might have lost by a dispersal of their industry."

Warren got quite excited by all this. He sat forward and smote his knee.

"Mr. Larsen, you've got something there! I believe that

is the solution. I believe that would work! But what about agriculture, down here? These countries are primarily agricultural—in Bulgaria they are pretty good at it. Can't you tie that in, some way?"

"But certainly. It must be tied in. In Yugo-Slavia they have already started to use their coal and iron and pigs, in combination, for a canning industry. Pork Goulasch, tinned hams. Already these are not so bad—they could be better. And it will pay them much more to produce articles of world export value than to sell their pigs as live or dead meat to Germany. At present, all these countries are economically in the pocket of Germany."

"That's right enough for Yugo, her canning," Warren said; "but these poor hicks produce pretty erratically. Some of their stuff's O.K., but some is very low-grade."

"Yes, what is needed is grading—under Government authority. See what Bulgaria has done with her white grapes. By having them properly graded and packed, she has captured the Eastern European market, in a few years. There must be grading; the purchaser must be able to count on a second and third consignment being of the same quality as the first—otherwise the price will remain low. Roumania produces wonderful clover and beetroot seed, but it is ungraded, so she gets about one-third of what it is worth; her beans go to Belgium to be graded! Economically, this is insane."

"I'll say it's insane! But I don't see yet just how you're going to get round it. These people are so backward and so individualistic, and always at each other's throats."

"Yes. It would take time and patience. These countries would need some financial assistance, and a great deal of unselfish and very wise advice. They would accept both. But it would not be necessary to change the *methods* of agriculture much; there is no need to go through such an agonising and disruptive process as setting up collective farms on the Russian model. Some improvements, yes. But if each State enforced grading for its export surplus, and consumed the lower-grade stuff at home, and if, further, some sort of inter-state Trading Commission negotiated all the sales for the whole of the Balkans, Balkans produce would take a decent place in world markets, at decent prices. They would not be, as now they are, economically at the mercy of one country."

Warren smoked and thought.

"Economic co-operation's easier than political, I guess," he said. "It might work, even down here. What else?" Warren was one of those unusual people who did not always want to put forward his own ideas, competitively, in conversation; if the other person's notions were interesting, he wanted to hear them.

"Two things—communications, and electric power. Balkan communications are puerile, at present. They should be made widespread, and good. And roads should *cross* frontiers, instead of avoiding them as a matter of policy. Also here, the possibilities of hydro-electric power are almost unlimited; and that means, or can mean, clean cities and factories. With hydro-electric power, there need never be a Black-Country, as in the English Midlands." Larsen paused, but as the other merely nodded, he went on: "With the potential water-power that exists all through the Balkans, each peasant's house could have also piped water and electric light, as they do in Switzerland; this comfort, this convenience, women could have here as there, without altering their wholesome peasant mode of life. There is nothing to prevent this type of development but the current superstition that city life is better than country life, and that to mass human beings together makes in some way for greater efficiency than leaving them to work in small groups. Pure superstition, this!"

Warren laughed again at his energy.

"You wouldn't find so many people to agree with you there."

259

"No, I should not. What is needed is for a prophet to arise and preach the gospel of individuality, real individuality, of the Good Life in the modern world, with industry and mechanisation strictly subordinated to human values, that is to say, to moral and aesthetic values. If such an idea were made politically fashionable, all these small nations would follow suit. As it is, they seek to follow the English or American pattern."

"Which is worst?"

"You forgive me if I say, the American—because mechanisation has gone further there, and in America there are no such countervailing influences as monarchy, as aristocracy, and the country life as an ideal. The retired English industrialist, what does he do? He buys a country house and sets up as a country gentleman—and the little shopkeeper retires to a country villa and digs his garden. In America, this is not an ideal."

"It is not—you're right there. A summer home on Cape Cod or in Vermont is about as far as it goes," Warren observed. "There wouldn't be much sympathy over with us for your ideal of village life. We don't have villages; we call them small towns anyway. I think we're pretty urban-minded. I'm not sure that I myself quite understand why you're so keen on villages—I mean, I see the results down here, but I don't feel sure why village life produces those results."

Larsen looked at him.

"This you will find absurd, what I say," he said—"but it is true. The village life is a *full* life, because it is interesting. The full life depends, not on the range of experience but on the intensity of the interest, the emotion involved, and on its being a personal interest. Life at second-hand, through the film, say, is wide in range, but shallow; not full. Such a full life these Balkan villagers enjoy who live in familiar communities and know their neighbours. I would leave them there, sustained by their traditions, but with their

260

methods of husbandry slowly improving, with their return for their labour slowly rising, and with the woman's burden eased by water and light in the home. One can have these," Larsen said quaintly, "without worshipping showers and radios, if one preserves one's sense of values. But humanity at present has lost its sense of values. And for this, I chiefly blame advertising. In the Balkans of which I dream—a dream which could come true—" and now he spoke with immense energy—"I would forbid advertising by law!"

Warren laughed.

"Why that last?"

"Because advertising confuses values, Mr. Langdon. By appealing either to fear, or to vanity, or to covetousness, it very skilfully insinuates false values. You are a better and more civilised citizen if you have a radio; more men will love you if you use Palmolive; if you do not use someone's tooth-paste you will have halitosis! Everyone in the Balkans has halitosis, because they eat strong-tasting food; but they do not have stomach ulcers or nervous ailments, and as no one minds their breath, they suffer no embarrassment. Advertisement," he went on, "is a purely parasitic activity; it forces goods for which there is no real need or demand on a foolish or even a reluctant public, always by appealing to their lower instincts." He leaned forward in his chair, his ugly intelligent face serious, earnest—Warren found him very appealing. "May I speak freely to you? For America is the paradise of advertisers."

"Go right ahead," Warren told him.

"What has two generations of high-pressure salesmanship and scientific advertising done to your people, Mr. Langdon? Do you realise, I wonder?"

"It's made them rich," Warren said, smiling. "But what else? I daresay it's done a lot that I don't see—one doesn't notice what's familiar. Go ahead and tell me—I want to hear. You've been to the States, I imagine, and seen us with your

261

old wise European eyes." He was not ironic, and Larsen knew that he was not.

"Yes, I have. Thank you. This is important, because of the great economic power of your country. I do not seek to provoke, or be offensive," Larsen said, pleasing the Bostonian more and more by the naturalness of his honesty. "It is because of the importance."

"O.K. Well go ahead and tell me," Warren repeated.

"Mr. Langdon, advertisement has destroyed the power of discrimination with your people—who are by nature shrewd and careful, for the most part. 'It's the name that counts.' 'You can rely on the brand'—these are the slogans. The Frenchwoman, in a shop, pulls the sheet, the stocking—tests the weave and the strength and the quality; she examines, because she *knows*. The American woman does not know, any more; and often she does not go to the shop; she buys by mail order a product whose name she has seen in glossy pages of magazines, or has heard on the radio. This is bad for her; she abdicates her human privilege of personal judgment; she is now at the mercy of clever and unscrupulous commercial suggestion. But this is not without effect on her other activities—and on those of her husband. They do not, either of them, listen to or read the news and form their own opinions, as the European bourgeoisie does; they read their favourite commentator, and take *his* views on events; they switch off the news, and switch on to Mr. Kaltenborn or Mr. Swing. These are good clever men; they are honest; they do their best. But man is a thinking animal—and if he lets even Mr. Kaltenborn think for him, he is foregoing his natural rights."

Warren laughed.

"I see you know us pretty well, Mr. Larsen," he said. "Carry on. I hadn't thought of that effect on our people."

"You are very kind. That—kindness—is a thing your people have not lost! But all this is also bad for the commercial men. In Europe, a product must be good, or it will not sell

262

in competition with other products; with you, it is enough to *say* that it is good, often enough and sufficiently loudly. The keenest competition is not in the making of things but in the advertising of them! When one of your soap manufacturers decides to launch a new product, what does he do? He does not find something new, or better—no, he has a Board Meeting to invent a new name!"

Warren laughed loudly.

"You do know the works," he said. "Go on."

"When he has chosen 'FLUFFOX, THE SUDSY SOAP'," Larsen pursued, grinning amiably, "he buys radio time and advertising space, hires a broadcaster with a name or someone to write a 'soap opera', and arranges a new packing. Only then does he begin to think of his product, which will differ little from the old one. I do not know exactly what are the relative costs of pushing an article and producing it, in America today—would you say fifty-fifty?"

"Around that. Maybe nearer sixty-forty. You see it's no good producing a thing unless you sell it, and selling is a terribly expensive business—you're quite right."

Larsen looked at him.

"Have you ever seen the advertisement of the Rolls-Royce car?" he asked. "It is small, like a post-card, and it just says—'Rolls-Royce, the best car in the world.' Yet I understand that these cars sell well," he said blandly.

The American laughed again.

"Fair enough. They do. They don't need a two-page spread."

"But why not?"

"Because everyone who knows about cars just knows that the Rolls *is* the best car in the world. That's all right, I give you that. That particular luxury product sells itself. But I'm not sure"—Warren was frowning and peering out at the sunny garden now—"that you could have got our tremendous expansion of industry in the United States without advertising. And I wonder if the effects are so bad as you think."

"I may of course be mistaken. You think it does not matter if people cease to discriminate, to judge for themselves?
I should have feared that this might put them at the mercy,
not only of clever salesmen, but of political charlatans also.
I mean this—if 'talking up' an inferior article of commerce
causes it to sell as well as a better one, do not words tend
to become more important than facts? This seems to me a
real danger. Are you quite satisfied with the political judgment of your compatriots?" the Swede asked, more blandly
than ever.

"No. I'm not. No one could be. It's immature and un-
stable; and we are very ignorant. A French peasant will give
you shrewder views on the current world situation than
most Congressmen," Warren said, his lined face looking
worried. "But we're a young nation, remember."

Larsen smiled, but said nothing. The American smiled
too.

"Thank you for not coming out with Oscar Wilde's crack
about the oldest thing in America being her theory of her
youth," he said. "I guess it was in your mind." Larsen continued to smile—it had been—but he said nothing.

"I'll have to think this through," Warren went on. "It's a
new idea to me; one accepts, in the strangest way, the con-
ventions in which one is brought up. But I can see that for
the Balkans of your dream—and it's a pretty good dream—
it would be as well to cut out advertising. I'm sure you're
right about tradition, too, being the thing to keep here. We
haven't it, and we tend to write it off as fettering. But it
isn't necessarily fettering—I've learned that. For old nations,
it's the roots to the tree. It nourishes. If you cut off the roots
you cut off the new growth; if you denounce the past you
kill the future. I guess that's what's wrong with Russia.
Sooner or later, she'll have to resume her past." He smiled.
"And we'll have to grow one! But now—won't you dine with
us, tonight? My sister would be delighted."

Larsen did dine with them, and Miss Anne was delighted

with him. Her definiteness responded to his. Warren introduced him as "a friend of Gloire's," and Larsen very politely corrected him with—"an acquaintance, please, Mr. Langdon." She liked his intelligence, his directness, and he was agreeably well-informed. After dinner they sat again in the garden-room, among the sweet scents moving on the light air, while the colours of the flowers outside became more poignant as the dusk dimmed them. And Warren raised the question of advertising again. His hyper-conscientious Bostonian mind had been working and worrying on the view presented by the Swede all the evening, and he spoke of it at some length.

"You could not get a comparable volume of business without it," he concluded.

"Yes, that is true. But for whose benefit is the business?—the manufacturers', or those who are cajoled or frightened into buying the goods?"

"Well, I would answer that the business gives employment, and having the extra goods at least does people no harm." He looked worried again. "You sound to me like a reactionary, and yet I would hesitate to think you that," said Warren, who by now greatly liked Larsen.

"Perhaps I am reactionary," the Swede said. "But I would like to make my position clear. There are forms of advertisement that are quite reasonable—it is fair to let people who live far from cities know what is available. When I was a boy, I stayed often with an English aunt of mine, and she used to buy her wool from a shop in Wales—I even remember the name," he said, smiling—"Price Jones. They sent out a small printed list of garments, of qualities of wool, and of prices—and she wrote and bought from them. This is reasonable. But in that catalogue were no pictures of glamorous ladies in woollen combinations, and no suggestion that one would die of pneumonia if one did not wear wool."

Miss Anne, who was knitting, smiled approvingly.

265

"Old-fashioned, I am," Larsen pursued, "for I am still concerned with such matters as religion and spiritual values. What I find most injurious to mankind in modern advertising is the constant appeal to material standards and values, the elevating of material things into an end in themselves, a virtue. Religion teaches us to sit lightly to this world and to material possessions, and to turn our hearts and minds to what is fair, lovely, and of good report. But St. Paul did not mean lipsticks, or nail-varnish or brassières! I would paraphrase what Lord Shaftesbury said about child labour in factories: if business expansion has to depend on the suggestion—the most skilful and unremitting mass suggestion ever devised, at vast expense—that material things are immensely desirable, and seeks to focus the whole attention of a nation on material things, day in and day out, then let business expansion perish! It is not worth having at the cost of a nation's soul."

Warren, more troubled than ever, sat silent; Miss Anne nodded approval, while her needles clicked and flashed.

"This is not only in America," Larsen went on. "The tendency is everywhere—but in America it is most, and in America most vaunted, advertising. The modern means of vast production and the desire for great sales have set the whole world this problem; but it must be solved somehow, or the soul of mankind will perish. I say to you, as I said in the train to Mrs. Thurston—'Where a man's treasure is, there will his heart be also.' I asked her, and I ask you—where is America's treasure?"

Unexpectedly, Warren laughed.

"Gloire is what every woman reader of magazines in the States would like to be," he said; "she's just the type they aim at."

"It's not a high type," said Miss Anne, knitting furiously.

"But internally, is not Mrs. Thurston most unhappy?" Larsen asked. "This was my impression."

"I think you were right," Warren said slowly.

266

"Of course he was right," said Miss Anne. "Idle, selfish people are always unhappy."

"But what do the advertisements in the American magazines suggest for the interior life?" Larsen asked.

"Nothing. And Gloire is the ultimate product of that view of life." He turned round to the Swede. "Tell me why you sent her here."

"I spoke at random," Larsen said. "Hungary, Poland, Albania—any one of these would have served to show her what I wished her to see. But it really did not occur to me that she would come."

"What did you wish her to see?"

"The foundations on which European civilisation is built —life lived in relation to the soil, with tradition and religion as ever-present, operative conditions. To see, to know, is better than to read or to be told. I thought this might help to clear her mind."

"Well, she's having a fine spell of seeing, getting stuck up there with the Lek-Gionajs," Warren observed, chuckling. "I've been wondering a lot how she's getting along. Poor Gloire, her mind could do with some clearing."

"You have known her long? You know how she came to be as she is? I wondered at her misery, her boredom, her despair," the Swede said.

"I've known her from a child," Warren answered. "But— don't you exaggerate? Boredom, yes; but misery, despair?"

"I think I do not exaggerate," Larsen said simply.

Miss Anne spoke.

"Gloire was always spoilt, Mr. Larsen. Her mother, who was an excessively foolish woman, with more money than is good for anyone, and no background, spoilt her to death. Spoilt people are always miserable, and if you are miserable long enough, I fancy you end in despair." Her needles flashed. "Gloire never had any discipline. No one ever said 'You must' to her, and she never learned to say 'I ought' to herself."

Larsen fixed his pale gaze on the Bostonian spinster. She was likely to prove more fruitful than his host, he thought.

"The husband?" he asked.

To discuss a family friend with a stranger was contrary to all Miss Anne's habits and principles; but she had taken greatly to Larsen, and was impressed with the degree to which he had taken Gloire's measure, and with the quality of his interest in her.

"A very fine man," she pronounced. "The best type of Englishman. Gloire had the quite undeserved good fortune to marry him—but then everyone is at the mercy of her type of looks! I fancy he might have made something of her, all the same. His death was a tragedy, in every way."

"She loved him—yes?" Larsen asked.

"She did," Miss Anne pronounced, with immense finality.

Warren fairly gaped. Anne speaking with such certainty about Gloire's love life was a portent in itself—but that she should do so to a man she had never met before that evening was incredible.

"And I do believe she tried," Miss Anne pursued. "Lady Mary—his mother—hated the marriage, pretty naturally, but of course she behaved perfectly. The British are much more tolerant of out-breeding than we are in New England; their men go their own way, and their society is strong enough to impose its own traditions on the wives they bring home. If Captain Thurston had lived, he would have made something of Gloire."

"Maybe Albania will do the trick," Warren said. "That's what you hoped, anyway," he said to Larsen.

"It is what I suggested," the Swede amended.

The Langdons were having a dinner-party later in the week, and next morning, on Miss Anne's suggestion, Warren rang up the Continental and invited Larsen.

"I am so sorry—no. I shall not be here," the careful accents came down the telephone.

"Isn't that too bad. You're leaving so soon? We had hoped to see a lot more of you."

"When I come back, I hope. I am only going up to Torosh."

"To see how much Gloire's seen?" Warren asked, grinning down the telephone.

"Yes—a little. And to see Lek-Gionaj. And my old friend, Miss Glanfield. There will be much to see," Larsen replied, unperturbed. "And it is too long since I walked through Albania in spring."

Later—"No, he can't come," Warren reported to his sister. "He's going up to Torosh to see the girls!" He was greatly amused.

"Which, I wonder?" said Miss Anne.

14

LARSEN enjoyed walking through Albania in the spring again. He travelled light, with an interpreter and a couple of ponies; he whistled as he climbed up on to the Malsi ridge, where the silvery verbascums which Miss Glanfield had picked in bud stood now as tall yellow candelabra; he sang as he ran, loose-legged, down through the woods to the Malsi spring, where he too drank; he lay there and smoked for a long while, listening to the nightingales, and then went on and camped at Shpali.

Larsen was perfectly clear as to which of the two women he was going to see—Mrs. Thurston. But he was extremely pleased to be about to meet Susan Glanfield again. He knew quite well that to meet someone after twenty years may easily prove a disconcerting experience, but he allowed for this, and did not worry about it. She might be grey; she might be stout; he did not expect her to be as she had been. She had been a delightful person, and he was confident that he would find her essentially delightful still. There had never been any hint of love between them; their talk had been all of books and poetry and mountains—and sociology, after the fashion of their day. Larsen never even asked himself, as he lay in his sleeping-bag that night under the great ash-trees at Shpali, whether he had been at all in love with her—he was so sure that he had not. But how enormously he had liked her. She had climbed beautifully, with strength and speed and great spirit; she had been charming to look at; poetry had breathed from her, apart from her pretty verses; she had been ardent and intelligent. And she had remained in his mind all these years, a tri-

umphant figure of youth and romance, with a virginal quality that held some antique spell. *Vera incessu patuit dea*—he
remembered how often the words had sprung into his mind
as he watched her, tall and slender, walking into a hotel
dining-room in the Alps, fresh from achieving some tremendous expedition. But there had never been any emotional nexus, and he looked forward with the old cool
pleasure to their meeting. Time has little power over the
qualities for which he remembered her, and he was not
afraid.

But Mrs. Thurston—her he had come to see. He had taken
these days off, deliberately, to come and find out what she
was making of Albania, and what Albania was making of
her—that very agreeable clever American was quite right.
Larsen had been greatly disturbed by Mrs. Thurston, and
greatly touched that she had taken his casual advice. His
thoughts turned to her, as he lay staring up at the ash
boughs with the stars burning through them, their tracery
as vivid and metallic a green in the light of his fire as it
had been when Gloire gazed up at them three weeks earlier.
Surely this place must help her! He thought of what Mr.
Langdon and his sister—a fine old character, that!—had said
of her: spoilt, futile. But the sister had thrown a little fresh
light on what the husband had been, and might have meant,
to her. He was glad she was with Miss Glanfield—just the
right person to help her, he thought.

He made a leisurely start next morning, taking a dip first
in the cold singing hurrying river; strode, sweating, up the
steep path out of the main valley, and drank and rested, as
Gloire had done, by the spring at the top. He paused, over
the crest above Torosh, to look down on the great church,
and up the wide trough of the valley, filled and glittering
with light—it was June now, and the heat was great. Larsen expanded his lungs, taking in the fine dry mountain air.
Ah, it was very good to be here again. Seeing a group of
women pass, in their gay and yet formal dress, he smiled

to himself—what on earth would Mrs. Thurston be wearing up here? Those ridiculous shoes and gossamer stockings, or beach trousers, or what?

He was soon to see. As he swung down past the church and took the small hot path beyond it into the ravine, he overtook two more Albanian women; he barely glanced at them and was striding on across the bridge, when to his astonishment he heard his name called—"Mr. Larsen!" He turned, and saw Gloire Thurston.

Larsen stood transfixed. What Mrs. Thurston was this?—in tunic and trousers and velvet jacket, her eyebrows growing, her face tanned? The black silk shawl bound over her head gave her curious square countenance a most extraordinary charm. She was quite lovely! He stood speechless, as she advanced upon him.

"Mr. Larsen! Well of all things! What on earth are you doing here?"

"I came to see you," Nils said, startled into the most unguarded truthfulness.

"Well, I hope you like what you see." She was gay; she was animated. "Look—this is Lisa—Miss Lek-Gionaj." She spoke a few words in halting Albanian to the beautiful girl with her, mentioning his name; Lisa smiled shyly. Standing together by the parapet of the bridge, the pair of them, they made a group like an antique painting, youth and health, glowing through the formality of their ample clothes; and again Gloire's radiance, as much as her beauty, struck him with astonished pleasure. "And guess who's here," she went on. "You'll never guess, so I'll tell you— Susan Glanfield!"

"I know—they told me in Tirana," Nils said tactlessly.

"Oh, what a shame! Who told you? Who did you see?"

"Mr. Langdon—and his sister. At first I thought it was you who was hurt."

"How are they?" Gloire asked, almost eagerly.

"They are well. They are so very nice," Nils said. "But"—

again he eyed her—"but how come you dressed like this?"

"Oh, I tore my slacks going after flowers for Susan, and I had to wear something, so Mme. Lek-Gionaj fitted me out. And I rather fancied it, so I've stuck to it," Gloire replied airily. "How do you like it?"

"It is beautiful. I never thought to see you look so," he said earnestly.

"Quite the Albanian maiden, I am now," Gloire chattered on as they breasted a steep slope through a wood of small pines—and now he noticed that she was wearing goat-skin sandals. How splendidly she walked, he thought—unconsciously she had quickened her pace to match his, and Lisa was falling behind. He had not been wrong about her walking when he first followed her down the corridor of the Orient Express.

"Where have you been?" he asked.

"Oh, down to the valley to borrow a finer shuttle for the loom—old Maria wants to start a piece of extra fine silk, and one of the married daughters down at Mastrokol has one. But Lisa walks frightfully slowly—just like a Swiss guide."

"Mountaineers always do," Larsen said. He was feeling extraordinarily pleased—there was an enchantment about this happy gay sunburnt Gloire, and the evidently intimate terms on which she was with Lisa and the family concerns delighted him. As they approached the house she and Lisa both went across to a group of juniper-bushes, white with linen spread out to dry; they felt the pieces knowingly; Gloire gathered up a bundle, and tucking it under her arm, rejoined him.

"I don't know where Lek-Gionaj and Madame are just now, but you'd better come right up and see Susan. Lisa will tell them you're here. We've pretty well mopped up the guest-room, I'm afraid, as a hospital—but they will fix you up somehow."

"I have a sleeping-bag—I need not be fixed," Larsen said.

273

Out of the heat, Larsen walked into the high-lit coolness of that upper room, and saw at first only a litter of feminine belongings, and a small white canopy, like a meat-safe, on a red mattress. Gloire ran across to it.

"Here, take that thing off!" she exclaimed, laughing— "I've brought you an old friend!" She whisked away the meat-safe and Larsen confronted Miss Glanfield.

For a moment both stared in silence. Miss Glanfield, the more surprised of the two, being a woman was the more self-possessed, and spoke first.

"Nils! How extraordinary! But how *very* nice to see you again."

He walked slowly towards her, studying the square pale face, the very blue eyes, the soft loose hair—above all the expression. Her hair—not grey yet; a sort of silvery lacquer on the chestnut he knew, in front. With his incurable simplicity, he spoke his first thought. "But you are beautiful, still."

To Gloire's amused delight, Miss Glanfield actually blushed. It had never occurred to her that Susan Glanfield was beautiful—looking with Larsen's eyes she saw that she might be accounted so, with the fine modelling, not yet marred by wrinkles, of her face, the clear skin, the gay sweet look.

"Nonsense!" Miss Glanfield said, without losing her self-possession, in spite of the blush. "You usen't to pay compliments! But what on earth are you doing up here?"

"I came to see how Mrs. Thurston likes Albania—and in Tirana I heard that you are here, so I had a double reason for coming," he said, sitting down on one of the upright chairs by the bed. His eyes were on her all the time. "How long is it since we climbed together?"

"Twenty years," said Miss Glanfield, with her usual total absence of coyness. "It was in Wales—do you remember? We made a new climb in Clogwyn-y-person."

"So we did! And were benighted trying to get down the

274

zig-zags from Snowdon. It was very black, and snowed. You were clever, and found the snow-steps with a match! And then they sent a search-party after us, and you were very cross!"

"Of course I was cross! It was such nonsense—we were only an hour or two late for dinner," said Miss Glanfield, with a sort of youthful naturalness that made Larsen laugh—it brought back that very dark walk down, and the girl who was so undaunted even by the prospect of a night out on Snowdon in winter. Gloire watched and listened, amused and interested, while they recalled episodes in their climbing past, which seemed to have been varied and extensive: they had climbed in the Graians, they had climbed and danced at Zermatt, they had met in huts above Chamonix and Courmayeur and Grindelwald; there had been episodes with guides, there had been excitements and dangers. They talked as if twenty months stood between them and those days, not twenty long years. Gloire marvelled and envied; it was extraordinary to see two particularly mature persons so engrossed in their common past—and how full that past had been of joy and adventure, and the peculiar intimacy which shared experiences confer. It must have meant a lot to both of them, she thought, for it to be so clear after such a lapse of time. Larsen, whom she had only known as rather judgematical, severe, was laughing now over those old adventures with a boyish eagerness and abandonment.

"Do you remember," he exclaimed, "that poem you wrote after we walked down the Val d'Anniviers, and slept at Sierre? The day we got so wet, and your skirt was left at the Trift Hut, because we had hoped to traverse the Gabelhorn back to Zermatt, and the porter took you for a young man?" He began to recite it:

> "Oh, do you remember
> Walking down to Sierre
> The puddles on the winding road
> The coolness in the air?

> The clouds that slowly came apart
> The deepening evening glow
> And on the blue hills opposite
> The freshly-fallen snow?"

"It was a very bad poem," said Miss Glanfield.

"To me, no—because it was so true. Then it went on about walking up to Ried, on our way back to Mürren. Do you remember the wild raspberries in the wood? And losing our way in fog on the Petersgrat?" He recited again—

> "How, when the light was almost gone
> We found the path begin—
> And then the food, and warmth, and light,
> And comfort of the inn?

Your brother was with us. How he swore!"

Miss Glanfield's bright look dimmed a little.

"What became of him?" Nils went on. "Where is he now?"

"He was killed in France, just before the Armistice," Miss Glanfield said. "I added another verse," she said slowly, "afterwards."

"Please say it," Nils said.

Still slowly, Miss Glanfield did as she was asked.

> "Oh, do you remember?
> For I cannot forget
> I see you walk beside me now—
> I hear your laughter yet.
> Though you lie cold in Flanders,
> What was it then you said?
> 'I know I shall remember this
> Long after I am dead.'"

That brought Gloire back into their company again. The bright tears stood in her eyes. Into the succeeding silence, neat and brisk, walked Dr. Crowninshield, humming a little tune; at the sight of the stranger she checked her tune, and stood still.

Gloire sprang up, animation returning to her face.

"Dr. Emmeline, this is Mr. Nils Larsen, of the I.L.O. Mr. Larsen, this is Dr. Emmeline Crowninshield." (Gloire had retained the outstanding American virtue of giving full and adequate introductions.)

Now it so happened that at no point had either Gloire or Susan Glanfield mentioned Larsen to the old Doctor. Since they were usually all three together, at meals and in the evenings, Miss Glanfield had hardly had a further opportunity of talking about Gloire to the old woman; they had smiled together, benevolently and pleasedly, over her Albanian appearance and the way in which she had settled down to Albanian life, but that was all. Now the pale old eyes glanced keenly from face to face, after she had shaken hands and expressed her pleasure at meeting, in evident speculation as to what this man might be doing in Torosh.

Miss Glanfield was, as usual, competent.

"Mr. Larsen is an old mountaineering friend of mine," she said, "and a friend of Gloire's too. He came to look her up."

"Well, we're quite a party here, as you see," Dr. Crowninshield said, sitting down on the edge of her brass bed. "I'm the doctor in charge!" Her eyes still ranged over the three faces; like Miss Anne, she was wondering which of the two women in the room had really brought Larsen to Torosh. "Do you know Albania?"

"Yes—I have been here several times. I have heard of you—naturally—though you have not heard of me," Larsen said, smiling. "It is a pleasure to meet you at last."

Valentino entered at this point, with cheese and raki, and a whispered communication to the old Doctor. Larsen's advent had put the Lek-Gionajs in a minor jam—with the guest-room a sick-room, where was the new (and well-remembered) male guest to be accommodated? Would he accept, Valentino whispered to Dr. Emmeline, a small room by himself, which could be cleared, and perhaps take his meals with Lek-Gionaj and the men? Or, if he wished to eat with the ladies, should Lek-Gionaj eat with him there? Would the sick lady mind? For it would be an obvious breach of hospitality for his host not to eat with him.

Dr. Crowninshield resolved this difficulty with her customary New England firmness. Conversation was now flowing again, and it was clear to her that Larsen was on excellent terms with both her fellow guests. Today, on his arrival, she told Valentino, he would of course lunch with his host. He should be given the small room to sleep in, so as not to disturb her patient overmuch: but, for the other meals during his visit, he would with Lek-Gionaj's permission eat with them here in the guest-room. He would wait on the Kapidan in a few minutes. When the servant had gone, she told Larsen what had been arranged.

"I have a sleeping-bag; I can camp outside," Larsen said.

"I don't imagine you'll be allowed to do that—anyhow come along now and meet your host," and she took him off.

They did not see him again till after the siesta, when Gloire, bringing up Miss Glanfield's tea, encountered him downstairs. "Let us go for a walk," he said at once.

"In just twenty minutes," Gloire said; "I have to give Susan her tea and bring the things down again. Do you want some tea?"

"No, thank you," he said, smiling at her busy-ness; he watched her as she went upstairs, carrying the tray, her tunic swinging round her knees.

When they set out, Gloire led the way. They took the Torosh track for some distance, and then turned out along another of the spurs of hill running down from Mali Shënjt, which projected far out into the valley; from its further end one could just see the tower of the church at Torosh, sticking up over an intervening ridge—across the valley, to right and left, spread the great white slopes of the opposite hills, flecked with black vegetation. The pinkish stony soil was warm under their feet, the air was full of strong aromatic scents from the stunted pines and low-growing sages and

278

junipers; the light on the slopes was growing rich at the end of the afternoon. Where the ridge fell away steeply below them they sat down on a sun-warmed rock. Nils took a long look at his companion.

"I like to see you so!" he said. "Tell me, are you happy here?"

"Yes," Gloire said slowly. It was the fact that for the past two or three weeks she had found herself content and happy as she had seldom been since her schoolroom days; and, oddly enough, her life at Torosh reminded her of them. Old Dr. Emmeline had a restful governessy way of telling her what to do, and Gloire found to her own surprise that she enjoyed both this, and the old woman's rather rare commendations. But besides being "bossed around" there was the general atmosphere of benevolent approval from both older women, which she found strange and pleasant, and the novel sense of usefulness. She had in fact begun to learn that it is really quite as agreeable to be liked and needed as to be admired and envied.

"Yes," she repeated, turning to Nils—"it was a thoroughly sound thing to tell me to come here. I did hear High Mass on Whit-Sunday at Torosh," she added, inconsequently.

"So. And what did you think of that?"

"Oh, it was just like you told me it would be, only more so. The clothes were perfectly marvellous. Outside, when the women stood under the church, they were like a sort of static ballet."

"And inside?"

"Inside was terrific. I've never known anything like it in any church I've ever been in." She remembered his words, or some echo of them, but she wasn't the sort of person who used words like that. "It was so real it was pretty frightening," she said, and left it at that.

Nils nodded. He was satisfied.

"I am glad you think it was right to come," he said.

"Oh gosh yes. I began to think that quite at the beginning, when I rode on that ridiculous pony into the wood at Rësheni, and the nightingales were singing like crazy things, just as you said—and the first night at Shpali, I knew you'd been right."

"And why did you know?"

"Oh, because it was a lovely place, and I felt so good, walking all day that way. And Susan said something just as we got in that brought it all out. You know how she always *expresses* everything that happens."

Larsen smiled. He was familiar with Susan's expressiveness.

"What did Susan say?"

"She said we felt so good because we'd been travelling all day in the old way, like people in the Bible, and Marco Polo, and all that," Gloire replied, airily. "She said doing that did something to you. I didn't understand when she said it, and I didn't have time to ask her, then—but now I know," she concluded.

"And what does it to you?"

"Oh, you must ask her that! I can't define those sort of things—I'm not an expresser! Susan can define anything; she hitches things together so that they mean something quite different, too. Isn't she grand?" she said, turning to him.

"Yes, very grand." But he was not really thinking much of Miss Glanfield, he was thinking how enchantingly pretty Mrs. Thurston was, tanned and strangely dressed and animated. He wanted her to go on talking. "How did you meet her? You have not told me this yet," he said.

"We met on the boat, going down to Cattaro; I thought her fantastically queer then, because she insisted on my seeing all manner of things, and told off a most comic little man called George to show me round. Then when I got down to Tirana we met up again."

"And you arranged to travel together?" Larsen remembered Warren Langdon's remarks about Miss Glanfield's mercifulness and thought he would like some details.

"It wasn't quite so easy as that," Gloire said. "I had the most frightful time fixing it. At one point I was just about in despair! Her trip was fixed all right, with the Robinsons; but that old General hadn't any more gendarmes to spare, and he told Warren I couldn't go along because I wasn't everybody's old friend! I didn't feel I could very well ask her to take me—even I wasn't brash enough for that!"

"What then did you do?"

"In the end I did exactly that!" She looked amused. Larsen, watching her face, recalled vividly the sulky misery on it that had shocked him in the train as they looked out on Lago Maggiore and the Borromean Islands.

"It was rather queer, that," she pursued. "The Carrutherses were giving a cocktail for her, and on the way over we met her on the road; she'd been bird's-nesting in the marsh, and she was in the most fearful mess, all over mud, even her face!—Miss Anne was shocked to death. And wildly late, of course. We gave her a lift, and somehow, she was so nice and natural, not minding being so dirty and odd, it made me feel maybe I could ask her. So I did, just like that."

"And what did she say?"

Gloire walked on to her fate, artlessly.

"Oh, she asked why I wanted to go, and I told her you said I should; then she said—'Well, I think you ought to go,' in that quick way of hers; and she fixed the whole thing. And here I am," Gloire said, with obvious satisfaction.

"This is interesting," Nils said thoughtfully. Gloire's recital had given him a good deal of food for thought, both about her and about Miss Glanfield. He sat silent for some time, smoking—looking now at Gloire, now at the hills opposite, and the valley slowly filling with shadow. Gloire sat silent too, perfectly content; it was good to be sitting there with Larsen, looking at these lovely hills that she was learning to love. She would have liked to tell him just how far she felt she was beginning to understand what he meant

281

by European civilisation—as exemplified by Mme. Lek-Gionaj and Lisa, and the household life. And by Lek-Gionaj too. Groups of men frequently turned up at the Kapidan's house; food was cooked for them, and they were closeted for hours with Lek-Gionaj. From Dr. Emmeline she always learned who they were: sometimes members of his own clan, but often of some other—he was the recognised chief of all the Catholic clans, and their problems were brought to him for advice and solution. She had watched the earnest faces grouped in the courtyard, and Lek-Gionaj's own anxious face, creased with thought, as he weighed and dealt with the difficulties of his people; she had realised his patience and his concern. Once he had had to go down to Tirana to represent their point of view to the authorities; this had been a very important occasion, and every one went about looking serious till his return. Gloire had in fact been seeing the aristocratic principle in action. But she couldn't possibly describe all that, she thought; only there were one or two things she must tell him, somehow; she owed that to him.

Shouts and barkings on the slopes high above made them turn their heads—the two rivers, the brown and the white, of goats and sheep were flowing down the mountainside towards the fold, towards food and security. They watched them in silence. But the Swede seemed to know that she had more to say; he turned his gaze back from the flocks pouring down the pine-clad slopes to her face, and said, smiling a little—

"Well, Gloire?"

She blushed at her name, but pursued her intention.

"Do you remember," she began, "what you said in the train about doing things with your hands giving *virtue* in some way?" Nils nodded—he kept his eyes on her face. "I thought that just funny, then," she said. "I suppose because I'd never really seen anyone working with their hands much, except my maid, washing and fixing my clothes. But I have

seen people doing that now—and I believe I understand
what you mean."

"What have you seen?"

"Oh, all manner of things! We took some coats down to
the braider at Torosh the other day—you know, those white
woollen affairs that don't fasten, that Mme. Lek-Gionaj
wears? Maria had woven the stuff and they got cut out
and sewed up here—but those fine, fine coloured patterns
round the neck and arm-holes and on the hip-seams that
look like embroidery are really a very fine braid, in all
colours. And we stayed awhile and watched the old man
stitching them on. It was fascinating. And then of course
there are all the other things they do—spinning and weaving, and baking the bread. Do you know how they bake
the bread, up here?"

Nils did know, but he said—"Tell me."

"They do it in the strangest way! They put the dough,
rolled out flat, on a great clay platter on some hot embers;
and then they put a thing like an iron meat-dish cover,
huge, that's been heated in the fire, right over it, and pile
more coals up around that; and that bakes the bread. And
they take such a pride in all they do—the Princess breaks
a piece off, after the baking, and smells it, and tastes it—
and if it isn't right, well! There is something to all that,
I guess—making your own things, and knowing if they're
good or bad. Why, even I sniff my wash when I bring it in!
—it smells so fragrant when it's dried in the sun, on the
junipers."

"Had you never washed anything before?" he asked,
curiously.

"Oh, just rinsed out a pair of stockings, if I was away for
a night or two, and hadn't Fraser with me. But"—she hesitated—"I laughed at you in the train for saying 'virtue,'
and I want to take that laugh back."

"Thank you," he said. He looked at her thoughtfully,
wondering how much she really did understand, how far

283

the change had gone, and—rather astutely—how much of it was due to Miss Glanfield, who clearly had inspired her with an enthusiastic affection, and how much to her close-up of Albanian life.

"So you like the life here?" he asked her.

"Yes—in a number of ways. There are a hundred things I'd want to change—I think the way they mew the babies up in those cradles is just frightful; they can hardly breathe! And I still like plumbing! And I loathe the flies. But—" again she hesitated—"oh well, they have got something. And they really are happy—I give you that! I wanted to tell you—and to thank you. Because but for you, I'd never have come. And actually I *have* been rather happy here."

Nils was extraordinarily pleased. A warm feeling flooded him. He took her hand.

"My dear, I am very glad. You need to be happy."

Colour came into her face, tears into her eyes.

"I could do with it, I guess," she said, with an attempt at lightness. "It's funny the way you and Susan seem to have understood, right from the start, what I did want. No one else has."

"Not the old American?" Nils asked, letting go her hand.

"Well, if she did, she hasn't done a thing about it, except order me around! But I like the way she does that, actually. She's grand," said Gloire. "The way she works and slaves for all these people here is just nobody's business."

Shadow had come up now, and engulfed the rock where they sat, and a cool air was rising from the valley; the pinnacles of Mali Shënjt glowed with a clear rose behind them. Nils glanced at his watch, and stood up.

"We should go back," he said. He took her hand again and pulled her to her feet. "Come."

He dined that night with Lek-Gionaj—it seemed indicated. Later, at the foot of the stairs, he encountered Mrs. Thurston coming down carrying a cup.

"What is that for?" he asked, pointing to it.

"Susan's milk. I always take her up a hot night-cap last thing," she said, as they went out. They paused in the court-yard, under the great southern stars; a glow came from the kitchen windows opposite—the air was sweet with all sorts of aromatic scents, and a gust of sheepy odour came up from the fold below.

"Did they fix you a room?" Gloire asked.

"They offered it, yes, but I prefer to sleep out of doors. The Prince knows this," he answered.

"Don't let the wolves eat you!"

"No—they will not. We shall walk again tomorrow, no?" he asked, looking at the pale shape of her face, and the glimmer of her white skirts in the darkness.

"Yes, surely. Goodnight," she said, starting towards the kitchen door.

"Goodnight. Till tomorrow, happiness!" he called after her.

" 'You will suffer!' is what Madame says on these occa-sions," she called back, laughing.

15

"WELL, how is the patient today?" Larsen asked next morning, when Gloire had ushered him into the big room, and flitted off again about her household affairs.

"Marvellously *im*-patient! Dr. Emmeline took a look at my leg this morning, and she thinks it would really be safe for me to go down in a few days, if we can rig up a sort of sling for the foot, for someone to carry, and go rather slowly."

"This is excellent."

"Yes. I ought really to be getting home. It's too wretched that I've missed Ochrida and the whole of the south, but it can't be helped. And besides, I feel I ought to leave as soon as possible—it's been so frightful for the Lek-Gionajs having us foisted on them for such ages."

"They have not felt this," Nils said. "Hospitality is second nature here. And they have especially enjoyed having Mrs. Thurston among them, so much like one of themselves; this rarely happens. They think it has been of benefit to Lisa to have her company—the Prince told me so."

"It's certainly been a benefit to Gloire to have Lisa's!" Miss Glanfield said. "Do tell me, what do you think of her now?"

Nils did not reply at once. He was a most unhurried person. He gave Miss Glanfield a cigarette, and lit one himself—while he did so, he was thinking of his encounter with Gloire that morning in the dairy. Coming up into the yard, cup in hand, from the fragrant hollow where he had slept under the stars among the dwarf pines and junipers, he had seen her standing among the particoloured throng

286

of girls and women, smiling, and talking in her few words of Albanian; and the profoundest part of him had rejoiced at the sight. He stood by the door when she went in, and watched her receiving bread and milk from the hands of Mme. Lek-Gionaj. She seemed slender beside that mountainous woman, but surely she was stouter—or was it just those full skirts? When she came out—"How do you like this sort of breakfast?" he had asked her, gaily.

"Fine. I'm putting on weight up here."

"You have a good way to go before you match her!" he said, grinning in the direction of their hostess.

"Yes, isn't she grand? Her hips must be a yard across!"

"And do you not despise her for that?"

"I don't despise her for anything—why should I? Do lay off that!" she had said impatiently. "I've told you I like the way she does things."

"I am glad," he said. "Yes, she has a splendour that the women in London and Paris, pulling rubber harness over their sterile pelvises to control their hips, can never have! I am glad that you are here to see it."

"Oh, I see quite a bit, for all you think me such a dumb cluck!" Gloire had replied and floated off with her cups and her slabs of dry bread. Formidable!

Now, to Miss Glanfield—

"I think well of her," he said, in his sober way. "She is happy, and this makes her charming."

The old Nilsian bromides, Miss Glanfield thought. But as usual she pursued her main theme.

"Do you think it's really made a difference? Will it last, should you say? I've tried—we talked about her husband; I knew him, you know, as quite a boy—to make her see that just hating the world because of his death won't get her anywhere."

"Of course not. I am glad you spoke of that. For her, this particular trial was peculiarly disabling because he was all the real hold on life she had. Women who have duties

287

and obligations which they recognise have these as a stable framework to support them, when such a blow falls. But she had not. Of all that by which most women live she had nothing! Do you realise the fearful vacancy, the emptiness, of the lives of these rich cosmopolitans, divorced from the land and from all duties?"

"My God yes, I do realise it!" Miss Glanfield said, with her customary vigour. "I couldn't agree more. It's something else, too—the frustrating of the creative impulse. Most women have that, lots of it, and the normal outlet, besides bearing and bringing up children, is all the work connected with a home: making clothes, making things for the house, making food—delicious food, so often! If a woman does all those things with her own two hands, the creative side of her life is nourished and strong and satisfied; but if she does none of them—and till she came here, Gloire Thurston never has—her only real outlet is the emotional one."

"That is true," Nils said thoughtfully. "I hadn't thought of the creative aspect. But through the emotional life people can also be led to other activities and outlets."

"Of course they can. And that poor child feels that. She said as much—she told me she felt that in losing her husband she had lost herself too."

"She said that? Most interesting! Then Miss Langdon was right," Larsen said.

"Oh, was she onto that? She's a very bright old bird," said Miss Glanfield appreciatively.

Larsen smiled at the phrase.

"She is—a splendid American of the old school. There are too few now like her." He paused—his mind had gone back to her remarks about the creative faculty. "Do you know the U.S.A.?" he asked. "You and I have not spoken of it yet."

"Yes, I've been in the States a good deal. Why?"

"Do you think there is a connection between the instability of family life there, the emphasis placed on the

288

emotions, the constant divorces, and this lack of a creative outlet for women? For in America, though there are few servants, most of the work in houses is done by machines, food comes out of tins, and clothes are bought, not made, as a rule. The American woman very seldom runs down the garden to gather a handful of herbs to flavour her soups and salads, as our housewives do—nor are they constantly knitting socks for their men, as in Scotland and Sweden. I had not thought of it, but might there not be a connection?"

"Oh Lord yes—personally I feel sure there is. I would say that the way American women—in all classes—go on about their 'love-life' derives directly from the mail-order system and the can-opener," said Miss Glanfield briefly. "Even if they do make their 'drapes' themselves, they copy them from a picture in *Vogue*; so that you'll see identical curtains in thirty thousand homes in any given year. That terrible uniformity of mass-production that Red Lewis wrote of so scathingly in *Babbitt* and *Main Street* helps to atrophy the creative faculty too." She paused, and then added—"You know, I believe Gloire has got onto that, at last. I think she sees the point of the way the people here live, for all their lack of plumbing, and that she's genuinely enjoyed doing a little real work herself."

"Yes, this is so."

"Oh, she told you?" Miss Glanfield eyed him with interest.

"Yes."

"Well, that's something positive, anyway."

Larsen lunched with them, and afterwards sat on, talking—chiefly to Miss Glanfield who, stimulated by a new person, was pouring out ideas and theories at a great rate. Gloire listened, working at her embroidery, and wondering when they were to go for their walk; the old Doctor smoked. But Larsen showed no sign of moving, nor Miss Glanfield of flagging, and at last Dr. Crowninshield took action.

"My patient has to rest in the afternoon, Mr. Larsen,"
she said.

Nils got up at once.

"Oh, I really don't need to always, Dr. Emmeline," the
writer protested.

"That's for me to decide," the old woman said, smiling
but decisive. "Anyway *I* want my nap."

"But of course—you should rest," Larsen said. He turned
to Miss Glanfield—"We will talk later,"—and then to Gloire
—"Do you rest also? or shall we take a little walk?"

Gloire was all for a walk, hot as it was, and they went
off together. Her pleasure in his company had become great
since his return; the mental alchemy which so often takes
place in absence had worked more powerfully than usual
because he was linked in her mind with this new conception
of life, this revolution in her scale of values. He must have
been important to her from the outset, she realised, or she
would not have heeded his words to the very drastic point
of leaving the train at Zagreb—but now she found him also
enormously attractive. Her relations with men were the one
thing—besides clothes—about which Gloire's mind was thoroughly alert, and she knew that she liked Larsen and might
at any moment be in love with him; she also, out of her
experience, recognised that he was interested to a considerable degree in her. But in this one case, all the familiar
technique of recognition of that fact and the corresponding
moves was confused by his being and meaning so much
more than the usual run of men who fell for her; she
couldn't apply the normal methods with him, she felt.
The word desecration was not in Gloire's vocabulary, except as something in history books that happened to
churches—but her instinct knew the thing it stood for, and
avoided it.

This left her curiously shy and inhibited, as they climbed
up through the woods below Mali Shënjt, treading paths
down which the flocks poured at sundown; a faint goaty

smell hung about them, penetrating even through the hot resinous fragrance of the pines. Tits zipped and chipped among the branches; the pine-cones were opening in the heat with a tiny dry popping sound, like a series of minute explosions. She walked in silence, unable to think of anything to say; nor did Nils talk much. He was watching her with immense pleasure—sun and shadow splashed her white trousers and tunic, against the reddish background of the tree-trunks, and struck brilliant as an emerald on her jacket, as she moved ahead of him, graceful and strong. His pleasure, silent as it was, communicated itself to her sharpened instincts; her usual delight in the movement of her muscles became keener, because she knew that he was liking the way she walked. In this silent pleasure and recognition, in great heat, they mounted to the limit of trees, and emerged onto the blazing splendour of open pastures and white rocks, where a breeze, cool and tonic even under the tremendous South European sun, fanned their faces, bringing the delicate fragrance of mountain flowers. At Nils' suggestion they sat down. Below them, a white speck, was Lek-Gionaj's house; down to the right the tower of the Abbey Church was visible, an elegant buff rococo pillar against a pink and white background of hillside; across the valley, the white slopes of the further ranges shimmered in the heat. Nils took off his hat and mopped his face; Gloire pulled out a handkerchief and fanned hers.

He watched her.

"You use no powder, now?" he asked curiously.

"No. I ran out. Anyway it would look funny with this get-up."

He was pleased at that—it showed a sense of the fitness of things. He studied her as they sat. He was interested to realise that her charm did not depend purely on a fashionable perfection of appearance; he had thought that it probably did, but he was wrong. It was based on something healthier, more fundamental.

Presently she pulled the black shawl off her head, complaining of the heat, and that remarkable heather-honey hair came down with it, a great coil of the dark-bold stuff falling over that green velvet jacket.

"I did not know you had long hair," he exclaimed in surprise.

She glanced at him sidelong under her lashes.

"My God, you are unobservant! I should have thought you'd have seen that in the train."

"The colour, I noticed," Nils said; "but not that it is long."

She laughed. She didn't bother to put the hair up again; Nils was aware of a very definite desire to shake the coil loose and plunge his hands in the deeply golden stuff. He changed the subject. Glancing down at the pine-trees through which they had walked up—

"That is surely *Pinus Pinaster*," he said; "with the very large cones, and the rough bark. This is within its range."

"This range of mountains, do you mean?"

He smiled. "No, its geographical range. Do you know *Picea Omorika*? That has a small range; in all the world it is only found wild within a few miles of Serajevo. It is one of the only two European spruces—and the other, the Norway spruce, covers the whole of Northern Europe. Strange, is it not?"

Gloire didn't really think it either strange or normal—spruces were definitely not within *her* range.

"Do you know a lot about trees and all that?" she asked, thinking how much she liked his face even when it was hot and shiny.

"Not a lot—a little. In any country, I like to know what grows, and why—the geological formations, the climate, that give it its vegetation. Does this not interest you?"

"I've never thought about it," she said. "I don't know the first thing about trees, or geology either—and I've never met anyone that did, except Susan. I've learned the names of a few of the flowers here, because I bring them in for her

292

to look at—and of course she always tells one their names," she added, looking amused.

But Nils too was thinking how delicious she looked, without powder, sitting there in the sun with her hair down her back, talking away about the Lek-Gionajs and Miss Glanfield and Dr. Crowninshield. About people she was quite observant and shrewd. She made it clear that she had never before met women like these two, and that she enjoyed them, though quite aware of their little foibles. Oh yes, she was *nice*—and alarmingly attractive, now that she was happy, whatever she wore! As they walked down, Gloire again in front, Nils found it necessary to exhort himself. I must be careful! he thought. She is the sort of person one falls in love with. This could happen—and then, for thirty years, what on earth should we talk about? She will never have much mind, nor care for the things of the mind —though her character might become charming. It would be a mistake to fall in love with her.

Such precautionary meditations are sometimes efficacious, and sometimes, by themselves, they are not. Possibly Paris used some such language to himself about Helen— unavailingly. But in Larsen's case they were reinforced from without by another element—the presence of Miss Glanfield.

He dined with the women that night, and sat with them afterwards, perched on one of the upright chairs; Gloire sat with her embroidery on the foot of Miss Glanfield's mattress; the old Doctor lay propped on the brass bed. As always, when foreigners met in Albania, the talk at dinner had turned on the future of the Albanian nation—what they needed, what could be done for them, what they must do for themselves. The subject was pursued when they had settled down.

"They seem very anxious to have more education," Nils said. "Every man I speak to always talks of the need for education, here."

"They talk of the need for it, but when they get it, they

293

don't use it," Dr. Crowninshield said rather tartly. She was tired—her old face looked pinched. "Any man here will gladly send his son to an agricultural college; but when he comes home, will he let him change the methods on the farm? No sir!"

"But that's only technical education, after all, and that hardly counts as education really," Miss Glanfield put in. "Is there a desire here for true education, for the humanities?—I mean as an end in itself and not as a means to a livelihood? If there is, something could be done." She looked towards Dr. Crowninshield.

"That's hard to answer," the old woman said, rolling another of her little cigarettes. "It's difficult for people who've only been allowed any education at all for less than a generation to be very precise about what they do want. Any sort of knowledge is education to them, and valuable—they don't differentiate."

"Miss Glanfield's point is important, though," Nils said, leaning forward. "There is that confusion between true education and mere technology in England and America as well as here, and on the whole the emphasis is laid on technology. Whereas in France, say—or in Poland or Hungary— the emphasis is on education in the true sense. But the laws of supply and demand operate quite as inevitably in the educational sphere as in the economic! The educational problem is not a question of schools or colleges, but of the social structure—of the esteem in which culture and learning are held, regardless of economic rewards. Where they are held in high esteem, even few and poor schools will supply a true education—where they are not desired or esteemed, hundreds of colleges, splendidly equipped, with Vitaglass in the windows!"—he grinned rather maliciously— "will not supply education in the sense in which Europe has always understood it. One has only to look at America and some of the British Dominions to see how little the multiplication of Universities can do towards the creation

294

of a cultivated society!—unless that society itself, in its most influential centres, really desires cultivation." He too looked towards Dr. Crowninshield. "Do you agree?"

The old woman sighed.

"Yes, I do," she said. "Culture isn't valued in the States much, today—not even in New England. When a Harvard student tells me, as one did two years back, that he is 'majoring in Accountancy and Music,' I know what to think! It's a complete confusion of standards."

"Europe used to differentiate, of course, and call technical education apprenticeship," said Miss Glanfield.

"That was right. And valued both, but did not confuse them," Nils said. "Also in apprenticeship a youth learnt not only the details of his trade, but the discipline of it. Today, discipline is gone out of fashion."

"Yes, the fashion is all for technology," said Miss Glanfield rapidly. "Commercial values are dominating the public views on education today, even in England. Mass standards are becoming the ideal aimed at—and mass democratic standards are commercial and debased. Fifty years ago the most altruistic and high-minded reformers believed that universal education and provincial Universities would produce a flood of hidden talent, and raise the intellectual standard of England. But it hasn't worked out like that. The standard of cultivation in the liberal professions hasn't risen, it has fallen."

"How do you judge that?" Gloire asked.

"Well, in one very direct way, by comparing the books written by leading men in the liberal professions today, Bishops and Judges, for instance, with those the same type of men published fifty years ago. They've gone back."

"But does that matter? I mean, why is it important that people should be so terribly well educated? Does it really make all that difference?"

"Yes," Nils said with emphasis. "And for this reason. Questions constantly arise and confront a nation to which

295

it is vitally important to find the right answers. But if the men in leading positions in that nation have not a wide philosophic outlook, if they are men of little intellectual ballast or anchorage, who tend to be swept away by the moods and catchwords of the moment—like the general mass of men who derive their cultivation from the public prints—the wrong answer is found. And this is a great loss, and peril, to any nation."

"It's more than that, isn't it?" said Miss Glanfield. "I don't mean that that isn't true; it's appallingly true. But— do you remember what Matthew Arnold said? That when in any nation 'the free play of the mind on all subjects'—isn't it a glorious phrase?—'ceases to be valued, ceases to be an object of desire,' the soul of that nation must perish of inanition." She turned to Gloire. "Your question is difficult to answer, because it turns the position. As soon as you start asking what education is *for*, what the use of it is, you're abandoning the basic assumption of any true culture, that education is worth while for its own sake. It's like asking what the soul of man is for."

"Mass-standards would ask just that, if they really believed man had a soul," Nils said, with an ironical grin. "The worst feature of democracy, to me, is this tendency to level education down, not to level it up. There is not only no enthusiasm for genuine education, there is a positive distaste for it."

"It's more than a tendency, it's a demand," said the old Doctor. "Though I don't agree that there is *necessarily* any connection with democracy. But there is that wish, in the name of democracy, to level down, because high cultural standards are despised and rejected, and even feared, in our Western Democracies. Don't let anyone else have what I've not got, or can't enjoy!—is the secret theory. A very large number of writers in the British and American popular press profess to be preaching democracy when in fact they are only trying to make envy respectable!"

The others laughed.

"Why, Dr. Emmeline, you're quite ferocious about it!" Gloire exclaimed.

"Yes, I am ferocious about it," the old woman said, her dry detachment for once forsaking her. "I see the world, drugged with ignorance and false conceptions and a town-bred passion for the second-rate, sweeping on to the most ignoble of destinies, a future of mediocrity and sham well-being; and jettisoning as it goes along all the things that might save it, all its main sources of strength and virtue—tradition, culture, religion, even beauty. Would you see that gladly, if you *did* see it? I live here in the old world, with the old graces, for all the poverty and the lack of hygiene—so I do see it. And I see that these things are being scrapped mainly out of ignorance and envy."

Nils glanced significantly at Gloire, while the old Doctor spoke, but her eyes were on her work. He felt in his pocket and pulled out the little note-book which she had seen in the train; he turned the pages, and then looked at Miss Glanfield.

"Do you recognise this?" he asked, and read out—

"Whatever the method of improving humanity and of raising men to a higher position than they occupy today may be, and whenever and however the millennium may be reached, it is not to be reached by declaring in favour of class consciousness and class antagonism, hatred between one class and another. The problem we have to solve is an educational and moral problem. No political constitution can enfranchise a people, no possessions can enrich them, no rank or title can ennoble them, unless they have solid, manly character and wholesome honesty, as the granite rock upon which they are built."

"No, I don't know that," Miss Glanfield said. "Who wrote it?"

"Whoever he was, he was a mighty sensible man," said Dr. Crowninshield. "If the whole world could be got to

297

grasp that, we might get somewhere. It's true—and it is the direct opposite of most of what is said and written today. Truth is very rarely popular."

"Who did write it?" Miss Glanfield repeated.

"It is from a speech of Sir Edward Grey, made in 1910," Nils said, stuffing the book back into his pocket. "So long ago, a great Englishman saw this so clearly, and spoke it. But his nation did not listen."

"The press spoke louder," said Miss Glanfield.

"Perhaps one day calamity shall speak louder still, and then all mankind must listen," Nils answered. He went off later to his bed in the hollow, thinking of the writer's words and the old Doctor's—they had a potency in some ways exceeding the potency even of green-gold hair and a beautiful way of walking.

And as the days passed, his initial thrill of pleasure—and it had been a real thrill—at finding Mrs. Thurston so transformed was gradually overlaid by his increasing pleasure and interest in his re-discovered friend, Susan Glanfield. Her great power of communication, the range of her experience, the breadth and fearlessness of her views and her pungent expression of them—all these were deeply satisfying to the Swede. And there was also that sheer uncajoling charm. He spent more and more of his time talking to her. Dr. Crowninshield often sat by, crocheting small garments —not for Mrs. Pieter's baby, but for those of poorer parents —with a curious rather wry folding of her thin mouth; Mrs. Pieter was much better, she was going to recover, and this left the old woman more at leisure. Gloire also sat there, listening and embroidering, with a faint and, as time passed, increasing expression of a sort of bewilderment which gradually deepened into a quite definite listlessness. Her walks with Larsen in the afternoons became shorter; he made a point of being back in time to share the tea which she made for Miss Glanfield, and then sat with her till the evening meal, and after it. At first, while the other

298

two talked, Gloire occasionally put in a question—rather trite and uninformed little questions—but gradually even these became fewer and fewer.

Dr. Crowninshield watched all this in silence for some time. Then, one morning when Gloire was out doing the washing with Lisa, she spoke. She had been looking at Miss Glanfield's leg and pronounced that she might safely start down as soon as they could collect a caravan of men and ponies. Sitting on the bed, she remarked—

"I guess you've forgotten what I said to you about Gloire, the day you came?"

Miss Glanfield looked up, surprised.

"I don't think so—no. I remember that talk vividly. Why?"

"You asked me then what I meant by saying that you and Gloire might come into conflict—what might come between you."

"I know. And I wonder more than ever now, when we've become friends."

"It hasn't occurred to you that Mr. Larsen could?"

"*Nils?* Good heavens, no." She was quite clearly astounded by the suggestion. "Dear Dr. Emmeline," she said earnestly, "I do assure you that there isn't the smallest emotional thing between me and Mr. Larsen, and never has been—oddly enough," she said, with her usual disarming candour. "We talk immensely, of course, but that's all."

"And it doesn't strike you that your talking might put most women's looks out of court, does it?" the old woman said, with a reluctant half-smile. "You're pretty naïve, for a great grown-up authoress!"

The colour came into the writer's square pale face.

"Actually, it hadn't occurred to me that Mr. Larsen was likely to fall in love with Gloire," she said, still with the quiet reasonableness that the old Doctor admired. "That, I suppose, is what you have in mind?"

"Something like it. I'd have liked her to have her chance, anyway."

299

"But Dr. Emmeline, she *has* it! Talking politics and falling in love are two *quite* different things, and they almost invariably happen with different people—except the Webbs, of course," said Miss Glanfield.

The old woman laughed outright, at that. But then her face grew grave, and even comminatory, again.

"Well, I told you you wouldn't know what you were doing when you broke her," she said. "You have been warned!" She got up rather wearily and went out.

This conversation greatly disturbed Miss Glanfield. She thought the old Doctor's idea unreasonable, actually; it would be madness for Nils to marry anyone like Gloire, and if he wasn't going to marry her, would either of them be much the better for falling in love? Possibly—she didn't exclude that; it was unlikely, though. But she was horrified at the bare idea of spoiling any chances that poor child might have, and shied away, as she always had, from entering into rivalry with any woman about any man. (Miss Glanfield had always been very take-it-or-leave-it in her relations with the other sex.) During the next day or two, while messengers went out to arrange for men and horses, and word was sent to the various gendarmerie posts on their homeward route, she tried, whenever Larsen was about, to be less in evidence; talking less and making brief friendly replies, when he started a subject, instead of her usual full and lively come-backs. Privately, she expected this to be useless, and it did not seem to work very well; the Swede merely studied her face solicitously and asked if she felt tired, or had a headache? When this happened she glanced, discreetly, in Dr. Emmeline's direction, but the old woman went rigidly on with her crochet.

Indeed the chief result of the writer's retiring from the evening conversations was less to make Larsen talk more with Gloire than greatly to increase his exchanges with the old American. He was eager to hear all that she could tell him about life in Albania, which he knew only as a summer visitor; though his knowledge of the country and its customs was intimate compared with Miss Glanfield's, it was superficial beside the old Doctor's, and night after night he drew her out. Feuds, birth customs, marriage customs—out it all came; Miss Glanfield listened enthralled. The accounts had a special interest for her when she could relate them to the Lek-Gionaj household; it enchanted her to hear how Pieter's wife (now on her feet again; she had been brought in to call on the writer by Mme. Lek-Gionaj) had come as a bride to the Kapidan's house riding on a white horse decked with garlands of evergreen and red bunting, escorted by her father, her brother, and a woman attendant; how Pieter's friends, in gala dress, had met her up on the pass, dancing round her in a circle and firing their rifles in salute till the volleys echoed down the valley—while Pieter in accordance with local custom had remained at home, doing his usual work and pretending not to know what all the fuss was about. This decreed coyness on the man's part delighted her, and she managed to refrain from drawing any of the anthropological parallels which sprang to her mind. The old Doctor had been present at the wedding feast, which lasted from noon one day till the following morning, and had heard all the special marriage songs—for the bride's ascent of the staircase to her room, for the serving of the various courses at the feast; both Nils and Miss Glanfield were impressed by the combination of ritual music with food and drink on such an occasion.

On another evening Nils asked about Christmas. "Do they make much of it here, with a tree and gifts, as we do in the North?" he enquired.

"They do make a great festival of it, but about as differently as possible from the Nordic or Teutonic set-up," Dr. Crowninshield answered. "There is no Christmas tree, and not much in the way of gifts, and they fast instead of feasting, on Christmas Eve."

"They fast? Really?" Nils said.

"Yes, unless Christmas Eve falls on a Sunday they eat no meat, only fish. The only ones to do any feasting that day are the animals."

"The *animals!* For goodness' sake!" Gloire exclaimed.

"Yes, on Christmas Eve the cows and goats and sheep, and even the chickens, are fed just before dark, and given an extra feed," the old Doctor said, smiling—"because of the Stable at Bethlehem, I guess."

Miss Glanfield could not restrain herself.

"How perfectly *golden!*" she said. "Do tell us everything they do."

"Why, all right. On Christmas Eve," said the old woman, "the housewife sweeps the house right through and white-washes it from end to end. She clears most of the ashes from the hearth, and at twilight she puts on the great log, like the Northern Yule log—that's pretty well the one thing our customs have in common with yours," she said, nodding her white head at the Swede. "When everyone has come in from work they dine, sitting in a semicircle round the fire; and after that the house-father lights a candle and says a prayer. Then he takes a spray of juniper and puts it on the fire—I really don't know what the significance of that is— anyway while it is crackling the family chants. When the chant is done the father pours a libation of wine on the log and on the four corners of the hearth; and for each of the corners he says a letter—K, R, Y, Q—that spells the Albanian name for the Cross. Then they bring an un-leavened loaf to the table, and the mother sets an apple with a sprig of olive stuck in it on the bread. The part of the loaf under the apple never gets eaten till three days are past—that's in memory of the three days in the Tomb."

"They seem to muddle Christmas and Easter up a good bit," Gloire observed.

"I should not call it a muddle—it seems to me rather profound, that they so recognise that the Birth led to the Death," the Swede said thoughtfully. Once again Miss Glanfield glanced at the old Doctor and once again the American would not meet her glance.

"But to my mind, about the nicest thing they do, up here in the mountains, is 'pledging the trees,' as they call it," Dr. Emmeline went on.

"What is that?" from Larsen.

"Why, fruit up here is pretty precious, they have so few vegetables, so every Christmas Eve, after all those ceremonies round the hearth are over, the father sends two of the sons out to the orchard; one takes an axe, the other hides behind each tree in turn. 'Will you give fruit this year or shall I cut you down?' The one who's hiding answers for the tree—'Do not cut me down; I shall give you much fruit'—and so they go the round of the orchard."

Again Miss Glanfield suppressed a reference to the customs of certain Pacific Islands.

"And what happens on Christmas Day itself?" Gloire asked—pledging the trees seemed to her a pretty dumb performance.

"Oh, at the first cock-crow the head of the chief house in each village comes out and cries—'Awake, oh villagers! Christ is born!'—and then all the men get up and come out and fire a volley for each household, one shot for each man."

"They seem mad on firing off their guns," Gloire observed. "Volleys at weddings, volleys at Christmas."

"Yes, that is one of their great ways of registering joy in public," the old Doctor agreed.

"Of course the Chinese fire off crackers on every sort of occasion," Miss Glanfield here put in, irrepressibly; "in theory it's to scare away the demons, but in practice I believe they like the noise! But do go on about Christmas Day," she added with a half-guilty glance at the old Doctor.

"Well, they attend Mass, of course—and then there is the special wheaten food. Overnight the mistress of the house puts a vessel of the finest clean wheat on the fire, and

303

leaves it to cook all night; and at the noonday meal on Christmas Day she pours melted butter over it, and they eat it. That's in remembrance of Bethlehem too—there is a legend that this was the shepherds' choicest food, and that they ate it in rejoicing for the Nativity on the first Christmas Day."

"On the whole, I do not think one can say they muddle," Larsen observed to Gloire. "They seem to have the Christmas aspect well in mind."

"The wheat reminds one of Buddha's porridge in China," said Miss Glanfield.

"What is that? In China, I never ate it," Nils said.

"Oh well, you wouldn't in hotels, and lots of Europeans don't know anything about it. But if your servants know you well on one special day in the Buddhist Calendar they bring you a most extraordinary mixture for breakfast—peas, small beans, millet, lentils, rice, every sort of grain, all boiled together. The legend is that in one village the Buddha was refused food, so he went and sat, hungry, under a tree outside the gates and slept; and while he slept all the birds and insects came and filled his begging-bowl with every sort of grain and seed."

"I like that," said Dr. Emmeline.

"It sounds rather nasty to eat," said Gloire.

"It is, horrible—but we always ate it down to the last chick-pea, because it was so nice of the boys to let us in on it," said Miss Glanfield.

The last night came. Larsen was going to escort them down, and in addition the General had sent Fran up again to wait on Miss Glanfield. That night, for the last time, Lek-Gionaj and Pieter dined with their guests, and before the evening meal Mme. Lek-Gionaj came and took coffee and raki with them, accompanied by Lisa and little Marte, and Mrs. Pieter, still looking fragile and big-eyed. It was a much less formal visit than the first evening. Dr. Emmeline acted as interpreter, but this time Miss Glanfield and the

304

Princess had subjects in common—her health, Mrs. Pieter's health, the baby, the imminent migration of the household to the high pastures (which had been postponed for a few days on the writer's account), gratitude, pleasure. Gloire for her part spoke and laughed independently with Lisa and Mrs. Pieter; though thumbs were occasionally twiddled, it was all much livelier than on the day they arrived. Miss Glanfield had decided to surrender her wrist-watch, a rather charming one with a gold mesh strap, in token of gratitude —this was duly presented and obviously gave great pleasure. It was arranged that Larsen should take it down to Tirana and try to get Mme. Lek-Gionaj's name and a suitable inscription engraved on it—for a gift without an inscription means little in Albania. Gloire slightly embarrassed everyone by giving Lisa the huge diamond bracelet which Nils had noticed in the train—it was a rather overwhelming present. However, after it had been duly admired on the dark velvet sleeve of the young girl's jacket, Mme. Lek-Gionaj impounded it, observing that such jewels were only for married women, and that Lisa would be able to wear it later on—at which there was giggling and blushes. The old Doctor, with her usual competence, had caused the messengers who went for the ponies to bring up a large linen bag full of silver leks—these Gloire, on her instructions, gave in handfuls to the children of all the household servants, the correct and rather pretty method of tipping in High Albania.

When dinner—a positive farewell banquet—was over, and the Lek-Gionaj men had gone, Larsen lingered a little.

"How much I wish that you would write a book!" he said to the old Doctor.

"Now why in the world should you wish that?"

"So that more of your countrymen could know Europe as you know it. It is beyond price, your knowledge and comprehension."

"If you do write one, have an English edition, too!" said

Miss Glanfield. "We could do with more of your sort of knowledge."

"In England you know more of Europe," Nils said.

"Of course we do—we're so much nearer to it. But our behavior, though it may be fairly well-informed, is often awfully stupid and insensitive and unimaginative towards little European nations. We don't really consider their needs or their findings, a lot of the time. That's why we alienate them, and throw away all sorts of chances. You must be well aware of that," the writer said briskly to Nils. "We mean well, but we are careless and lazy and ignorant, fundamentally. At this moment we could buy the Italians right out of this country with a loan of five million pounds— Frasheri was talking to me about it—with all that that may mean in the future both for the Balkans and for our own interests. But Albania won't get that loan—it won't seem important enough, either to the Foreign Office or the Treasury! And all the prestige we've got through running the gendarmerie all these years will go by the board and we shall let the Italians have their way and allow our control to be terminated. Afterwards we shall be sorry, of course— when it's too late, and the Italians are in full control."

"Anyway, though, you do take a hand," the old Doctor said. "The British have the tradition of responsibility for Europe—the way you're talking yourself, right now, shows it. We don't; we stand aside. And yet we keep on telling the world how to go on. If I were a European I would feel the American strictures and exhortations to be *insufferable*, in the strictest sense of the word! If you are going to be like Pilate, and wash your hands of the world, then go the whole way with Pilate. Pilate asked what Truth was?—he didn't keep on telling folks what he thought it was, and washing his hands at the same time!"

The others laughed.

"I think your press is partly to blame, that your people know so little," Nils observed.

"To whom do you say it! Of course it is. We have more reporters, and pay them more highly, than any country on earth—and know less! But that's because of our false conception of what constitutes 'news.' Facts aren't news," the old American said bitterly, "and good solid *reportage* on the elements of a situation, such as you get in even quite mediocre European papers, isn't news either. News is sensation, or gossip, or attacks on some nation or person. If there is a piece of straight news we have to sensationalise it, in other words, to distort it. Why, men—our star reporters —are actually specially engaged and paid high salaries precisely for their known skill in dramatising—and distorting— what goes on. Our very phrase, a 'news story' gives the whole set-up away. When I was a child, telling a story meant telling a lie! And it still means that, I guess."

"Yes, but you know that tendency is growing with us," said Miss Glanfield. "And I deplore these huge circulations, too. One man, or one group, shouldn't have the power to mould the political conceptions of eighteen million people, as a paper with a daily circulation of two or three millions does. I would like to see the circulation of all papers limited by law to, say, 100,000 each. Then the rewards would be so small that people wouldn't buy papers as a commercial speculation, like factories, and the power wielded would be too modest to tempt the political adventurers. And yet you would preserve the freedom of the press."

"Well, you may get that, but we shan't—money talks too loud," said the old Doctor. She rose as she spoke. "Now," she said firmly to the writer, "you're going to bed before your travels. Goodnight, Mr. Larsen, and goodbye. I hope we meet again some time."

When Nils had departed the old Doctor took out her despatch case and wrote for a long time, while the others prepared for bed. Gloire had settled Miss Glanfield and was already under her own red quilt, smoking a last cigarette, when the old woman finally screwed on the top of her

307

pen, snapped her case to, and came over with an envelope in her hand.

"I thought maybe I would worry you with some chores to do for me, when you get back to Tirana," she said.

"Why, of course, Dr. Emmeline. What is it?"

The old woman put the envelope down on the bed.

"There's a list in there of a number of things I need—dressings and drugs and so on. Some you'll get in Tirana, maybe; the others you'll have to order from Bari. You'll just have to hunt around. There's a cheque in there—if it isn't enough, I'll send you along another; if it's too much, you can send me back the balance."

Gloire was slightly taken aback.

"You're sure I'll know what to get? I don't know much about dressings and all that."

"Pretty well anyone can buy from a list, if they give their mind to it," the old woman said brusquely.

"Why, yes. Well anyway I'll try," Gloire said, fingering the envelope hesitantly.

"Don't open it till you get down, either," said the Doctor, "or the cheque will fall out and get lost."

"O.K. Oh, how will I get them up to you?" the young woman asked—"Where will you be?"

"I haven't an idea! You'll just have to find that out," said Dr. Crowninshield, still brusquely, but with a queer little smile.

Now what's she up to? the writer thought; she had watched the little scene with interest. Gloire seemed rather an odd choice for this task. But she was sleepy, and only gave it a passing thought. Before the American had completed her old-fashioned and rather elaborate nocturnal toilet, Miss Glanfield and Gloire were both asleep.

16

THEY made an early start next morning, for the journey was to be in easy stages. Lek-Gionaj had lent a sure-footed pony of his own for Miss Glanfield's use, with a better saddle than those of the usual caravan ponies, and one of his own men to lead it; the leg, still in a splint, was supported in a broad canvas sling with a loop to pass over a man's shoulder—Fran and Larsen took turns at carrying this, or walked beside the writer, to steady her if the pony should stumble. A couple of gendarmes from the post at Torosh were to escort them half-way to that night's camp; these included the cheerful corporal who had given Gloire coffee and played the accordion to her before High Mass on Whit-Sunday.

They took the steep path through the pine woods up onto the pass; then, after a rest, followed a track which contoured round the head of the valley, keeping practically to the watershed. From the pass onwards the country was new to all of them; there were splendid and unfamiliar views, back towards Mali Shënjt and Torosh, ahead and to their left out over Kthellë, to range upon range of huge tumbled mountains; bare limestone ridges, a cold blue in shadow, with black blurs of forest on their lower slopes. The forests interested Larsen—a lot of felling had recently been done, rather casually, to his trained Scandinavian eyes, of *P. pinaster*, but there was no sign of re-planting; this appeared to be left to the processes of natural regeneration. However these seemed to work fairly well; everywhere where clearing had taken place a healthy, if patchy, undergrowth of young trees was springing up.

At length they reached a spot where a track plunged down towards Kthellë e Epër—Upper Kthellë. Here fresh gendarmes should have met the party, but there was no sign of them, so they lunched, and waited. And here the forestry-minded soul of Nils Larsen was vexed by the behaviour of the pony-men. There was at this place a fine growth of young pines, about six feet high, in the clearings; having eaten, the Albanians pulled long knives from their belts, and proceeded to cut off the leader of tree after tree, just below the junction with the first lot of lateral shoots. His interpreter at his earnest request elicited the reason for this wanton destruction of future forests. The leader, soft and tender still, could be hollowed out to make the stem of an excellent pipe, and one of the lateral shoots, cut short, would be similarly scooped out to hold tobacco—indeed, Fran proceeded to fabricate the rough draft of such a pipe on the spot, to demonstrate.

"That's clever!" Gloire said admiringly, watching Fran's brown hands at work.

"For the trees it is disastrous," Nils said sombrely.

Presently, hot and out of breath, there appeared on the track above them one gendarme and two peasants, the latter in the customary fancy dress and even more heavily armed than usual—their belts bristled with long-barrelled revolvers and daggers, they carried their rifles in their hands, not slung at their backs. All three were evidently in a high state of excitement, and gabbled out a long story to the corporal from Torosh, of which Larsen's interpreter passed on the gist to his employer. They had been waiting further along by the head of the track down to Kthellë e Posht; the two peasants, the single gendarme explained, were stout-hearted men, who had come to guard the travellers; no more gendarmes could be spared, for a murder had taken place between Kthellë and Rësheni that morning, and they were all out hunting the murderer.

This news produced a highly stimulating and agreeable

sensation. Fran, the caravan men, and the two Toroshi gendarmes gathered round the newcomers, pressing them eagerly for details. The aggressor, it seemed, had just completed a term of three years' imprisonment in Scutari for attempted murder, and had returned home the previous day, when he had got his rifle out of the thatch, oiled it and loaded it, and gone off at daybreak that morning to lie out for the enemy whom he had failed to finish off on the previous occasion! And this time he had got him, on the long valley track between Kthellë and Rësheni. No, the man was not quite dead yet; he had been carrying a satchel of bread on his back, which had slowed down the bullet—"but he will die" the men said, in tones of gloomy satisfaction.

Rather to Larsen's surprise, both his companions seemed to find these tidings almost as exhilarating as the Albanians did, when the interpreter gradually unfolded them.

"Well good for him!" Gloire exclaimed, slender and European once more in her shirt and renovated grey trousers.

"How fascinating!" Miss Glanfield, *more suo*, observed. "I suppose we ought to be sorry for the poor man with the load of bread, but really it *is* rather fun to run into a real full-grown feud and murder. Do try, Nils, to find out what it was all about, originally."

But there they failed. After the first burst of excitement, the clannish suspicious caution and clam-like silence of the mountaineer descended on their escort. They would tell a compatriot, they might have told Colonel Robinson—but they were not going to tell foreigners, or a townsman from Tirana like the interpreter, any more than they could help. The Toroshi gendarmes saluted and departed on their homeward road and the caravan pursued its way, dropping down through pine woods into the summer green of deciduous trees, and emerging from these onto valley fields and pastures, where the hay was cut and flowers few. Below an open slope of grass starred with bushes, still some distance above the valley floor, where a grey river sang its

311

loud song, the gendarmes showed them the suggested site for their camp—a level lawn-like space of smooth turf, at one side of which stood a single tree, some species of pear or plum, with a surprising spread of branches and a strong elegant trunk. Here Miss Glanfield was lifted off her pony and set down on the grass; the tents were pitched, a fire started, and Fran, after serving tea, produced the usual delicious supper. They sat—Miss Glanfield reclined—round an upturned case which served for a table; above the green of the valley pearl-pale hills rose into a pale sky of tenderest grey-blue—sharply cut, behind them, by the grey-green of the slope down which they had come; the bushes on it, in the muted late light, detached themselves from their background as dark significant shapes, of a beauty impossible by day.

Gloire was rather silent at supper. She was heavy with emotion; half-stifled with it, to the point of finding it hard to eat. This was her last night in these pale mountains that she had learned to love, and it might well be her last night in Larsen's company. She was considering, with a painful urgency, whether she could inveigle him into a stroll in this singing valley, loud with the river's voice; she wanted, for once and finally, to tell him what it had all meant to her, to thank him. Oh yes, she had done that once already, on the spur below the Kapidan's house, the evening that he arrived —but it was different now. He was more important to her now.

She succeeded. Aware of a slight reluctance on his part to leave Miss Glanfield, nevertheless she persevered; among the bushes about them the grey-green shapes of gendarmes were occasionally visible, mounting guard—returned from their fruitless pursuit of the murderer, they had closed in to protect the foreigners, in a silent unobtrusive circle. This in itself put a curious little edge of tension onto the evening—but it also made it reasonable to leave the writer. Larsen fussed over her, propped her up with coats against

312

the tree-trunk, asked if she was all right?—Miss Glanfield, amusedly gracious but brusque, shooed them off for their walk.

Poor Gloire! She was happy in a way when they set out—happy and yet burdened. It mattered terribly to her, tonight, to know if she would see the Swede again, and if so, when, and when he was leaving Albania—and she didn't know. She had got to find that out, and she wanted to tell him all those things she had thought of at supper, thought of so hard that she couldn't eat. She must use, skilfully, this moment that she had manœuvred for and obtained, this exquisite evening in an exquisite place. They walked along the slopes above the river—the nightingales were still singing, but less furiously than five weeks before; only delicate isolated voices, sending clear jets of liquid notes out into the cool evening air, like violin solos above the orchestration of the river's strong music.

But she could not do it skilfully, when it came to the point. She did it pathetically badly. She had become defenceless where Larsen was concerned; even her little futile fortifications of boredom and contempt were no longer available to her. Her very spiritual development stood in her way; for, as on the day below Mali Shënjt, she could not bring herself to employ the devices of physical attraction, or the deliberate appeal of the pathetic. Gloire had stopped using vulgar means to any end, even a high one—and for her a high end was involved. Paradoxically, she was frustrated in her attempt to make a fundamental communication to Larsen by her sense that he was the one person living who could be to her and do for her what Tony had been, and could have done. And—insistent, bitter, and urgent—was the feeling, pulsing up through all her endeavours to clear her mind and say what she meant, that she *couldn't* lose him, just *couldn't!*—and perhaps she had got to.

All this confused her and hindered her speech, never

313

good. She was banal. Nils recognised some at least of the feelings that lay behind her inadequate words, and he was moved—but by the pathos of them, not by herself, as he had been when they met on the bridge below the church. And gradually her sixth sense for men made her aware of this. Still she struggled on—this wasn't just the ordinary straightforward battle of the sexes; it was worth struggling on. But at last one thing told her that she was done. Nils, honest and tactless, perhaps a little perversely blind, to show that he understood what she was trying to express quoted a sentence from one of Miss Glanfield's books, with acknowledgements—"it is the sort of thing she puts so well."

The young woman turned away sharply, at that, and put her face into a flowering bush; she pulled off a spray and held it before her face, sniffing at the white scentless blooms, before she attempted to answer. The pathos of that particular gesture was lost on Nils; he thought she was hesitating over her words, as she often did. And when at length she said—"Yes, frightfully well, doesn't she?" in a conversational if slightly stifled voice, he was perfectly satisfied.

Nor did Gloire, even then, feel it was Miss Glanfield's fault in any way, this defeat of hers—as perhaps it wasn't. She just accepted it as inevitable. She lay outside her tent, the Methodist chapel—it was so warm—later that night, watching the stars through the fine small branches of the spreading tree, thinking how wonderful Miss Glanfield was, and how natural that a person like Larsen, who was wonderful too, should be unable even to concentrate on anyone else while she was around—especially when she was his friend, and of such long standing. She, Gloire, had probably been a fool to think that he might ever fall for her; she wasn't his type. Only, she needed him so badly! The hot tears slid out over her tanned cheeks; she brushed them away, and went on doing some pretty hard thinking. She had got something out of all this; she had got a lot—and she would just have to do without the so much more that

314

Larsen might have given, and carry on with what she had, alone. Gloire was quite unclear as to what form this carrying-on should take, but quite definite as to the internal substance of it. But doing it alone, but losing Larsen—that, as she faced it, was a heavy, a gnawing pain. She felt *tired* with it—and after a time, in that fatigue, slept.

Miss Glanfield, while they strolled, had been thinking about them. She saw much more clearly than Nils what was going on in Gloire, and she didn't think she would make the grade, poor child. But her thoughts presently turned altogether to Larsen. It was a most curious business, his turning up again like this—and it had been a very happy thing, finding him again. He was part of her youth and her past—her lovely climbing past—and a very important part of it. She was convinced that there had never been any emotional nexus on his side; and on hers, he had been so much mixed up with the whole emotional and spiritual adventure of mountaineering that she had never been able to disentangle them. She had been so young then, too, she reflected; and her generation, the educated young women of the first decade and a half of the century were singularly unemotional while they were young. There was none of the intellectual curiosity about sex which the films and the psychological novels had brought in immediately after the war, let alone the cheerful mixed discussion of it, over drinks, which was now so prevalent. A good thing or a bad thing? She didn't know, and to her immediate thoughts the question was irrelevant. The point was that in her youth, emotion—how deliberately she could not, at this distance of time, be sure any more—had been kept out of the picture in one's relations with serious men, as a rule; and indeed the avoidance of it had been quite as much on the men's side as on the girls', unless they decided to marry you.

No—with herself and Larsen the thing between them had been that they were acutely in sympathy about almost everything, but about mountains and the meaning of moun-

315

tains above all. And since for her, for many many years, mountains had taken the place of religion, had satisfied her religious sense, her need for adoration and worship as no service in any Cathedral, however sublime, had been able to do, he had come to take an almost hieratical place in her mind. You could not call this love in the ordinary sense; and she had not, and did not now call it that—but looking back over the other men with whom, awakened by marriage, she had been avowedly and specifically in love, she realised, as she too lay awake under that tree in Kthellë, how much more important Nils Larsen had been to her interior life than any of those others. They had become dim in her mind. Nils had never become dim; the idea and the picture and the atmosphere of him had always remained vivid and potent to her.

This seemed to her queer, and very interesting; she lit a cigarette to consider it. This was a thing you couldn't put into a book and get away with, she thought (the unloved and unwished-for writer in her butting undesired into her thoughts as she so often did)—because people just wouldn't believe it, the importance a man and a woman could have for one another, without any question of love entering. And yet it was true; and fascinating, the strange durability of such a relationship, lasting on and on through the years—through separation, through other most searching experiences, like marriage and children. It almost looked as if a relationship upon which the physical had never so much as breathed were the most perdurable of all. One returned to it, as she and Larsen had returned, to find it untouched—only enriched and deepened by their separate experience; one began again where one had left off, with no sense of the lapse of time, and no need to feel one's way or pick up threads. When they were together, at once there they were, their old selves.

This struck her as being immensely reassuring and she lay quiet, thinking how rich and satisfying and strange life

316

was, and how it went on and on, always producing some new facet or aspect, some fresh revelation of an unguessed-at experience. She fell asleep on this note, without so much as thinking again of Gloire. Larsen, healthily fatigued, had fallen asleep some time before, without thinking of either of them.

The fact was that Larsen, as a rule, thought chiefly about politics and social problems; he did very little thinking about individual people unless they confronted him with a problem of some sort. Mrs. Thurston, in the train, had so confronted him, but now he regarded her problem as practically solved—Susan Glanfield and Albania had done it between them. He had been pleased with what she told him, and with what he could see for himself, but the thing was done. To what use she would put her revised outlook he had no idea; it would mean a long struggle with habit and circumstance, but time would make some issue to that clear, and he had no doubt any more but that she would win. Poor Gloire!—her very struggle to tell him where she now stood had only served, so to speak, to put her on the shelf in his thoughts. He recognised his initial share, of course, and that to some extent it would be a continuing share in her mind; but—again perhaps a little perversely, a little deliberately—he limited that share to the original impulse. He did not allow his mind to recognise how much more than that his share could have been.

He was in fact much more interested in Susan Glanfield, the ardent, poetical girl of his youthful admiration, turned by time into such a mature and satisfying and entertaining person. Like her, he was happily impressed by the ease and permanence of their renewed relationship. But he was beginning to be in a hurry, now, to get back to civilisation— to hear what the Italians were up to and what line England was going to take over the Abyssinian *fait accompli*. As he shaved outside his tent next morning, his bare feet on turf agreeably cool with dew, he thought with great satis-

317

faction that he would be in Tirana that evening, able to go round to the Scandinavian Legation and hear the latest news, and perhaps on to see that nice American, Warren Langdon, and discuss it all with him.

The track down from Upper Kthellë to Rësheni is long, hot, and dry; much of it passes over stairlike blocks of granite, on stretches of path so narrow that Nils found it extremely difficult to squeeze down them alongside the shoulders of Miss Glanfield's pony while he supported the sling. At one point the teamsters clustered round the gendarmes with a great chattering and gesticulation, and the interpreter showed Nils a dark stain on a rock beside the path—blood from the murder of yesterday. Shortly before noon they reached the first houses of Rësheni, which is a long straggling parish, and by the church they encountered the priest, a curious figure to Western eyes in the sort of black yachting-cap which Albanian Catholic priests wear out of doors—it looked so odd above a soutane. The priest invited them to inspect his church, and Gloire and Larsen did so, while Miss Glanfield rested in the shade. It was large, and in surprisingly good order: fresh paint and gilding and whitewash, fresh flowers in the chapels and before the images. But the Swede was almost painfully moved by the offerings at the various shrines, they afforded such touching evidence at once of piety and of poverty. On the ledge below one statue lay a single egg, before another a sock, skilfully knitted in black and white wool; in front of a third, two lumps of sugar on a green leaf. Larsen commented on this to the priest, a rather simple man with a charming rugged face, who had been educated at Ulm and spoke excellent German. Yes, his people were poor, the priest said —bitterly poor; under-nourishment was chronic and acute. Larsen asked how he managed to keep his church so fine? The priest smiled with unaffected pleasure. Ah, it looked nice, did it not? Well, he saved and scraped, and his one or two rich parishioners made presents; and he had written to friends in Germany—and now the church was "worthy." Nils was struck by the happy devotion with which he pronounced the word.

The saving and scraping was acutely in evidence when he took them into his presbytery for coffee. They climbed a ladder-like wooden stair to a very poor dwelling indeed: one rough wooden armchair with a worn and faded cushion; a little shelf of books, a deal table and two or three kitchen chairs, a crucifix. No carpet, rug, or curtains—and no other furniture save a pair of wooden sugar-boxes nailed together, with a piece of figured cotton hanging in front, which served as a cupboard; from this the priest took a supply of the local hairy tobacco and handed it to his servant, with some coffee, for the entertainment of the caravan men downstairs. The walls stood in sore need of a fresh coat of whitewash; they were fly-spotted and stained with damp. Even Gloire was struck by the contrast between the dinginess of the priest's house and the freshness and smartness of his God's. The only beautiful thing in the room was a line engraving of Ulm, and even that was neither expensive nor valuable; only the grace of the city's profile, spire and tower and high-pitched roofs, gave it beauty. The priest eyed it wistfully, as he sat and talked. Did they know Ulm? Ah, a beautiful city! And such cultivated people—one never lacked for conversation, there. And the music! Glorious services; concerts! His tired eyes glowed. An old lady whom he had known during his student days there had sent him that picture; she would never know the pleasure she had given. "I return,"—he said, gazing, "when I look at it." Loneliness, he admitted, mental isolation, was his worst trial.

Nils, always practical, asked if nothing could be done to raise the level of subsistence? Was the soil actually too poor? It didn't look so, down here in the valley.

No, the priest said, the soil was not the crux; it was poor, but not as poor as all that. It was the habits and preferences of his flock that kept them so ill-fed. And he related the

319

lamentable story of his attempt to introduce the potato into his parish as an article of food. He had procured seed potatoes, dug a plot outside the Presbytery, planted them, hoed them up, showing his parishioners each stage of the process. Finally he summoned them to be present at the lifting and they exclaimed with delighted wonder at the numbers of tubers where but one had so recently been planted before their eyes—1200 per cent, at least! they said. Then he gave them a banquet of potatoes—boiled potatoes, baked potatoes, potatoes fried and stewed in milk; and they ate them with relish. Yes, this was excellent food, and they would greatly like to have some themselves. Accordingly the following spring the enterprising little priest procured, with immense trouble, seed potatoes in bulk from Bari, and distributed them to each household in the village—and each household cooked and ate them forthwith!

Gloire and Larsen laughed, in spite of the priest's distressful face; but they agreed that the Albanians were not an easy people to help. "Capital is what's wanted here," Gloire observed as they went away; "obviously he can't do much alone, poor little thing. It needs a whole team of people, with lots of cash, to keep on and on giving them potatoes, and to sit over them and just *make* them plant them! Dr. Emmeline could, if she had the time. Goodness, how I should like to fix that priest's house for him; get it painted up, like his church, and give him a decent armchair, and more books, and a good radiogram with plenty of records. It wouldn't cost anything, really."

"No. For the price of two of your dresses, you could do that," Nils said.

The colour came into her face.

"Well, maybe I will," she said.

An ambulance was waiting when they reached the end of the motor road at Rësheni, but not the car for Larsen and Mrs. Thurston. While Fran paid off the caravan men Gloire strolled across the meadow towards the little wood of oaks

320

which hid the Fani Vogel. It was well into June now, and mid-afternoon; the nightingales were silent. She stood still, remembering her unexpected happiness as she rode across that meadow six weeks before, and her sense of expectation. Well, a lot of things had happened, but not the one wonderful thing. When she met Larsen on the bridge at Torosh, she had thought maybe it would happen—but it hadn't. Rather bitterly, she wondered why. And then she remembered how on that other morning, so cool, so fresh with birdsong and dew and anticipation, she had heard her first Albanian proverb—"Don't measure your importance by your morning shadow." She smiled a wry little smile. "That's a pretty smart proverb," she muttered to herself, as she walked back towards the cloud of white dust which heralded the car.

17

"NOW don't talk in that perfectly dumb way! Of course you're staying here!"

Thus Warren Langdon, a few hours later, to Larsen, in the garden-room over drinks. Gloire and the Swede had shepherded Miss Glanfield into the Legation at Durazzo, and handed her over to Lady Carruthers' competent care; and Larsen had of course taken Gloire to the Langdons before going to the hotel, and had been hailed in by Warren.

"Go along and collect up your traps, if you won't let Cyril do it," Warren continued—"but you're staying here! Anything else just doesn't make sense."

Larsen was rather touched by the warmth of this invitation. And certainly the Langdon ménage offered a good deal more comfort than the Continental. He did as he was bidden; returned with his effects, revelled—grinning to himself—in a hot bath in his own bathroom, and reappeared before dinner in the garden-room fresh, hungry, and to Gloire's eyes startlingly sophisticated in a dinner-jacket. She was there alone, mixing cocktails.

"My, you look clean!" she exclaimed.

"I feel it. Almost surgically clean. What do you make, there?"

"A Smiling Duchess. I thought it would be a change from raki."

Gloire herself had paid a flying visit to the hairdresser, and was dressed once again in her old exquisite clothes; there was lacquer on her nails and make-up over her tan. She looked very lovely. Warren, fussing in, calling instructions about the icing of the champagne over his shoulder to his Swiss butler, eyed the pair of them. Yes, she looked grand, did Gloire; that sunburn suited her; but she had changed somehow. Warren didn't stop to analyse his impression; he just said to himself that she looked, someway, like an orphan-school child all dressed up.

The drinks were admirable, the dinner excellent. Warren had the passionate hospitality of the Bostonian host (once he has decided to receive you into his home at all) and had decided, happily, to make a little celebration of Gloire's return. He did it all so nicely, Nils thought—even his fussing was a welcome in itself, untiresome. How nice nice Americans were! That warmth—of interest, of affection, of benevolence—was a quite precious trait. Surely they must, in time, abandon their false gods and grow up into the maturer virtues and qualities too. It could only be a question of time, he thought, warmed by the champagne and the intelligent kindliness. And then was chilled by his mind's sudden question—will there *be* time? Can the world wait for them?

The beginning of dinner was devoted to Torosh, the Lek-Gionaj family, and all the adventures there. Warren knew of Lek-Gionaj as an important figure in local administration, and was interested to learn about the man himself, and his family life. Nils and Gloire supplied details in strophe and anti-strophe—both stressing the personality of the Princess. "She's great!" Gloire said more than once, with unaffected warmth. But presently Nils turned to his host with a question about the external situation—"I have heard nothing for ten days. Does anything happen?"

Warren's face grew gloomy.

"Oh, there's the most appalling mess-up in Abyssinia. The Italians are cruel bastards, as well as being pretty mean citizens."

"What has happened?"

"Well, they're using mustard gas all over the place, and burning the villages with incendiaries from the air. The

323

Ethiops have no defence, of course. Oh God, how I despise and hate the Italians!" Warren exploded. "They put on a show like this, just an exhibition of pure beastliness, about once every decade. In 1911 it was the Massacre of the Oases, when they were invading Tripoli; in 1926 it was the Massacre of the Senussi, when Graziani had the sheiks dropped alive out of planes, to burst like a bag of flour in their own villages. They're a mean, trumpery, wicked nation. Do you know that the Italian Minister here bribed two chieftains to murder Zahg? Sent them the money, with instructions!"

"Good Heavens! And what happened?"

"Oh, the pair of them came hustling down to Tirana, bribe in hand, and told the King all about it, and asked what they should do with the cash? The King laughed a great deal, and told them to put it in the poor-box."

"This is fantastic."

"The Italians are fantastic. Oh yes, and—to go back to Abyssinia—they're shooting up the Red Cross units that go to help the poor wretched blacks—flying low and pouring fire into them at point-blank range, so no one shall live to report on what they've done."

Nils was horrified, asked questions.

"I'll tell you some more later," Warren said, with a significant glance at his sister—"but they've touched a new low this time."

"And what does England say?—and France?"

Warren shrugged.

"Pious horror—no action. The British seem to be weakening on sanctions anyway—what was left of them."

"This is true?"

"Sure. Mr. Chamberlain, their Chancellor of the Exchequer, went down to the city the other day and made a speech to British Business at the Guildhall, and referred to sanctions as 'this midsummer of madness.'"

"Sanctions are no longer the policy of the British Government, then? But this is a most important change."

"It's the first intimation we've had of it, anyway. I don't know for sure if the Government have changed their minds. Maybe Chamberlain just meant to kill sanctions on his own."

"But this is distressing," the Swede said. He was deeply concerned. "I cannot conceive the need for such a change. Why should Chamberlain make such a démarche?"

Warren shrugged again.

"He's a business man. They don't always make the best statesmen. We should know," he added, smiling a sour little smile.

Politics dominated the conversation for the rest of the evening—Gloire and Miss Anne for the most part listened in silence. But Warren frequently glanced across at Gloire, languid and graceful in her swing, listening—with a slightly puzzled expression often on her pretty tanned face. And again he had that curious fancy about a dressed-up orphan.

When Gloire went to bed, leaving the two men to their highballs, she opened the old Doctor's letter; she had been too hurried with unpacking and the hairdresser and her toilet to do so before. She sat on the edge of the bed and read it. It was long, in a pointed spidery old hand, on fine paper—the handwriting was much older than Dr. Emmeline herself ever appeared to be, except when she was very tired; it gave her age away. Most of the letter consisted of a formidable list of medicines and dressings, which Gloire didn't even skim through; she was appalled by its length and by the long difficult words. But there were two sentences, one at the beginning and one at the end, which claimed her full attention.

My dear Gloire [the letter began],—If you can and will procure these things for me promptly, either in Tirana or from Bari or Rome—and some will certainly have to come from Italy—you will be doing a real service to people for whom, I think, you have begun to feel some affection, as well as helping a very tired old woman!—I get more and more oppressed by the extent of the need here, and my own inadequacy to cope with it.

325

And at the end, above the delicate wavering old signature, were these words:

Thank you in advance; and if you should feel inclined, any time, to come back to High Albania, remember that I can always do with an assistant!—you are not a doctor, I know, but you have a number of different sorts of wealth—energy and health and capacity—that you could harness to anything you had a mind to, I guess—and there is a need for just those things here.

Gloire sat for a long time with the letter in her hand, after reading that. Then she read both sentences again. Curiously enough, it was the priest at Rësheni and his bare shabby room which came most sharply into her mind. Oh yes, there was a need here, right enough—and she had the health and strength and she had money too. And Nils was going down to Corinth next week to go across to look at the silk mills at Broussa—she had heard him tell Warren so; and anyway he would never think much about anything but politics—and Susan. She put the letter down and began to undress; but by the time she had thrown off her clothes, creamed the unwonted make-up off her face and got into bed, the question which had been unresolved only the night before, under the tree in Kthellë, was suddenly settled. The next step, at least, on the road along which she must travel alone was clear.

Gloire continued to puzzle Warren during the next day or so. Except at meals, he saw little of her; she was either going round the chemists' shops with Cyril, returning laden with packages, or else borrowing his typist and dictating long letters to other chemists in Rome. And she made rather a fuss about seeing the General and getting a letter sent off by hand to Dr. Crowninshield—though what it could possibly contain to give it that much importance was a mystery to Warren. He was genuinely anxious to find out what had happened between her and Larsen up at Torosh; that something had passed between them he was convinced, and he tried once or twice—very tentatively and with elaborate circumlocutions—to draw Gloire on the subject. But Warren seldom had the courage of his intuitions, and he shrank from the friendly directness that might have achieved a direct response—Gloire rather sweetly eluded him, as so much of life had eluded him always, and always would.

Of Larsen, on the other hand, he saw a great deal; and the more he saw of the Swede, the more his respect and liking for him grew. There was an honest simplicity and openness about the man which was very bracing to Warren's shivering delicacy and, baffled by Gloire, he turned at last to him for enlightenment. It was a tribute to Nils' quality that the Bostonian found it almost easy to say to him, one day in the garden-room—"I feel it might be quite a plan if you were to marry Gloire."

Nils, who was smoking and drinking, comfortably extended in a long chair, never turned a hair. He took another sip from his glass, smiled equably, and said, with great deliberation—

"I had rather marry Miss Glanfield."

Warren was thoroughly flummoxed.

"Why—but hasn't she a husband?—and a family?"

"I believe so—unless he is dead. I only said I had rather," the Swede pursued imperturbably, still smiling.

So that disposed of that. Larsen was a pretty smart guy, Warren conceded inwardly—too smart for him, anyhow. But it left him convinced, just the same, that there *had* been something there. Poor Gloire! What was all this racket with chemists, anyhow? However, twice baffled, he fell back onto the much more congenial subject of international politics. He and Larsen ranged over the whole field, coming back, always—as was natural enough in their case—to Albania and her specific problems, and to her main menace, Italy.

"This is insane, what England does, to call off sanctions," the Swede said at one point. "If she had put on oil sanctions in the winter, the Abyssinian campaign would now be over. Your country would have come in?"

"I guess so. But whether we did or not, as the British and the Dutch control over seventy per cent of the world's oil tankerage, they could have cut off fuel supplies effectively themselves."

"Yes. True. Or Britain could now, this spring, have closed the Suez Canal. This would have had the same effect."

"The French wouldn't have liked that."

"Possibly not. But what could they do against England? To me, this is incomprehensible! England is not Finland." Warren laughed. "No, but Mr. Langdon, this is such dangerous folly. To give Italy a free hand in Abyssinia is to invite gangster practices everywhere. Germany shall follow suit— you will see; and then Italy will come here."

Warren frowned worriedly.

"I know. You're plumb right. It was such a chance, last September, getting all those nations in on sanctions together; it looked as though the conscience of the world had really waked up and gone into action. People at home were very much impressed."

Larsen smoked.

"France again," he said at length. "She had her secret agreement of January '35 to give Italy *la mano libera* in Ethiopia. But Britain had no need to give in to France. It is a mystery."

"I guess Britain's *foutu*," Warren said gloomily.

"Oh no—no, she is not. Britain is never *foutu*," the Swede replied, tranquilly. "Though the good God alone knows why not! But this country here," he went on—"I care so much for it. Could America not help? For twenty million dollars you could set the place on its feet, start your fruit-farms, buy out the Italians, and make it an American sphere of influence. Could not the money be spared for this?"

"My dear man, you forget the Monroe doctrine—and still more the Monroe doctrine in reverse!—no Old-World entanglements. Congress fears Europe's ancient wickedness more than it fears the devil!"

Larsen sighed.

"Ah yes. However, a time will come. The world is one world now, however little we may like it." He leaned towards his host. "I am glad you are here—you and that old Doctor."

"Dr. Emmeline's a whole heap more use than I am!" Warren said, with a gloomy smile.

Over at Durazzo, too, there was curiosity about Gloire.

"Well, and how did your glamour-girl enjoy herself in the wilds?" Sir Arthur asked, when Miss Glanfield's own experiences had been thoroughly canvassed.

"Quite enormously. She got more out of it than any of us."

"Oh? How so?"

"She made tremendous friends with the Lek-Gionaj girl, Lisa—in fact with all of them; and ran about doing whatever they did. She got a real insight into their life."

"But how did she talk to them?" Helen Carruthers asked.

"Oh, she picked up quite a bit of Albanian, and made signs and so on; she's very good at languages."

"But did she enjoy it? Didn't she miss the fleshpots and the fashion-plates?"

"No, Arthur. I was right about her and you were wrong. She really enjoyed it—except the flies, which no one could enjoy! And she was absolutely invaluable, as it turned out. She waited on me hand and foot, gave me my bed-baths and made tea and things—I should have been wretched without her."

"Well, you surprise me," said Sir Arthur.

"That's only because you're so silly, Arthur. You're frightfully borné and unexperimental about people—diplomats always are," said Miss Glanfield with finality.

But the writer, lying out on a sofa at the far end of the long terrace, under the awning, spent a lot of time thinking about Mrs. Thurston. She was sure that she had done a lot more than enjoy herself and be useful up at Torosh—she was convinced that some re-orientation had taken place and, always practical, she wanted to ensure some useful outcome from it. Gloire had better do something—and start doing it at once; and if she had really suffered a bit of heartbreak over Larsen, she would probably be quite ready to start, the writer thought shrewdly. But what on earth could she do? Miss Glanfield turned over possibilities and schemes in her head, but nothing seemed quite to fit. The only thing to do was to talk to her, sound her out and see what she felt like. And pulling the worn despatch case which Gloire had first seen on the boat to Cattaro onto her lap, she indited a note, asked her young friend over to tea.

Miss Glanfield's own plans were taking shape. A pair of crutches had been procured from Italy, and she was learning to hobble about on them; the Military Attaché was coming over from Rome for one of his flying visits, with his wife—and on their return they would escort her to Bari, and put her on the Paris train in Rome. She would be met in Paris, and would manage all right. Miss Glanfield usually managed all right; the counterpart of her own constant impulse to put total strangers in the way of seeing Roman remains and iconographic paintings was that other total strangers, when she had need of help, sprang up from between the paving-stones to her assistance. With the measure that ye mete withal, it is measured to you again.

Her note—a kind, clever, affectionate little note—reached Gloire soon after she had received a second letter from Dr. Crowninshield. The old Doctor had come down to Kruja on another baby case, so a wild-faced boy in goat-skin sandals popped over with it. It was neither so clever nor so expansive as the writer's, but it filled Mrs. Thurston with a profound satisfaction.

Why yes [the old woman wrote],—I will love to have you. I was hoping you would say just that. Come right along when you have got some kit together. You will want your own bed and tent and sleeping-bag and basin and what-have-you. Get some *soft* luggage—strong canvas hold-alls. They are easier for the ponies. And some appropriate clothes. These people appreciate skirts! Maybe you could wait and bring my things along with you, when they come.

I will be very glad of your help.

The young woman took a curious pleasure in burning her boats. Without a word to Warren or anyone else, she telegraphed to book a room at an hotel in Rome, the nearest place where she could acquire "appropriate clothes" and canvas hold-alls and camping equipment. She telegraphed notice and a large compensatory sum to Fraser, her maid, still languishing at the Lido; and she telegraphed a comprehensive and peremptory order to her husband's bailiff in Northamptonshire for a ton of seed potatoes, an armchair, and a radiogram "with heaps of batteries" and "enough paint and distemper to fix a small house"—all to be consigned to Durazzo via Trieste. When she had done all this, and not before, she wrote warmly to Susan Glanfield, promising to come over to tea. And two days later she borrowed Cyril and the Cadillac and went.

Bowling along the dusty road, she leaned back thinking of the first time she had driven along it, and the idle mood of boredom and pre-contempt which was her normal state of mind before a party with people she didn't know. She did feel different now, Gloire thought. There was a solid lump of pain in her, connected with Larsen—Gloire's mental similes were of the simplest—but the rest of her was pretty content. And sort of tough. She was going to have a real job, something to do, instead of floating about like a jellyfish, carried here and there by any old current of whim or emotion. Even that lump of pain was a sort of anchor, she thought. The car topped the rise, and there before her was the lagoon, with a white fleet of pelicans on its blue surface, mere specks in the distance; and beyond, the piled-up pinkish-buff rectangles of the old houses of Durazzo, climbing the side of the pale little hill—the hill at which she and Susan Glanfield had stood looking from the Legation terrace on that momentous day when she asked if she could join the party to Torosh. Gloire sat up, recognising fully at last just how momentous that day had been. Susan had made a whole lot of difference—first taking her along, and so causing her to meet the old Doctor, but also in herself: all those things she had said about Tony, and about doing something for mankind. That had given a pointer, had directed the—well, the new feeling she had about things, that Albania and Nils between them had given her. It would be nice to see her and say goodbye, and tell her the new plan. Gloire was still entirely without resentment against Miss Glanfield on Larsen's account—so much so that as they drove along the causeway she peered anxiously out, trying to identify the spot where they had seen her standing with Mr. Hickson, all wet and muddy; because that had been a momentous meeting too. She couldn't be sure, and sat back as they entered the town, still in that strange security and contentment that was yet half pain, and went on thinking about the work that lay before her. It wasn't a very grand job—not glamorous in any way. Planting potatoes and washing things for an old American woman and waiting on peasants—that was what it would amount to, mostly. All very humble things—beginning at the bottom. Gloire had always hitherto despised the bottom, and those who either began or stayed there—she had despised the humble too, whether things or people. Yet she contemplated joining their ranks with a very positive satisfaction, at this moment. It made her feel safe, and somehow strong. This struck her as very queer, and she was still pondering in her untutored way on how queer it was when the car pulled up in the narrow lane, and she got out and went in through that funny little courtyard under the city wall, climbed the outside stair, and was ushered through the long cool passage dining-room out onto the terrace, where the blue glare of sea and sky hit her once again under the striped white-and-orange awning; and there at the far end, on a sofa by a spread tea-table, lay her friend—she felt that indubitably—Susan Glanfield.

They took tea, and talked of this and that. The Carruthers were out, to Gloire's relief. They both frightened her, called her old tiresome defences into action—and she didn't want to be on the defensive today. Susan alone was charming—amusingly gay, as she had come to know her.

But after tea Miss Glanfield got down to it. She did it very nicely and carefully, and of course with her usual rapidity, which made interruption almost impossible.

"Gloire dear, I've been thinking such a lot about you. I feel you've gone a long way lately." Gloire nodded obediently and sympathetically. Well, she had gone a long way! It was like Susan to know it.

"And I feel you will want to express that, somehow, in action—*do* something; something concrete." Gloire nodded again. Susan, as usual, was quite right. She was generally quite right.

"But just what? I've been wondering. Is there a job, do you think, on your husband's property? Infant Welfare, and the miners' wives, and all that?"

Gloire was quite unprepared for this organisation of her future. She stammered, rather feebly—

"No. I don't think that would do. I'm too American to be any good to the British. And anyway the property all went to Tony's brother, as we had no child." Her mouth twisted a little. "Tony wanted me to learn to climb and a pregnancy would have cut into that so. And there seemed such lots of time."

"Of course." Miss Glanfield was all sympathy. "But I have a feeling that it would be sound to do something almost at once," she went on, "while the impulse is fresh. Forgive me for being so sure the impulse is there," she said, smiling.

"Sure," Gloire said, "but——"

333

"But then, what?" Miss Glanfield pursued rapidly, thinking of secretaryships to Almoners in hospitals, or school Care Committees. "Can you type?" she asked. "And have you thought where you *would* want to be?" It was awkward if Gloire wouldn't work in England—she could so easily have fitted her into a job in England.

"Yes, I'd like to work here," Gloire said, beginning to smile—this was getting quite funny.

"Here? Good gracious! But my dear child, what could you do?"

"I'm going to teach the Albs to grow potatoes," Gloire said, grinning. "I've ordered a ton of seed. But that'll only be part-time—what they call 'seasonal occupation.'" She grinned more broadly than ever. "The rest of the time I'm going to help old Dr. Crowninshield—do chores for her. I'm going across to Rome in a few days to get my kit. It was her idea," Gloire ended cheerfully. "I do hope you approve."

If Miss Glanfield didn't actually blink at this information, her expression amounted to it.

"Good Heavens!" she exclaimed, and for once had no follow-up.

"Don't you think it's a good idea?" Gloire asked. She was too firm in her own conviction of the excellence of the idea to be damped by the writer's surprise, but she rather wanted Susan to think it a good idea.

Miss Glanfield recovered herself—she was as quick at that as at everything else.

"Actually, yes—I think it's a marvellous idea," she said warmly. "I think you'll be a great help—and pleasure—to her; and she's getting old, and needs help. And I think you'll enjoy it—and there couldn't be a greater need anywhere." Suddenly she laughed, her loud spontaneous laugh. "Have you really ordered a ton of seed potatoes? Where on earth from?"

"From England," Gloire said, smiling happily—"I've told

the bailiff to send them. I said he should write to Kew or the Ministry of Agriculture or somewhere and find out what potatoes grow best in South-East Europe. And he will—he's very smart. Tony thought the world of him."

"And when was all this hatched up?" Miss Glanfield was genuinely curious.

"Oh, she suggested it in that letter she wrote the last evening, with the list of drugs. So I wrote back and said I'd go. And I heard two days ago from her—she sounded pleased."

"I'm sure she did."

"You see," Gloire pursued, earnestly now as well as happily, "actually this could be a much bigger thing, if money were put into it. I don't know, but I don't fancy Dr. Emmeline is all that rich. Well nor am I, but I have quite a bit of money. And when I've been here a year or so and know the whole set-up, I don't see why I shouldn't finance two or three more units to go around. Dr. Emmeline could help me to choose the personnel. The ideal thing, I guess, would be to train Albanians to do it—doctors and orderlies and nurses. It would be quite an organisation."

Miss Glanfield fairly gaped at her.

"My goodness!" She paused, digesting it. "Gloire, you really have got onto something there," she said, as the possibilities unfolded in her mind. Yes, that was a thing Gloire could do extremely well; she could cajole anybody to do anything already, and if she gave her mind to organising something, doubtless she could do that too. Anyhow cajolery was always the better part of any form of really successful organisation! She leaned back on her sofa—excitement had caused her to sit up—and gazed thoughtfully at her young friend. Gloire was looking delicious today, fresh and finished in a tailored frock of some heavy expensive white stuff, with green-and-white sandals, green belt and turban, and emerald clips; but Miss Glanfield, who had seen her in tunic and trousers and a black fringed shawl,

335

looked beyond the Parisian figure before her to that other Gloire, and noted with real gladness the firm confident expression on the pretty square face, that was so reminiscent of the typical faces of South-East Europe. Funny that Gloire's bones should be the most European thing about her!

"Yes," she went on, much more slowly than usual—"you could make a tremendous thing of it, Gloire. And you seem to be planning to do it in such a wise way—beginning from the bottom, learning the ropes thoroughly, and building up gradually. So many frightfully worth-while enterprises fail from being begun on too big a scale, from the top, and without local and individual knowledge. Oh," she said, her generous enthusiasm growing as she envisaged the scheme more and more fully—"oh, *dear* Gloire, I think it's quite brilliant of you and Dr. Emmeline to have thought this up. It's the ideal thing for both of you—and it will be wonderful for Albania. Oh, I am so very glad."

Gloire was delighted by all this. Warmly, happily, presently, they exchanged addresses: her publishers for Susan, Brown Shipley in Paris for Gloire; and it was a moving moment for both when they took their farewells. Miss Glanfield might not be a real lover of humanity, as the old Doctor was, but she was a warm-hearted and generous person, and where her rather choosy and capricious affection was given, it was given whole-heartedly—and it had been so given to Gloire. The diffused general benevolence, too, had operated in Gloire's case with really dynamic results. And Gloire herself was fully aware of this. She owed much to Susan Glanfield, and in her unsophisticated simplicity she looked—wisely, perhaps—only on what she had gained by knowing the writer, not on what she had, possibly, lost. Simplicity is in some ways a blessed state.

Gloire drove back to Tirana in an even more contented frame of mind than she had driven out. She found the passage outside her room full of cases and parcels—some from the local chemists, two from Rome. She looked them over,

336

half with excitement, half dismally—she supposed they would have to be unpacked and the contents checked, a lousy job. Perhaps Warren's secretary, who was accustomed to such things—but then she gave herself a little shake. No, she must stop being so lazy, and shoving the boring tiring jobs off onto other people. She would do it herself, tomorrow. Larsen was leaving tomorrow, on the Corinth boat—when he was gone she would have nothing on earth to do. I guess I'll live to be glad of those cases, she thought, as she turned into her room.

She had not yet made up her mind whether or not to tell the Swede about her new "design for living," but she dressed and went downstairs early on the off-chance of catching him alone, merely to be with him—Warren always drank Old-Fashioneds till the last possible moment, and then went to have his shower, change, and be comfortably late for dinner; his household knew this, and arranged soufflés and the like accordingly. So little time left, Gloire thought, as she drifted downstairs—only this one evening. She had not been able, very humanly, to refrain from putting on one of the loveliest of her dresses, all beige lace and tulle and semi-revealings, a work of art in its own genre. There was no one in the garden-room when she got down, and she went out into the garden. The dress really wanted some coppery-orange flowers to set it off; she had a brooch at her breast to pin them with. She wandered about, looking for the exact note of colour; the garden was brilliant with flowers, and presently she found some roses of the perfect shade; she picked a few, arranged them, and was pinning them on when she heard Larsen's voice behind her—"Do you garden in this dress?"

She turned, unsmiling.

"No, I'm getting some flowers for it."

"That is charming," he said, when she had done. "Perfect. The dress is very beautiful. This is a thing you do extremely well—dressing. It is a contribution, too."

337

"To what?" she asked, smiling in spite of herself, as they walked down one of the paths.

"To civilisation," he said, grinning at her. She made a face at him.

"Where I am going, at Broussa, they make lovely materials," he said. "Silks, and cut velvets. Shall I send you some?"

"Yes, surely. I'd love that. Will you truly?"

"Yes. What sort of thing?"

"Enough cut velvet for a jacket with long sleeves—in very, very deep red," Gloire said, thinking of Lisa. His wish to give her a piece of stuff gave her extreme pleasure.

He took out his little book and noted that down methodically, making her smile.

"And you, what do you do, now?" he asked, stuffing the book back into his pocket. "Do you go on to Istanbul?"

"No. I'm staying here."

"For now, yes, but later?"

"I'm still staying here. For quite a time—perhaps for keeps."

Nils stood still and faced her.

"What does this mean?" he asked, suddenly grave—in Nils surprise was often expressed by gravity.

"Only that I've got a job. I'm going to help Dr. Emmeline. I don't know the first thing about medicine—it'll just be donkey-work, of course. But I shall learn Albanian, and I'll learn my way around down here."

He stared at her. "You mean to do this?"

"I certainly do."

"And it is settled? She agrees?"

"She suggested it," Gloire said dryly—she was hurt by the last question. He proceeded to hurt her more.

"And for how long do you mean to go on?"

"If it works out, perhaps for ages. I might put some money into it later on, and get some other units going. There'd be room for them."

338

"Indeed there would," he said. But he went first, as always, for the practical aspect. "And how would you staff these other units?"

"What I would *like* to do would be to train Albanians for it, men and women—endow them, or whatever you call it, to learn English and get their medical training over there, and then bring them back and pay their salaries and all that. But I'll have to see if I find the right people. I'll know, after a year or two here."

He looked at her now with a sort of deep grave pleasure.

"This is very splendid news," he said; "this is more than the best." He did not say—"that I had hoped for," but with his kind eyes upon her, Gloire knew that that was what he meant. "That old American," he said thoughtfully, studying her face above the lovely dress—"she is very wise. She is quite right. You shall do this well. And it shall make you very happy."

She was touched at his saying that; tears sprang to her eyes. And when he took her hand and kissed it, the bright drops came showering down. He saw them, and said very simply—

"Dear Gloire, you have made me so glad."

She stood among the flowers, looking at him.

"Well, in a way you've made me happy," she said rather quickly. "You said you wanted to, in the train after Trieste—and I told you it was quite an undertaking. But you've done it. Though why you ever wanted to be such a missionary beats me! But you're responsible for the whole thing—" and she broke away and floated back to the house, leaving Nils to follow slowly, sighing a little as he went along the sanded paths between the bright borders.

He left next day. Gloire occupied herself with the unwonted drudgery of unpacking, checking, and re-packing her first instalment of stores. Fagged but satisfied, she went down unchanged, long before dinner, in search of Warren's company and a drink. After a cocktail she felt expansive—

339

and anyhow the time had come to tell Warren that she was
going to Rome next week, and wanted to come back. She
did this, adding:

"I'm going to stop on and work here, Warren—understudy
Dr. Emmeline."

Warren sat up.

"Well for Heaven's sake! What do you want to do that
for?"

"Because I do."

"Well, I be darned! And what does the old Dottoressa
say?"

"Says she wants me."

"Well I be darned!" Warren repeated, staring from his
sad deep-set eyes at his pretty guest.

"Oh Warren, don't keep on saying that. And stop staring!
I know I don't look like it, but I'm sure I can do it. Don't
go blowing on it, and being a toad," Gloire said, half plain-
tive, half impatient. "Miss Glanfield thinks it a great idea,
and so does Mr. Larsen. Don't you think it's a sound plan?"

"Why yes—I'll surely think it's great, when I've had time
to get accustomed to the idea," Warren said. "Only *you*
drudging around waiting on sick peasants seems kind of
queer, just at first."

"If it works, it might mean a lot," Gloire said. "I think
Dr. Emmeline would have liked to expand some while back,
if she'd had the money. Well I *have* the money." She expanded herself, telling him of her schemes for the future.
In Warren, as he listened, the old affection for Gloire welled
up, tinctured as it was, inevitably, with scepticism.

"Yes, I'm sure you could do it, Gloire," he said as she
finished. "And it wants doing. I think it's swell, really. You're
a great little girl." He paused, puffing at his long cheroot,
his eyes wistful. As so often, he saw someone else, someone
tougher and more enterprising, doing something for which
he saw the need, but lacked the toughness and the enterprise. He startled her by saying, "If you're really going to

put money into this—and I can't imagine a better use for your mother's dollars—I suppose you hadn't thought of going in for a bit of fruit-growing here, as a side-line?".

Gloire laughed. Warren's absorption in fruit-growing in Albania was an old joke between them by now.

"Oh darling Warren, no! I'm going to teach them to grow potatoes—not for export, but for food."

"You're *what?*"

"Going to make them grow potatoes. I've got a ton of seed potatoes coming." She rose as she spoke, went over, and gave him a kiss. "You've always been an angel to me, Warren, and I know I've mostly been a pest to you. Well, I'll go right on being one, I guess, while you're in this country." She went off to change, leaving Warren muttering again to himself that he would be darned.

Steaming down the coast of Southern Albania, Nils Larsen watched the mountains turn paler and paler blue, grow dim and faint against the pale sky beyond the soft green flatness of the coastal plain. Standing at the rail, watching that lovely outline recede and fade, he thought of Gloire, and—most vividly—of Dr. Emmeline. Splendid old woman—modest, industrious, selfless, wise. If Gloire would stick it, she could do much under those auspices—and she could not be in better hands. A curious turn of events. He had certainly never expected this when he told Mrs. Thurston in the train that to learn about European civilisation she had better come to Albania. But it was a good thing—certainly for her, perhaps also for Albania. It seemed to him very strange, as he turned away from the now almost invisible mountains, that he should be leaving *two* American women in there, both bent on good works! And one already understood Europe, and the other stood a good chance of learning. As for the good works, modest small-scale individual efforts like this usually produced much more in the way of results than was ever achieved by Commissions and press campaigns and huge impersonal expenditures of

341

money. He strolled to the other side of the ship, and looked out across the Adriatic, whipped by a rising breeze to a dark steely blue, and thought about Italy. Poor Italy! With their graceful gift for gay and civilised living, their lovely architecture and their charm, the Italians were allowing themselves to be drugged and beguiled and driven along a disastrous and alien road, the road of imperialism and conquest, for which they were as a race wholly unsuited, causing untold misery to other wretched and innocent nations on the way. His face darkened as he thought of what Warren Langdon had told him of their doings in Abyssinia. And the tragedy of it was that they would fall by the way; they would never reach their wicked silly goal. Empires were not achieved like that, self-consciously and deliberately; they were built up in bits and pieces, in a perfectly *ad hoc* manner—opening a trading or a coaling station here, fighting a little war there, negotiating a Treaty somewhere else. That was how the British Empire had been built, and the American Empire too—the annexation of California, the Mexican War, the Louisiana purchase. Nils never fell into the vulgar and uneducated error of assuming that an Empire is only an Empire if it lies overseas; he recognised the truly imperial quality of United States expansion on the North American continent in the nineteenth century, and of Russian expansion in Asia during the same period. All three were Empires, and all created in the same way and for the same reasons—commercial reasons, strategic interests. The British was the more spectacular because of the distances involved, seas and oceans and diversity of races and climates—and because of its amazing and temperate success. But they were all Empires, all right.

He leaned on the rail, a little heavily, thinking about the future of the world; thinking, as he so often did, about America and her place in it. Perhaps America would be one of the great Empires of the future—she could hardly fail to play a big rôle. Nils, a purist, distinguished sharply between words and their meanings; he knew the difference between big and great. An enemy of size, he admired greatness. Would America learn enough, in time, be humble and wise enough to make her rôle in the world not only big but great? He wondered. Would men come forward, her aristocracy of character and intellect, to lead their country, as the aristocracy of England had come forward?—to bear the burden of drudgery and ill-will, at home and also abroad, in filthy climates, in isolation and desolating homesickness, to carry the torch of justice and decent administration and personal liberty? Did that torch burn for them, really and truly?—and would they sacrifice their personal lives to it, as the English did? Or would they seek to impose on the world, by their immense economic strength and technical supremacy, a lower order—of mechanised living, of advertisement, of the selfish pursuit of comfort, of high-sounding suicidal greediness? Greediness and selfishness were infectious, contagious—but how suicidal, also. Even greedy agriculture was suicidal—look at the Dust-bowl! Would they learn, would they see?

Nils Larsen sighed, and walked back to the other side of the boat. Nothing was now to be seen, above the darkening waters, of the Albanian mountains. But somewhere in there were two American women, both unselfishly pledged to the service of others. It was a good omen. He turned, breasting the cold evening wind, and walked briskly forward along the deck.

Edinburg, October 1942—Edinburg, September 1944.

Ann Bridge is perhaps the best known pseudonym of her generation of writers. The person who uses it is the wife of a distinguished member of the British Diplomatic Service. She was born in Bridgend, Surrey, of an American mother and an English father. She spent much of her girlhood visiting relatives in northern Italy, was educated at home and at the London School of Economics, has spent many years in northern China and in Dalmatia with her husband, and has two grown sons who served with the R.A.F. and the British Navy during the war.

As the background of her novels ranges from China to Dalmatia, so her personal interests and enthusiasms range over a wide field. She is an enthusiastic gardener; she has a knowledge of archaeology rare in her sex; she is a keen mountain climber, and at the age of nineteen became the youngest member of the Ladies Alpine Club; she is a devotee of sailing, skiing, and swimming; she speaks fluent French, German, Italian, and Chinese, and a smattering of other languages, including Mongolian; and she is exceedingly accomplished in her own craft of writing.

Ann Bridge was wise enough to wait until her powers had matured before having her first novel published—"Peking Picnic," which won the Atlantic Monthly Prize and took her immediately into best-sellerdom. That was in 1932. After "Peking Picnic" came another Chinese story, "The Ginger Griffin" (1934); but her next novel, "Illyrian Spring" (1935), showed that she could move as easily in Europe as in Asia, and incidentally started a

(Continued on back flap)